THE
SOLDIER
AND THE
WAITRESS

The Soldier And The Waitress

Copyright © 2025, Kerri E. Murray

ISBN: 979-8-218-60897-2

Book cover design and interior layout provided by Self Publish Me Publishing Consulting and Book Design Services for Independent Authors. www.selfpublishme.com | email: info@selfpublishme.com

THE
SOLDIER
AND THE
WAITRESS

KERRI E. MURRAY

EDITED BY
KAREN SUE REDLACK

A Kerala Jade Brand

Part One

My Grandmama Blake wanted to name me something different the morning I was born, but Mama would have a different saying in my name. It's infrequent and uniquely done.

So, she named me Kerala Jade. I was born to John and Barbara Blake. I was the only girl and the baby of the family. I have two older siblings named Shane and Noah. My Uncle Joel and Aunt Martha Connor had three boys: Joshua, Dexter, and Kyle. Uncle Joel is my Mama's big brother. As for my Daddy, he only had one brother named Gabe. Gabe and his wife, Donna, had no children. As for them, my brother and I were their kids. Uncle Gabe and Aunt Donna owned the bar in town. My Mama and my Uncle Joel were very talented musicians. They had their band together. Listening to their music was normal around the house when I was growing up. I didn't get to meet my Mama's parents. They passed away before I was born. My parents had a small farm just outside of town. We lived in the last Victorian house that was still standing in our county. My Grandmama Blake always told me that there are significant dates in your life to remember. They are the day you get married, his birthday, and your children's birthdays. My family didn't have a whole lot, but they worked hard for all we had.

Grandmama Blake always told me that a rich man isn't different from a poor man. He's going in the same hole as you. It's just that his casket will be a bit fancier than yours. During the summer months, while Daddy worked at the mill and Mama worked at the sewing factory, I would spend my days with Grandmama Blake. She would teach me how to cook and sew. She always said to me, "If a man goes back for his third plate, it means you've done something right." When I was six, Pappy Blake passed away. As a child, I noticed it was a little more challenging for Grandmama Blake. It might have been tough, but she rolled up her sleeves and worked like a man. The lessons she taught me will always be part of my life. My parents gave me my first bicycle on Christmas of 1989. Uncle Gabe and Aunt Donna bought us a Basset Hound. My brothers and I named him Ace. I was disappointed that I still didn't get a Teddy Ruxpin, but Grandmama made my Pound Puppy dog and Cabbage Patch doll. As spring of 1990 came, my brothers and I were on spring break. I asked Mama if I could ride my bike into town to Uncle Gabe's. Mama told me I could after I got the house cleaned for her. Well, at about 10:00 AM, I started my little ten mile journey into town. As I was leaving, Ace was tagging along. While I was riding by our crazy neighbor's house, he stopped me. He picked up Ace and told me it was his dog and that my Uncle Gabe had stolen Ace from him. I told him that was a lie. He locked Ace up in his car and popped me in the back of my head with his hand. My last words to him were that I would get my Uncle, and he'd be sorry. I was still crying over him hitting me in my head and it hurt. When I got to Uncle Gabe's bar, we always had to go in through the back. As I was about to go in, I was still crying. I saw Mr. Doven, who was the town's alcoholic. He fought alongside my Daddy and Uncle Gabe in Vietnam and he asked me why I was crying. I told him, "Mr. Amos took my dog away from me and hit me in the back of my head." Mr. Doven told me,

"I tell you what, Kerala. Why don't we go and get your dog back instead of messing with your Uncle Gabe? But here is the deal, you go inside and grab me a bottle out of there and I'll help you get your dog back. I'll be right back here so we can get your dog." So I went in without Uncle Gabe seeing me. I grabbed one of the closest bottles I could reach and quickly went out the back door. Mr. Doven was pulling up with his vehicle. When he put my bike in the back of his truck. I got in and a box was in the seat next to me, with green and blue wires. Along the way, he told me, "I will ensure no one else messes with you in this town again. Yes, ma'am, we're getting that dog back for sure. Yes, ma'am, we are for sure, for sure, yes, ma'am." When we pulled up to Mr. Amos' house, Mr. Doven busted out the window of his car and he said, "Hold on, Kerala, we're not done here yet." I watched him do something to the car and out came the funny box with green and blue wires. He asked me, "I hope this is gonna be good enough for you?" I said, "Yup, good enough for me." He told me, "Now, when I ask you to push that hammer into the box, I want you to get down because what we are about to do will get me three hots and a cot and some cool air for the summer months." When I did what he told me and a big boom came out, I realized that I had just blown up Mr. Amos' car. Mr. Doven told me, "Okay Kerala, get your dog and go." So I did.

As I was peddling out, I saw Mr. Amos. I stopped and turned around, flipped him off, and told him, "I told you I'd get my dog back." I sat on the front porch with Ace in my arms. The explosion was so big that it knocked the courtroom clock off the wall. It cracked every window in the house. When Daddy pulled in, he was checking on us, and I couldn't hear him. My ears rang and muted words were all I could hear. But when Sheriff McCain pulled up, Daddy walked out to him, and Sheriff McCain pointed his finger at me. Mama pulled in. That's when Daddy started walking back up to me, pulling his belt off. I knew what was coming for me and I didn't run. All I saw was muted words come out of their mouths. When Daddy whipped me, it hurt ten times worse than what we would usually get. When I saw Grandmama I knew I was safe with her. Within three days I regained my hearing and my family sat down for Sunday supper to discuss me. Mama told Daddy it was time to put her in the church choir and teach her music. Grandmama said, "That's a Sunday thing to keep her busy, which leaves us two days of busyness." Daddy said, "Well, she can sled pull with Shane and Noah on Saturday." Grandmama said, "I got something else to keep her busy."

So, during the weekdays, after Mama was done with dinner, I had voice lessons. Mama taught me to play the guitar, piano and write my songs. I was too advanced to be with the youth choir, so they put me in the adult choir. Mama and Uncle Joel got me, Kyle, Dexter, and Joshua together to learn music once a month, every month. Before summer started, Grandmama bought me a horse and told Daddy this would be a great activity for me to compete in barrel racing. Daddy asked who was going to take me. Grandmama said Gabe would whenever he was busy with the boys. They brought this beautiful sand-colored horse home to me. There was a small mark, like a tulip, on the forehead so I named it Flower. Every day that summer of 1991, I worked with Flower to get us ready. On the side, I would meet up with my cousins to learn music. I would ride with my Dad to go sledding with my brothers. My life was full of doing things. Still, shortly after I was 12 years old, Grandmama Blake passed away. I was heartbroken. When I reached the age of 14, my cousins and I formed our band. We were good at contests and our local festivals. My parents and Uncle Joel raised enough money to let us make a few demos. Uncle Joel and Mama sent them to the local radio stations, and they played us. During one of our festivals, a big wig from the city came and told my parents that he had a contract to sign, so they set up a meeting. About three days later, my Daddy told me, "You don't have to do this if you don't want to, but go in there and let's see what this is all about." As my Mama and Daddy were having a small chat with this guy, I was doing some reading on the contract. I asked him where my cousin's contract was and he said, "Oh, sorry, but we are only interested in you." I came out and said, "No cousin's, no deal." My parents told him I thought you said the boys were going to be with Kerala? He said, "I'm sorry, but they were only interested in her." So I walked out of there. I was mad and it hurt, but my family came first. I told Mama and Daddy I couldn't do that to them if there was no contract for them. I'm not doing this. And Daddy said, "It's not being selfish, Kerala. That's thinking of others and that's being human." My cousins and I were bummed out about it for a while. The whole town, they made a big deal out of this. So I shifted my attention to sledding. I started getting better. My Daddy was excellent friends with Marv and he owned numerous sleds. But one night, my anger got the best of me, and I asked my Daddy for help. He told me if you want to run, you'll learn how to work on stuff yourself. So I got mad at him. With Noah's help, I got him to help me. Soon, it was my turn to go down the track. I was last in line to go. When I hooked up and got the green light. I heard popping and metal grinding. And I pulled the sled outside the gates. It was a full pull of 94.9 yards. I came to find out I had broken the sled gears and busted the weights. I apologized to Marv for breaking it. He said, "It's okay, Kerala. This is one for the history books on sledding. Black Betty is due for retirement. Besides, I have others at home." That weekend, I won $4,000.00. My parents put it away for me to use later. I finally got Flower to run well in the barrels during this time. So my dad figured it was time for me to race Flower. My first run wasn't that great; I had knocked over a barrel. My Mama told me to keep trying. So I did. By the year's end, I received a buckle for my first win. But as the spring of 1995 came, my cousins and I were helping to earn money to help Uncle Joel get us a small recording studio. My Mama and Uncle Joel paid for our demo recordings. So once a month, my cousins and I would record a demo and give it to the radio stations, where my cousins and I played many genres of music, Country, Pop, Gospel, and Rock. I wrote the lyrics for most of the songs, with the help of Mama, but I loved singing the hell out of them high notes until it made me lose my voice. As the rodeo season came into play, I and the other girls were waiting for the barrels to start. While we were back there, many bull riders were standing around and talking to each other, until one of them walked up to me. He said, "Hi", and I said,"Hi" back to him. During that period, Cole Caney was gaining popularity around the county as one of the best bull riders. He said, "That's a nice Quarter Horse you got." And I was being nice to him and said, "Thank you!" When they called my name out, I said to him, "Gotta go." I had made an impressive run, too, winning another buckle, saddle and $1,800.00. When I received my money,I took it to my Uncle Gabe to put away for me. We brought two of my friends, Hope and Valerie. My Uncle told me, "Good job on your winnings. Have a seat, and let's enjoy the rest of the show." Hope and Valerie checked out the boys as I watched the main event. And I told them, "Boys will get us into trouble and I'm focused on other things." A few weeks later, I saw Cole again. And we were having small talk about the next rodeo. He said something that made me laugh. My parents and his parents were acquaintances. Daddy had some small business with his father, but I did grow up in a town where everyone knew your business. Cole was nine years older than me, and it was normal for us younger kids to have an older friend who hung around with the younger crowd. As the Fall Festival of 1995 came, my cousins and I entered the talent contest. While I was standing there on the stage, I saw Cole. And I noticed that he was at every event I attended. When I got off-stage, I ran into him again. And he said, "That's a good song." And I said, "Thank you." He came out and said, "You know, you're a pretty girl. I'm surprised you don't have a little boy hanging around you." I told him, "I'm focused on what I'm doing now." It was nothing but a friendly conversation between us. During the past few months, I had noticed that Cole was hanging out with my brothers and helping my Daddy out around the farm. Around November, as I got off the bus, Cole, and my Daddy sat talking on the front porch. As I walked up the steps, Daddy stopped me and said, "Kerala, Cole asked me permission to date you, and I knew that you were getting into those stages of dating. You're almost 16 years old. I permitted him to date you. That is if you're interested in him." I thought for a minute and said, "Kind of." My Daddy said, "Well, I'm guessing Cole would like to take you out tonight." I said, "Hang on and let me get changed." So I did, and as I changed my thoughts were, okay, let's see where this leads. So, we left. We grabbed a bite to eat and shared a friendly conversation between us. And I had to admit that I was crushing on him a little during that dinner. When we returned to my house, he told me, "You're a beautiful girl." I said, "Thank you," to him and he kissed me. It kind of felt forced, but it was, after all, my first kiss. The next night my cousins and I hung out and found some old spray paint. What better way to spend the weekend than to climb to the water tower. And my dumb ass sprayed, in bright hot pink, on the water tower along with them and wrote 'The Hometown Of Kerala Jade and the Bomb Band'. I had some Jolly Ranchers in my pocket. Kyle had recently just broken up with his girlfriend because she had a car and he didn't. It was about 25° outside and Kyle said to me, "Kerala, give me some of your Jolly's. I saw this on that old show so let's try it and see what happens." So, I handed him some. He licked a few and placed them on her

12

front windshield. Well, the next morning came. Mama busted into my bedroom and said, "Well, the whole town knows when the Blake and Connor kids get together and do stupid shit." I tried to play it off, and she said, "The hot pink spray paint is all over your hands, and yes, your Aunt Donna called and said you were up on the water tower last night with your cousin's. You can't lie to me because your name is up there now." I told her, "Well, it has a nice ring to it, and it does match the black water tower." Mama said, "Kerala Jade, get your butt ready for church." As Kyle's ex-girlfriend's car passed by us, I saw the window busted out, and I was fascinated by that. But as Mama and I were walking into the church doors, the town Mayor came up to me and said, "If you wanted your name up there all you had to do was ask me. I would have proudly had it done for you. We are very proud of our most talented person around here." I apologized to the Mayor, and he said, "Oh, it's nothing. You're just being a kid. I was one once." After church Mama wanted a picture of it. The sign said, "The Hometown of Kerala Jade and the Bomb Band". I was laughing and Mama said, "I'm going to let you slide on this one since the Mayor didn't have a big fit on you." During the coming months, Cole and I were starting to be a couple. After four months of seeing each other something in him changed on a Wednesday. Mama dropped me off for a Wednesday church service and Cole would pick me up after service. Isaac and I had many classes together in school and he was the pastor's son. Isaac asked me, "So, have you been studying for your driver's exam?" I told him, "Yes, I passed the written exam. But when it came to driving, I made an Illegal turn, so that's what failed me. I will go back in two weeks to try again." Isaac said, "Oh, that's uncool. The exam has some pretty tricky questions. Well, at least you're admitting you failed. The other classmates are too embarrassed to say that they messed up." I told him, "There's nothing wrong with telling the truth to people." Then, I saw

Cole pull in. I hugged Isaac and told him, "See you tomorrow." As I got into Cole's truck, I could feel his mood change. When we got down the road he said, "You should be ashamed of yourself for hugging all over the Pastor's son." I said to him that we were just friends. Cole pulled the truck over. He started hitting and choking me until my nose began to bleed. When he stopped, I was shocked, and he told me to start cleaning myself up. Cole said, "I'm sorry, darling, please don't tell your Daddy what I did to you. I'm sorry for what I did. Seeing you hug another guy just got me upset. I've had a bad day at work." When I got home, I was still shocked at what had just happened to me, and I looked at Noah. Cole told my dad that I fell on the corner of the concrete, and my Daddy believed him. About three days later, Cole came around and begged me to forgive him, which I caved in to and about a week later, I said something wrong to him. Cole did it again, but only slapped me in the face. As we were in church the next morning, I noticed his Mom was attending, and Cole came in with her. He stood beside me and placed his arm around my waist like nothing had happened. We were singing the morning hymns. Cole whispers to me, "I see you looking at the Pastor's son again. You're about to piss me off now. I'm with you because I'm looking for a good woman, but it looks like I'm going to have to break her first. From now on out, keep your head down, and I better not see you looking up again. Do you understand me?" When he said that to me, I had a feeling that if I didn't do what he told me, I would get hit again where no one could see. I felt him pinch me so hard on my right side as we were leaving the church. I kept my head down until we got closer to the Pastor, Cole pinched me harder, and I raised my head up. Shaking the Pastor's hand was his way of ensuring I understood him. When the spring rodeos came around, I ran Flower and put her away. As I was walking to get a seat, Cole told me, "You better go get a seat and stay there, and don't you move without my permission." As I sat there, I had to go to the bathroom so badly that I was about to pee on myself, so I quickly ran to the bathroom. When I returned to my seat, Cole stood there waiting for me and told me, "You missed me riding. Let's go." When we got into his truck, I felt a full-blown fist hit me a few times. He asked me, "Where did you go?" I told him I had to go to the bathroom. He said to me, "I don't care if you shit or piss yourself, you better stay where I told you." I started getting good at hiding the bruises from my family and friends. When summer came, I passed my driver's test and received my license. Mama and Daddy gave me the money I had earned through the years, a total of $14,000.00. I bought myself a two-year-old car from an old lady. It was a nice car. All she wanted was the pay-off and I bought it from her. I was proud of that car and it was all mine. When June came, I figured I'd take Flower for a ride, but as I was almost at the end of the road, I saw Cole coming. I could tell he had been drinking when he stopped and he ripped me off of Flower. My head hit his truck and I felt him hit me with a full fist. When he kicked Flower, to make her run away, he threw me in the truck and took me straight home. He pretended that Flower hurt me. Daddy was furious and quickly took Flower to sell her. When I saw Shane, I shook my head and told him that's not what happened. The next morning, I cried so much over my horse that it felt as if my child was ripped out of my arms. That horse meant so much to me. It was the last thing Grandmama Blake bought me. I cried every day until I couldn't cry anymore. Around 1997, every weekend, Cole would physically, mentally and verbally abuse me. It got to the point where I was like, let's get this weekend beating over. And to the point of the thoughts of killing myself. One morning, I got up and went into the cotton loft. I stuck a pitchfork into the ground and climbed onto the loft where I sat there and cried momentarily. As I was about to start running, I felt like someone was in the loft with me, and as I started running, Noah came in and asked me what I was doing. I told him nothing, just getting out some saw horses for my saddles. But as October came around, Cole started doing other things to me when he took me down a dead-end road and jerked me out of the truck. I was ready for his fist. But when he ripped my shirt off, he cut my bra with a knife, exposing my breasts and started rubbing them, he pulled his pants down and started playing with himself. After he was done, he beat me. His words to me were that this should be easy soon. About a month later, here we were again on the same road. He unbuttoned my shirt and forced me onto the bed of his truck, climbed on top of me, and placed himself in between my breasts. I was disgusted. Three days after my 18th birthday came, Cole took me to his house. As soon as the door closed, he told me, "I've been waiting for this day for a long time. I think it's time to turn you into a full-blown woman, so go on and take your clothes off." When he said that, I told him, "No", and he said, "What the fuck did you say?" I said, "No." He told me, "If you don't take your clothes off right now, I'm going to get a rope around your neck and drag your ass all over this town. So, go on and take your clothes off, so I can turn you into a woman. If you say no again I'm fixin' to do what I said. I'll go and kill your Mama and Daddy." So I took my clothes off and started crying. When I was undressed, he grabbed me by my hair and dragged me into his room. He placed himself inside my bottom. The third time was different. He had beaten me, and kind of started ripping my clothes off and pushed me down in the bed facing him, and he started jerking off and opening my legs. I started crying because I didn't want him to have my virginity. When he inserted the tip of himself in me, it hurt. I heard him sigh and felt him let off in me, then he laid down. I laid there beside him in tears. When he passed out, I told myself to get up and run. So I carefully got up and got what clothes that weren't ripped and quietly put them on. I ran out the door. As I was running down a county road, with no shoes or a coat on, I saw a truck coming up behind me. I stopped running. When it pulled up behind me, I turned around and saw it was Kyle. I started crying in his arms. He picked me up, put me in his truck, and asked me where the motherfucker was. I told him at his house. Kyle told me to stay in the truck when we returned to Cole's house. When Kyle went in, I heard scuffling sounds between them. Then a gunshot went off. I went a little hysterical, thinking Cole shot Kyle. When Kyle came out, we left, and he asked me, "How long, Kerala, has this been going on." I said nothing, and Kyle screamed and asked, "HOW LONG Kerala?" I told him that since we started seeing each other. He asked, "Does Uncle John know?" I told him,"No, I've kept it hidden." Kyle said, "Well, he's fixin' to find out now." When Kyle helped me in the house, my Daddy asked me what happened, and Kyle got in Daddy's face and told him, "I'll tell you, he beat the hell out of her and has been for years." I had already gone upstairs, passing Shane and Noah along the way. As they looked at me, I went into the bathroom and ran the bath water. I could still hear Kyle and Daddy yelling at each other. Mama was knocking at the door and asked me, "Kerala, what did you make Cole mad at you about?" I laughed until I started crying. I didn't tell my family that I had been raped on three different occasions by him. I sat in the water until it was cold. The next morning came and my Daddy walked into the room. I could see that he was upset with himself and asked me what I wanted to do. I told him to leave Cole alone. I wanted him to never set a foot back on this property. I'd go to my grave with this and I didn't want to speak about it again. As February approached, I went to Wednesday night service and asked to speak to the Pastor privately. We went into his office and I started to break down and confess what had happened to me. He excused himself, ran into the chapel, and got Judge Shafer and Sheriff Anderson.

He told me I had waited too long to report this matter, and Judge Shafer asked me how he could help me. I told him to keep Cole away from me, and he looked at our Pastor and said, "Buck, we have to help Kerala." The Pastor said, "Yes, and we do it by getting her confidence back first and having small counseling visits after service."

Within a month into February, I was very sick and couldn't hold anything down. Mama shoved me into the doctor's office. When they asked me about my monthly, I told her it was coming, and she said we have to check. So, as I watched the test strip go positive, I knew I was pregnant, and by a man I didn't want in my life. My mama said, "Well, I think you should say something to him that you're pregnant." And I told her, "NO, I don't want him to ever touch this baby."

As the week progressed, I knew I better find a job quickly to support myself and this baby. On top of all that, I was still in high school. Three months before graduating, I applied at this small downtown café. Joe, the owner, hired me immediately. I worked there after school and on the weekends. When there was no school, I was working the morning shift. I had given Joe a heads-up that I just found out I was pregnant, and he said, "I'm still going to hire you." As I was leaving downtown, it was swamped since the military outpost had reopened a few months back. There was an extensive write-up in the newspaper that they used this post as an overflow base. Uncle Gabe and Aunt Donna were praying for their business. As the week passed, I was getting down on being a great waitress. A week later, Joe gave me the night off. I had plans to join Noah and Shane with their new girlfriends, Mia and Layla.

Before my cousins took off to return to work, Dexter came in the shop door and said, "Kerala, you will not believe what the fuck I just saw." And I had to stop to get out and look at him. It was Cole on the ground, passed the fuck out with a needle in one arm, a crack pipe in the other, and beer cans all around

18

him. When Dexter told me that, I had to see it for myself. So, I picked up the box of demos and left. When I pulled in, sure enough, there he was, just like Dexter said. So I put my foot on his throat and stood on him for a few seconds. I found his knife and cut him close to his throat. It wasn't deep, but it was a light cut. Then I spit on him and left. We had some recent demos done a few weeks back with my cousins before they went back to working shutdowns. So, I asked my brother's to help me place the names of the songs where they needed them to be. Uncle Gabe would pitch in with his helping hand, and he said, "I can't believe that he's on the shit." I told him, "Yup, I had a feeling that Cole was on the shit. And all that matters to me is this baby and his nasty paws stay away from me. He'll never see the light of day of this baby." As we were putting the demos together, the regular barflies were showing up, and I'm guessing it was getting time for them to be off work. Layla said, "I don't recall this song." I looked at it, went over, popped the instrumental in, and started singing it. Man, of the high-note songs, it was sad, but it was just. Still, I hit it right when I was done.

I grabbed the box and told them later. I bolted out the door to get the new demos off to the radio stations so we could get paid. As I was walking in, Jack saw me coming in, and he gave me $500.00 for my demo recordings. When spring break came around, I had my regular customer in the morning, which was Judge Shafer. Naomi was a lazy old bitch that was into everyone's business except her own. Naomi and Mama went to high school together. As for Lynn, she got stuck here, passing through. She decided to stay years ago and has yet to leave. As the sun started rising, my normal customers were coming in, mainly older people who like to gather around and sit and bullshit until lunch. Before Judge Shafer walked out, I fixed him a coffee to go as he liked it, a hint of hazelnut with two spoonfuls of sugar and a dash of milk. I poured Mr. and Mrs.

Harrison's coffee and ensured their food was perfect. I looked up and saw four military guys coming in from the outpost. I quickly looked and didn't see Naomi or Lynn around to help them. As they stood there, I just said, "Have a seat anywhere. I'll be with you in just a moment." So I went and put the coffee back on the warmer and grabbed some menus. As I looked up, this guy from the outpost stood out. In my head, I thought he was handsome. As I walked up to the table and handed the menus, something told me to look at him. When I did, oh my God, I smiled at him, but I didn't realize that I was flirting with him. As we locked eyes, I had a crazy vibe with him. Somewhere, my soul left my body. While I was standing there, my soul slapped the shit out of my body, but as I looked at him again and smiled, I noticed his eyes were hazel. I felt this small asshole vibe from him and he started flirting with me. So I started flirting back at him. As I took their order, I couldn't get over how built he was, with his black hair and nice tan. As I returned to the kitchen, Joe smiled and said, "I saw you flirting with him." I smiled and said, "I was just being friendly." Naomi came out and said, "You shouldn't be doing that in your condition. Besides, he might have a wife or girlfriend somewhere." Joe said to Naomi, "So what do you want Kerala to be like, you cold, bitter bitch? That can't get over shit. You need to butt out of her business, she's still a kid." I started fixing their drinks while Joe was on Naomi's ass about me. When I went out, Lynn said, "Thanks for covering my tables while I smoked. I heard everything. Girlfriend, he watched you walk away." I giggled. I said, "Oh? See, he's kind of got my head a little fucked up. I mean, look at him." Lynn said he was cute, but too young for her. But the General looked just right for her. I told Lynn I had to focus on my baby right now and make sure we were secure in life. I brought them their drinks, placed them down and I walked off. At another table Mrs. Parker was getting upset. She was in Naomi's area, so I walked over to her and asked if she needed anything. She said, "This is the fourth time Naomi left me hanging. Tomorrow, I'll be sitting in your section to get service." I apologized to her on Naomi's behalf. As I came into the kitchen and told Joe that Mrs. Parker was pissed off and said she would not be sitting in Naomi's Section again because Naomi wasn't there for her needs. Joe said, "Well, I'll make Naomi bus your tables and wash dishes since she's not taking care of people." As I had grabbed my table food I walked back up to the soldier and touched him. It felt something like I had never felt before and we locked eyes again. We both flirted with each other. When they left, I told them to come back again. When I went home, I found myself standing in front of the mirror, looking at my pregnant belly. With me being almost nine weeks, my stomach was a little bit bigger, and I had a small bump that was showing. The next morning came and I was serving Mrs. Parker. Lynn came running up to me and said, "They are here again." I had begun to blush, felt my heart sink and beat faster as he walked into the door. As I stood there, I was mind-blown by how tall he was. He smiled at me, and I remembered what drinks they had from yesterday. So I fixed it and took it over to the table. I saw his last name was Nicholas. He asked me, "What's your name?" I came out and said, "I'm sorry, my name is Kerala, and I'll be your waitress today." He said, "Well, Kerala, that's a unique name you have." I told him, "It's infrequent." He said to me, "Well, Kerala, my name is Steve." I said, "Well, it's nice to meet you." I asked them if they would have the same thing as yesterday, or if we needed a menu. I looked at the General, and he said, "Yes, ma'am, the same thing as yesterday." So I returned to the kitchen. Joe was smiling at me and he said, "Kerala, you're the cat's meow out there." I laughed and said, "Joe, that is so 1920's." And he said, "I think you have impressed him." I told Joe, "You're a mess." He hugged me and kissed me on the top of my head while saying, "You're like the daughter I never had." I walked around and checked on my tables. When their food was done, I took it to their table and remembered who had what from yesterday. When Steve touched my hand again, there was this crazy vibe between us. Like there was something there and a feeling I couldn't describe. I looked at his left hand, which told me one thing: no ring. I told them to come back again as soon as they left. Steve smiled at me and said, "Oh, I'll be back very soon." I had to keep telling myself to stop thinking of him and that he was out of my league. I needed to focus on my unborn baby. Naomi came out and said, "Hun, he could have a wife or a girlfriend somewhere. If he's looking for a one-night stand, you can't because you've messed yourself up. No man wants a package deal when he could have an unopened party package to play with." I just shrugged it off because she was right. That is how Southern women are. Once you get pregnant in the South, then he leaves you, that means no one wants you. I just told her, "Hell, it's just wishful thinking and he could be hiding his wedding band." But I had blown it out of my mind and how he looked at me was driving me crazy. By that afternoon, I started cleaning up at the end of my shift. As I was wiping my last table off, I looked up. There he was, walking in with a small bouquet of flowers. He walked up to me and handed them to me. He asked if I would like to go and do something with him, go for a walk, or something. I looked at him and the flowers. They were my two favorites. Tulips and carnations with blue baby's breath. And my dumbass said it a little rude to him, "I hope you know that I'm pregnant and fixin' to be a single mom." And he said to me, "So what? That doesn't stop me from wanting to hang out or do something with you." I caved and said, "Wait here." My shift was about over so I walked into the back to finish up. And Joe said, "Kerala, get the hell out of here and have fun with him. He seemed like a nice guy." So I clocked out, grabbed my things, and overheard Naomi asking him why

Steve wanted to be with me, "She's pregnant, and plenty of single girls in this town are not soiled." Joe put her in her place and told her that it's none of her damn business. I thought, shit, he just put her in her place. So I walked out, and Steve looked at me. He opened the door for me. And as we started walking, he asked me, "So, what's your story?" Then he quickly apologized to me. And I said, "No, no. Baby daddy became a drunken drug addict. He decided to be with a few crack whores, so here I am, pregnant and preparing to be a single mom. Steve asked me why I thought I would do this alone. And I came out and said, "Look at me. No man wants a package deal." After I said that, it kind of got him upset. And he told me, "You'd be surprised." When he said that to me, it shocked me by the way he said it. As we were walking, I asked him if we could sit down. And he said, "Yeah." And I had asked him, "So why did you join the military?" He said, "My grandfather is a veteran and I figured I would put his shoes on for a while. I have been in the service for the past four years now. I'm a drill sergeant. I intend to retire after serving our country." I had asked him, "Where is home for you?" He said, "Arizona." I said, "Oh, one of those wild west guys." Steve said, "Kind of", and I asked him, "So you got a girlfriend back home?" Then I said, "I'm sorry, I shouldn't be in your business like that." He told me, "No, you're asking me the right questions." As he was about to say something, my brothers passed by and yelled in the street, "Kerala Jade, what in the hell are you doing?" I shrugged my shoulders at them and apologized to him and told him, "Sorry for that. They are my brothers." and He said, "Jade, uh, that's a cute middle name for a girl. As for the girlfriend back home, I have an ex-girlfriend I broke up with many years ago. Back in high school for a lot of reasons. Still, I am interested in getting to know this girl I'm very interested in, and she's given me a chance." As we spoke, I smiled and kind of blushed and thought holy shit, did I just hear the words? He wants to go out with me. And I said, "I'm glad I'm giving you a chance." He said, "As for siblings, I have two myself, a brother and a sister." He asked me how old I was, and I told him I was 18. He said, "Perfect for me. I'm fixin' to be 21 in a few months." And then he said, "Sorry, I should have asked that question initially." I told him, "That's okay." He said he figured that this place would have crazy names for people like Wilbur and Bobbie Jo. I laughed and said, "They live over there on 1st street." He looked at me, and I said, "Claude and Brenda live on Marlin Ave." He said, "You're kidding me, right?" I said, "Nope." I laughed until he caught on to the fact that I was joking. While we were talking and getting to know a little bit about each other, I felt so comfortable around him. I felt the asshole vibe from him go away. As we sat there laughing and carrying on, we realized no one was walking or driving in the streets. He looked at the time and it was close to midnight. I told him I had to open it in a little while. As we walked to my car, he opened the door for me. I said, "Thank you for the flowers." He said, "I think a gorgeous girl like you deserves it." I got in, closed the door, and left him standing there. When I got home, Mama and Daddy were already in bed, so I put the flowers in a vase on the dining room table and went on to bed. When I got to work the next day, Joe asked me about my date last night. Joe said, "I saw you glowing, and the smile on your face said it all." I said it was good. By mid-morning, Sam, the flower shop owner, had delivered some more flowers to me. Lynn was dying for me to read the card, and I did. "I had a great night with you. I can't wait to see you again! Hopefully, we can meet at the café on Friday night at five." Naomi had to rain on my parade and said, "You bought them and had Sam deliver them." Sam said, "Nope, a big, tall, built, white guy came in this morning." Joe said, "Naomi stop being a fucking cunt to this child. Matter of fact, Kerala, I'm going to let you have Friday and Saturday night off, so enjoy your weekend." When I got home that afternoon, Daddy said, "Kerala, Shane and Noah told me they saw you sitting on a bench with a guy from the outpost." I said, "Yes sir, they did. He asked me out on a date on Friday." Daddy asked me if he knew I was pregnant, and I said he was fully aware of my mama status. Daddy said, "I thought you'd returned to Cole because of the flowers on the table." I told Daddy, "When hell freezes over. Those are from Steve." Daddy asked if that was his name, and I said, "Yes." When Friday morning came around, I had taken my time with my hair and makeup. I was putting myself back together before the thought of Cole tore me down. As I dug inside my closet, there was this cute sundress with the tag still on it. I put it on and found a pair of matching shoes by 4:00 PM. I checked myself in the mirror and saw that the baby bump was showing. So I ran out of the house to my car and left. When I got to the Café, I sat down, and Lynn was working. When I saw Steve pull in, I thought shit. I'm dealing with a rich asshole jock. He had a brand-new truck, and his clothes were name-brand. He looked different, was in civilian clothing, and brought more flowers. I sat at the counter and when Steve walked in he didn't recognize me. He sat down. I looked at him and I asked him, "Are you waiting for someone?" And he looked at me and said, "Oh, hey, I'm sorry, I didn't recognize you there." I saw him quietly say the word "WOW" to himself. And he said, "I didn't expect you to look like this with makeup fully on. I hope you are hungry. The General told me about this place on East Blvd." I said, "Oh, Barlow Steakhouse." As we walked to his truck, he opened the door for me, and I got in. He closed it. I put on my seat belt and he looked at me as he got in. I saw him blushing as he started the truck. The local radio station was playing. It was our mixed radio station where they played rock to pop. DJ Double Dave came on and he said, "We all know this dynamite kid. She's just released their new album to us, so let's give her a Double Dave play tonight in our hometown." My song, 'Giving Up the Fear' started playing. Steve turned up the radio and said, "They play this band a lot. I've been to the retail stores looking for this song." I didn't want to tell him. But I did say to Steve, "You're not going to find it because it's a demo album." I couldn't resist because my favorite part was coming up. I sang it in a lower tone. Steve looked at me. And I smiled and said,"She is I and I am her. That's me and my band." This impressed him. He said,"That's you?" I said, "Yes." I told him to look at the water tower as we sat at the red light. And he said," WOW, that's cool." I reached into my purse and handed him one of the demos. I told him, "Please don't let this get into other hands." And he said, "You bet it won't. Thanks for it." As we pulled into the steakhouse, I had forgotten it was my senior prom. I wasn't interested in going because they were using the Banquet Room. Steve said, "Oh, I'm hopeful of getting in," as he helped me out of his truck. He said, "I don't mean to kind of sound like a broken record to you, but you're beautiful." I smiled and said, " Thank you." As we got a table he asked me how long have I been singing? I told him ever since I was ten. As we sat there, there were things that I didn't want to say to him, and a lot was about Cole or how he would beat me. I wanted to go to my grave with it. Our first date went great. I was very interested and attracted to him. As our fourth date came to the end of the night, he took me back to my car. We did not want the night to end, but we had to go to work the next night. As he opened my car door for me, I turned around and looked at him, and he asked me,"Are you and I officially a couple?" I smiled at him and said, "Yes, Steve, we are." He carefully picked me up and set me on the hood of his truck. He placed his hand on my cheek and leaned into me, and started kissing me. This feeling of electricity felt like it was flowing between us, my heart fluttering. In my mind, I thought, what the fuck is this shit? Where is this feeling coming from? I had never been kissed like that before or ever had those feelings from just one kiss. As he played with my hair, he kissed me again. The chemistry between us was there. When he set me down, I felt like I was high as a kite. Before going our separate ways for the night, he told me he would see me in a few days. I had a doctor's appointment the day we would see each other. As I got into my appointment. When we started doing my ultrasound, the midwife said, "Oh." I said, "What's the oh for?" She said, " Congratulations on having twins." I said, "Say that again." And I looked. I'll be damn, there they were. And she said he has a friend. And I thought shit, I thought I would only have one. And Mama said, "Kerala, it looks like karma is coming for you." I told her, "Well, I guess I will sell my sled truck to pay for them. And Mama said, "I'll tell your Daddy." Mama asked when they were going to meet Steve. I would like to know who my daughter's mystery boyfriend is. And I told her this weekend, since Shane and Noah were sledding. When I met up with Steve that night, I had a lot on my mind about how I would pay for two babies, and Steve asked me if something was on my mind. I hesitated a little and told him my little sidekick had his own sidekick. He said, "You're having twins?"

I said, "Yup, two boys." He told me everything would be okay, saying, "I've got us, so trust me, I'll ensure it." and he held onto me. I didn't question what he said the next night. I brought Steve to the county fair. I introduced him to my parents. As Layla and Mia were talking to me, Mia said, "Damn, girl, you traded up good. He's not from around here, is he?" And I told Mia, "No, he is not." I smiled at her, and then I looked at Daddy. He and Steve were chatting away. When I saw Daddy slap Steve on his back, I knew that Daddy approved of Steve. As the show started, I explained how the competition was done. While I watched my sled truck go down the track without me, it burned that I wasn't in it. Daddy had just sold it to Marv. He has a small lot of sled trucks on his property, which he buys and sells. As we sat there, I focused all on Steve, and Daddy started having a fit. I looked, and Cole was standing in front of me. My heart dropped, and I started breathing heavily. I was afraid he was fixin' to do something stupid to us. Instead he grinned at me, started shaking his head, pointed to me, and started walking off. Within a few minutes, Steve excused himself, so I figured he would go to the restroom. About 25 minutes later Steve came back and I could feel him being tense. He wrapped his arm around my waist and kissed me on my cheek. Out of nowhere the babies started moving. I looked at Steve and we smiled at each other. It was a weird feeling inside me. As the show ended, Steve walked me to my car. And as we were talking, he told me I will be at your house tomorrow for dinner. Your dad invited me. I said, "Well, I'm guessing you impressed him." Before we parted we kissed and he said, "Please be careful going home." When I was almost home, my car belt was screaming and starting to heat, so I punched it to get into the driveway, where it died on me. Something told me Cole did something to my car, and when I walked in, I said, "Daddy, I think Cole did something to my car. It was running fine when I parked at the fairground." Daddy said he'd look it over in the morning. My dog Ace had been missing for the last few days, and we had been looking for him. Daddy said, "I don't think Cole liked what he saw with you wrapped up in Steve's arms tonight. I have good vibes about that boy. He has you where I like to see you, happy." I smiled and said, "Goodnight, Daddy." As the next morning came, Daddy started working on my car. I had a bad night with one of the babies on my bladder, so before Steve showed up, I laid down for a while until I felt someone brushing my hair. When I opened my eyes Steve was sitting in a chair next to my bed. He kissed me on my cheek, and I smiled at him. He told me, "Baby, I'm here; your mom said you had a bad night." I said, "Yes, coming home my car tore up and I have had a baby on my bladder just about all night." And he told me, "Well, I helped your Dad with one issue, but inside you, I can't help you out." He helped me out of bed and we left my room. I said, "Well, let's get the photo thing out of the way before they embarrass me." He snickered at me and helped me down the stairs as we walked into the den. That's when Daddy was fussing at me about me being up and down all night. As my brothers showed up for Sunday supper, I knew I was about to be embarrassed. Still, during dinner, Daddy and Steve were chatting away. Out of nowhere, Daddy started telling stories about me and we were laughing about my foolishness. By the end of the night, Steve had to leave. Before he left, he and I kind of made out, and I was starting my first full week of the morning shift as the summer months had come to a close. Fall was on the horizon. Naomi had a fit about working the morning shift and I was almost nine months pregnant. Joe and Steve were getting worried about me. Joe told me, "Kerala, I hate doing this to you, but I'm just going to have to get you off the floor." He said, "The only thing is can I get you to come in at night for a few hours, fold the silverware, and refill the shakers? I'll still pay you full-time wages." I told him I would. The night I started doing it, when I closed up with Joe, I walked out to my car, and that was when a hand grabbed me and slung me against my car. When I saw it was Cole, he was about to start choking me, and that's when I saw Joe point a shotgun at him. He told Cole, "If I ever see you again, I'm going to kill you. Stay away from her." When Cole let go of me, Joe said, "I'm calling your Daddy and staying on the phone with him until you get home." And he did. Three days after the incident, I had plans with Steve, but as I was doing the silverware, Steve came in and told me,

"Kerala, I'm sorry, baby, but I have to do night training. I hate to cancel on you." I told him I understood, and he said, "At least I get to see you just for a few minutes. I'll make it up to you next weekend." After Steve left, I looked up and saw a big storm coming.

As Joe had locked up, I felt a stabbing in my stomach. As I was getting in the car, it hit again, and as I tried to start my car, it wouldn't start, so I got out to see if Joe was still in the café and saw he was already gone. It started raining when I got back to my car. I felt this big burst of water going on. I knew what had happened. With this and the pain kicking in, I held onto my car door. Even so, I had fallen to the ground. As I laid there trying to get back up, a Military Police (MP) patrol vehicle stopped. He asked me, "Ma'am, are you okay?" I told him, "No, I'm in labor." He got me up, put me in his vehicle, and he asked me if there was anyone he could call. I told him to please find Steve Nicholas. He said, "You mean Drill Sergeant Nicholas?" I said, "Yes." When this MP got me to the hospital, they took me to the Emergency Room (ER) and started putting an I.V. in me. I was waiting for the doctor to come in. As I lay there waiting, Dr. Fletcher finally came in and said, "My c-section case. Having twins tonight, aren't we Kerala?" I looked at him and said, "I guess so." He said, "Okay, let's get a room ready." As they were fixin' to take me upstairs, Steve came in and he was soaked. I told him I was sorry, and he said not to be. As I lay there, Steve came out and said, "Marry me? I want to be the boy's father." This shocked me and I smiled at him and said, "Yes." Steve kissed me and got excited. When the first baby came out, they handed him to Steve. He brought the baby around to me so I could see him and the nurse showed me the other baby boy. When they put me in a room, Steve sat in a chair, and I fell asleep. As I was sleeping, I had a dream about Cole coming in there and taking the babies from me. I woke up and saw that Steve wasn't in the room. My anxiety kicked in and the thoughts of Cole coming in and doing something to me scared me. When the door opened, Steve walked in, and he said, "Oh, I see you are awake. I was in the nursery feeding the boys. I figured I'd let you rest." He asked me what their names were, and I told him I was naming them after my grandfathers, Andrew Connor and Lucas Blake. He said, "That's cool you named them after your family." He asked me, "So you know that last night wasn't the way I wanted to propose to you, but I felt it was right to ask before the babies were born. So when are we going to go and get married?" I told him we could go to the courthouse on Monday morning. He said, "Baby, if that's what you want, then we'll do it." I told him I didn't want Cole anywhere near the babies or me, and he said, "No, I don't care for him. I want to adopt them and raise them as my own if you want me to adopt them." I told him, "Yes, I do." I told him my car wouldn't start last night, and he said, "We'll get it taken care of this afternoon, but here in a bit, I'm fixin' to have to go and get changed. I can't be in uniform for too long." I told him I understood. And told me, "I'll run and get your car fixed and get your base passes set up." As we were making plans, the nurse brought the babies in and handed me one of them. I opened up the blanket and saw a mark on the left side of his foot, so I had chosen him to be Andrew. I laid him down and looked Lucas over. Steve picked Andrew up and held him as Mama, Daddy, Aunt Donna, Aunt Martha, Uncle Joel, and Uncle Gabe came into the room. Daddy walked over and picked up Lucas. Steve said, "Kerala, I'm going to run and get your car and take care of other things. I'll be back within the next few hours." I told him, "Okay." Daddy asked what was wrong with my car. I told him it wouldn't start last night, so Steve was fixin' to get it towed. I rubbed my nose. Aunt Donna gasped and said, "What is that on your finger? That's a big rock on it." Mama looked at the engagement ring. I told her, "Mama, I need you to go and pack up my stuff. I will not return home because Steve and I are getting married on Monday." When I said that, Mama looked at Daddy and said, "John, did you just hear what your daughter said to me?" Daddy said, "Barbara, I knew about this because he asked me for permission for her hand." Mama said,

"We know nothing about his family." Daddy said, "So what? It's Kerala's choice, not yours, Barbara." Aunt Martha said, "I'll get a cake made tomorrow night and we can have a small reception. This is wonderful Kerala. At least it isn't Cole." Daddy said, "That's for damn sure." Uncle Gabe said, "Well, Donna, I guess we should pitch in and get our girl a nice dress for Monday." Uncle Joel came out and said, "Let's give our only girl the little wedding that she deserves in the courtroom chapel instead of the mess she has gotten into, at least she's marrying a man that's accepting her for flaws." I told them Steve wanted to adopt the babies. Mama came out and said, "Oh, thank God." In this conversation, I had a small feeling that Mama was still learning about Steve. As they discussed planning for Monday, Aunt Martha said to Kerala, "I'll close up my beauty shop. Come in and I'll do your hair and makeup." My aunt Martha owns the small beauty salon in town called 'Hair Today Dye Tomorrow', but my uncle Joel calls it the clucking shack because that's where all the older women go to gossip in town. I asked if anyone had asked me what I named the boys and they said, "Oh." I told them they are both named after Grandpa Blake and Grandpa Connor. I said, "The one with the birthmark on his foot is Andrew Connor and the other one is Lucas Blake." They said that it was sweet of me to name them after my family. Steve came in as they sat around, passing them back and forth. Mama got her camera out and started taking pictures. Steve and Daddy started talking away. My aunts and uncles said, "Well, we better go. We have a lot to do today before everything closes." When they walked out, Mama asked Steve,"So you're marrying my baby on Monday?" Steve said, "Yes, ma'am." Mama asked if he wanted to meet her to get some things. Steve said, "Yeah." When Sunday morning came, I told Steve to get some rest for the night, so he did. By mid-afternoon, Mia came by, and my baby blues kicked in. Mia asked me, "Kerala, why are you crying?" I said to Mia, "I'm

afraid that Cole will come in here and take the babies away."
Mia said, "Oh no, he's not. Your daddy slapped a Restraining
Order against him the other day, so you have nothing to worry
about with him. That Cole is a psycho retard. And what he did
to you, your Daddy wants to hang him. Noah saw him the other
day so strung out. And as for Steve, he can't stand him." I said,
"Mia, can you please promise me if I tell you something you
won't say anything to anyone?" She said, "Yes." I told her Cole
had raped me and she said we figured he did. Just Noah, me,
and along with Kyle that have been in our minds. Because we
knew that it wasn't like you. We just can't figure out why you
stayed with him. I told Mia he controlled my mind and me. I
told her I was worried about when Steve and I would get ready
to be together. She said, "Oh, that subject. Kerala. With Steve,
it's just going to feel natural for you two. Because I'm sure he
will be easy on you and love you instead of being beaten and
then having sex the wrong way. This with Steve will be
different for you and will be your real first. I'm happy that you
found your person. And the way he looks at you, Kerala, he
means the business of love with you. I mean, come on, the guy
is a beast and gentle with you. That's all that Noah is happy
about for you." I thanked her for talking with me. She said,
"Well, you have a big day for yourself tomorrow. I think you'll
love the little setup in the chapel. Your Aunt Martha has asked
Joe to use the café for a reception. Your Uncle Gabe was going
to use the bar, but with food, and you just having the boys,
someone might be coming in to disturb us." After Mia left, I
went to sleep. By morning, Mama, Aunt Donna, and Aunt
Martha came in. I took my first shower, after having the babies,
and those staples hurt when I lightly washed in that area.
When I got out, I put on a hospital gown, and Aunt Martha
said, "Kerala Jade, I'm fixin' to have to cut some of your hair off,
girl." So she cut it up to my shoulder blades. When she did, I
had to go and re-shower. When I got out, Mama and Aunt

Donna held Andrew and Lucas. Aunt Martha started putting on my makeup. Steve wanted to be at the courthouse at 2:00 PM. When Aunt Martha finished fixing my hair, Aunt Donna unzipped the bag. She said, "Your Mama and I went on Saturday night. I got this for you." When she pulled it out, it was a lovely gown, nothing fancy, no beads or lace, just a pretty beach wedding dress with spaghetti straps. When I put it on, my breasts were swollen. It looked like I had big boobs. As I was about to put the heels on, Mama placed a silver sixpence in my left heel and told me, "Do not lose it. It's been our family for years. It's yours until you pass it on to your daughter or one of the boys." She brought out her necklace with a blue pendant and matching earrings, and Mama said, "This is your blue and borrowed." Aunt Donna said, "Your cake topper is very old. It was Grandmama Blake's when she got married. It's yours now. Your Uncle Gabe had it when given to him, so now it's yours." 12:45 came. The nurse came in and said, "Oh, I see you've got big plans after leaving here." And I said, "Yes, don't make me late." The nurse said, "Hence, I'm not. I have your discharge papers right here and I brought you two bags of diapers and six cans of formula. I'm not supposed to, but the babies will need it." When I looked over there, Mama and Aunt Martha were packing everything they could get their hands on. They put me in the chair with Andrew and Lucas in each arm. Out the door we went. When we got to the courthouse, Daddy and I stood out front, and Mama and my aunts had taken off inside. I saw Steve's truck as Daddy and I stood at the courthouse chapel doors. Daddy asked me if I loved him. And I smiled at Daddy and said, "Daddy, I have never had this feeling of being so comfortable around someone and there's a feeling with him that I can't explain. We do not choose who we love. Our souls desire it for us. When you realize you want to spend the rest of your life with somebody, you want the rest to start as soon as possible. I never knew what love was until I met him; every moment in his arms, I feel safe, loved, and cherished, so Daddy, if you're asking me if I love him, yes Daddy, I do." Daddy said to me, "That's all I needed to know, but I'm going to miss my little girl around the house. I believe Steve will be good to you Kerala Jade. One more thing, I love you." I smiled at him and said, "I love you too Daddy." When Daddy opened the door, I took a deep breath, and we walked into the chapel. There stood Steve. When I stood beside him, Judge Shafer smiled at me. Steve and I said our "I do's" and signed our marriage license. Steve and I asked Judge Shafer how we could keep Cole far away from the boys and what was needed for Steve to adopt them. Judge Shafer said, "Kerala, Cole is downstairs in the jail for beating a woman the other night." He looked at Steve and asked him, "Do you want to adopt the babies?" Steve said, "Yes." Judge Shafer asked me if I had put the father's name down when I named them. I said, "No." Judge Shafer told me that Steve was well with him. Steve put his name in as the boys' father, and Judge Shafer said, "I will fill out the forms for their birth certificates and strip Cole's rights away. He is unfit to be anyone's father, and I'll waive the fees as a wedding gift." After we signed all the documents, the boys were officially Steve's and had Nicholas' as their last name. Before we walked out, Judge Shafer said, "Kerala and Steve, I wish the both of you peace and happiness together." As we left, we went to the café and had a small reception. While I looked at the cake, I told Steve to be careful because the cake topper was older than both of us, and that it was my Grandmama Blake's wedding centerpiece. He said, "That's fucking awesome, baby." I told him, "It's going with us now." He said, "Family tradition is great." After the reception, Steve and I headed to his apartment. As we parked, Steve said, "Let me get the babies in. I'm coming back for you. So I sat there for a few minutes and he came out the door. When he opened the door, he picked me up, carried me in, put me on the couch, and told me I was off tomorrow. I have someone covering for me. My General is a good guy. I noticed my stuff had made it, and two bassinets were in the living room. Steve said, "Baby, I'm sorry, but I need to get this crib together. I got one done last night and started on this one this morning." He was putting the boys inside the bassinet as he told me this and he said to me, "I put some of your clothes in the dresser if you want to change." I said to him, "Oh, already playing around with my unmentionables?" I saw him blushing and he laughed saying, "No, ma'am, I left them alone." So I went into the room, saw my dresser, and opened up where I put my pajamas. There were four new pajama sets and a note of a gift from us. Noah, Shane and I set it out with a matching tank top. My boobs were on fire and I was hurting, so I removed the dress and put it away. I put the pajama's on, and the tank top made my boobs pop out. So I put on my robe to cover myself up. I looked at the bed and saw that it was new and well-made. As I returned to the couch I sat there looking around. Steve got up and checked on me once he got the crib set up. I fed the boys, entered their little nursery, and put them to bed. I could hear the shower running as Steve put Lucas and Andrew down. I got a drink from the cup I used earlier. I figured it was time to spend my first night with Steve. As I passed the bathroom door, it swung open and Steve stood there without anything on. I looked down at him and my face flushed red. He smiled at me, walked up to me, and said, "I'm not ashamed of showing you my body. It will be odd for us both because we're still getting to know each other better." As he smiled at me, he kissed me and said, "Baby. We have the rest of our lives to explore each other." As he walked off, I thought, holy shit, Kerala Jade. What in the hell did you just marry? That is not normal between his legs. My face was still blushing. I had taken off my robe and forgot that I had the tank top on with my boobs showing. I thought, oh my God, Kerala, this is a slutty move, but yet here he is showing you his package, and I thought again, yeah, that's your package, and you have a big man and well-built to play with. As I got into bed with him, I placed my head on his shoulder, and he said, "Baby, you looked beautiful today." I told him, "Thank you. I finally got you home with me." As I laid there, I fell asleep on him, but around 1:00 AM, I woke up to the boys crying. So I got up and had to change them while figuring out the best way to feed them simultaneously. I got a binky, put it in one mouth, and fed it the other. As I got one fed, I picked up the other. Once I had them settled, I went back to bed. Steve carefully moved me closer to him and he kissed me on my cheek. I went back to sleep when the morning sun hit the window. I got up and took care of myself. I noticed the washer and dryer were in the bathroom, so that was settled in my mind. I stood in the shower for a long while. As I got out, I cleaned up my blood mess and got dressed. I looked at Steve and he had one son in a bounce and the other in his arm. He saw me and said, "Look, boys, Mama is up. Both of you wore her out last night." I walked up to him, kissed him, and said, "I'm sorry I didn't hear them." He said, "Naw, baby, I got them out. They were still sleeping, so I figured you needed some sleep before bed." Steve had given me my identification to go to the commissaries and some money if I felt like going.

As 1:30 AM rolled around, the boys were up and ready for feeding and changing, so I got up and fed them. It had taken me 45 minutes, and when I was almost asleep, Steve's alarm went off. I felt him get up, go into the bathroom, and go out the door. I saw the time was 3:00 AM. As I went back to sleep, I found myself dreaming and fantasizing about me and him. I heard one of the boys crying, so I got up, walked to the chair I had set in, and looked out the window. While feeding the babies, I heard the morning workout from the base. It sounded like a swarm of bees with echoes of yes, sir, no, sir. As the sun rose, I could see them doing exercises. I put Lucas back in the bassinet and placed him back to sleep. Andrew was my fussy baby.

After 45 minutes of getting Andrew comfortable, I quietly slipped off and got my first cup of coffee. Lord, after my sip, I realized why my Mama ran off to drink her coffee. I slipped out onto the small back patio to enjoy a little bit of "me" time. I saw where I needed to unpack my stuff, looked through the kitchen cabinets, and saw hardly any cookware. In the fridge was nothing but beer and leftover takeout from the night before. As tired as I was, our little apartment was dirty. So I went and got ready to walk to the commissary store. It was just a five minute walk, and I saw where Steve put together the double stroller.

I was still craving food and wanting a pot roast. As I was getting ready, I saw one of my sundresses, so I put it on. It had a light blue color to it. Once I was ready, I placed Lucas and Andrew in their carriers and put them on the stroller base. I noticed a storage area under the carrier and a small place to put a shopping basket. I double checked that I packed everything for the boys. I had money from my paycheck, so I decided to get some dishes and things we needed. I couldn't believe what was there as I walked into the store. The prices were cheaper than at the grocery store. It was like a small strip mall. So I picked out some dishes, pots, pans, and cooking utensils. I checked out of that area, placed them in the bottom of the stroller, walked into the grocery, and got cleaning supplies. I got excited about having a dishwasher in the apartment. All my life I had hand-washed the dishes for Mama. I chuckled over being excited about an appliance and now understood why the household ladies got excited about it.

As I got our food for a few days and walked out, I could hear boots stomping on the pavement and chanting as they approached me and turned on the block. That's when I heard whistling and catcalling. I heard, "Hey baby, why don't you return to my bunk tonight?" Then a big scream came out of nowhere. All the troops came to a sudden stop. And someone asked while screaming, "Who the fuck is being disrespectful?" As I started to walk off, the Drill Sergeant came around from the other side. It was Steve with this crazy ass look that I had never seen before and he was screaming, "Who is catcalling? You better step the fuck-up?" Just as his troops stepped away from those who did it. Steve looked at me like he was mad. I felt my heart drop, fearing I had pissed him off in the way he had looked at me. Did I make a mistake with what I had on? In some ways, I was scared to death. He told them, "By disrespecting my wife standing there, you just disrespected me, and I want you to apologize to her right now." As they apologized, I just smiled, and Steve made them drop to do push-ups while screaming in their faces as they were on the ground. And with all that going on, it woke the boys up. So I found the nearest bench and started caring for them. Steve walked over to me and just smiled at me, but still had this crazy-ass look on his face. He said to me, "Baby, go home and rest up. I'll be there at 1700." I smiled at him, got up, and started walking away. I had just read the rules. Steve couldn't touch or show affection to me while in uniform. But it blew my mind. What kind of man did I marry? As I got back into the apartment, my fear of feeling like I was with Cole again came to the forefront. I had to feed the babies and put them in their bassinet. I started putting things away. I found my Grandmama Blake's handwritten recipe book. She gave it to me before she passed away. She wrote it when she was a teenager. It is very old and an essential book to me.

I started cleaning up things and placing my whatnots in the places that I had in my room. When I was done, I started making dinner. As 5:00 PM came around, I had my mess cleaned up and dinner on the table. I placed his drink next to his plate. Just as I was setting it down, the door came open. I was scared of him. I stood stiff by the table, with the fear of getting my first ass chewing by him for the way I was dressed. Still, a different person came into the door instead, and when he saw me standing there, he quickly greeted me. I apologized, and he told me to please not be ashamed of myself or apologize for what happened this morning. He said, "I'm training idiots that are not well mannered, which is rude. I'm sorry, Baby, you had to see a side of me this morning that I never wanted you to see. I'll try not to pull that side out of me here in our home. If I do, please set my ass straight."

I apologized for wearing the dress I wore, and he snapped at me and said, "No, you don't stop being yourself. Besides, I thought you looked beautiful in what you have on. I'm sorry I snapped at you, but I love the color on you, and dammit, this food is fucking awesome. Where in the hell did you learn to cook?" I giggled for a few minutes as he got up to get another plate. I told him, "My Grandmama taught me how, so you're eating my Great-Grandmother's pot roast." After his third plate, I knew he was fixin' to make himself sick and miserable. I also knew I did well. Grandmama always said if a man eats more than one plate, he appreciates the meal and your cooking. After dinner, he got up, walked over, picked Andrew up, and said, "Did you all miss Daddy because he missed you two today and Mama." I cleaned up the remainder of my mess.

When we got in bed, he told me, "I'm sorry that I scared you today and that things are moving fast for you these last few months. We're still learning our habits and getting to know each other, but I want you to know I love you. I may not tell you that I do like I should be. Still, I'll start a habit of telling you like I should as we lay here." I told him, "My heart belongs to you and only you. I love you and I feel safe with you. Being in your arms I feel like I belong here."

I spoke my love and feelings for him and poured my heart

out until we understood each other. The following day was the same routine, but he kissed me before he left and said, "Good morning, baby, and I love you." When I got up, I cleaned and cared for the boys. I had done too much the day before, so I sat around and got dinner ready. Like clockwork, Steve came in the door and kissed me and told me he'd missed me today. I smiled at him as we sat down to eat. I sat back and watched him make a fool of himself again, and he said, "Are you feeling okay about going out for dinner tomorrow night?" I told him I was feeling up to it. After Steve ate, he went straight to the boys. I sang to them primarily throughout the day. They had been awake most of the day, so I hoped they would sleep through the night. And I was blessed that night. I was scared about 1:00 AM, so I got up and checked on them. About 3:00 PM that afternoon, I was up to get myself and the boys ready. I wanted to leave the apartment, so we got to the restaurant and sat down. Harper Ross waited on us, and she was Cole's cousin. She was being a bitch and said, "I see that you had your babies. And got married." I said, "Yes, we did. So here we are." As she was about to say something else to me, Claudine came up to the table. Claudine told Harper, "Bossman said it's time for you to take a break." Claudine said, "I got this table," when Harper walked off. As we ordered, I was glad. Claudine is Aunt Martha's sister, so she knew the story. Harper walked off. Steve asked me, "What's that about? Harper was a bitch." Harper was consistently rude when Claudine brought out our food. I had a feeling she went and called Cole. She was why I didn't talk to anyone besides my best friend, Hope, during school. If I did, Harper would tell Cole what I did in school. As we left, sure enough, Cole was coming in. While we were driving off, I didn't say anything to Steve. When Saturday morning came, Steve was working on my car. When he came in, he said someone had been tampering with your vehicle because your Dad and I just fixed the belt on it. Somehow, your wires were cut, so it would not start. I figured it was Cole. Steve said he was helping my Dad and that the alternator wire was on there good. I told him I tried to start it, and it wouldn't. Steve said it was just a quick fix and that he had fixed it by the end of the day.

When I got my staples out, I was happy to have them gone. Aunt Donna met me, but it was only briefly, for about one hour to sit with the boys. I disliked the appointment time. It was too close to time for Steve to be home.

As seven weeks passed, things between us were perfect. I asked Steve if there would be an issue if I went and saw Mama and Daddy. He said, "Baby, you are way overdue for a visit with them. You have been in this apartment too long, so go visit." The next morning I packed Andrew and Lucas's playpen, diapers, and formula. As I pulled into the drive, Mama and Daddy weren't expecting me. So I got the boys out and their bags. It felt odd that I was no longer living there. As I walked up onto the porch, Mama met me and said, "It's about time you come to visit us." I smiled and said, "Sorry, I've been busy with them." Daddy was sitting in his chair, telling me to give him his grandbabies. I handed him Andrew, and told Daddy, "This one here likes to have his fits and piss on me all the time." Daddy started laughing about it, and he shooed me away. So I went into the dining room, where Mama was shelling the last of the summer peas. I grabbed a handful and joined her. I asked her, "Well, what's the gossip?" She told me that Mr. Doven passed away. I was a little bit saddened by that news. I said, "There goes my bombing buddy. At least he's taking care of Ace for me up there." She asked me if Steve was good to me. I told Mama, "That the man treats me like a princess and spoils me. Unlike the stupid one I got rid of, he is a big old teddy bear." She said, "Speaking of that piece of shit, I found out something. That a friend of yours, Hope Hopkins, is messing with him." I told Mama, "I told her she shouldn't mess with him." Mama said,

"She's the woman that put his ass in jail." I told her, "Isn't that something? I got married on top of his dumbass." Mama said, "You certainly did." It made me mad that Hope would do something like this. Mama said, "Hope was working at the Russell's Pizza Place." I said, "Really?" Mama said, "Look at my pictures."

I looked at the wall, and she had an 8×10 of me and Steve on our wedding day. She said, "I have yours on the hutch already in a frame." I said, "That's a good picture of us." She said, "I put that one in the newspaper announcements and your scrapbook." Mama and I visited until about 1:00 PM that afternoon, then Mama said, "Kerala, you look exhausted. Why don't you let me have the boys until after the Sunday service?" I told Mama, "Steve is very attached to the boys, and besides, I don't want Tilley getting a glimpse of the boys." Mama said, "She hasn't been to church since Cole did that to you. I could show them off." I sighed, caved into her and said, "Fine, but you're going to have to go and get diapers. There's a can of formula in the bag, and these boys are a handful." Mama said, "Kerala Jade, I think I can handle it. I raised the three of you." Before I left, I held them for a few minutes and put them in the playpen. As I walked out the door, it broke my heart that I was leaving them behind. It bothered me because they weren't in a heavily protected area. As I was driving, the thought of Hope came to mind, and I thought I would grab us a pizza since it was Friday. I was mad at Hope for not listening to me in the first place, so as I walked in, I saw Chris Russell Chris's dad owned the pizza place. He said,

"Hey Kerala, how have you been doing?" I asked him, "Where is Hope?" He told me she was out on a delivery and would be back soon. I asked him if she was still messing with Cole. And he said, "Yeah. God Dammit, I told her not to mess with him." Chris said, "I'd told her also, I'm glad you got away from him." I asked him if it was obvious that he beat the living fuck out of me every weekend? Chris said, "Yea, our whole class knew. Oh, by the way, congratulations on your babies and getting married." I said, "Thank you and I needed to go ahead and place an order." So I did. As I was standing there, Hope came in the door. and I came out and said, "I told you not to mess with Cole. Look at you now. You didn't believe me until it happened to you." She said, "Well, you've stuck with him since you had his babies." I told her, "NO, they are not his. They are Steve's babies." The look on her face was shocked at what I just told her. I said, "Hope, my advice to you is to get in your car, fill the tank up and start your life there when you run out of gas. If not, you're going to be trapped here." I reached into my wallet and handed her a $100.00 bill. Chris said, "If you want Hope, I'll go with you. I'm ready to blow this place anyway. Can we leave tonight?" Chris handed me the pizza, and I told them, "Life is full of never knowing. Take that chance and do something with your life, but not here. Leave."

As I got home, I grabbed a piece of pizza and figured I would go and soak in the bath since I didn't have the boys. As I was sitting there relaxing, it hit me. I sat up in the tub and said, "It's been almost eight weeks since you had the boys, and Steve was teasing me for the past few weeks. I had just finished with my regular monthly and I began to fantasize about us. So I made up my mind. I was ready to give myself to him. I cleaned up and got out of the tub and noticed that it was about ten minutes until he got home. So I found this cut-off old tee that I had, put it on, and put on a pair of my favorite thongs. I covered myself up and made sure the curtains were closed. I thought, how am I going to ask or say what I want to do? I thought for a minute, put some food on a plate, got a beer, and removed my robe. I was running around about where to place myself when I heard the door unlock. I stood behind the wall. When he came in and the door closed, I presented the plate with a beer. I stepped from behind the wall. When he saw me, the keys dropped on the floor. He threw the plate on the table along with the beer. He picked me up and he asked me, "Are you ready for what's about to happen?" I smiled at him and said, "Yes." He placed me on the bed and started kissing me. I had already taken off my shirt and he started undressing. When he dropped his pants, it was fully erect and bigger than what I had seen. When he suckled on my breasts, I began to breathe a little harder. As I watched him kiss me all the way down, he started foreplaying with me until I couldn't take it any longer. He began kissing me all over again and he said, "Baby, are you sure about this?" I said, "Yes." He said, "If I'm hurting you, please let me know." I shook my head at him and he placed me the way he wanted me. And as he placed himself inside me, I felt my hymen rip. It felt like it was my first time. As we continued making love, the pain started turning into pleasure and he was making sure I was comfortable. This throbbing sensation hit me, taking a little bit of my breath away. I felt him let go inside of me. It was amazing. He carefully slid me into the bed. We cuddled up to each other, not saying anything, just looking, kissing and touching each other. I found that romantic as ever until I fell asleep in his arms. I woke up in the middle of the night and cleaned myself up. I was sore and I went back to bed. When morning came, I was ready for round two. Hence, we did. By that afternoon, he asked me where the baby boys were, and I told him they'd be here tomorrow. Tonight they were with their Nanny and Papa. Steve said, "Oh, so we get to have fun with each other." I said, "Yes, we do." He told me, "I hope you're not planning anything for Thanksgiving because we're flying out to see my parents so you can meet everyone." Steve talks very highly of his Grandmother. She was the one I was looking forward to meeting, but the word flying had me thinking second thoughts. I had never been on a plane. But leaving to go somewhere else had me quite excited because I never went anywhere out of my home state. We spent the whole Saturday being selfish with each other. By Sunday morning, Steve was ready to get the boys. We both figured we would make a grocery run before going and getting them. As we got to the store, I started getting what we needed. I headed down to the frozen food section. Steve and I heard a baby crying. I said to him, "That kind of sounds like Andrew pissed off." Steve said, "I know it is." So he walked away from me, and I started looking for coupons that I clipped. I looked up and saw Cole standing there. and I could tell he was about to hit me. I heard Steve say, "Look, Mama, look who I found, he is ready to be with Daddy." I looked at Cole, and he started walking off. Mama came up behind me, and I asked her, "Did they give you any trouble? " and she said, "Not too much. Lucas is your quiet baby, but Andrew wants to be seen and heard." Mama came out and said, "Oh, Kerala, someone robbed the pizza place and took Chris Russell and Hope Hopkins. Bert went to check on them. It looked like a struggle. The money and Hope's car are gone." I said, "Really?" As Mama and I talked, Cole came back by again and stood there. Steve looked like he could kill Cole, and Mama said, "Well, kids, the two of you better get home. There's a storm tonight." I looked up and saw the Military Police (MP) and thought, oh God, now what, and I saw Cole run like a scalded dog. An MP saluted Steve and said, "Sorry, sir, but General Aldridge has asked us to come track you down, ask for your service, and help the public find two missing individuals. General Aldridge has asked you to get your squad to help. You must report at 1600. That gives you enough time, sir?" Steve told them, "Yes." We took the kids from Mama and checked out. When we got to my car, Steve put the boys and me in the car and locked the door. I was bothered by many things and I couldn't believe what Hope and Chris did. I was quite mad because it pulled Steve out of the house when Steve got in the car. He didn't say a word about Cole other than don't open the door for anybody when we get home. So, as he got ready, I put away the food. Steve came up behind me, held onto me, and said, "Sorry baby, but this is one of the perks. I'll be home in the morning. I love you." I told him to be careful and I loved him too. As he walked out the door, he locked it behind him. As I went to bed, I dragged the boys in their bassinet into our room. At about 3:00 AM, I felt Steve get into bed. I left the lamp on. I felt him pull me into him and start kissing me. Before Steve returned, I laid there thinking of Hope and Chris and wondering how far they made it. But I couldn't believe he trashed his Dad's pizza place.

The morning we got on the plane, I was nervous. I put chewing gum in the boy's ears, but mid-flight, I started getting sick, and Andrew was starting to get fussy, so I sucked it up. As we landed, I wanted to kiss the ground. Steve rented a car for us to go to his parent's house, but along the way, I was sightseeing. Steve was showing me around as we pulled up to this gate, and he pushed in a code. When the gate opened, and we started pulling in, I knew right then that he was raised differently than I was. The houses were fancy. Looking at them, I felt Steve placing his hand in mine. And he kissed it. I was confused and understood his family owned a prominent real estate development company. I told myself, don't touch a fucking thing, but your babies. As we pulled up to this house, Steve asked me to stay in the car and he would return to get me. As I was looking around, I was a little bit uncomfortable. These people were out of my league. Within five minutes, Steve comes out with people. He opened the door and said, "Mom, Dad, this is my wife Kerala, and I have a surprise as well. Meet your grandsons, Andrew and Lucas." His Mom came out and said, "What?" As I looked at her, she said, "Steven, you're kidding me." As I looked at Steve, he had his wedding band off, and I wasn't happy about that. As I watched him put his band on, his Mom said, "I'm sorry, I'm Shelby, and this is my husband, Phil." I said, "It's nice to meet you." His sister came up and said, "Sorry, but my little brother can be rude sometimes. I'm Amy, and this is my husband, Wyatt. This is our brother Bradley." I politely said, "It is nice to meet everyone." His Mom hugged me and Steve started getting the boys out of the car. His sister grabbed Andrew as we walked in saying, "I didn't know which baby to go with." Shelby came out of nowhere and said, "You're welcome to follow me into the kitchen." So I did and she was holding on to Lucas. She got on the phone and called someone by the name of Mary, and she demanded that Mary come over and not poke around. After she hung up, she said, "No one will believe I have grandchildren now. I can't believe it. Steven said nothing about you, these babies or getting married." Amy asked her what she wanted the boys to call her. And she said, "Glamy." Amy said, "That's suitable." So when Mary knocked on the patio door, Shelby posed in front of her and said, "Look what I got." Mary said, "Where did you get that?" Well, I suppose my new daughter-in-law, and she gave me two grandsons, whereas the other one she asked for is in Phillip's arms. These are Steven's babies." Mary looked at me and said, "Now, what's your name?" Shelby came out and said, "Mary, this is Kerala; Kerala, this is my long-time friend Mary." I came out and said, "It's nice to meet you." Mary's first words to me, "You're not from here. I can tell by your accent." I said, "No, ma'am, I'm not." And that's when she drilled me about how I met Steve. So I told her, but I kept the baby's real Daddy out of it. I put his ass in the dirt. I sat back and watched them talk. Amy said, "I finally have a sister-in-law." I said, "I finally have a sister." I told her that I was the only girl, to which she said, "Oh my God, I feel like this is crazy that we grew up not having sisters. I love the way you speak." I told her, "If I ever say 'Bless your heart' that means I'm calling you something else in Southern English." She said, "I want to know." I told her it was an insult to mitigate its severity. I explained my southern words to her, and she thought it was funny. We laughed at each other's words. As we talked, I noticed that Shelby was a little bit hyper and just a happy person. Amy and I clicked. Shelby and I got to talking about who I was and she brought out albums of family. As I looked and saw his high school friends through there, I saw why Steve had some small scars. He had an accident when he was 17. I turned it over and there were some obituaries. I quickly read bits and clippings of two obituaries of the same kids in the previous pictures. I put two and two together. Oh, shit, they died, and Steve survived. I flipped over and read the newspaper clippings of how it happened. Steve was speeding when a drunk driver hit them head-on. The car rolled several times before coming to a stop. It ejected one of his friends and killed them instantly, so Steve has Survivor's Guilt. Shelby said, "Steve has never gotten over losing them." I was looking at Steve as he came into the kitchen and sat down. Shelby closed the book and I noticed he was a little upset. He kissed me on my cheek, got up, and walked away. Amy said to me, "I think it still bothers him to this day. He was in a dark place during that time." I felt for him as I saw the time. It was rather late. I came out and told them I hated being rude, but I had the twins on a schedule, and I was happy to know they understood. So I got the boys ready for bed and stepped out where Steve was talking with his brother. I politely told them good night, walked back into Steve's old bedroom and gently closed the door behind me. As I walked over to the playpen, the boys were smooth out. They had a big day of meeting new people. I saw a Jack and Jill bathroom, so I took advantage of using the shower and slipped into appropriate clothes instead of wearing my normal nightwear. I got into bed and fell asleep until the next morning. I woke up and saw the boys weren't in the playpen. So I freaked out until Steve had me in a body lock and kept telling me they were fine. I relaxed, but as we lay there, he started stroking my hair. He said it was just now 2:00 AM, the boys were in Mom and Dad's room. He had just now laid down his brother and noticed the time had passed by quickly. So I went back to sleep. When the morning came, I could hear the boys chatting with each other, so I crawled over on top of Steve. Midway, I woke him up. He wrapped his arms around my body and smarted off, "Oh, we will start the morning with you on top of me. I can work with this, but not here. Just wait until we get home. I will turn you inside out." I leaned in and kissed him and he gently put me on my back and told me, "I don't ever get to love on my baby like I want to, like she deserves." I just let myself have him. We had to stop before we got carried away because we both knew it was inappropriate to do it at his parents' house. Soft and better words were spoken between us. As we stopped, we thought we had better get up and make the best of it. While sitting there, Shelby and Amy invited me on a shopping trip, so I agreed to go. Steve handed me the credit card, which I didn't like to use. So we packed the boys, and I left with Shelby and Amy. When we got to this strip mall, we went into a baby clothing store. I couldn't believe the prices of the clothes, $25.00 for one outfit. I was a little taken aback by it. Shelby and Amy had a handful of clothing in their hands. I found at least two outfits for the boys. When we were checking out, Shelby took the clothes out of my hands, and as the total priced out, she had blown $6,000.00 on the boys in one store. I said, "Thank you for the boy's clothes." She said to me, "Oh, don't mind me. Those are my grandchildren. I will spoil them, whether you or Steve like it or not." When lunch came around, I was worn out, but as I was sitting at a lunch table, a group of ladies came in and I could tell they had never worked a day in their life. Still, one kept looking me up and down as we put Lucas and Andrew back into the strollers. We got up, and she started looking at me hard. As I passed by her, I could tell that her makeup and blonde hair had the look of being a snobby rich bitch written all over her face. As we left and returned to his parent's house, I was worn out that women could shop that much. Steve and I sat on the couch with Lucas and Andrew, playing with them and watching them talk as the doorbell rang. Steve smiled at me and said, "I have a surprise for you. Come out here with me." Hence, we got up, and he opened the door. There was that same woman from lunch, so Steve grabbed my hand. We walked out. This woman tried to make herself known to Steve, but he ignored her. I put two and two together. The ex-girlfriend, Asha, and Steve told me, "Baby, this is what I got you." As I was standing there, I was shocked. Steve bought an SUV, and this bitch came out and said, "I'm sure Ellie May, here, is going to love it." I couldn't hold my mouth shut. I giggled at her and said, "Bless your heart. I'm guessing my husband told you my name, or are you too stuck on my southern accent that you must think I'm dumb?" As I said that, he snickered, and Amy stepped in and thanked Asha for bringing it by for them saying, "I'm sure my sister-in-law can find her way around this SUV." I looked at her and she didn't get the hint that she needed to leave. Shelby came out and said to her, "Well, I'm glad you dropped it off, but dinner is almost ready here. I'm sure Kerala and Steven would love to explore their new car by themselves." By this time, Asha had taken the hint. As I looked up, I saw Steve watching her walk away and I smarted off, "Do you still have feelings?" He said, "No, ma'am." As I looked at the SUV, my concerns showed, and I asked Steve if we could afford it. Steve told me, "Baby, don't worry about the payments. It's my job to worry about what we can or can't afford." I smiled at him and said, "Thank you." Shelby and Amy pulled me into the kitchen. Shelby told me, "I'm sorry, Kerala, but I'm guessing you figured out who she is. I told her, "Yup." Shelby said, "I saw her at lunch today. I'm guessing she's in for the holiday's and ran into Steve at her father's dealership. He owns just about everyone in town." As she told me, I thought to myself, okay, Kerala, we must clarify this mess. Phil came out and said, "She tried to throw herself at Steve and he told her to get lost. Amy said,"She's a psycho. There's another issue of why he dumped her in high school." As we were talking about Asha, Steve's ass had been saved from her desires. Phil said, "We avoided Ed's dealerships until Steve saw the SUV, so we stopped. Steve wasn't happy about it when she popped out." Later that night, as Steve and I were getting ready for bed, I handed him the credit card back, and Steve said, "Did you get yourself something?" I told him, "Your Mom, overbought for the boys." Steve came out and said, "Baby, I know this is a little overwhelming for you to be in this type of environment. I've seen my Mom blow money like it was nothing and I've been around homes that are bigger than our apartment, but this lifestyle isn't what I want for myself. And yes, I did buy you the SUV today because my baby deserves it and I'm looking forward to having it later on." And I told him, "I was guessing he was looking to be the black sheep." And he said, "Well, yeah, if you kind of want to put it that way. I don't want to ask my parents for anything. I want to earn what we get. I don't care for their lifestyle. If I work in a factory to ensure you and the boy's needs are met, so be it. I hope you understand what I want for us." I told him I understood, and he said he was happy we had this subject out of the way. Steve said, "Let's discuss another subject that happened. I don't want Asha ever to degrade or bully you again. In reality, now I can't stand her, and to be honest with you, as a kid, I never should have messed with her. I know you had that quick thought: did you mess with her today? No, I'll never mess around with you. I married you because I fell in love with you, and nothing will change how I feel about you. So I hope we have this all clear and out of the way." I told him, "Yes, we do."

The next morning Steve and I put the boys in the stroller.

We walked down to his Grandmother's house. As we were walking, I could hear two older women going at it and arguing. I heard this woman say, "Evelyn, you're stupid as fuck. If you think you still got it, your whale hole is dead." As we made it to the fence. The two were cussing each other out; one was drinking and smoking, and the other one was sitting on her side of the fence. Steve opened up the gate to the one that was cursing and drinking. She saw Steve and told the other lady to shut up. My grandson is here, and she stood up and hugged Steve and said. "Oh my big boy, I'm sorry that I missed you yesterday. I had a doctor's appointment and my rummy game was scheduled for yesterday." Also, she looked at Steve and me and asked him if this was her. Steve introduced us. I told her it was finally nice to meet her. She asked, "Are these the boys?" Then she told Steve, "I didn't say a word to your Dad. Well, let's get in the house before Evelyn starts to get up in my business. Steve, can you get me another beer before you sit down?" So he went and got her one. She told me, "Kerala, you have a beautiful name. To top it all off, you're gorgeous." I thanked her. She said, "You're from the southeast, and it's about time we get a Southerner back in our family. My husband and I grew up in Mississippi until we met in college. I went to school for marriage counseling and sex therapy, and when Hudson and I got married, we moved out here. He and Shelby's parents went to become partners, so what do your parents do?" I told her. She said, "Hard workers." I said to her, "Yes, ma'am," and she said, "That's honest people." As she sat there, she said, "Excuse me." At the same time, she stepped outside to smoke, and Steve followed her. Now I knew where Steve picked up his cigarette habit. Steve isn't a big smoker, just here and there. But I was falling for his Grandmother, whom they call Bebe. We visited for a while. I kind of didn't want to leave. The day after Thanksgiving, Steve and I headed out. I was a little bit glued to the scenery, but a short time after we stopped for lunch, I started getting sick. After driving for 11 hours, Steve was getting sick so we checked into a room for the night. The next morning I still felt like shit, and he was fine. When we got home, I felt as if someone had been inside our apartment, so I walked around as we settled in for the night. I was still sick and miserable when Tuesday morning came so I went to see the doctor and ran all the tests they suggested. The only thing that came back positive was that I was pregnant. As I returned home I sat there thinking of how was I going to tell Steve when he walked in he said, "Kerala, I've been transferred to North Carolina, and we have to move within two weeks. Does that bother you?" I told him, "I married you. I go where you go, but there's something I have to tell you." He asked, "What's that?" I smiled at him and told him, "I'm pregnant." He was a little stunned, and he asked, "So you're carrying a piece of me inside you? My flesh and blood?" I told him yes again, and he picked me up and said, "Oh my God. I can't believe this baby. Our family is growing." He was so damn happy that he had walked over to the boys and said, "Did you two hear Mama? We're going to have a little brother or sister." I had fears that since I was carrying his own child things would change for Andrew and Lucas, but in the last few days of me telling him, it didn't. He is very attached to them, very protective of them, and has been since they were born. During that week, Steve started packing so the movers could come and pick it up. We didn't have very much and Steve hired a guy to transport his truck to a place where he could pick it up when we got there. As Sunday came around we went over to Mama and Daddy's. We had dinner with them and Daddy told me and Steve that Cole intends to kidnap the boys according to what Frankie heard. Frankie told me the other day. Steve told Daddy he'll die trying. Steve made the announcement that he had been transferred to North Carolina and Daddy said to us, "You know by you two leaving here it might be a good thing for the boys." I said, "Well, just in case you're wondering about the other news we have for you, Steve and I are going to have a baby." The news to them was good, but what bothered me was the fact that my parents were going to miss a lot of their lives. When we got back to the apartment, Steve was a little on edge, and I knew why. By the end of the week, Steve and I had driven through town. I got one last look around and we were out of there. A few days later, we arrived at the new base. Steve and I were looking for the address of the house. When I saw the address I said, "You're kidding me." It was a nice house and Steve said, "Baby, we're not on the base. We're just on the edge so we can have family visit us, but they're paying for it. As we pulled up Steve's truck showed up where it wasn't supposed to be. Steve had it sent to a storage unit until we got there. A day later the movers showed up. I tried to pick up some boxes and Steve snapped at me saying, "I better not see you pick up another box." So I just sat back and barked orders at him of where I wanted things to go. After we were settled in, within the first two days, I completed all of the paperwork. I found a new brochure guide and maps of the area in our mail slot. I looked through them and one thing the brochure had stuck out to me. I could be benefiting by taking nursing college courses. I put some long thought into it. I needed something to say I had done something with my life other than just making babies. As I was making dinner I did some reading on the nursing course and the degrees offered. It struck me even more as Steve walked in the door and I had myself buried in the article. He circled around me and asked me, "Are you deeply interested in what you're reading?" I apologized to him and just hit him with it. I told him, It's time to do something for myself, make something of myself instead of sitting around." He raised his voice and said, "No wife of mine is working in a damn restaurant." I told him, "No, I'm not aiming for that. I want to take some college classes." He got quiet and we discussed the issue that it would be a good idea if I wanted to proceed with my education. I told him, "There's an in-house day care and if you get moved my credits move with us." He told me, "Baby go for it, I support you on this if this is something you want to do." So I filled out the application the next morning and went to the post office. I figured I would make my first store run. As I was walking through there I realized it was our first Christmas together and the boy's first ever. So I got us a tree, some decorations and I figured I would get a few gifts. I wanted to kind of decorate the house a little. Once I was done, I felt like I was with Shelby when I returned home. I played with the boys for a few hours after I put the food away. When they went down for their nap, I put the tree up and decorated it. It was placed near the front window. As I started getting housework done, my morning sickness began. I pushed through it and made dinner. When Steve came home, he saw what I had done. And I quickly told him that I was sorry for over spending. He told me, "Baby, I'm not mad. You are just trying to make a hollow house into a home." I could tell he was in a good mood and I had asked him how his day was. He told me, "Baby, it was good. I ran into my buddy, Aiden, that I lived with in Germany. He's here." I said, "That's nice to know." As we were sitting there talking, Andrew and Lucas were blabbing away with each other. Steve got down and started playing with them until they were out for the night. Within two weeks of waiting for some response, I finally got a letter that I had been waiting for. I had been accepted into school. When Steve came home that afternoon I was excited about it. During this time frame, Steve was working 14 to 15 hour shifts, and I tried not to bother him too much with things. As January came around and my first day of school, I was a little bit nervous. As I was sitting in my seat, this girl sat down beside me and said, "Hi. My name is Eliza. I said, "It's nice to meet you. My name is Kerala. And Eliza said, "Is this your first class?" I said, "Yes it is." Eliza said to me, "My husband and I just recently got married last weekend. He is still in training, so he has to stay in the barracks until his training is done. He slipped off base, and we ran and got married." I said to her, 'Congratulations." As she was talking to me, she was fussing to me about his drill sergeant being an asshole and how big of a hard ass he was. I chuckled as she was talking to me, and she said, "So is your husband in training?" I looked at her and said with a smile, "He is a drill sergeant." She got quiet, and I told her, "If your husband has mine as a drill sergeant, don't worry. I know how he is out there." Her face got bright red and I told her, 'Don't worry. I'm not going to say anything to my husband." During lunch she sat with me and a weird craving kicked in of a chocolate and cheese chips mixture. She looked at me crazy and I told her, "I'm three months pregnant, and I have almost five-month-old twins that are in daycare while I'm here." She asked, "So how long have you and your husband been married?" I told her, "For about five months. We have been together for almost a year in March. We got married three days after the twins were born. But for Steve, he has been in the military for years now. So it's nothing new here for him. As I was talking to her the cheese chips and chocolate were working well. Once it was gone, I was still wanting more, but as soon as I got the boys I went to the store and got some more. When I was pregnant with Andrew and Lucas, it was nothing but pineapples. With this one, shit, when I got in the door another crazy craving hit. So I started dinner and that wasn't what I wanted. So I cooked some ramen noodles and I seen some sour cream and I mixed it together with chili powder as I was mixing it up I didn't notice Steve had came home I was busy mixing my concoction together, I had my Nacho cheese dip and melted chocolate mixture and I turned around Steve had scared me that I had dropped in the floor, and he looked at me, and I was disappointed that it was in the floor, and I was about to cry about it and he seen my face, and he said oh no baby I'm sorry so where in the craving stage and I said yes, and he said I thought you heard me and I told him no, my thoughts were on fixing this and Steve picked me up and said I'm sorry, baby I'll make it right and happen when he put me down he took off out the door, and after I cleaned up he within 20 minutes he was back with it what I had I was happy as several weeks had past Steve had gone with me to the sonogram at I'll be damn, there was two more little boys coming, but we really didn't care as long as they was healthy. As August 1999 came, Lucas and Andrew was full speed two: legged chatter boxes, and they loved to get into stuff and Andrew was the leader, but when Steve came home, that was it and as they said daddy the man and Steve started them on that mess, and they would tell me to open the door so they would run out to him the day Steve got granted maternity leave for a month so we had played smart and paid everything ahead and gotten our needs for a month. Shelby and Phil were flying in for the birth of the babies. I had just been ordered to be on bed rest for two weeks before my due date. Steve and I were in bed. As I was sleeping, I had strong cramping in the abdomen, groin, and back, as well as an achy feeling. As I lay there waiting for it to stop, I woke Steve up. He was all over the place and ready to go. It stopped, so I figured that I started getting ready for labor, and I told him I'll let you know when it's time to go. It was back and forth with light pain. It wasn't until about 6:00 AM that I went back to sleep. But as I was awakened by Steve, he helped me sit up and he sat behind me. The pain kicked in and I didn't realize that I had dug my nails into Steve's arm. He got me comfortable again and I went back to sleep. After I was sleeping a while, I woke up, and my water broke. I called for him. I told him we needed to go. Before I could get out of bed, Steve picked me up. I saw Shelby and Phil, but did not get a chance to say anything to them as we were going to the hospital. I had to calm him down a few times. Once I got in there, Steve was trying to throw his weight around until I had to tell him to calm down again. They were all set up for a C-Section. As the first baby came out, he was big. Whenever they got the last baby out, he was big also. I looked at Steve and told him, "You name them." He asked me if he could honor his friends, and I told him yes, but at least name one of them after you. He named them Seth Wesley and Chase Michael as I looked. Steve said, "Well, one of them has a dirty blonde with a reddish tint, and this one would be Chase." So we were amazed by his hair. After three days, when we got home, the boys wanted me to pick them up. I couldn't do anything for them, but they were very interested in their little brothers. After Phil and Shelby left to fly back home, Steve and I had our hands full. My energy level was gone.

A few weeks passed, my ass was being handed to me, but I was sucking it up and going with the flow. When November came around, Steve told me that he and Aiden had plans to go hunting and man, I wanted some deer meat, so I told him okay. I cleaned up some hunting gear for Steve. I told him not to come home empty-handed the morning he left, and he said, "Yes, ma'am." But it wasn't until around 3:00 PM that afternoon Steve returned to the door with three bags full of meat. I was surprised that he got a deer. But the truth is, it wasn't only one deer, so I cooked some. This would be Steve's first time eating wild game. He did what I had told him to do. I was proud of him.

By December, we joined Mama and Daddy for Christmas. As we walked into Mama and Daddy's house, I set Andrew and Lucas down. They looked at their Papa and looked at me then took off to him. I had been teaching them who is who through family photos. As I pulled off Chase's little hat, Mama saw his reddish-tinted hair, and Steve had pulled off Seth's, and Mama couldn't believe it. Daddy picked up the boys and took off outside with them. I saw Steve a few minutes behind him. I told Mama I needed a few minutes, and she said, "I understand entirely. Don't worry. I have them here. Good Lord, I don't see how you're doing it all." I told her, "I just make it happen." As I put my coat on and walked out of the house, I started walking down the road. It was just a tiny break from the boys as I stood in front of Mr. Amos's old house. Standing there, I looked around where Mr. Doven and I had blown up his car. I saw tiny pieces of shrapnel on the ground that were still around. I picked up the piece that I saw and placed it inside my pocket. As I was standing there thinking of that day Noah and Mia pulled up. Noah said to me, "Reliving that day?" I turned around and he got out and hugged me, and he said, "It's been too long, little sister." I told him, "You think?" And he said, "Come on, I want to see what my nephews look like." I told them, "So when will you make me an aunt?" Mia said, "We could just use your kids as our own." I said, "Oh, really, Uncle Gabe and Aunt Donna's story." She laughed at me, and I told them, "Boy, I could tell you this, if there were a contest of changing diapers my ass would win it!" We went to laughing about it. As soon as we returned to the house, Noah and Mia looked at Seth and Chase. Noah asked me, "How many months are they?" I told them, "They're four months old." He asked me what they do. I said, "They're at the stage where they can laugh and kind of talk to you, but it's not like Andrew and Lucas." Noah was laughing about them. As I looked up, Steve and Daddy were bringing the boys back in, and Noah got down on the floor with them and started playing with them. As Shane and Layla came busting in the door, Andrew and Lucas had taken off to Steve, and Noah said, "Dammit, Shane, why in the hell do you do that? The boys and I were playing hard on the floor until you came in and did that."

We had a fun visit, but I explained to Steve that we don't buy much from the stores. We hand make most of our gifts. It's been a family tradition of ours for years.

When the year 2000 came, we returned to North Carolina about a week after the holidays, and Steve came home. He told me he had been transferred to his home state, and I started getting boxes ready for packing. While I was packing, I felt we had acquired more things since we moved from my home state a year ago. We had everything loaded and we were gone. Within three days, we arrived in our new city and stayed at a hotel. Shelby found out about it as we stayed there, and she told Steve that his other Grandmother's house was just sitting there. No one in it, but Steve refused until she had a slight fit with him. The two made a minor deal with each other. We were waiting for housing, but the deal with his Mom was sweet. We moved into his Grandmother's house, a four-bedroom house. Steve wanted to turn the garage into a main bedroom. He didn't feel comfortable sleeping in his Grandmother's old room, which gave four of our boys a room. I was happy that Bebe lived down the Street and Phil and Shelby lived across the street. His siblings lived one house down from ours. We had two elderly neighbors on each side of us, and one was Ms. Margo, one of Bebe's friends.

Within a month of moving into the house, I was pregnant again. When I told Steve that I was pregnant, the smile on his face was happy, but he and I had discussed that we needed to play it safe for a while, and I told him yes, we do. I was still waiting on my transcripts from North Carolina, which gave me some time to get to know my sister-in-law better. She and I discussed how I should get this piece of furniture that would fit perfectly in the living room. I told her that Steve and I couldn't afford anything right now with me being pregnant again and the bills. And she said to me, "Yea, right, Kerala, not unless my little brother has blown his million dollars already." I looked at her crazy and kind of laughed and said, "We don't have a million dollars." Amy said to me, "Bullshit, Kerala, yes y'all do. Steven got money after Grandpa passed." I still was in shock, questioning. Amy said, "Oh shit, Kerala, he didn't tell you. Oh my, I'm sorry, but it's something that he should have told you." I was getting mad about it, but I kept my cool until she left. I went into our bedroom where Steve keeps the bills and bank statements. Sure enough, there it was, a million dollars. I was pissed off. I just didn't understand why he had hidden this from me. When he came into the door, I was still pissed off, and I could see that he was in a bad mood. Generally, if he is in a bad mood, I try to turn his mood around. But his mood and mine didn't mix that night. So, as he walked in, while I was cleaning up the bottles and sippy cups, something just hit me. I started throwing the shit around, and he asked me if there was something wrong, and I told Steve in a hateful tone," NOTHING." He asked me again. I came to him and said, "You know, I thought we were supposed to talk to each other over our finances. Yet here we are, struggling a little, and I found out today that you are hiding money from me. And it's not just a little, it's a lot." He asked me, "Who fucking told you?" I didn't say anything to him. He got in my face and started screaming at me and asked me again, "WHO FUCKING TOLD YOU?" For some reason, I flinched and closed my eyes. I felt as if I was about to be hit. He stopped and started walking out. As he was leaving, he slammed the door. I knew that I had pissed him off, and this was our first fight ever. It bothered me a lot. I should have approached him better, but he got a taste of me when I got mad about something. He was hiding something from me, and the worst part was that my pregnancy hormones were all over the place when I saw him over at Amy's. I guess he put two and two together. Standing in the kitchen window, I watched him walk down to Bebe's, and I knew she would put him in his place. I fed the boys, bathed them, and put them to bed. In reality, I wasn't concerned about the money. It was just that he was hiding it from me. After I calmed down, within a few hours, he walked back into the house, and I still didn't want to say anything to him.

I just couldn't figure out why I didn't want to speak to him, but as he grabbed me, I saw him in a calmer tone. He said, "Baby, I'm sorry that I screamed at you. I should have told you about my inheritance money, but it's set up differently. A lot of it is for the boys. It's in accounts being built up for them, and the rest is held back for emergencies and medical bills. I told Steve that it was only money. I got mad at him for not telling me, and I'm worried about the bills and medical bills. He told me again not to worry about it and that it was his job to worry about it. We both apologized to each other and promised that we wouldn't try to get into arguments. That night, we discussed if one of us felt unhappy about doing something, we should talk about it to see if one of us was uncomfortable. So Steve and I started setting our rules and boundaries for each other. He knows firsthand when I get mad now.

When October 2000 came, Steve and I welcomed our third set of twin boys. I saw him upset that we didn't have a girl. I told him we would try one more time for a little girl, and if it was another boy, I was done having babies for us. We discussed that I wanted a year off from having kids, and we agreed that we needed to practice having safe sex. He told me after you're done, I'll let you see about getting one of those mommy makeover things. The morning I delivered via C-Section, out came two small baby boys we named Kaden Jade and Matthew Steven, weighing 6 and 7 pounds. None of our twins are identical twins, but I can say that when Bebe and Shelby came in to see them, she looked at them and said, "Well, I see that both of them look like Steven from his baby pictures." After three weeks of bringing them home, I started feeling overwhelmed, so Steve told me I should leave the house. All I did was go to school and come home. Amy and I made plans to get acquainted with Bradley's new wife, Leah, who he recently married. The morning I got ready, I asked Steve three times if he could do this, and he told me, "Baby, just go. I've got this. So, as I walked over to Amy and Wyatt's house, and we got in the car, Amy told me that she had some good news. She had just found out that she was going to give birth for the first time. I told her, "Well, congratulations! At least it isn't me this time. We're taking a year off." As we were leaving, we talked about the weather and how this cold front came in. It was odd for this time of the year. It was about 25 degrees outside, still early that morning. But as soon as we got to the store, and I was looking through a rack, I saw Asha, and she came out and said to me, "I've been told that inside every fat person, there's someone beautiful... I'm just wondering who the hell you ate?" When she said that to me, it made me mad, so I walked away from her and went out of the store. I was so mad at what she said to me. I somewhat felt that she made it to the point of me being her target. So when I got back to Amy's ride, I dug around in my purse and noticed I had a pack of Steve's cigarettes and some Jolly Ranchers. It hit me that I remembered what my cousin Kyle did to his ex-girlfriend years ago. So I looked for her car and there it was her little red BMW with her name on her license plate. I walked over there and licked the Jolly Ranchers and stuck them to her windshield. When I saw Amy and Leah coming out of the store they saw me walking away from her car. I got a cigarette and lit it up. I've never smoked a day in my life, but boy it hit the right spot and took some small stress away, so I stood there smoking it. They asked me, "What in the hell Kerala did you put on her windshield?" I told them, "Sit back and let's watch the show. I'm getting my revenge on this bitch. The bully is about to meet the bully. She's about to bite off more than she can chew with me." So about ten minutes of us sitting there and we watch Asha come out of the store. I said to them, "It's showtime." As Asha got in her car and she saw the Jolly

Ranchers on her windshield, she got a scraper out of her car. And as soon as Asha started scraping it, the windshield shattered. I started laughing. Amy and Leah looked at me and said, "Oh my God, I love you." Amy said, "She was mine first." I said, "Sorry ladies, but I'm Steve's." They were in shock and awed by what the fuck I just did to Asha. I told them, "Do not tell Steve what I just did to her." Amy said, "After what she just said to you, I think that bitch deserves it." I told Amy I got a helluva lot of revenge and rage in my ass. If she wants to be my target, so be it. I've got a better plan. Why don't we go back to the house and have a family night and I'll cook dinner." I was feeling home sick anyway, so I had made plans to cook a Goulash. They thought that was a good idea, but when we walked in the door I was still pissed about what Asha had said to me. It was fully out of line and Steve was asking why we were back so early. Amy just came right out and told him what Asha said to me and this pissed him off. He came up behind me, wrapped his arms around me and told me, "I love you a lot. You know that, right?" And I said, "Yes." He told me, "You know you're beautiful to me and that's all that matters to me. Don't worry about what others think of you. I've already told you not to let her get to you in your head. I married you because I love you." As he was holding on to me, I understood him. I told him, "I'm fixin' to start dinner so your parents and Bebe can join." As he stood back watching me cook, I wasn't thinking about what I was doing. But the thought of this bitch wanting to put me down, and made a fucking beeline to come and say something about my weight. But with me, jollying up her windshield was fucking classic. As we all gathered that night, I was happy to make Bebe feel good about her roots. It reminded her of home also. She told me, "I haven't had this since I left home," which pleased me. After dinner, Steve made sure Bebe got safely back home, but he was still hot about Asha's dumbass remarks.

By mid-November, I started doing clinical, which was fantastic. I started having my sights on becoming more than just a nurse; I wanted to be a Pediatric Nurse Practitioner. You could say I had the wants of the White Coat Syndrome. I wanted it badly, so I made a goal for myself. If I wanted it, I had to make it happen for myself. As Monday morning came around, I got up and did my best to get the kids rounded up. Chase was being a mean little shit and he had kicked me. It surprised me for him being only a year old. So I had to give him a little swat on his leg as he was trying to go out the door. Steve had just left. Chase ran over and kicked the shit out of me and had a fit over his Daddy leaving. When Steve came home, he asked me if I wanted to go and have a date night. And I told him sure. During that whole week, during clinical, I had a bossy ass nurse that was shoving her weight of attitude around on me and a few others. I wanted to tell her off. I was damn sure glad to see Saturday in my sights because that Monday, we were going back into the classroom. But when Saturday morning came, I fixed the boys and my big boy some breakfast. I cleaned up and went into our room and started messing with my hair. By that time in my life, my hair was past my ass, and it was tricky to fix. So I fixed it the way I wanted, put on my makeup, and got ready to go to this restaurant. As Steve and I started to talk, he asked me why I saw a very overwhelming wife. I told him I was sorry, but I've been feeling overworked here lately. Steve asked me how I liked clinical, and I told him I liked it. I was in the children's ward. It's a somewhat fast pace for me, and I asked him how things were going on his side of the job, and he told me the same shit different days. I'm learning new people and who they are. I told him I know it's been an adventure for both of us.

And I hit him with a question and asked him how his mental health was since Kaden and Matthew arrived. He had told me it was stable. He told me that he had to whip Lucas the other day. He had to run behind my back because Lucas didn't mind him. I told him, yeah, I've been waiting for you to do so, and Chase has been acting up a lot lately. When you left the other morning, he was trying to walk out of the door, and I wouldn't let him. So he was as mad as ever and kicked me. I had to get him. As we were talking, this guy called out to Steve. I looked over at him, and he started talking to Steve. I listened to them talk. They were talking about whom, why, and where they had been. This guy was sitting there next to me while I was trying to eat, spitting his food in my hair.

I noticed Steve was attempting to break his attention away from him, but this motherfucker wouldn't shut the fuck up, and Steve's leg began to shake. I knew he was getting upset. I grabbed his hand, and I let the fuck lose on this guy and said to him, "Excuse me, I hate to interrupt you, but you shouldn't be ashamed of who you are. That's your parent's job. And by the way, you need to wipe your mouth. There's a tiny bit of bullshit around your lips. From the looks of it, you are just slightly exaggerating. It's more of you thinking you have won a competition over my husband, for which I'm very proud of him, and his goals and accomplishments. It sounds like whatever he did to you in the past, you can't let go. So it's best that you behave yourself before I unleash my pit on your ass." I shocked myself with what I had said to this guy. It's kind of like my life is better than yours, kind of thing. After I said that, Steve paid, and we were out the door. I knew it was wrong of me, but I had a shitty week. When Steve placed me in the car, I looked at him, and he laughed. All I could do was just smile and say I didn't mean to say that. All Steve did was giggle the whole way home over what I said. Still, once we got home, we both told Phil and Shelby thank you for their time. I started putting Andrew and Lucas to bed. Once I got them down, Steve told me to go on and relax for a little bit, so I did. However, I could still hear him laughing about what I said as I got out of the bathtub. I opened the door, and he pulled the sheets back, so I got in. We started loving each other and picking until Seth and Chase entered the room and we let them in the bed with us.

As the week of Christmas came around, we packed up the boys and went to Mama and Daddy's. They would get to meet Kaden and Matthew for the first time. When we got to my home state, I could tell that the place was going downhill. But I did have a worry that Cole was out of prison, yet he got sent because he had big plans to do something to us. Cole tried, but burnt down a damn daycare that was sitting a few doors down from our old apartment. Once I stepped inside Mama and Daddy's house, I could tell they missed me being around there. I got caught up on the latest gossip. And Mama said we should take the kids to the Christmas Parade. I thought that was a good idea, so she and I made plans. The next night, we did go, and I was shocked when I ran into Hope and Chris. It surprised me that they were married and living in the next state over. I told them, "I guess $100 or more got the both of you really far." She told me, "Thank you for your advice on getting the hell out of there." She asked me where I was living, and I told her, and she said I see that you got out of this place and I had told her yes. She told me the reason they had to show face due to they were about to be declared dead, but she told me when Chris walked into his Dad's pizza shop the other day we had to explain to him of our actions, and I had told her yeah it was a big deal when you two did leave town and I told her it was good to see her, but I needed to attend to my boys before one of them get out of hand. I was happy to know how they were doing in their lives and how far they had made it, but as we had got a spot the mistake was the fact we were at my favorite display, the Thomas Kinkade Christmas figures. I could look at those for hours just looking at it, Steve bought me a laptop computer for Christmas which I appreciated. As for my gift for the boys, they really shied away from everyone until we got ready to leave. They all four started showing out for Mama and Daddy. At the start of May 2001, I can say that we had a very eventful year. I was out for summer classes, and I had looked up out of the dining room window. I could see down the street at the corner of Ed and Lizzy Welshmen and Shelby's best friend Mary going into their home. I was trying to watch, and Bebe came in to see the boys, her daily thing to do. I asked her how good Mary and Shelby are friends, and she told me very well. And I said, well enough that she knew Shelby doesn't like Lizzy and Asha? Bebe said yea, and I had told her to watch down there at their house and tell me who in the fuck comes out. As Bebe and I watched, Amy came into the house to let Marcelina play with the boys, and Bebe said, "Look, Amy Kerala has a better view of the nut house, and your Mom's so-called best friend is in it. As we were watching, and we waited around, Bebe said to us, 'Well, I'll be damn that bitch Mary is down there in the Welshman house." Amy was shocked to see Mary come out of there. She said, well, that's how Lizzy is getting the Information about you and Steve now, through Mary, I looked at Amy and said, well, do we need to do some dirty deeds? Bullshit, and Bebe said, what are you two talking about?" Amy said, "Bebe, our Little ol' Kerala here can be quite a little devil behind closed doors." I had told Amy some bullshit.

I'm an undercover gangster; I fly under the radar by doing things where I'm not seen and just sit back and watch the action after I do this shit. As it was just about noon and my mother-in-law had come in from work early and stopped by, Bebe had told her everything of what we just saw. Shelby yelled out, "That Bitch," and Bebe asked, "So Shells, What are you going to do?" I could see evil in my mother-in-law's eyes, wanting revenge, and I said, "We could reverse the role. You approach Lizzie's best friend to find out what the fuck she's up to. Either way, it's your choice. Amy said her mom provided her with information about us, and she's giving it to her, so Asha can be involved in Kerala and Steve's business." Shelby said, "Let's hold off and see what she's up to. Let me go and call this bitch to see if I can get anything out of her." I told her, "Well, if you need to play dirty, please let me know, and I'll show you how it's done. The right way of doing it." She looked at me and said, "We're not playing dirty until I say so, Kerala. I know you busted out Asha's windshield. I said," No, that wasn't me. It was the Jolly Rancher." Shelby said, "I wish I could have been there to see that shit go down." As Shelby left, I knew what she was going to do. Within 45 minutes, Shelby returned to our house, looked at me, and said, "Kerala, I'm trying to figure out if she's friend or foe?" I asked her if she had given her any info about Lizzy. Shelby said,"No." Bebe said, "Well, now you know all those years your best friend betrayed you." When I looked at Shelby, she was pissed and said, "So what can we do, Kerala?" I told her, "Get some raw meat and a few raw eggs. Place them in a mason jar, mix it up, and poke a hole in the top. We bury it for a few days, and we go from there. Shelby asked me, "What will it do?" I told her, "We get it and put it in between the window of the car door. That shit will stink for days and it won't leave. And you are in luck this week because Steve has night training on Friday. It's only Wednesday, so if you want to do it, Friday night is your best, so we can go in and do both cars, Mary's and Lizzy's. Let's see how well they get along. Lizzy keeps her car out because she'll usually have someone from her husband's dealership wash it in the drive." Shelby said, "Amy, your Dad, and Wyatt have an out-of-town meeting Friday and won't be back until Saturday evening." I looked at Shelby and said, "Sounds like my mother-in-law is making plans for her revenge." Shelby said, "Yes, I am Kerala." So I had Shelby make the mixture up, and we buried it.

Within three days, I saw Steve off for his night training.

Shelby, Amy, and Bebe came over. After Steve left, we both looked out the window, and damn, what a sweet treat this is. Asha had come in, and Shelby said, "Oh shit." I said, "Well, this will be fun after all." So at about midnight, we dug that stinking ass mixture up and grabbed a small, light rubber, syringe that I used for the kid's medicine. I'd grabbed some cheese from the icebox, some Jolly Ranchers, some sugar, and salt from the house, and some Liquid Drano in a balloon. Along the way, I found piles of dog shit. Shelby asked me, "What in the hell are you doing, Kerala?" And I had told her, "My part of the fun." So when we got to their house, I watched Shelby put the mixture shit inside the window. She was about to get sick of how bad it smelled.

As for Asha, I stuck cheese all over the body of her car and more Jolly Ranchers. Then I placed the dog shit in her wipers, and dumped the Liquid Drano off in her gas tank along with the sugar and salt. As I grabbed my mother-in-law, who said, "This shit should be fun in the morning." I told her, "Breakfast at my house?" She said, "You're damn right. I'll be there to watch it front and center." My mother-in-law had too much fun doing this. We took Bebe back to her house, and Amy went home herself. I showered, cleaned up my evidence, and got into bed at about 4:00 AM. I had felt Steve get into bed. I knew that shit was fixin' to hit the fan within a few hours, about 6:00 AM, I got up. I kept telling the boys to be quiet and that Daddy was still asleep. So I fixed my coffee, some breakfast, and Amy came in with Bebe behind her. Within about ten minutes later, Shelby was too excited to see this, and Bebe said to Shelby, "Calm the fuck down. You'll wake Steve up. So let's sit here and have breakfast with the kids as a typical family would." About 9:00 AM rolled around. I opened the window and Andrew asked, "Mama, why were you out last night?" I told him to shut up, and Bebe said, "Your Mama had to chase the boogie man away since your Daddy was gone the previous night."

71

I felt my grandmother-in-law's southern accent come out on Andrew. She told him, "Boy, don't ask any more questions than what you should be worried about." Within 10 minutes, after nine outcomes Asha. All of us sat at the dining room table watching her be miss prissy ass in disgust and looking around as she removed the cheese from her car. She didn't dare touch those Jolly Ranchers, but I had ensured she would. When she got in her car, we saw her turn on her wipers. The dog shit got smeared all over the windshield. When she got out and touched it, she bumped the Jolly Rancher, and the windshield blew. She smelled her hand and realized it was dog shit. Man, the childish fit she had.

As we laughed, I could hear her scream echoing off the houses. At about 11:00 AM, the guy who washes Lizzy's car comes in, and needless to say, he doesn't want to touch it. As we were sitting there watching this shit go down, Ed came in. He was trying to figure out what was going on. He started Asha's car, and within a few minutes, boom, her car engine blew up. I looked at my in-laws and said, "My ladies, this is how you get shit done." As the three of them were trying to figure out who would do this to them, they started prissing their asses over to Mary's house. I said to my in-laws to hold tight because this might blow back on us, so get ready. As we watched Mary get slapped Shelby realized that Karma came to play off what Mary thought of being on the other side. Shelby said, "I don't think I have time for her now." About noon, as we were still laughing about what we had done, it got quiet. I knew that Steve was towering over me as I sat there. I could feel the heat from his body, and he came out and said, "You know I would like to get some rest, but with this little party that I'm hearing from the dining room, it's not happening for me." That's when Bebe said, "Well I think I could go and give Ethel hell. We're sorry that we woke you up." Within a few minutes after my in-laws left, Steve looked at me and said, "I thought I would have a quiet nap, but who could sleep with you ladies laughing and carrying on? Baby, I'm exhausted, so I guess I'll go and lie down again." I told him I was sorry. I didn't mean for it to get so loud. I told the boys it was time for a nap and told them to hurry up about it.

Close to an hour after the boys laid down, I figured I would go and play makeup to Steve about the noise this morning. When I did get back into bed, he said, "Now this is what I'm thinking about." So I could get some sleep during that week, everyone was trying to figure out who trashed their cars/ My ass wasn't saying one word about it nor did my in-laws say anything. By mid-June of that year I let the boys out in the front yard to play in the sprinklers. I mean it was hot. I had to try to find things for a two year old, one year old and an eight month old to do together. As a boy mom I'm going to get out there and show them how to do it. Andrew and Lucas thought this was amazing. So as they got an understanding of what to do, Chase and Seth started following along behind their big brothers asking for Matthew and Kaden. I had to hold both of them while teaching the older boys how to play in a sprinkler along with their toys. About lunch time, I turned the water off and figured it was time for them to go and take a nap. They weren't happy about me turning off the water. When I had the boys dried off and fed them lunch, they were worn out from playing outside. So it was no issue for them going down for a nap. As their napping hour kicked in, I started to clean things until the doorbell rang. When I opened up the door this guy came out and said, "You know the rules." I said, "I'm sorry, what are you referring to?" He said, "The toys in the front yard are part of the Homeowners Association (HOA) rule and you can't have any toys on the front lawn. You need to go and pick them up. The wagon isn't supposed to be on the front porch." So I said, "Fine, I'll get them in a few minutes." He told me, "Now." I looked at him and said, "There's never been a problem before about the wagon on the front porch." He said, "Well, I'm the HOA President and the code enforcer." So I said, "Give me a moment, and I'll go and pick them up." He said, "If you don't pick them up, I can do a lot to you and your house. I can make you homeless and sell your home right out from under you." So I got mad and went and picked up the toys. He said, "Your children aren't supposed to be playing on the front lawn with the water." And I told him, "I have six toddlers. You're not going to tell me what I should or shouldn't do with my kids." When I picked up the toys and put them away under the hidden bench seat that we have on the front porch, I told him to fuck off and grabbed up the wagon and put it in the living room. When Steve came home that afternoon he asked me, "Why is the wagon in the living room?" I told him, "This rude ass, so called president and code enforcer from the HOA, came here and told me that I needed to pick the toys up and get the wagon off of the front porch." That's when Steve told me, "We are not in an HOA, the old part is not on it. The new part of the community is. But when my grandparents built this area, they made sure that this part wasn't a part of the HOA." I knew this would piss him off, so the next morning, I had Steve put the wagon out on the front porch because I had just made Bebe a pie. I intended to go to her house to give it to her by mid-morning. I gathered the boys and we briefly visited Bebe, then returned to the house where I left the wagon on the front porch. I went into the house and figured I would get Steve to bring the wagon in by that afternoon. Here is this guy again cussing me about the wagon being where it is and handing me a letter saying what we must pay. When Steve came home that afternoon, I gave him the letter and told him what happened to me. He was getting pissed off more, and he told me not to worry about it. All during the week; this guy kept attacking me, and each time I would tell Steve about it. By Saturday, Steve had to work a half day. It was about noon. The boys were already down for their nap and I had gone to shower. As I was standing in the shower, I felt as if someone was in the house with me, and I knew if it were Steve, he would let me know. While I was getting out of the shower, there was this big flash, and there stood this fucker in the house. I quickly got my robe on, and I told him to get the fuck out of my house. I kept pushing him until I saw Steve pulling in. When I reached the front door, he tried pushing me back, and Steve grabbed him. Steve choke slammed him against the wall and asked him what he was doing. He told Steve we were violating HOA. Steve said, "Oh really because this is not a HOA house, so why in the fuck are you in my house." He told Steve, "To ensure there has been no remodeling of the house's layout." I told Steve, "I stepped out of the shower as he took a picture." Steve grabbed him by his throat and told him, "I could kill you right now with my bare hands, right?" While Steve was choking his ass, he threw him down on the ground and Steve told him, "If I catch you back in my yard again, I'm going to hurt you." When Steve came back from Bebe's, he told me, "You don't have to worry about him again." I asked him, "Where in the hell did he get a key? Because you know me, I have the door locked at all times when I'm here alone." Steve looked on the porch and our spare key was gone. So the next morning Steve changed the door knobs on the house putting in new locks.

On the morning of September 11th, I was getting myself and the boys ready for school. As I was about to open the door to leave, the phone started ringing. I picked it up, and Steve told me, "Kerala, I need you to listen to me, and I need you to stay home and turn on the news." He told me, "Baby, do as I tell you." So I walked over and turned on the TV, and that's when I saw the towers fall.

After the towers fell, I turned off the TV. I couldn't watch any more. It made me worry about my husband and what it meant for him.

I had so many questions by that afternoon when Steve came home. I asked Steve what this meant for us as a family and for him. Since that happened, he told me truthfully about the possibility of war. During those first few months, I stayed worried, fearing that if he left, I wouldn't ever see him again.

When February 2002 came, I told Steve that our last baby was coming. But, of course, this was our only planned baby. I told him he was a little too excited. As soon as August came around, I decided to put Andrew, Lucas, Chase, and Seth in pre-k and a head start program. I knew this would save us some money on daycare, but when the morning came for us to take them, I was a little heartbroken because they were getting so big. Steve was laughing at me about it, but it hit him when Lucas told him bye. I saw it in his face as we went to Chase and Seth's classroom. Those two had to be peeled off of us. During this pregnancy, we were getting what we

prayed for a little girl. It was a back-and-forth thing with him over the names. It wasn't until I placed them together that I would announce it to him. But when we got home from taking the boys to school, we had Glamy to watch Matthew and Kaden. So when Steve walked in, he wanted to play with them. Mama's boys get a little rough sometimes, so rough that I have to pry them off of their big brothers. When Kaden reared back and hit Steve, it surprised Steve that Kaden could pack a pretty good punch. I sat there and giggled about what just happened. When the boys came home from school, they looked worn out, and I was glad they could barely hold their little heads up to eat dinner that night. Within a few weeks, Steve and I went to my doctor's appointment, and my blood pressure had spiked. The nurse said, "Well, it looks like this one here is ready to make her debut." So, within three hours, Steve and I had our little girl. We named her Savannah Ketria. When we brought her home, Seth wasn't happy about Savannah and he had a slight fit on us until Steve told him, tough shit, that she was his sister if he liked it or not. And I can say Steve is very picky about Savannah; it had taken the boys a little time to get used to another girl inside the house. Still, within a month of her being home, I placed her inside the crib and left, taking care of things I hadn't done yet. When I looked up, Steve had come into the room. He was laughing about the boys and told me that all six were having a meeting around Savannah's crib talking about how they needed to protect her. I laughed and thought it was funny. With Halloween around the corner, I figured I would call Mama and tell her what the grandkids were doing.

When I called her, she told me that she would have some little outfits for them when they arrived at the house. I pulled them out of the box with a note saying this was the only thing I could come up with since you told me about the boys holding meetings around Savannah's crib. She made one for Savannah. Mama made little mafia outfits for them, and I was guessing Savannah was the boss. When Steve came home, the boys were very excited. But when I put Savannah's on, Steve thought it was cute what Mama put together. I got tickled at him because he parades Savannah around so much that sometimes I have to make excuses to get her, so I can spend time with her. Steve is very picky about his daughter. Within three months, we had plans to go to my parents' house for Christmas, but with the boys and Savannah coming down with colds, we changed it to staying at home instead. Many things were getting to me during this period because I sent money to Mama and Daddy to come out and meet Savannah a few months back. They sent me the money back, saying they didn't have time, and they weren't going to take money from me when I could use it on the kids. The note bothered me also. When I told Steve about it, I could see that he didn't like the fact that they weren't coming, and it was kind of unfair.

As March 2003 came, Steve and I poked around so much,

about getting ourselves fixed, that the morning I had things scheduled for myself we received a surprise. When I went in and did a quick sonogram, the nurse looked at me and said, "Are you sure you're done with having babies?" I told her, "Yes." And she said, "Oh, your body has other plans for you." When I looked up at her, she turned on the heartbeat. She said, "You are pregnant." So she printed out the picture of baby number 8. When I walked out, I started laughing. Steve began to laugh because it was our fault for not being protected during sex. But Steve had told me, "Kerala this one was meant to be our baby."

After a few weeks, I dropped Savannah off at daycare. That Friday morning, I could tell Savannah was moody when I got her up and had taken the boys to school. I had gone to school myself. When I picked Savannah up, one of the caregivers told me that she had been on it all day. So when I put her in her car seat, I looked at her gums. They were swollen, and I knew she was teething. When I got home, I grabbed a washcloth from the freezer. When I would sit her in the high chair, she would have a fit, so the only place she wanted to be was me just holding her. The boys didn't understand what was happening to her until I told them she was getting her teeth in, so she would have them soon. I held on to her while trying to cook dinner. When Steve came in the door, Savannah saw her daddy and she started crying and holding her arms out for him. I told him she was teething when he took her out of my arms. The way Savannah does her little sniffles is cute because she does this face thing. After dinner, Steve and I tried to fix Savannah so she could get some sleep, but nothing was making her happy. So I told Steve to get some sleep. I stayed up with her until at least about midnight. Steve got up and took over when the boys and I got up. Steve and Savannah were out on the couch. I quickly fed the boys, gave them some old baking pans, and sent them out back. I noticed that Savannah was out of teething meds when I saw Steve get up. I told him that I was fixin' to run to the store and get some more meds for Savannah, and the boys were content out back. He told me she just wasn't having any of this teething mess, and he tried everything with her last night. I told him maybe tonight will be better and I needed to study for my finals. He told me at least I'm not working half a day and it is the weekend. I went to the nearest store to our house, so I could quickly be back, so Steve could get some rest. When I got back I saw Steve out front talking to our brother-in-law and his brother. I went in and checked on Savannah and went out back and sat down with the boys for a few moments. The boys made some mud in the backyard playing with the water hose. Kaden came up to me and said, "Mama me and Matthew are making you something." I thought it was pretend baking and I said, "Okay, I bet it is going to be good. I can't wait to try it." I told them that I needed to check on their sister and I would be back out. So I got up, went inside, and heard something clicking in the kitchen. I walked around and heard it again. So I walked over to the oven and opened the oven door. There was a mud mess inside my oven. It was full of mud and turned on, so I quickly turned it off and grabbed the baking pans. I took them out and ran out the front door with them. Somehow Matthew and Kaden started baking the mud pies for real. But they also cleaned up the mud off my floors, so there was no sign of them coming into the house. When Steve saw what was going on Bradley and Wyatt were laughing about it. But it really wasn't a laughing matter because Savannah was in the house. When Steve got on to them about what they had done, the rest of the boys pointed their fingers at Kaden and Matthew. Steve didn't get onto them that hard because they don't get into much trouble. All he did was spat their little hands. They didn't like it much, but with them being two three-year-olds, they were learning, and Steve told me they spend too much time watching you cook. I told him, "Well they are my baby boys as well. As a few weeks passed, and it was another weekend before bed, I saw the boys had their coloring books out before bed, so I figured I would just leave them out when I woke up. I laid there. I wanted a little time with Steve, and I noticed that Savannah wasn't up yet. When I looked over at the monitor, she was still asleep. So I rolled over to Steve, and when I did, I heard the boys were up, and Andrew said, "I'm not getting in trouble for you." Something told me to get up Kerala. When I quietly walked into the living room, there was Seth with a green marker drawing on the wall. When he saw me, he dropped the marker and ran over to play like he was watching cartoons. When I started raising my voice a little, I felt Steve standing behind me. That's when they pointed the finger at Seth. When Steve grabbed him up and took him into the bedroom, I knew what was fixin' to happen to him. Seth was fixin' to get his butt whipped. When I told the rest of the boys it's best that you go and play in your rooms today because it seemed like Seth put Daddy in a bad mood. Steve and I tried to clean the marker off the wall all day, but it wasn't working at all. Steve had to paint the wall that Seth had drawn on. When Steve asked Seth if he wanted his marker back Seth told him, "No sir. I don't like that color any more." During that summer Steve and I found something active for the boys to do, summer T-ball. We were busy with them going back and forth to their little games. As the end of summer was coming around, Shelby and Bebe wanted to tag along to go school shopping for me and the boys, which I was fine with, and with it being a weekday. Shelby took off work to go just as I was getting the kids into the SUV. I looked up and saw Asha leaving. Like clockwork, the bitch flips me off as she drives by the house whenever she's visiting her parents. As we left we met up with Bebe and Glamy so we started shopping for me. I have this little boutique shop that I like to go to. After I got my clothes, it was a bunch of maternity clothes, Glamy and Bebe came up with the idea that they would each take three of the boys and take off with them. I knew that they were fixin' to go out in the water from there because the two women bought nothing but the best and they took off inside the mall. Glamy had Andrew, Seth, and Kaden while Bebe had Chase, Lucas, and Matthew with money in their pockets to burn. I had the money to buy their clothes and if I try to give it back to them, they always have a fit on me. I learned through the years to just give in and let them go. So Savannah and I walked in the mall a little bit, until I bumped into Amy with Marcelina, and she was like, "Wow, how in the hell did you get off without the boys?" And I told her, "Your Mom has three and Bebe has the other three." She told me about school shopping with the two of them last week. I came back here for a backpack that they didn't have last week and I said,"You know your Mom." Amy said, "Yup, shop until you drop, and I can see my little brother's face now at the amount that Mom and Bebe is fixin' to drop." I told her, "I know, and he gave me the credit card last night for them. It makes me feel guilty." Amy said, "Don't be. Mom is spoiling them while she's here. Some day our butts will have our own and I imagine we'll be doing the same." I told Amy, "I'm sure we will." She told me about this outfit for Savannah. So Amy and I walked down to that store. As we were walking we passed by this nail salon. Amy looked inside and said, "I knew that bitch was home," I looked and there was Asha. So we both just walked on, and we had other shit going on in our minds. So as we made it to the store I picked Savannah out a few outfits and some for the new baby. Steve and I just found out that we were going to have another little girl.

As we go out of the store and I saw Asha, she yells out, "I fucked your husband last night." I just laughed at her and smarted off, "What, you mean to tell me your dildo wants nothing to do with you? And Hun, I doubt that you screwed my husband last night because he was too busy screwing his recliner with the back of his eyes and holding our daughter in his arms. So, try again, dumbass." I just wasn't in the mood for her dumb shit. She had circled around and started walking behind me and Amy. I felt her kick me, almost knocking me down, when I almost knocked Savannah out of the stroller. When I got up, she saw that I was pregnant and this scared me. She said, "I hope I just hurt the baby you nasty pig." As I was about to grab her, Amy stopped me and told Asha, "Bitch, you better run now because we will tell the cops what you just did to her." I began to worry about the baby and Amy told me, "We better go and get you checked out just in case." We called Shelby and told her what happened. So we got into my SUV and went into the Emergency Room (ER) As Amy and I were sitting there, within fifteen minutes, I was checked out and everything was fine. But Steve was blowing up Amy's cellphone and Amy had told him everything. When I got home Amy and I saw Steve was home and she and I told him everything again. As Steve sat at the dining room table, looking down there at the Welshmen's, I saw fire in his eyes. When Amy left I sat down next to Steve and something kept telling me to get dinner started. As I got up, Steve told me not to worry about dinner, so I ordered out for us. As he and I sat there, I saw his leg shaking, and I knew he was very upset. When I saw Phil come home, I watched him. Phil didn't go inside the house, but walked down to the Welshmen's house. About half way, Ed comes out and starts walking up our street. That's when Steve gets up and steps outside. I wanted to hear what was fixin' to be said. As Ed and Phil were coming up the walkway, I watched Steve start pacing the porch. That's when Steve let loose on Ed with Steve screaming at Ed, "I heard everything. If your daughter lays a hand on my wife or my kids, I swear to God she'll be the only woman in my life that I would ever lay a hand on, and she needs to stay away from us." Ed came out and said that he would make sure that she would keep her distance when she's in for a visit. Did I have it out for her now, you gawd damn right I did. Steve was still in Ed's face and when he was done, I watched Ed walk back to his house, but kept looking behind him. Within 40 minutes, I watched a little argument between Asha and Ed, then saw her leave.

When Steve came into the house, I had propped my feet up on our bed, and he sat down on the floor, kissing and holding on to me somewhat. Steve held on to me a little bit tighter that night. I just knew numerous things were going through his mind.

When school began, I started my last year of clinical studies. Alongside my classmates we had the white coat syndrome, bad, and we were so glad this was our last year. During the summer months I took the opportunity to advance, ahead of my class, since I would be out for a few weeks. When the new baby arrived we would almost be done, but as winter came around Steve and I welcomed our last child into our lives we named her Stephanie Michelle. As I was on the table, the Doctor was cutting my tubes and burning the hell out of them. Steve sat there watching him and making sure we weren't going to have any more babies. But our baby girl is beautiful. When we brought her home the boys said to us,"Not another girl Mama." I said, "Sorry, but she's the end of the line and no more."

As spring of 2004 came, Steve and I had a pretty big day for the both of us. That morning, the kids and I attended his Stripe and New Rank Ceremony. Once it was over with, I went back to the house and got myself ready for my White Coat Ceremony. I was happy that I had been accepted in the Pediatric Ward at the hospital. But once again, it hurt my feelings that my Mama and Daddy weren't going to be there to see my accomplishment. I can tell you this, I had one proud ass husband. When they called my name and placed my white coat on me, I knew that all my hard ass work and goals that I set for myself was done. After it was over, we all went out and ate together. After the weekend was up, I was excited to start work. I would be leaving for work early. When I dropped the kids off at daycare, they weren't happy that it was very early in the morning. But as I made my way up to pediatrics, when I stopped by the nurses station, they gave me a warm welcome, but the shock was when they called me Dr. Nicholas, and it was something that I had to get used to hearing. As a few weeks had gone by, I made a few new friends, but one morning I had come in and Dr. Ferris was needing a small relief. He was our labor and delivery Doctor, so I stepped in for him. As I walked in, there was a very young couple. She looked to be about 18 years old, and I looked at her chart and I had asked her if this was her first baby, and she told me yes, and I had told her oh, well, congrats on your first. I have eight kids ages 6 years to 4 months old. The first six were twin deliveries and my two daughters were singles. I made a joke and told them I drank too much of that weird water that our Mama's told us to stay away from. I began joking and getting her to laugh, I noticed that she was nervous. I understood how she felt, but as soon as Dr. Ferris came back into the room and asked me if I could assist him because most of his staff hadn't come into work yet. He said, "We are using what I could round up," as we placed all the tools out for the arrival and this girl was yelling for her significant other to wake up. So I stepped over to him and told him, "Hey, it's that moment that you could miss out on. Within a few moments a few staff nurses had come in to give a hand, so I stood by Dr. Ferris. When the baby came out, he handed this baby to me. As I started to walk over to weigh it, I looked down, and it stopped breathing. I started checking the baby out and trying to clear its lungs and airways and still no signs, so I started CPR on the baby. I looked at Dr. Ferris, and he looked at me and said, "Well, I did my part so it's your turn now." So I started barking orders to get this baby somewhere to do what needed to be done. When I saw Dr. Crosser had taken over, I walked over there to see if I could help. About 15 minutes went by, and she looked at me and said Kerala, "There was nothing that anyone could have done. The baby was going to die either way." I told her what Dr. Ferris said to me. This floored her and I had asked what happened. She told me the baby passed away due to Neonatal death, but was going to go and tell the mother what really happened. I walked out and to me, it had fucked me up a little bit. When I went to my own stationed area, I told them what just happened and they couldn't believe what Dr. Ferris said to me. When Candy stopped me about midday, she asked me if I was okay. I told her I was, so this is part of the job that I have to get used to. Before the end of my shift, I showed a little compassion to the parents and I clocked out for the weekend. When I picked the kids up, I held on to them a little bit tighter, but for later on that night, I couldn't sleep at all. So I dragged the bassinet into our room, placed Stephanie in it, and watched her sleep. It had taken me a while to go to sleep when Steve woke up and saw she was in our room. He didn't care much that she was in there with us and in the bassinet because we had just taken her out there to place her inside the crib. It had taken me a few weeks to cope with understanding this was part of my job, and they don't teach you this shit in med school. When summer came around, we were just sitting around the house and Steve's cell phone rings. When he hung up, he told me Aiden is in town and I thought oh okay. Then on second thought, oh shit, here we go again. A few hours pass then Aiden and Steve take off. Well I didn't say much about it, but when 1:00 AM comes around, I'm starting to get worried. So I wait up another hour and here Steve comes in, drunk as a dog. I was a little mad at him and I told him, "Get your ass on the couch." When he did, I noticed that he got a tattoo. So I turned off the lights and went to bed. When the next morning came the boys were standing around him, looking at him. When they saw me up, they knew I was mad so they scattered. I asked him, "So does your head hurt?" And he said, "Yup." He had shaken his head and I told him, "Well good then, I'm going shopping and you're watching the kids." When I returned home, he was sick as a dog and I saw the tattoo on his arm. I started laughing about it because it was a fucking unicorn, and he wasn't too happy about it. When Christmas came around, I figured I would cave in and go see my parents. But Steve and I were avoiding this one thing, and that was buying a MiniVan. So we both caved and Steve went and bought one. The morning we left I knew this was going to be a long trip home and it would be Savannah and Stephanie's first time meeting Nanny and Papa. It still bothers me at the fact that my parents never even tried to come and meet their granddaughters. When I would discuss the subject with Steve, he would get a little heated, but he and I see it the way we do. It works both ways and he and I are very busy people.

By Saturday morning we arrived at my parents' house and as we were passing through town I was looking around to see if anything had changed. The boys were so antsy to get out of the van. They had been cooped up in the van for a while and were ready to go and play, but as I noticed a few things had changed. The place was starting to be a little run down as we were pulling in, Steve told them, "We are going in first so Nanny and Papa can see you after that, you can go play." As we walked in, Mama was looking me over. She looked at the kids and I hugged Daddy. He said, "Oh my Kerala, they have gotten so big since the last time we saw them." I said, "Yes, they have." Mama said, "I don't see how you do it." I just told Mama, "Steve and I make it work." As Mama and I sat at the dining room table, I felt as if we were interrupting something. It seemed to me, Mama was throwing a little bit of her attitude towards me.

I started talking about the kids, and she said something that kind of rubbed me the wrong way. Mama said, "I wish you didn't live so far away so I could really get to know your kids. I don't really know them like I do Shane and Noah's." A little bit of my mouth opened and I said, "Well it's your own fault. I had sent you and Daddy some money to come out and see us. I'm sorry that my husband's career moves us around." And she told me, "Well, you should know that your Daddy and I don't like to go to far off places." I said, "Yeah, I know." I wanted to drop the subject because I was getting mad about what she just said to me. The fact that she was picking and choosing which grandkids she wanted to spend time with. Both of my brothers had nothing but girls.

As we had headed off to bed that night, I stood looking outside the window in my old bedroom, thinking and feeling I was just an outsider inside my childhood home. I said to Steve, "Do you ever get the sense of where you don't belong anymore in a place you knew your whole life?" And he told me, "Baby, you have been gone from here too long, and yes, you are going to have these feelings of being improper, and you know this is no longer home. It's coming home for a visit." I told Steve, "It's that I kind of hate it here in a way and in a way I don't. It's like coming back to see if anything has changed. Steve had told me, "Baby it's the same. It's just that it's getting run down." Steve asked me, "Are you and your Mom getting into it over something?" And I told him, "Kind of. It's how she put it and I might have taken it the wrong way. I would rather not tell you what it is because it will get you upset as well." When I told Steve this he said to me, "Baby, please keep me out of it until you need me to be in it." The next morning, I helped Mama get breakfast ready. The boys were using every bit of manners that Steve and I taught them. And while I was fixing their plates, Mama had a small fit on me saying that there wasn't enough food on their plates. I told her if they wanted more I would get them more. What surprised Mama was when they were done eating, they got up, taking their plates back into the kitchen. But when I helped wash up the dishes Mama was bragging about how well they had acted when I had heard Shane come in the door. I wanted to see my nieces. I hadn't seen them since they were babies themselves. Shane and Layla's daughters' names were Dakota and Phoebe. When I walked up to Dakota and bent down to say hello and kind of tell her who I was, she slapped me. It pissed me off. I jerked her up and whipped her little ass. This stunned her in a way. Shane told me about how he has tried to whip her, but Layla and him would kind of tie into how she should be disciplined. I told my brother, "If you don't start it now, there will be issues with the both of you and her later. Shane said to Dakota, "See, I told you that if you acted up before coming in here Aunt Kerala will rip you a new one, and you didn't listen to a word I told you." Shane came out and said, "It's about time somebody really tore into her. Every time I tried to, Layla gets on to me. This is her first butt whipping ever." I lectured them that if they don't get a hold of her now, then it'll be ten times worse later on whenever she becomes a teenager. During our visit, I felt as if I was whipping Dakota's ass every 15 minutes. My niece is a spoiled little brat. When Christmas morning came around, she was the only one who was very ungrateful for her gift. She didn't like what I bought her and it was kind of hurtful in a way. But, in a way it wasn't. Whenever she started having her fit and she didn't like what she got, she was trying to take Phoebe's away from her. I decided to rip her up and really show her who was boss. It bothered me the most that Shane and Layla didn't even bother to try and discipline her the whole time that we were there for the visit. Each time that I would really rip her ass my own kids would run in fear. They would look at their Daddy and be confused as to why she was getting her ass whipped. But, as for my brother Noah's daughters, they were genuinely grateful for what I got them after they opened their gifts. It surprised me they gave me a hug, and they turned around and hugged their Uncle Steve for the gifts. This put a little shock on Steve himself. After the holiday, Steve and I were so ready to see the four walls inside our own home.

As life moved forward for us as a family, the kids were growing into their own little personalities. Two years had gone by and the year was 2007. Each kid was from the ages nine to four years old. When I picked the kids up, Andrew, Lucas, Seth, and Chase walked in the door and grabbed a tennis ball and started throwing it around the house. I had taken it from them once. So they started in rough housing around with each other until I got on to them. Well, it stopped for a while, but Steve walked in the door. I knew that he had let asshole Steve come home with him. And that man, I really don't have anything to do with him when he is in one of those moods. I prefer to run from him when he gets in those moods. But after dinner, Kaden and Matthew had homework along with Savannah and Stephanie. Steve and I were helping them with it and the older boys were getting louder and horsing around. Chase started crying, Steve got up and separated them, but it didn't take long, and they started in again. I looked at Steve and I could tell he was getting agitated. That's when that crazy look on his face came out. I had seen that look when I was disrespected by a couple of soldiers. The man that I never wanted see stepped his ass into the door behind him. When the boys broke something Steve whipped up out of his chair and saw the boys had broken something important. That piece belonged to Steve's Grandmother before she passed. It was the glass in the tower clock. That's when Steve let loose and whipped them for the first time. After he had done so, he made them stand in a single file line and told them to start heading to the bathroom. I had gone on and gotten their clothes out. Once they got out, he had them line back up again, and he started chewing on their little butts again. He told them, "Look at Mama. She's always cleaning up our shit. Well, it's fixin' to change. If Mama tells you to do something, you better do it." As I started cleaning up the broken glass, needless to say, it put the fear of God in those boys. After Steve got a hold of them, he sent them to bed. I finished going through sight words with Kaden and Matthew with their sight words by 8:00 PM. When I finally laid down that night, Steve was still awake, which is not normal for him. He said, "Was I too hard on them?" I told him, "No, but the man you promised would never show up in our home just opened the door and you let him in." He told me, "I know I've had a bad day today and I forgot to leave that person at the door." I reminded him that, "They need discipline, and you need to distill that in them. If not, you and I will pay the price for it later on." Steve and I noticed that the boys had been acting out a lot here lately and we both wanted to get to the issue of why. When Steve came home the next afternoon, the boys knew not to fuck around and play games with him.

One night in April, about 2:00 AM, I'm dead to the world and I could hear Steve's cell phone ring. When it woke me up, he was up and had walked out of the room. I had a small bad feeling that it was his call to go overseas, so I waited a few moments before I got up and saw Steve sitting at the dining room table. He looked a little bit upset, so I walked up behind him, wrapped my arms around him and that's when he told me that Aiden was killed in a Humvee explosion. I said to him, "Honey, I'm sorry about this."

Steve and I attended the services, where I became acquainted with his wife, Rachel. Throughout the years, after the service, Steve really wanted to go get that tattoo changed up a bit. While we were in the tattoo parlor, I was laughing my ass off about the tattoo and listening to the stupid story behind it, but somehow, in a way, in my heart, Aiden knew that he was leaving to go overseas for a while. This was something for him and Steve to share and laugh about if he made it through, the way I looked at it. Aiden gave Steve something to remember him by and that's how Steve sees it also. But while we were away, our four trouble-making boys decided to do a little trouble of their own in school. My cell phone kept ringing and stuff and I kept ignoring it. Then I noticed it was the school during the last time it rang. I'd answered it and the school principal told me what the boys had done. When I told Steve he was a little bit furious about it. He called his parents, and they had just brushed it off as boys will be boys. That shit does not fly well with Steve. I had already been to the principal's office. The principal and I don't get along very well. It was over some petty bullshit. When we flew home and got the boys in the house, Steve really got into their asses about misbehaving. I knew that all four of them were hanging out with one little boy, and I just couldn't figure out which one did not have the best discipline in them. The next morning we were in the principal's office, and they knew that at one time Daddy was sitting in there. But with me, they knew they really fucked up. What they had done was TP'd the bathroom and set off the fire alarm. The boy's excuse was that they had a spelling test and a math test that they didn't study for so they didn't want to take the test. I was on their ass to study a few nights before we even left to attend the services for Aiden. When the physical education teacher came in, Steve and him were talking up a storm, so I figured that those two knew each other from the past. He was talking about Steve's former deceased friends, Seth and Chase, and how they used to act in school themselves. When the principal came in, he started treating me like shit. To me, it was going in one ear and out the other. All the boys got was an in-school suspension, but I could tell by the expression on Steve's face that the boys were fixin' to really have it tough around the house.

As July rushes around the corner, Steve comes home and tells us that we are having to move, that he has been transferred. I asked him why and how come we couldn't stay? Is there any way that he could try to stay? The only reason why is that we built our lives here and were stable here. But, then again, I had to remind myself I did marry a man that's part of the military and I did tell him years ago I go where you go. When he told me that we were having to move to Missouri, it didn't bother me as bad because I knew I'd be a little bit closer to my own parents, and he had promised me that this would be our last move ever. I started researching for places to live closer to the military base in Missouri. The only thing that I could find for rent was a three-bedroom little house. From the pictures of it, on the internet, it didn't look too bad. The rent was cheap for us to live in temporarily, until I could find something better. Packing up things I'd made sure that my Grandmother's handwritten recipes were safely secured, along with a ceramic cake topper and a Sixpence that's been part of my family for years. Those are the things that are very valuable to me, and Steve, other than his guns. A few weeks passed, and the last box was coming out of the house. We sold the house for nearly $500,000. It really broke my heart. I didn't want to say goodbye to something that was in our name, and we had made so many memories. Yet this really hurt my in-laws so much that we were moving because they were no longer going to be in the boy's or our daughters' daily lives.

But I can say that the time that we lived there, both my sisters-in-law and mother-in-law, along with Bebe, gave Asha and Lizzy Welshmen hell. My in-laws and I are really close to each other, but Steve had told me that if I found us a home, and I liked it, buy it because it will be our forever home. When we got to the rental house the look on Steve's face was one of not pleased with what I had just gotten us into. He told me, "Kerala, you better get that little monkey inside your head peddling fast and find us something better than this fucking shit." My husband has this little joke, which is now the family joke. When I go into my thought mode or something is on my mind, he makes a joke about a monkey being inside my head. About a week after we moved in I quickly got the kids enrolled into school, which was just down the street. In the meantime, I was bored off my ass and trying to find a job. So after I walked the kids to school, I looked through the help wanted ads in the newspaper. I saw where this clinic was needing a full-time Pediatric Nurse Practitioner, so I called the number and asked if the spot had been filled, and a lady told me no. I had given her a little of my resume over the phone. She told me it sounded good and asked if I could come in first thing tomorrow morning for a better interview. I agreed. When the next morning came, I got up and got ready. What was a killer was that it was in a few towns over, so it was a little bit of a drive there. When I got to this little town it just felt like I was home again. But my hometown was 500 miles from here. When I found the clinic it was the only one in the town. So I went in and told them I was there for the pediatric interview. As I walked back to this office I saw the Dr.'s name was Hannah Granby and I had seen pictures of her and her husband. He was in the Military. When she walked in she asked me, "Is your husband in the military?" I told her, "Yes." She told me my husband, Bodie, just got a new drill sergeant a few weeks back. All he does is come home and talk about this guy named Steve." I smiled at her and said, "If his last name is the same as mine, he belongs to me." And she said, "Oh my God, I think my husband finally found him a friend." I said the same to her and she and I sat there for a few hours talking about her husband and Steve.

Just before I left, she told me, "Be here on Monday and

your hours are 8:00 AM to 5:00 PM. We are off on Fridays' and welcome aboard because I'm just getting started in this doctor mess myself." I told her, "I've been at this for a while." She told me, "I'll let you hire your own staff." I told her that it would be great, and she told me you'll have this one side of the hallway and your own office. As she showed me around it looked like a boring old doctor's office and what got me tickled was that I would have my own patients. When I got home, I was so excited that I had a job. The fall months passed and I was loving what I was doing, no hospital bullshit. But, at this time, each house I looked at just didn't feel right for us. Steve was getting frustrated until I had gone to work and one of my nurses asked me, "Are y'all still living in the house?" I told her, "Good Lord, yes, we are." She said, "I have the perfect place that my gg's friend has. And it belongs to her parents. You should go see it. I'll call her and let her know if you're interested." I told her, "I would like to look at it to see if it can fit us." She told me, "I'll give her a call." When 4:00 PM kicked around, I had an address. I had spoken to an elderly couple to let them know that I was coming. When I started heading out of town, I thought, okay this is good in a way, but as 45 minutes passed, I wound up in the country. I saw the mailbox and a gate, with an archway, with the owner's name across it. I thought this can't be right. This is a ranch. So I proceeded to go through the archway and the crazy thought came to my head of a horror movie. Within two miles down a small, private, dirt drive the house appeared. It was a two story that looked like it needed some work, but I saw potential in it. But when I walked up to the porch, the elderly couple was excited to show me around. I knew I could work with updating the inside and I started falling in love with it. There was a small mountain view and a river running behind it and a barn. That's when the old man said to me, "This is an 800 acre ranch. If you buy it, I'll leave the 2,500 head of cattle."

When he said that to me, I knew this would be good for the kids. But when he told me that him and his wife were ready to move, and their children didn't want this place, I understood where he was coming from. When I had asked them how much, he said with the house, land, cows and equipment, $90,000.00. I thought, what, I'm stealing his land. So I had asked him if everything was ready to go because I had cash in hand. When I told him that, he was ready to get the money. I told him that I was off on Friday and we can get this done. He agreed and asked me, "Do you have children?" I told him, "Yes, I have eight." It had taken him back a little and I told him, "I have three sets of twin boys and two girls." He told me, "This place will be great." I told him, "I think so." When we agreed on making the exchange, I was giddy as ever. Along the way home I grabbed some take out and rushed home. The boys had ransacked the kitchen and were crying over no food in the house. I told them if you didn't eat most of the snacks in one sitting, you would have something. I noticed Steve hadn't made it home yet. The boys saw what I brought home and were fussing. My nine-year-old, Seth, came around the corner while I was at the sink. The rest of the boys were giggling. I figured they found something funny and just out of nowhere I felt this big hit on my back. Seth came out and yelled, "Mama, I smacked you on your ass just to watch the wave." I was pissed. I grabbed him up and took him and the rest of the boys outside to the grass. I asked them, "Which one of you put him up to it?" They told me, "He did it on his own Mama." I told them, "Just wait until your Daddy gets home." I told them, "So drop and give me the number of push-ups for your age times two." My older boys knew the drill. Steve and I used this method for punishment. But, as Seth refused, he stood there until the boys finished theirs and that's when he knew I was getting angry. He finally dropped and did it. As he was starting, Steve comes home and bends down on the ground and told him, "You did something didn't you?" Seth said, "Yes, Sir." Steve said, "So what did you do? Finish up and tell me." When Seth stood up, Steve asked, "So what did you do?" Seth said, "Well Dad, I walked up behind Mama and hit her on the butt to see if she has a wave." When he told Steve that my husband went to laughing his ass off. Seth told him, "Well Dad, you were not home yet, so I was doing my part of being the man of house taking care of Mama like you do." Seth had Steve rolling I had found it funny after it was said and done. Steve was kneeling and trying to look at Seth with a straight face, but couldn't. He told Seth, "Your job is to protect Mama, not doing things like that. It's inappropriate to hit girls and giving Mama hugs and kisses is my job. So if you do it again, it will be more than push-ups. Steve and I stood there, I had told him, "I found us a house. We will go and sign it on Friday." I told him, "The elderly couple are ready to move as soon as possible." When Friday morning came around and Steve met up with us at a lawyer's office, Steve quickly just came in, signed and left. He didn't know what I really just got us into, but in reality I was ready to get back to my own roots. We had just bought 2,500 head of Black Angus cattle and those bastards are worth a lot of money. I thought this would be good for the kids. Steve thought the house was in the city. Boy, I had him fooled. Once the elderly couple moved out Steve and I loaded the kids up and took them out to see the house. When we got there Steve kind of started freaking out on me and asked me, "What the fuck did you just spend money on?" I said, "To buy a house." Steve yelled, "But NOT A GOD DAMN RANCH." Just as we were getting into a heated discussion, I reached up, shut him up and said, "Listen." It was pure quietness and the boys were spread out down by the river. I turned Steve around and sat down in a chair that was left behind. I told him, "This is what they need. This is where you can teach them how to do things and there are no city noises, no nosy neighbors. And we don't have to worry about the kids getting hit playing in the yard or worry about them getting kidnapped. This is just us and 800 acres." He said, "I know nothing about cows or how to be a farmer." I told him, "You better learn quickly because we have 2,500 head of cattle that needs to be fed soon." He looked at me in shock and I told him, "You got this!" He asked me, "How much did you pay for this?" I told him, "$90,000.00." As I stood there watching the boys play by the river, Steve comes up from behind and hugs me and tells me it's going to be a lot of work. He said, "Get this house the way you want it. I don't care if you have to scrap it to build us a new one, we have the money to do so.

As we stood there in silence, he said to me, "Oh my God, I can hear myself think for a change." I told him, "Yes for once." He told me, "I'm going to go and take a walk." So the girls and I went in and explored the house better. I saw there was a basement and I knew that I could turn that space into guest rooms. My plans were to rip the whole house ends off and make them bigger, then gut the house down. On the outside, I wanted a log home feel with a fireplace in the living room and a carport when I step out of the house. Needless to say, I tore the house down and rebuilt the home I wanted. Steve was in this recently built shop that the old man had done. As I was walking down there I could hear him messing with something. As soon as it started up, Steve pulls out in a tractor trailer. My jaws dropped, and he jumps out and said, "Look baby, there are all kinds of stuff in that shop that I can mess with." I told him, "Yes, they left just about everything for us." By the time we were getting ready to head back to the rental house the boys had a fit to not leave. I knew this was our forever home. When we got back to our rental, the kids were all passed out. They were tired, and I knew that our new house was going to wear them out. Everynight before Steve came home he would run out to the ranch to feed the cattle and check on things while we were rebuilding the house. Each weekend, Steve and the boys would take off to the ranch. They would come back with stories to tell me. It had taken us nine months to get the house remodel finished. Steve and I decided that we were getting new furniture. We built a 15 bedroom and five and half bath home with a small apartment home for Bebe. I wanted to decorate our home with a country lodge feel. With the money left over, we got a good size in ground swimming pool with a hot tub and made the patio big that connected to the swimming pool. We moved into our last home in 2008. Andrew and Lucas were ten, Seth and Chase were nine, Kaden and Matthew were eight. Savannah was six and Stephanie was five. While the house was being built, Steve had taken it upon himself to learn a little bit of Veterinarian information and he read just about every book he could get his hands on about cattle. He thought he was stupid about the care the cattle needed and I told him that he shouldn't feel that way, saying, "It's okay to learn something that you're not very knowledgeable about. It's okay if you really don't understand something, just ask me." I'll tell you the day that we moved out of the rental house, Steve told me, "We are just taking our personal belongings and getting rid of the furniture." We had enough money to get new, enough for new dishes and enough for me to decorate the house. I fought him tooth and nail over my kitchen. I ordered Industrial appliances for the laundry area. I wasn't going to stand there all day doing laundry when I can just throw it in and get it over with. And feeding a family of ten, that's like feeding a small army. I decorated the house in a rustic country with antiques. I loved every minute of putting the house together, but there was just one thing that I couldn't find, and that was our dining room table. I wanted it big enough to where when we have family over for visits, everyone can have a place to sit. Because if everyone visit's at once, it's 33 people inside the house, including our nieces and nephews. So when I went into the last store to look around, the salesman told me about one of his family members that builds custom tables. I gave him a call and he understood what I wanted for my dining room. He got the job done. Once he was done with it, it fit perfectly. As for the rest of the house, our two oldest took the bedrooms downstairs. Down there I placed a game room with a workout area and some of the guest rooms with a full working bathroom. So there's about five bedrooms downstairs and two bedrooms in Bebe's little makeshift apartment. One bedroom I had made into something that my own Mama and Daddy would feel comfortable in, was on the first floor, next to Savannah and Stephanie's rooms. They took the bedroom's across the living room from mine and Steve's bedroom, the rest of the boys took the upstairs bedrooms. Steve and I made sure that our bedroom was far away from the kids and I really got down to business when I designed our master bedroom. I made sure that Steve had a place to secure his guns and built a huge walk-in closet. As for our bathroom, I had an area where I could put on my makeup. I made sure the bathtub had jets in it and it was a big bathtub with a walk-in shower. I made sure I got an office, so I could do some charting from home on my days off. As for our backyard, I made damn sure I got a big swimming pool with a hot tub in it. We have a pretty big patio, with a sound system, so when we're in the pool we can listen to music.

As spring of 2008 came, Steve was getting the hang of things, but one day Steve and I were putting up a fence to keep the cows out of the backyard and Steve looked up, and he asked, "Baby, I thought you had plans for when the family was supposed to come and visit?" When I looked up, there was Phil and Bradley walking down to us and up on the patio stood the rest of my in-laws. I told him, "Yes, but in a few more weeks." Steve and I kissed each other and as I had walked off, I greeted

Phil and Bradley. From the way my father-in-law looked at me, he wasn't happy about something. So I hugged them and said to them, "Y'all see him." As I walked up to the patio, I hugged my ladies and showed them around the house. But Bebe wanted to hang out on the patio. Shelby couldn't believe that I designed every inch of the house and I told her, "I started drawing on a big cardboard one night. Once I was done, I talked to a contractor. I showed them every room in the house." I also said,"I haven't seen the boys as much since we moved here." About an hour later, everyone went out onto the patio and I had started fixing some dinner. When Steve came in, I could see some mixed emotions written all over his face. That's when he came out and said, "That man right there, who is my own father, doesn't understand me. For him to come barging in and he wants to pick a fight with me over the way we live now." When he said that, I had to stop what I was doing and listen to him fuss about it. As I was listening to him, he came out and said, "Why do I need to get his approval of things that I do in my life, and this shit hurt all my life. I have always felt that nothing is ever good enough for him. He thinks our lifestyle isn't up to his standards. I told him that I'm not into his office lifestyle and rich people's parties. I love the old fucker, but there are some times when he gets under my fucking skin." I knew whatever was said between them hurt Steve. I knew that there were some things that Steve and his Dad didn't see eye to eye on. But picking at my ways of how I was raised bothered me and I told myself that one day Phil will see, and one day Phil will understand. The one thing that I could come out and tell Steve was maybe you need to really settle on what his issue is. The only thing that I could really come up with and tell him is that I thought his Dad was really upset about us moving here. Phil is really close to our boys. During our last Christmas visit, with my parents, they became interested in what Papa does for his hobby, that's carving out things and making knives. I try to support Steve when it comes to things like this, but all I can do is give him a listening ear.

By the end of the summer, I noticed that Steve had the ranch running the way he wanted it. I could tell he was loving every minute of it.

As fall came around, Steve was excited to take the boys out to the woods to teach them how to hunt. This was his way to spend time with them and to get them to understand things about life. He shared his knowledge of survival skills so they would be ready if they were somewhere and didn't know what to do. I was proud of my boys when Lucas came in with his first kill of the season.

As 2009 came, Hannah was encouraging me to go and finish up getting my full doctor's degree.

We settled into our lives together. The kids were going to a great school and had good friends. Things between Steve and I were starting to be at a loss for both of us. He and I would fight over small, petty shit, that didn't make any sense. But, then again, it was really no longer Steve that came home anymore. It was asshole Steve and I really didn't care for him. But I had chosen to live with him. We just managed to get through our day to day life.

When 2011 came around it got to the point where I was feeling lonely as fuck. He and I might have been speaking to each other, but the way he treated me when we first got married was gone. I felt as if it was the way I looked. I was overweight. Looking at myself in the mirror, I was disgusted at how I looked. I felt as if I was no longer good enough for him. But on this one particular night, Steve hadn't come home yet and dinner was long over with. I placed his plate in the oven and I went into my office and started doing some charting. With our families joining us for the holidays, I was pretty stoked about my parents' first visit with us and I didn't want to be disrupted. Hannah and I were going to close the office for about a week and a half. When Steve came home and was leaning against my office door somewhat. I just smarted off like I have never done before to him. I told him, "You're late and your dinner is in the oven, just give me a minute and I'll get it out for you." It felt as if a switch had been turned on inside me and it pissed him off with the way I said it. During this time period in our marriage we were heading for a sexless marriage. I would get up and go to work. I mean we were talking to each other, but the physical touch between us was no longer there. When I went to bed that night I laid there watching him sleep thinking, how did we get here? And on top of it all, I was starting to feel like a maid. I felt as if I was being run over by our own kids. I got out of bed and went into the bathroom and as I stood there, tears started rolling down my face and I started looking at my body. It didn't matter what diet I tried or how much exercise I was doing, that fat on my body wasn't leaving me. A lot of reasons for why I was crying was because I was hurt. I felt as if my own husband didn't love me anymore. But as I stood there, Steve walked in, and I covered myself up and walked out of the bathroom.

When I heard the alarm go off, I just laid there. I wasn't ready to get up and go to work, so I laid in bed with my eyes closed. To me, it was the start of my two weeks off. But when I felt Steve slowly run his fingers down my body, I couldn't resist. I wanted him so badly and I called his name out. He started kissing on my neck and when he and I started kissing, he asked me, "So, are you hot and bothered baby?" All I could say was, "Uh huh." He asked me, "Do you want me to take care of it?" Before I could say anything else he placed me underneath him. Just as we were about to start making love, Lucas came bursting into our room, got his bow and walked out of the room. It turned us both off, so Steve and I got up. He headed off to work and I had to go in for a half day. I gave my patients enough chances for their parents to bring them in, just in case they got sick before we closed. When I got home, I could tell that Lucas wasn't back from bow hunting. My boys are very active hunters ever since Steve has taught them, but as soon as Steve got home I had felt as if I had a little bit of the man I married come home to me. But once again as we were about to go for it, we got blocked again. Two days before Christmas, my parents showed up. First, it was a long drive for them. Steve and I had the two weeks off and this would be the first time that my parents stayed in a house together in years. It would also be the first time that my parents would be meeting my in-laws. I'm cleaning up the house and preparing rooms for everyone. Since we moved, we don't see much of the boys. I do have trackers sewed in their coats, especially for Lucas and Chase. Them two are heavy hunters. As a mom, I worry about them getting hurt. When my side of the family showed up, they had shown their proudness of what I accomplished in my life. We started dinner and I began catching up with my sister-in-laws. We were waiting on the boys to come back from their adventure when Matthew came slowly into the door. He was freezing. Now Matthew is my baby boy and the smallest out of all six of them, so I pamper him a little. Matthew came out and said, "I left their butts." Seth and Kaden came in after dinner was set on the table. I stepped outside and started hollering for Andrew and Lucas. It was getting dark fast and just as I was fixin' to go find them, they were walking on the north side of the ranch. Just as I was getting my coat on, Andrew came in with blood on him and looking winded. Andrew said,"Lucas has blown his lungs out." I flipped my shit and asked him, "What?" Andrew said, "Yea. Lucas got Dad's M24 Carbine this morning when y'all weren't looking." When Steve heard that he jumped up and went outside. My heart was starting to shatter. I asked Andrew, "Where is Lucas?" Andrew said, "Mama, no one is hurt." He looked at his hands and said, "Oh snap, Mama. I'm sorry. Lucas finally landed that deer he's been after." I saw Steve out there on their asses. I told Andrew, "There's no way in hell that Lucas could have shot that gun. It's a high-powered military rifle." That's when Steve opened the patio door and said, "Andrew Connor, get your ass out here now." When Andrew walked outside, I was still trying to figure out how Lucas shot this gun. When Steve fired it off once, the recoil from it didn't look good. Steve was screaming at the boys so much that it caused my Daddy to get up. My Daddy started getting on my ass and I told him to step back. My Mama said, "Man, he is one scary man when he gets upset." I told them, "It's fine y'all." When Steve calmed down he walked over, grabbed Andrew, Chase and Lucas and hugged them. He told them they better not ever touch this gun again. Steve turned to Lucas, congratulating him. The boys were dragging that deer from the field for hours on end. They were cold and tired, but when he was done, I had popped him hard in the head for scaring the shit out of me. Lucas realized the real work was about to start. I grabbed a few pictures of him and his first deer. It had a beautiful rack. So Steve stood back while Lucas cleaned his first deer. That boy cleaned it by himself, with no help. It was as if my Daddy understood why Steve was a little hard on the boys. Dad said to me, "Steve is making some fine young men out of these boys." The older the boys get, the harder Steve gets on them. I told my Daddy, "We are trying our best to see them succeed in their life. Teaching them nothing is free and you earn your keep." After they cleaned the deer, Lucas came to me and said, "Mama, I'm sorry we scared you and Nanny, but I shot that sum bitch dead on the ground." When he cussed, I popped him in the back of his head, but he was proud of himself. He corrected himself for cussing, then he came out and said, "Can I cook some of my deer? Can you teach me how to cook it?" I got giddy inside because the only three helpers I have are

Matthew, Savannah and Stephanie in the kitchen. I told him, "Yes." Lucas patted me on the back and told me, "Don't worry Mama, it'll be alright." I had enough of the day, so I carried my ass to bed. When Steve came to bed, and as he got in, he asked me, "Are we going to discuss this or just throw it under a rug?" I asked him, "What's on your mind? You're telling me, there is no fucking way that this kid could have shot this gun." Steve said, "I cannot believe he fucking snipered that deer. The older I get, the more I'm starting to feel like a fucking asshole bastard dad. I've become one of those fucktard people who haven't really let them be kids. I have drilled those boys since they were born. And to you, I have been more than most asshole husbands ever. All you ever know of me is the asshole. You don't really know me. You just married the asshole me. I have been a bastard for the whole 13 years with you in our marriage. I am so sick of the person that I have become in the last few years and you deserve better from me.

I don't tell you the things that you need to hear from me. Hell, I feel that our marriage is a train wreck because of me. Hell, my wife is a doctor. As soon as she steps in the damn door, it's mom mode and a drill sergeant wife." He stopped for a second and turned to me and asked me, "Are you happy and do you love me because sometimes I see you have this look on your face when you are alone. It's a look of unhappiness and God-damn it kills me. I really want you to know the real you just like I want you to know the real me."

After he was done talking, my heart sank because he was in the middle of trying to figure out life. I sat up and turned to him, telling him, "The old me died years ago. I'm a mother of eight kids. I have a blown out body that I'm disappointed and disgusted with every time I look in the mirror. I have a DNP license that I busted my ass off to get. I have this new mom that comes in to my fucking office and tries to tell me that 'Dr. Google' told her to do this to her child and tells me how to do it to mine. When I get home, one, I have to rush my ass off to clean little boys piss off the bathroom floor, have the fucking laundry done, alongside dinner for a master drill sergeant that comes in and demands every little item be clean. If not, we will have this whiteout moment with you, me and the kids literally having to walk around on eggshells just to make sure you don't flip out on us. All I want to do is come home and say fuck the dishes and fuck the laundry. All I want you to do when I walk in is love on me, give me affection and hold me tight. As for your answer if I'm happy, yes, I am. Do I love you, yes I do." I placed his arms around me and told him, "I want more of this." I kissed him and said, "And a lot more."

As I was about to slip down into the bed and into his arms, I heard our bedroom door rattle as if someone were about to come in. So I got up and opened the door. There stood Andrew and Seth. I snapped at them and told them to get their asses to bed. I closed the door in their faces and I told Steve, "I also want a little more privacy, meaning more quality alone time with you." As I got back into bed, Steve wrapped his arms around me. I was pissed off and that's when he told me, "I'm opting out early. By February I'll be a civilian. I'm just tired of it. I don't know what I'm going to do yet, but I'm done with the military."

I didn't even know what to say other than, "If this is what you want, I'm here for you." That was the last thing I had said to him. When I got up that morning my brother had coffee made and was sitting outside on the patio. I joined him. Somewhere in the mix I let him know I was pissed at Steve for no reason other than feeling like I was a damn door mat and I felt like I was in a marriage contract with him. As I was sitting there I grabbed a cigarette off of him. I found myself smoking, and I haven't even touched one in years. I smoked when I did that thing to Asha. Now Steve still smokes cigarettes and cigars. My brother came out and said, "You need to get back into the family hobby, little sister, when are you going to let the wild you back out again? All you do is work, come home and also work here. Why don't you come upstate New Year's Eve and help me at the truck pulls. Hell, I heard Marv still has your old rig." As we were talking, Shane came out and said to me, "You're off-duty from everything today, and you're getting drunk." I told Shane, "I don't drink. Even when I was a teenager, I never touched it." He looked at me and said, "Today you're going back to be a teenager just for one day and to just enjoy something that you never did. Live a little before it's too late." I told him, "Okay, just this once." As soon as I said that, he said, "I'll go start breakfast and you just enjoy the day off. Hell Kerala, it's the holidays. It's the best damn gift I can give you." As he got up, I sat there. Just as the door swung open, my brother grabbed Matthew and told him, "Leave your Mama alone boy. She needs time to herself." Shane closed the door. I got up and turned on the hot tub. Within a few minutes, my own damn brother was catering to me and I thought this should be Steve's job. When my brother brought out a plate of pancakes, I ate every damn bite of it in peace. I saw my brother's cigarettes still sitting on the table, so I lit it up and smoked it. The temperature was dropping more outside, but our heated patio was putting off the best temperatures. My brother stepped back outside and asked me for my choice of booze. I looked up at him and said, "Why don't I just try all of them." I grabbed my phone, turned on the pool radio and bluetooth on my phone. I played George Thorogood and told my brothers to line those fuckers up. I disliked them all, but one. Both of my brothers, Shane and Noah, along with my sisters-in-law, Mia and Layla, and I sat there and mixed up this German drink I fell in love with. As it started snowing, I stripped down to my bra and underwear and ran my ass to the hot tub. I hauled ass with the bottle. I started becoming an ass myself, and I didn't even give a shit. Somewhere in there I blacked out. When I woke up, I was hugging up to the toilet and Steve was holding my hair back. I found myself embarrassed and still drunk. Steve picked me up and we got into the shower. It was cold water as he stood in there with me. I looked up at him and told him I was sorry. He said, "Thank you for letting yourself out. She's kind of mad-wild. I hate to say this, it kind of turned me on." I started throwing up again. When Steve put me back to bed, the room was still spinning and my head was killing me. When the morning light came around I laid there. Steve turned over and hugged up to me and asked me how I was feeling, and I told him like shit. There was pounding on our bedroom door, and it was Chase. The door swung open and as I looked up, there stood Bebe. I sat up and Steve was in shock. Bebe walked in, closed the door behind her and said, "Look, I got a phone call from Kaden the other night during our normal weekly calls and heard you two yelling and exchanging heated words. I flew 1,300 miles to come and straighten you two out. It's fucking Christmas. Plus, I beat your Dad and Mom here. So, what's the problem?" Steve tried to lie to her and said, "Bebe we're not having problems." She snapped at him and said, "Steven Wesley stop lying to me. I think I know what the issue is. When was the last time you dated your wife?" Steve sat there dumbfounded. The door busted open. Savannah, Stephanie and Kaden came in with coffee for the three of us. Bebe told the kids, "Thank you. Now get your butts out of here." She got up and locked the door, turned around and said to us, "Now you see how simple that is, Steve. I'm still waiting on your answer. When was the last time you dated your wife? You never have and it's starting to shatter this marriage. When the both of you got married y'all hit the ground running. You started making babies without taking the time out for the both of you to date each other. Maybe it's time that you date each other again and relax with each other." The embarrassing question she asked us next was, "When was the last time the two of you were intimate with each other?" I told her, "A year and half ago." She quickly said, "Shit. Hun are you tired of him?" I told her, "No Bebe you're saying things that he never asked me, and yes, that was the argument that we were having. I'm tired of the same routine day in and day out. Just once in a while I want to be selfish and have Steve to myself. Is it wrong for me to ask that every time I think I am about to have some time alone with my husband one of the kids ends up needing me or Steve is sleeping." As I was talking I came out and really said, "I'm lonely in that department."

After I told her that, she told us both her thoughts, "Well, I think the two of you need to stop and breathe. Steven, it means a lot to a woman in love with her husband when he does small things for them. Stealing kisses from each other to have small moments together, even if it is just a split second." After she spoke to us, it kind of all made sense. As she got up she turned around to us saying, "I think y'all need to talk to each other to make things better for the both of you." As she walked out the door, Steve and I looked at each other again, and he said, "Baby, I'm sorry that I've had let this asshole inside of me take over and Bebe is right. I haven't given you the time with me that you've deserved. I told you the other night things are fixin' to change here. I can guarantee you that asshole Steve will show up from time to time while I'm trying to kick his ass out of here." I told him, "Yea, it's time for some changes. Well, I hate to be the brew of a bitch, but your ass is mine tonight." But right about now it's the day Before Christmas Eve and Steve jumps up out of bed saying, "Oh shit, baby I got to go, but I'll be back here by 1 I've got to run into town and do you need anything?" I told him, "No, but last-minute shopping sucks." He said, "No shopping, it's the puppies. I've got to go pick them up and the horses will be here tonight and Mom, Dad and the rest will be here in a little bit. But yes, you and I are going to bed early." As soon as he walked out the door, I got up, got dressed and started putting on my make-up, which I rarely do on the weekends. I decided that it was time to start trying to take better care of myself and putting on make-up to make me feel good about myself. My hair was so long that it was past my hips, so I fixed it a different way. I decided to play a little game with Steve. So I placed a love note for him and I wrote: There are so many ways to tell you how much I love you that I don't really know where to start.

After I wrote it, I put it on his bedside. I kept my promise to Lucas and he and I together made deer stew. With it being cold outside, it was perfect. After we put it in the pot, I think I had him hooked on cooking. After everyone showed up, it was a full dining room table of everyone talking and getting to know each other. They were swapping childhood stories about me and Steve. The conversation caught my pre-teen's attention. I walked into the laundry room, which is a never-ending story. I had my back turned to the wall, folding clothes, when I hear the door behind me close. I figured one of the kids had closed it as they walked by and that's when I felt Steve wrapping me up with his arms around me. He started kissing on me and said, "Baby I forgot to tell you this morning that I love you." As I told him the same, we both had to stop making out before we screwed each other in the laundry room. The laundry room was a few feet away from the dining room table. He just picked up some laundry and was about to walk out. I turned around and changed my tone of voice, calling his name and walked up to him, I kind of squatted down and pretended to go down on him. He said, "Awww, baby, are we really doing this?" I jumped up and said to him, "I think I'm going to really enjoy teasing your ass for the rest of the day." He yelled out, "Awww, come on baby." As he was walking out, I said, "Steve." He looked at me as I was pointing at his pants. I started giggling at him and I could see the frustration on him as he walked out. I had gone on about what I was doing.

When dinner came around everyone had a seat. As for me and Steve, sitting out of our normal dinner chairs felt odd. Bebe was setting next to me and Steve sat across, in front of me. No one knew what they were eating, except for my side of the family. Lucas is hooked on those words, you eat what you kill, and Steve instilled that in the boys. They were sure bragging about the stew that Lucas had made, I made a cheesecake and as I sat back down to eat it, as I was looking at the spoon, I had a teasing idea. I grabbed a bite and suckled on the spoon looking directly at Steve. When Steve saw me doing so, his jaw dropped, and I just started smiling. While I was doing this mess, Bebe was rubbing and patting me on the back. I looked at her, and she just smiled at me and snickered. I thought you dirty old woman. But I didn't forget that Bebe is a retired sex and marriage therapist. This morning's talk helped us a little bit more.

When Steve got up, that's when Bebe got up. Bebe yelled out at Lucas and said, "Young man, that is the best deer stew that I have ever had." When she said that, the dining room got quiet. She looked around and said, "Oh shit, it's not going to fucking kill you. That's a survivor's skill that a young man has." I looked at my brother and we started laughing. Bebe is a mess. She reminds me of the character Sophia from the Golden Girls, but with a dirty mind and mouth. When I looked up, I saw Bebe and Steve talking. My Mama and mother-in-law were deep in conversation with each other. Both of my sisters-in-law were doing their own thing. I got up to start the dishes and Bebe told me, "You have 15 kids sitting here. I'll bark orders, you go have a nice hot bath and rest up. We have a lot of food to cook tomorrow for

Christmas dinner." As I was about to walk off, Bebe pulled me closer to her and said, "I hope you two have fun tonight." I blushed and yelled out, "Goodnight everyone." They looked at me and said, "Already?" Bebe said, "There is so much to do tomorrow so somebody's got to get into bed early." I closed the bedroom door.

As I got my bath ready, I heard my beeper go off so I answered a call. The mom was demanding that I come to the hospital and care for her sick baby. I told her, "I'm sorry, but I'm out of town with my family. If you can make appointment with me after the new year..." She got mad and hung up on me, so I resumed what I was doing. I rushed out, dried off and put on my robe when I heard the bedroom door open. There stood Kaden. I looked again and Steve was standing over him and telling him to, "Get your ass out of here damn, Mama is trying to get peace, and it always gets fucked up." When the door slammed, Steve locked it. I took my vanity chair and kicked it into the middle of the floor. Just as soon as he sat down, I opened up my robe and things went from there. We both didn't rush. We stopped to cuddle with a second round of each other until we tired ourselves out.

When morning came, Steve and I didn't rush out of bed, When we did, Steve was loving all over me. As I looked up after fixing our coffee, Steve grabbed my hand and I saw he had a big blanket. We walked out to our fire pit and we wrapped ourselves up in it as we watched a beautiful Christmas Eve sunrise. He said to me, "If I had to choose between breathing and loving you, I would use my last breath to tell you I love you, you're my everything." When he told me that, it put a smile on my face. After hearing those words I told him, "I love you so much that it hurts. You have been and always will be the carrier of my love and heart." I felt like a giddy teenage girl again with being wrapped in his arms as he was holding on to me. He started to love me and pick on me at the same time.

When I looked up, Shelby was walking out. I really didn't want this moment to end between us.

As I looked up, Mama came out, and she was fussing about how cold it was. Within a few minutes, Steve got up and walked back into the house and Mama asked me, "Kerala how many more weeks of school do you have left to fully get your Pediatrics MD license." I told her,"About three more years. I'm also studying for my autism license as well. And Shelby said, "I just don't know how you do it." I told her, "I just take things one day at a time." Shelby and Mama started talking, so I told them, "Well, I have to go and start breakfast or we will be having brunch instead of breakfast." As I walked back into the house Bebe called me, we walked into her room, so I sat down with her in her little apartment. She said to me, "You're glowing again, and I haven't seen that on you in the last few years." I told her, "I was really enjoying what was going on between us this morning." She said, "I know. I was watching the both of you from the window here and studying the both of you. And Kerala, it's not you doll, it's him. It appears that you're welcoming everything that he has given you. I know my grandson too well, just as you do, and you and I both know that there's two different Steve's. It appears that he has let moody Steve take a hold of this marriage." I told her, "Yes, but he knows that I'm here for him if he needs to let it out. But it's like both of us have just bottled things up so much that we have forgotten to share with each other how we feel." Bebe said, "I think he needs to be re-taught of what I taught him in his teenage years. You just sit back and let him work for his love for you. If he wants you badly enough, he'll start showing more affection to you in your marriage. The only advice I can give to you right now is let him work for it, but for those little moments don't reject them. Even if you're busy, include him in it and make it fun. I'll give Steve some books and tools that he needs, just work with him on it. If there's something new that he intends to try with you, go for it. Spice things up. If he is uncomfortable with it, encourage him to at least try it once." After Bebe had a small session with me, I understood what she was saying to me about us. A lot of it is him, not me. Later on that morning, while I was cooking, I looked up and Steve was barking order's to Andrew, Chase, Lucas, and Seth. I thought, what the hell is he up to and got in his ass when I saw the gun. He told the boys to come outside. I watched him go outside. I stepped outside and asked him, "What are you doing?" He told me, "I'm going to teach them how to clean it." When Steve tore down the gun it impressed the boys, and he was talking to them about how to clean it thoroughly. They were really getting their asses chewed out. But after everyone had gone to bed, and we placed the presents under the tree, Steve handed me something. When I opened it, I didn't understand it at first. It was his promise to me years ago for a mommy makeover. I looked at him and said, "I thought you had forgotten about it. He said, "No baby, I was just waiting on you to tell me when you were ready for it. I was happy about my Christmas gift. Steve and I agreed that this was our biggest Christmas ever. But as I stood at the bar in the kitchen, watching the kids open up their presents, I felt Steve standing behind me. I saw this necklace come around my neck, then he placed a nice ring on my finger. I loved everything that he had given me. I got him a few enjoyable things. But when the kids saw the keys for the ATVs, it was said and over with. After everyone ate dinner they were worn out from the day. I was in the kitchen cleaning up a few things. When I looked up, there was Steve, and he started helping me put things away, and I started flirting. He and I were using crazy ass pickup lines to each other and we were laughing and carrying on. We had each other laughing so hard that he had tears rolling down his face. It was so bad that we couldn't catch our breath. Once we settled down and stood toe to toe in front of each other, he picked me up and put me on the counter. There's a corner spot inside the kitchen that's hidden from the living room near the fridge. We had a stolen moment with each other, stealing kisses, complimenting and telling good things about each other. I was enjoying our moment until his sister snuck up behind us and said, "You two still act like teenagers. You know the both of you have a bedroom." Steve smarted off to her, "And we do, but this is my kingdom after all. You're standing in my queen's kitchen and trying to tell us where to go inside our house to have a private moment." He was basically telling her to fuck off, and she came back at him with, "Excuse me!" Steve got hateful on her and I said, "Hey." Steve turned around and snapped at me. When he did, I got down off the counter and walked outside. He had just let asshole Steve come into the house again. Yes, Amy was out of her place telling us what to do. I love my sister-in-law, but she has the tendency to open her mouth where it shouldn't be sometimes. I was walking down the fence line. I wanted to see the horses. As I was looking at them, I thought of Flower so much, and for some reason I wanted to ride. But when Steve was slowly coming towards me, that mad feeling clicked in me again, and I told him, "Come here." He told me, "Baby, I'm sorry." I told him, "I'm letting you slide this time, but if it happens again you and I are going to have just a little bit of a problem. Amy was out of line and in our business, but come time for you to go back to work you better not bring asshole Steve back home with you." When I told him that he fully understood my frustration with him and the asshole Steve that's inside of him. He told me, "I will leave his ass there baby, I promise." When the next morning came I found myself so ready for everyone to go. When my side of the family was the last people to walk out I felt as if I slammed the door. By the next week, I had to cancel my plans with my brothers because of the weather. We came down with a small virus. By mid-January, the thought's had came to my mind of what my

115

brother had said to me about Marv still having my Sled truck. As I sat in my office at work it hit me I wanted it back. So I called Daddy to get his input and thoughts on some thing's. I asked Daddy, "I want your thoughts on what's on my mind." Daddy said, "Well Kerala, tell me." I said, "Well Daddy, Shane told me that Marv still has my sled truck." Daddy said, "Yes." I said, "Well Daddy, I want it back." When I said that to him he said, "It's about damn time you and I get to back to bonding together." I told him, "Yes it is, but I'm not so sure about how I can tell Steve that I'm wanting back in the family hobby. I mean I have the money to buy it back. Daddy said, "Baby girl, I tell you what, why don't you send me the money and I'll work out something with Marv. When you're ready to make your grand entry again, it will be here when you say so." I told Daddy, "I have a few surgeries coming up." Daddy said, "Girl, you sick?" I said, "No sir. I'm doing this mommy makeover thing where I can get my 17-year-old body back. Speaking of that, you know Daddy, When I lost Flower as a kid, I felt as if I started losing everything that I worked so hard for." Daddy said, "Yes, you did. It's that sorry piece of shit that did it all to you, but don't regret the boys. They have Steve there to guide them to a better life." I told Daddy, "I couldn't ask for a better man to step into my life when he did. Don't say anything that I'm buying my sled truck back to anyone. This will be our little secret between us." Daddy said, "You just let me know when you're ready to go. You can meet up with us, and I'll talk to Steve from there." Before I hung up I said, "Well Daddy, I have another patient to attend to. I love you, and I'll talk to you later." Each day that I have been coming home Steve has changed a little bit. He has been giving me a little more attention and affection. He started using the tools and reading the books that Bebe sent to him.

Part Two

By February of that year, Steve said goodbye to the Military lifestyle. And I was glad to see that asshole Steve go. But for that month, he surprised me twice. I waited until it was warm for me to start teaching the girls how to ride a horse. It was during a Super Bowl game, so the girls and I walked down to the arena. I told them to let the horse do the work, and you just ride. They are getting to know you and you're learning them. So the girls were just riding in circles in the arena. As I looked up, there stood Steve. I thought holy shit, he left the game to come down here. He asked me, "So what do we do?" I smiled at him and said, "Come here." We walked into the stables, and I handed him a halter and asked him, "Which horse?" He said, "Him, I think I'm going to call him Blue, So Steve got him out, and I said, "Saddle him up." I had to teach him how to saddle the horse and showed him the no zones of what's okay, and what's not okay. I had to do a lot of explaining to him about horses. I told Steve, "See this area on him? Do not kick him there on the flanks because he will throw your ass off of him. He has feelings too. If you're hurting him, he will hurt you. You have to treat him like your best friend. And right now, your best friend is letting you on his back, and he's your work buddy too. When I put the bit into the horse's mouth and

117

handed the reins to Steve I told him, "Easily move back onto his back." So he did. I got on and out of the stall we went to ride together. I placed Steve's hands on my hips and I knew he was getting excited, but he was a little freaked out. I told him I needed him to relax a little bit. When I got off and placed Steve on the horse on his own, I went back into the barn and saddled up one of the other horses. I figured the one I picked needed a good run, but the horse I picked out, her name was Lily and she was Kaden's horse. She was ready to go for it, so I let this horse show me what she could do. I came flying by Steve, and he just sat there on his horse watching me ride. It felt good to be on a horse again. A few weeks later came around, and I didn't pay any mind to the day other than that it was just Valentine's Day. To me, it was simply another work day. Just before lunch I was working the shit out of my side of the hallway of patients. It was one room to the other and Hannah was working her side of the hall. Chloe, who was a 20-year-old receptionist, was young and dumb. It was getting around lunch time. Normally, Hannah and I would just sit in the lounge and try to catch up on patient reports while we ate. On this particular day, Hannah jerks me into the nurse's area and tells me, "That little bitch is gone. By the end of the day." I looked at her and said, "Why?" She said, "Steve is in your office and Chloe tried to flirt with him, but he told her that he was here to see you." So I told her, "I'll see what's up." When I walked into my office, I closed my door and Steve told me, "That little girl up front was a little bit of a whore. As soon as I said something about you, she just shut up and let me back here." I was surprised that he was here. She broke one of the rules besides flirting with my husband.

Yeah, she's got to go. Steve said, "I'm here to take my baby to lunch." I told him, "Okay." As he sat there, behind my desk, I noticed that he bought me a bouquet of my favorite flowers. It was points up for him. It was odd for me seeing my husband in civilian clothes and it was something that I had to get used to. It was hard on him to get adjusted as we sat down to eat. And, yes, we moved to another little town where everyone knows everyone. The town gossip of what was going on was in full swing and everyone stopped by our table to chat as they were leaving. As we sat there, I asked him, "So what have you done this morning?" He told me, "Well, I fed every animal we have, tinkered with that big truck that we have and came to town bullshit with the locals at the feed store. Then I thought I'd come have lunch with my baby before I head back to the house." Then he said, "Oh, I've talked to the other cattle ranchers around here. They said Buddy, who used to own the land, would haul cattle once a week to places. I've been thinking of doing that. I'll only be gone three days out of the month and I can put that truck to good use. I mean, if it bothers you, I won't do it." I said, "If that's what you'd like to do then I support you, but I can support our family now." He told me, "My wife isn't going to do this alone." I told him, "Okay." He told me, "I wonder if we can finance a trailer or two for my options? I'm keeping them open, but for the ranch that's priority work. I just want to be my own boss. I can't handle someone bossing me around. I've already got one. I don't need another, but I'm not doing it until after your surgeries." After lunch, Steve brought me back to my office. Since he has retired, he's making excuses, saying that he didn't get his morning kisses from me. He is still asleep when I normally kiss him as I'm leaving for work. He tells me, "If you don't do that before you leave for work I will have a bad day." I thought he was being silly, and he tried to pull that on me because my lipstick mark is still kind of there. I gave him a kiss before I went back into the office. By the end of the day, Hannah and I pulled Chloe to the back and told her that her services were no longer needed. She asked, "Why?" I told her, "We are a family office and this isn't a place for your flirting with our patients, families members, or our spouse's. So please pack your belongings and leave the property immediately." As I laid her off, I asked Hannah, "Was that too hard?" She said, "No, that was more professional than me." Once we locked up for the night and I got home, I could tell Steve had the house in shape. And had the kids doing their school work.

During this era in our lives, Steve was in the middle of trying to figure shit out. When March came, I had my surgeries. Within two days later I came home. The boys finally pissed me off within minutes of me walking in the door. Right behind me getting pissed, Steve stood back and let me handle them. As I walked in it was Mama, Mama, Mama, I need you to do this and that for me. I snapped and told them, "If you wanted something done you should have it done by yourself. I'm not a fucking door mat for your demands. If you don't do your own laundry or pick shit up in your room I'm throwing it out. If your laundry isn't washed, I'm throwing it away. If your beds are not made, it's getting thrown away. If you don't put your dirty dishes in the dishwasher, you'll get a sandwich for dinner while the rest of us eats a meal. I'm fucking tired." After I said that, Steve started clapping and helped me into bed. I just got my stomach cut and my boobs straight. As Steve helped me into bed he said, "Baby, I've been waiting for the last few years on you to snap on the boys. It is time for them to take care of themselves instead of you running yourself ragged." As the weeks went by, I kept my promise of what I told the boys and Steve enforced it. Needless to say, two went without eating and another slept with no blanket and no clothes. They had to wash the same pair of clothes until he got the hint. My plan was working. As for Savannah and Stephanie, they were way ahead of the boys and that was impressive for their age. When May came around, I helped get Steve off on his three-day cattle run. I was proud of him. By June, my body was losing weight in the way I wanted my boobs to be perfect, and my back was great looking. I was pleased with how my body shape was becoming more like my younger self. I have still hidden my body a little bit, but I had a great diet and work out plan with my very own favorite personal trainer. Steve wouldn't let me have a cheat day on food or a day off for exercising, but Steve and I both were starting to treat each other better, seeking to meet each other's needs. Things in our marriage were looking better and we were discovering who we really were. Bebe was right. We did hit the ground running. He and I both can make each other laugh. Since Steve wasn't hard asshole Steve, I was falling in love with him all over again. I was really crushing on the way he looked. He started growing his hair out and changing his appearance. He said what he meant to me, that he was a different person than whom I first met. But as for the boys, he was still a hard ass to them. But they were also seeing some small changes in him. As fall of 2012 hit, our four boys, Andrew, Lucas, Chase, and Seth had their first junior football game. As we were walking into the stands these two guys were talking shit about me and Steve. I heard them just as well of what they were saying about us, and I disliked what they said about us.

And they were talking about our height and said, "I wonder how that works in the bedroom." I wanted to turn around to them and tell them it works just fine, if you are eager to know, but I didn't. Steve and I held hands on our way in and Steve and I were just looking at each other and smiling because we know how it works. But as we sat down, Steve said to me, "Others shouldn't be worried about what happens in our bedroom." I said to him, "Let them talk." When Hannah and Bodie found us Hannah and I were scouting for our patients. We were discussing who is sick. I looked down under the stands and there was this mother that is jacked up on pot all the time and telling me the baby has a constant cough. Hannah pulls out her phone and starts to record what she was doing. I smelled pot and there she was blowing the pot smoke onto this child. I was getting pissed off and I told Hannah, "You watch, she's going to be in the office come Monday morning. When she does, I'm calling child protective on her." Hannah said, "Do what you think is safe for the baby. I just filmed her doing this so it can be proof that she did blow smoke on this child." After the game, I checked the boys over before they went to bed. But when Monday morning came around I was on the warpath about that baby. Sure enough, she was on my schedule to see today. She had made a 3:30 PM appointment. Therefore, I called the Sheriff's Department, showed them the video and told them that she would be in at that certain time. By 3:00 PM the Sheriff's Department and Child Protective Services (CPS) were in the back area waiting for her to show up. I took care of the baby and checked it out, acting like everything was fine. When she figured out that it was me that set up a sting on her ass, I had told her, "I'm only here to keep this baby healthy, and you're hurting it by abusing it."

By that Tuesday evening, Daddy calls me and tells me, "The deal is done, and it's the last show of the season." I asked him, "When and where?" He told me and I told Daddy, "I'll rent us some rooms. You just come up with a plan to get me out of the hotel room." So we had a plan set. When I got home that evening, I talked to Steve about my day and brought up the subject of going to the last sled show. He told me that we can go and show family support, and it would be awesome for the kids to see their Uncles do some cool stuff. When he said that, I smiled because I was really skimming myself. The day that we left, I was really excited to set my butt slide back into my old sled truck again. But as we got to the hotel and got everyone settled in for the night, I really couldn't contain myself. I was ready to see it. The next morning I got my make-up on and French braided my hair. When Daddy saw me I nodded my head to him and told him I was ready to go. As

Daddy approached Steve, I don't know what he said to him. Before I knew it I was sitting inside my Daddy's truck and Daddy said, "Boy he is in for it tonight." I told Daddy, "Yeah that's another issue. I'll need your help with smoothing this over." Daddy said, "Don't worry. I got what I wanted to say to him in mind." Daddy was so tickled at the fact that I was getting back into the family hobby. When we got to the stadium, I couldn't believe it. There she sat as I walked up to the truck. I got a little bit emotional over just seeing it. When Noah walked up to me, he said, "Don't cry, little sister. I know it's been a long Journey of getting you back to your truck, but that's all about to change now." As Noah and I were standing there, he said, "You better beat the hell out of someone tonight. But hell, you're a legend anyway with Black Betty." As we stood there looking the truck over, Marv just about broke his neck to come and hug me. We hugged each other. He told me, "I always knew there would be a day you would come back, that's why I just stored your truck for you until the time had come. Everyone wanted to buy it, and I always told them, hell no, we are just waiting for her to come back." I asked him, "What about the money I owe you?" He said, "Shit, don't worry about it. Just look at it as a gift." I just smiled at him and said, "Thank you for what you have done for me." Marv said, "Oh hell Kerala, it isn't no big deal. I just kept her stored next to Black Betty." I asked, "When are you going to bring that old sled out of retirement?" He told me, "Someday." And he told me, "I replaced the alcohol engine in it so you're good to go to give me a helluva ride tonight, but don't bust the sled gears in buster here." I told Marv, "I'll try not to." Marv told me, "Well Kerala J, I'll catch up with you later on." I told him, "You definitely will."

When Noah and I opened up the body latch and I had climbed in, everything was still in its place just like I left it. I somewhat felt like a teenager again sitting in that seat, but with better knowledge. As I was sitting there, Shane came up and said to me, "Fits like an old glove doesn't it?" I told Shane, "It certainly does." As the day went on, two hours before show time, they held a meeting. After telling us the new rules, wishing us good luck and having fun, I went on and suited up. As we stood around talking with everyone, I started checking things over like Daddy taught me. Daddy was standing by me just in case I needed a helping hand. Small crowds started coming into the stadium. Daddy came out and said to me, "Uh oh, there's Steve. You just hang here and I'll go have a chat with him. The rest is on your own after that." I said to Daddy, "Thanks old man for pushing me out of the wagon. I thought you were really going to smooth things over for me." He said, "Not in your marital world, I don't belong there." After Daddy said that to me, my jaw dropped as Daddy walked up to Steve. I stood there and Steve was looking at me. He would look at Daddy, but I couldn't watch them chat anymore. My boys came up to me and said, "Mama??? What are you doing?" I told my boys, "See, Mama has been doing this way before you were even thought of, you just thought you knew your Mama. Think again boys." My boys wanted to start to try and take advantage of my truck and I had told them, "NO this isn't a toy. It is in a way, but it's just for entertainment purposes only. I have had this truck ever since I was a teenager." Chase asked me, "So Mama, you mean to tell me that you're a professional driver of this thing?" I told him, "Yes." The boys saw their Daddy walking to me and Seth came out and said, "Ugh guys, do you see that look on the big Mack 10 there that we call Daddy?" They said, "Yea, we need to go check out the other truck. Mama we love you and good luck. Now I have something to brag about my Mama." When they said that I giggled about it, but Steve's facial expression didn't look too well. When he and I stood toe to toe, and I looked up at him, I told him I'm pulling tonight and told him don't worry I know what I'm doing," He had said to me, "Why did you hide this?" I had said to him, "If I had told you from the beginning, you wouldn't be as surprised. I'm sorry, I just wanted to show the kids that Mama isn't just Mama and I wanted to have a little time with my Daddy here and there. Our bond is broken." I turned to the truck and told Steve, "I've had this sled truck since I was 13. Daddy sold it when I was carrying Andrew and Lucas, the night you met Mama and Daddy. I intend to gain back things that I've lost, and I want you to walk with me on this because I don't want to do this alone." Steve said to me, "Baby, I love you. Stay safe and have fun. I kind of support you, but I need you to make me change my mind." I understood what Steve was saying. I had to show him what I could do, and by God, I was going to. Before he walked off from me, he kissed me and told me,"Well, we better go and get a seat before it's too late to get a good one." One by one I was watching the other trucks take their turn with the sled. The closer it got to me, the more my heart started to race. As the driver next to me was hooking up I got in and got ready. My heart was racing more, and I was shaking a little. Shane said, "Shit Kerala, it's just riding a bike again, you got this." When I started it up and had a big smile on my face, I told my own truck it's just like old times being here my old thing. As I was hooking up, I took a deep breath and when I saw the green flag and didn't let the fuck off of it, I got in the middle of the track and let harder into it. I did a full pull as Noah went down the track. It was heartbreaking to see that he only got halfway in the track and that's all he had. As for Shane, he did a full pull, and we waited on the other drivers to see what they came up with. It led to me and Shane. At the end of the night I was going against my older brother, and it wasn't easy. My brother depended on the money. I, on the other hand, was financially okay. But I had to place. We agreed on, no matter what, we're still brother and sister by the end of the night if the time came for one last round. As for my parents, it wasn't easy to see their baby out there with her big brothers competing against each other. When Shane took off, he didn't hold back on his rig and I thought, OK, let's go with it. I guess I got on it too hard because I pulled out of the gates. I felt guilty until my brother came up to me and said, "I let you win. It felt good to do it." I had an Audience Fully Standing in an arena Cheering, but after the arena was empty, I gave my brother the prize money. Shane needed it more than me. When we got back to the hotel, the boys and Steve were hyped up about me showing them what I could do. As we returned home, Steve was into watching so many sledding videos that he would ask me all kinds of questions about sledding. Two days later, he said, "Baby, we need a hobby together, and it would be awesome if we did sledding together." So I told him, "Well, we need to go and see Marv." When we went over to Marv's house, Steve picked out his rig and I knew what he was going after. It was a diesel hybrid. Marv and I tried to tell him why Alan got rid of it, but I told Marv, "Sometimes we just have to let others learn the hard way." In a way my husband is no damn dummy when it comes to mechanical stuff. He loves tinkering with shit. There are days when I have to pull him out of the shop just for him to come and eat dinner. Once he got his rig set up and running the way he wanted it, Shane and Noah came up and taught him how to pull. I would have taught him in a wrong way which would have caused a fight. That's one of our rules together. To try and not fight with each other. We have this big arena at the house. It was a good opportunity to put it to use once Steve got hooked. Within weeks he and I bought two trucks to pull. This made it a hobby for us to do together. We agreed that we would only do it once month. It did give the kids something to look forward to. As Thanksgiving came around, we stayed home because the boys wanted to go hunting. The Friday before Steve and the boys left, Hannah and I decided to close the office for the week.

We never have that many patients during that week. So the girls and I were fixin' to have mom and daughter time. I called and got us a hair appointment. It was time to cut this mess off. My hair was down to my knees and the girls had never had a haircut before There used to be 'mommy cuts' where I just trimmed the dead ends off. They were excited. So when Monday morning came, I decided I wanted something different. The girls got their hair trimmed up to their shoulders. As for me, I dyed my hair and got a light perm. They cut off about 25" of my hair, styled it and showed me different ways of fixing it. After we had left there, I was on the hunt for new make-up and to help get Savannah started in make-up. I let this young lady put my make-up on me and got Savannah started. As for Stephanie, lip balm is far as it goes. She would be trailing behind, but as for Savannah, she was collecting make-up during this time. Steve and I made a rule that when they turned 13, they could start wearing it. We went shopping in clothing stores. I got frustrated by trying on clothes. I went from 180 pounds to 102 pounds, wearing size 0 clothing and D cup breast. I got a whole new closet full of clothes along with the girls. I let them have a few things. But damn, that was a sticker shock of three grand. The girls and I ate out and headed home. Their little friends started calling them to come over to stay the night, so I rushed them to the house and let them pack an overnight bag. I was disappointed, but I had figured I was taking this opportunity to study and finish my finals for my doctor's degree while the house was quiet. After the girls unloaded and put things away, I ran them to each of their friends and came back to the house. I started studying until I fell asleep. By the time Thursday morning came around, I got myself ready and started in with cooking Thanksgiving dinner. The girls and I started last night baking stuff, so we sat around cooking. By noon, Chase came in and looked at me and asked, "Where's my Mama at?" I said, "I'm here." He smiled at me and said, "I like it, but Daddy is out there fussing over the money you spent. I think he'll shut up now when he sees you looking good because it's been a long time coming on the hair." As I started digging for a pan and talking with Chase, Steve came in, asking Chase, "Where is Mama?" He told Chase, "Tell her to meet me in our room. We need to talk." Normally when he tells the kids that it's not going to be good. As he walked into the room I got up and walked my butt in there for an ass chewing. When I closed the bedroom door he started in on me, "Baby, you better explain to me why you have spent a lot of money." As he was waiting for me to answer, he stepped out of the bathroom, and I just shrugged and smiled. He smiled and said, "Well damn, hey and what the hell! You looked so beautiful. You changed and cut your hair." I told him, "Yes." As he looked down at me, I asked him, "Are you okay?" He said, "Well, kind of. I'm trying to look into my wife's eyes to see if she's in there." I told him, "I'm here." He said, "I'm really loving this new look." I just came out and said, "Hey, I'm sorry for spending the money." He said, 'No, don't worry about it. I shouldn't fuss about it. You've deserved it." As Steve picked me up in his arms he asked me, "Can I play with you later on, after the game?" I smarted off, "I'll be your player." After I told him that, he smiled, and I told him, "I really missed you in these last few days." He said,"I bet you have. That's okay. I'm getting in bed tonight." I told him, "I know you are, but right now, I've got to cook to feed you and eight others. You need a shower." So he kissed me and put me down. As I walked out, all six boys were sitting on stools at the counter looking at me, like buzzards. They came out and asked me, "When is it time to eat?" I told them, "When it's ready, I'll let you know." Seth came out and said, "I'm glad to know that Daddy is going to be in his own bed tonight." I looked at him crazy, and he said, "Well Mama, the first night Kaden was on his air mattress next to him and Daddy pulled him out of his bed trying to cuddle with him. Kaden had to wake him up. He was reaching for you. So the next night we put Chase in Kaden's spot and he did the same thing. So that morning we had to do the shortest straw, so poor Matt got it. He slapped Daddy and made a female voice, and he thought it was you. He had too many beers. Matt told him to lay down and not to touch him." I thought it was funny. Steve's dirty habit is reaching for me while he's asleep. I was laughing and told them, "Well don't sleep next to him." Lucas said, "Yeah we started messing with him until he got mad at us." I just shook my head and told the boys, "Y'all stink. Get a shower." After they flocked off, my bigger buzzard came out clean and loving up on me. He told me, "I caught Andrew smoking, so if he's coughing it's because of it. Don't worry baby, I took care of him and the issue. I told him next time I'll be taking him to a lung clinic to let him see how they're breathing." I told him, "Well, you smoke too." He looked at me and said, "I have seen you smoke a time or two, but he is still a kid and curiosity gets to the best of them. I hope he learns." As we sat down for our Thanksgiving dinner and said our blessings, small talk at the table was normal for us. After we all cleaned up, just before the game started, I put in some laundry. I walked back into the kitchen and looked over at Steve, he motioned me to come there, so I walked over and sat with him. He covered us both up, and whispered in my ear, "I have a dirty mind and right now, you're running through it... Naked." I giggled and told him, "Do you want to run with me?" He asked me, "Can I do bad things to you?" I giggled and told him, "Bring it." I think he paid more attention to me while we were flirting with each other than watching the game. Just as the game was almost done, I got up and made my way to bed. There was Steve, hot on my heels. He couldn't keep his hands off of me and I welcomed it. As soon as I got into his arms, I melted and gave myself to him. Ever since Bebe gave us a talking to, things were getting better in our marriage. It didn't feel like a contract marriage anymore between us. We entirely changed for the better. We communicated better in what we wanted and our goals for each other. The next morning, Steve surprised me with a nice, hot bath, and he kissed me good morning. As I was getting in I had asked him, "Where are you running off to? It would be nice to share this bath with you." When I invited him in, he jumped at the invitation. It was less of showing him my better body, and I could tell he was digging it. But as we got out, I thought I would take Lily for a good run, so I put on one of my new jogging suits. When I came out of the bedroom, I could have sworn I heard Steve stutter his words a little bit when he asked me if I had anything planned for myself and I told him that I was going to ride Lily for a few hours. He told me well we can go and ride Blue together to my deer stand, so I thought ok. As we started walking down to the barn there was Blue showing out for me. I love spoiling all of our horses. But for Blue, Lily is his girlfriend, and he is the alpha out of all of our horses. We mounted up on Blue and along the way Steve just couldn't keep his hand to himself. I welcomed it, but along our way to his deer stand he and I had a deep conversion with each other. It was a bonding conversation of our fears and what's changing in ourselves and our marriage. It was nothing bad. It was good that we spoke towards each other and how we feel. He and I built each other up. When we got to his stand, he helped me up there, and I got in his chair and sat there looking around. I found it peaceful in his blind. I stayed quiet until I could see that he was getting bored and so was I. He asked me, "Do you want to shoot the gun?" I told him, "Sure. It has been a long time since I went hunting. The last time was with Uncle Joel, my brother's and our cousin." So he and I sat up there. Steve was sitting behind me, with his hands on my hips. I was getting set up. I'll be damned it stood out of nowhere, a deer. As I shot down it went and Steve got a little bit over excited. He tried to play it off and told me good job baby, good job. As we got down from his blind and walked over to the deer Steve made sure it wasn't going to get up on us. So he tied a rope on the horse and we dragged the deer to the house. The closer we got our boys saw what we had and Steve said to them, "Mama killed this one." We got off the horse and the boys were fussing because I wasn't cleaning my own deer, especially Seth. I went into the house and fixed Steve something to drink and used the bathroom. When I came back out I didn't really care much about what I was hearing, especially out of Seth's mouth. They were basically talking about how to treat a girl and from the way I was hearing it, Seth sounded something like what Cole would say to me. So as I was standing behind him, it hit me in so many ways that I drop kicked his ass to the ground to where he could face me. Seth is a 6-foot, 13-year-old teenager and when I had him eye to eye, I got in his face and told him if I ever catch you mistreating any damn female that comes across your path, I'll be there to beat your ass every step of the way. Your Daddy and I didn't raise you this way. Not this ego bullshit. No girl wants to be done that way." When I saw a small smirk come upon his face, this made me even madder, and I slapped the shit out of him. When I did, Steve came out and said to me, "Mama, what the fuck did you just do to him?" I wasn't done with Seth and I told him, "Seth, the reason I slapped you is for a good reason. To remind you when you treat a girl like shit that's what it's going to feel like when she slaps the living fuck out of you." He came out being a sarcastic smart ass, saying, "I'll just hit her back on the ass and watch it jiggle." When he said that I got a little bit disgusted and walked off. I was also a little mad at the fact that Steve snapped at me in this mess. As I was walking up to the house, I just couldn't believe that I had slapped my kid. Something from an old memory hit me of what Cole had done to me. As I went to my office, I sat there in tears. I was so mad about my child saying what he said. But when Steve walked into the office he had said to me, "I had a better talk with Seth. With you slapping him, I have mixed feelings about it. I'm sorry for snapping at you." I came out and said, "No, I shouldn't have done that to him." Steve mentioned to me that's a slap he will remember so don't worry. I had a talk with him. Maybe this will change his way around girls."

After Steve walked out of the office, Seth came in and he and I had a good talk. The next morning, I still felt guilty for slapping him, and he had a damn good bruise on his face.

When Sunday morning came around, Steve was leaving out to cover for Bodie and had decided to go on and do his normal run. Also, after he was off, I started studying for my exams. I got tired of studying so I walked into the living room and I said to the kids, "So who's bored?" They said to me, "We are." So I told them, "Well let's get on the ATV's and go find something to do." They were stunned by what I said. We bundled up and took off. When we reached an area on the property, I saw this mudhole and I went into it and started playing around with Steve's four wheeler. The kids followed me and I did a few donuts in the mud. They thought Mama had lost her mind, but I was only teaching them to have fun and boy did we. When we got back up to the house, I told them to, "Clean up Daddy's four wheeler and put it away, and we are not ever going to talk about what y'all seen Mama do. If your Daddy sees the mess we made he is going to lose his shit a little." Lucas said to me," Don't worry Mama, we'll take the blame and get it over with." I told them, "Well, I will go and get this mud off of me and make us some dinner." As I got up the next morning, I was trying to find fun things to do with the kids so we could make the week fly by. After work I made a quick run to our local Walmart and I saw these bumper balls where you get into them and horse ass around in them. I bought about fifteen of those things just in case we got a little rough we would have extra. I grabbed take out and brought it home and the kids were just too busy with their school work that we didn't get a chance to mess with them and I needed to study myself because my exam was tomorrow when Steve called me he told me that he was going to do a ten-hour break at Mama and Daddy's house for the night and get started on his run. I told him that it would be good for him to get out of the truck.

When the next morning came I had to drive up to Springfield for my testing, but once I got in there I took my time on both tests. I messed up a few, but still passed both of them. The examiner came out and said to me, "Congratulations on becoming a board certified pediatrician with an autism license." When he told me that I finally started breathing. When I called Hannah and told her the good news, she thought I was going to leave her and start my own office. She and I had a great relationship with each other and she asked me to partner with her, so I agreed. But when I got home, the kids were bored. So I called Steve and when he picked up, he said, "Hi baby. Everything OK, how did you do on your test?" I told him, "I passed and guess what? I have even more crazy news. Your wifey here has passed and has a license to study Pediatric Autism." Steve said, "I'm sitting here looking at your Uncle Gabe and Shane along with Noah." When he told me that I knew he was at Uncle Gabe's bar, which I didn't mind. There's no telling what Shane and Noah were doing other than talking about sledding. Steve was still pretty heavily into it, and he said, "Baby hang on a second and my Uncle Gabe started talking to me, and he asked me, "Kerala, if I have an open mic night, will you come in and sing when you come during your visit for Christmas?" I told him, "Well if Aunt Donna will make my favorite dessert." Uncle Gabe told me, "I'll make damn sure she does." I told Uncle Gabe, "Well, it's a deal but no dessert, no singing, and he says, "God I'll make sure it's done if I have to crack a whip on her. I'm proud of you Kerala Jade and I can't wait to see you soon." I told him I couldn't wait to see him also. As I was about to start talking to Steve again, Savannah comes running in the house yelling, "Mama, the boys are doing something stupid again." When I looked up outside, I saw one of the kids flying in the air with the bumper balls. I started to lose my shit,flipping out, and I noticed that they had some of their friends over as well. I started yelling, "Oh my fucking God. The six of you are going to kill me one day with your foolishness." I had to quickly get off the phone and said, "Steve, honey, I have to go. The boys and the entire football team are here. They have those bumper balls out and are horsing around with them." He told me, "Okay baby I love you, and I'll call you later." I told Steve, "I'll video it or post it on social media for you to watch what these little shitheads are doing. I love you too." I started to video them for a while until Chase came up and told me, "You know Mama, it would be a gas if we could do a football game in those things." Andrew said, "Yeah, it would be. You know we have the arena and Christmas is coming up in a few weeks. The Coach wants us to do a food drive." Drew looks at Chase and says, "Little brother, I have an idea." I looked at them and Chase said, "Why don't we do a bumper football game to raise money for our community, to help buy toys for the kids that are less fortunate?" When my boys were sitting there discussing it, my jaw dropped as my heart was warming with their thoughts and them thinking of others. So I told them, "Well, why don't we call Coach Barker and see what he thinks of this?" So Chase and Andrew did. The coach liked the idea that instead of the food drive, it would really get each team member and the community involved. I told them, "We can use our Arena. It's about the size of three acres with heat lamps to keep the kids and everybody warm." He said, "That's even better Dr. Nicholas. I will see if I can get the school involved to help out with some of the concession donations and see if I could get any volunteers." He asked Chase and Andrew when they would like to put this on and the boys looked at each other and said, "This weekend." The coaches said, "You two are throwing me and your own Mama under the bus and the whole community." Andrew said, "The shorter time, the better." And Coach Barker said, "Let me put some phone calls in, and we'll go from there." When we hung up, I told the boys, "Well, as your Daddy once and always tells you, that part is done. Now the real work starts." I can say that we had a pretty big day around the house. Before bed I sent Steve a text telling him good night, I loved him, and sent the video of what the boys were doing. When I went to bed, I just felt normal about passing my test, but in my mind I was patting myself on the back. The next morning, I went to work. I had spoken to everyone in the office about what the boys wanted to do to help raise some money. Hannah came out and said, "Well, why don't we set up something inside the school's gym to do a health check?" And I told Hannah, "I'm all ears and up for it." By lunch that afternoon the coach called me back and told me it was a green light to go. I told him that Friday afternoon I would be willing to feed the kids before practice and he told me that sounded like a great plan. By that Wednesday afternoon, before I even came home, I realized my two sons were on the channel news about the game. They were explaining to the public their ideas and how it all came about. I can say that Mama got a little credit on the Bumper Balls. Before Thursday morning came around it was all over social media and the boys had numerous donations. Things were starting to get a little bit out of my hands, but that Thursday night the boys went down to the arena and cleaned up. They got some things prepped up. I figured I'd better start doing our own dinner and figuring out what I was going to feed those kids. With it being cold outside there is nothing better than making dinner rolls, soup, salad and sandwiches with fresh fruit. But for my own household, since Steve will be home, I would make one of his favorite dishes, chick pic with sweet baked potatoes, roasted veggies, along with southern mac and cheese. With the fruit that I had left over I made a fruit cream cake and I placed it in the fridge. I felt better knowing that my own family's dinner was prepared and done. After I was done in the kitchen, I looked around, and I was the last one to go to bed. When I got to bed it felt a little lonely. Steve wasn't home. Being alone in our queen size bed just felt too big for me. About 3:30 AM I heard Steve come home. He woke me up by bringing his loud truck by our bedroom window and I heard him unlock the front door. About 4:00 AM, when he came to bed, I felt him pull me into him and kiss all over me. But there was something different the way he had pulled me into him, and he was holding on to me a little bit tighter. I waited until he was fully out, and I figured I better get up and start making lunch for the team. So I started coffee and made myself a cup, got a cigarette and bundled up. I went outside and enjoyed a little bit of me time. When I saw the time was about 6:00 AM, I figured I better go and get started on making my scratch chicken noodle soup and the dinner rolls. I figured I would make the salad and knock it out of my way. When I saw Savannah get up and go into Stephanie's room, I knew that it was time for them to get up. My hardest kid to get up is Matthew. I saw Lucas was up and Seth was trying to get everyone else up and out the door. I gave them the responsibility to get up and get out the door because they don't really want to get their Daddy up in case they miss the bus. Matthew has done that a time or two. When I saw them leave out the door, there was Matthew dragging behind, and I told him, "You know there's going to be a day that your job, or whatever you do in your life, is going to require you to get up far earlier than what you are doing now." I looked at Matthew. He was just shuffling his feet along as he got a muffin and walked out the door. Steve and I let them ride their ATV's down to the gate so they could catch the bus. When Matthew closed the door, I started making the soup. Once I got it all in a pot, I started making the dinner rolls. Once I had them just about done, Steve came into the kitchen, sneaking up on me and scaring the shit out of me. I told him, "You really need to stop sneaking up on me before I hurt you." And he told me, "Never. Why are you baking so much?" I told him, "Well, we are hosting a Bumper Football Game tomorrow night in the arena. The entire football team sold tickets. So I've had to whip it into high gear. The money that they collected will be going to the unfortunate kids in town so they can have something to open for Christmas morning. This idea came from Chase and Andrew. When they pitched the idea to me and asked the Coach the other night, I offered the arena. And it's a big deal around the community. I know it's last minute to spring on you and I know you're tired. I'm sorry, but the positive thing is the boys have raised $7,000.00 so far. The other morning the news station interviewed Andrew and Chase." When I told Steve what was going on, I knew that it felt as if I had thrown him under the bus just like I was. But if it's for the kids, Steve will drop everything that he has going on and jump in to help them. And as I was telling him everything, he put on an apron, jumped in and started helping me. I told him, "The kids are coming here to practice in the arena in about 45 minutes, so I have to feed them lunch." Steve told me, "Kerala you're going to make these boys miserable." I smiled and said, "Well, I need to take care of them. There's no telling which one of those kids might not get a meal after school." And he asked me, "What was the most difficult thing watching your parents struggle with?" I told Steve, "Watching them make the choice of food or bills and sacrificing their needs to make sure there was something under the tree. That's why homemade gifts are a family tradition. To remind us that the fancy things are not necessary, it's family, and we have each other. He asked, "Do you think we can help a few families out?" I told him, "You know I was going to talk to you about this subject to ask if we could possibly put together something like paying a families utility bill and a dinner so they can have a nice meal together. Hannah and I had thought of doing a health check." When the bus arrives at the door, in comes Lucas, telling his Daddy, "I know what's in that oven, and it's a regret for you later on." I smiled and Steve looked at me. I smiled at him as I started handing out the food and drinks. Coach was praising Steve and I on how we are raising the boys and being thoughtful of others. Steve and him started talking, so I tried to stay busy with the kids. One boy came out and said, "Yo, you Nicholas boys didn't tell me you have a fine-looking Mama!" Chase said, "Uh um, you better not let my old man hear you say that. He is very territorial over Mama. Not in a possessive way, but in a loving way, and he is very protective over Mama." This kid said, "Yeah I gotcha. If I had a wife that looked like your Mama, I would beat everyone in town if they looked or said anything wrong to her." Seth said, "Well, you just described our Daddy in a few words." I just snickered and walked off. After the kids were done eating, the coach had the kids clean up. Once when I went back to see if there was any soup left, that pot was bone dry and there was no food left over. So cleaning up was a breeze for me. When the boys had taken off down to the arena, I sat down and I started dozing off. Steve called my name and I looked, crawled my ass down to him on the other end of the couch, and climbed on him like a baby. My ass was handed to me, and I was out. When I heard the kids come in from school, it woke me and Steve up, which was a good thing because he and I wouldn't be able to go to bed. I got up and waited for dinner to get done. I sat there and watched Steve make a fool of himself. When he was done eating, he was whining and crying over how much he ate. I told him, "You do it every time

I make one of your favorite's."

The next night of the bumper game, Steve and I couldn't believe the impact. Our two boys brought two communities together. They had a fun night, and it was fun to watch. They raised $10,000.00 and Steve and I matched it, along with Hannah and Bodie buying bicycles. About a week after the game, the team did some toy and clothing shopping, mainly coats, and they had wrapped it up for the kids. They had a boy bend and a girl bend built. When we passed out the gifts it was pretty remarkable to see how many families we helped that were in need. Hannah and I did a health check on some adults and kids. I was surprised at the number of people who couldn't afford health care and just qualified for Assistant Healthcare. It made me a little mad about our system. By the time we were done handing out gifts we were wiped out from our day. By that Thursday morning we packed up and left to go spend Christmas with my parents. Steve was a little bit upset at the fact that he had a set time that he wanted to leave and we missed it. I always fall asleep during road trips. Somehow around 3:00 PM, Steve woke me up and told me we made it. I started to look around, and I said, "Well nothing's changed." As we were driving by Uncle Gabe's bar, there was a big ass sign telling everyone that I was coming home. I really didn't like that at all because it was informing Cole that the boys were here. He had a big sign saying 'Welcome home Kerala. She's singing on Saturday night. Come out and see her.' Steve didn't like it that much either. Normally, when we come to visit, I try to keep a low profile. But all I could say about it was damn him. Steve reminded me I promised I would sing for him. I said, "Not like this." I came out and said, "Can't I just come home to see family and not be treated like a damn famous person? Hell, all I did was leave this shithole with you." Steve said to me, "Baby, don't be such an ass." I looked at him, snickered and said, "Well maybe with me being home I'll knock the county queen off her high horse that Mama said she's been living on for the last six months. She's been strutting around here like her shit doesn't stink. Nah, I'll just be me and go find an old cat, take a wire bush, rub the cat's ass with it." When I said that Steve looked at me, I told him, "You know I'm joking, right?" Steve said, "I definitely hope so." He started laughing a little bit once we pulled in. The kids bailed out of the van and disappeared, but as we walked into the house Daddy started in on my ass about this coming weekend. He told me, "I hope you know that since you are here now, Kerala, you need to prepare for Saturday night. So tomorrow you'll have your Aunt Donna take you over to the shop to practice with your cousin's. Your Uncle Gabe is over the moon about this. He financed his bar for this, so you better do a damn good job so he can get his money back. To have your cousin's playing live behind you again now. That's something you haven't done in a long time. It is a treat for us as a family, but Gabe has blown it out of the water. I don't like this any more than you do, but I encourage you to put one foot in front of the other and do it and get it over with." I thought, what the fuck has he done and why?

So the next morning came and Aunt Donna picked me up. She couldn't stop hugging all over me and when she told me, "I'll get that bread pudding done tonight so you can have it for breakfast. And sure, we'll break a lot of your Mama's no singing rule." When she told me that I said to her, "We sure will." When she dropped me off, and I walked into the shop there was no one there. I walked around, thinking about all the memories and music that was created in this homemade studio. I pulled out my new booklet of lyrics. During the entire time Steve and I have been married I have continued to write songs in my alone time. I saw my old lyric box so I pulled out some books. Found the songs that Mama and I had written, so I walked over to use Uncle Joel's guitar and turned on the mic and plugged up his acoustic guitar. I started singing and playing this song that I wrote. I don't really sing that much anymore, around anyone. Not even around the house, unless I'm alone. The song that I was playing was about how a married couple is no longer communicating with each other. As I was singing it, Josh came in and joined me. It's like we just set everything down, walked back in and picked up where we left off. I haven't really seen my cousin's in years. We always kept missing each other. Once I was done singing, that's when Kyle and Dex came in. We hugged each other. They said, "Well, we have a radio interview at 9:00 AM, so we better get to stepping. We can catch up when we get back. I said, "Why not along the way." So as we were heading to the radio station, Josh came out and said, "You know Kerala, Dex's big ass was too afraid to come and get you." I said, "Why?" Kyle said, "Because of your husband." Dex said, "That dude is scary looking. He looks like if you want to play games, he's the predator, and you're his game. I'm not being mean to you Kerala, but looking at the pictures on Uncle John and Aunt Barbra's wall and on both of your social media pages, that fucker seems like he can snap my fat ass in half." When Dex said that I was laughing my ass off and said, "Steve isn't anything but a big old teddy bear. But I'll tell you this, let one hair fall off my head and let's see how that goes." Dex said, "See, that's the shit I'm talking about." We were laughing at Dex and Dex said, "I mean come on guys, look at him, he is like he-man all buff and shit." Dex had our ass's rolling. I had tears rolling down my face and as we were driving by the water tower. Kyle said, "Look Kerala, they're redoing our names up there, but in a professional way. Aww, to be almost famous and still get treated like we are celebrities in our hometown. I just rolled my eyes about it. Once we got to the radio station, we walked in for the morning show. There sat Justin doing his thing. We got a chair and he pointed at the headphones. We put them on. He was jabbing away and then he said, "You will not believe who I'm looking at inside the radio station. It's a big blast from the past, it's Kerala Jade and the Bomb Band." Justin said, "Okay Kerala, the public wants to know where in the heck have you been in the last 15 years. We see Josh, Dex and Kyle around, but you, that's the question?" And I said, "That's Dr. Kerala Nicholas to you. I've been flying under the radar when I come in for a visit. But for the last 15 years, let's see, I got married and had two awesome boys before I left this place. And along the way, Steve and I were together and had eight kids. That's three sets of twin boys and two single girls. We have been here and there. Along with all the moving, I worked on becoming a Pediatrician. Believe me, there's not a dull moment in the Nicholas household." Justin said to my cousin's, "So have any of y'all done any recording in the last 15 years?" and we said, "No. Matter of fact, this is the last time that we have seen each other in 15 years." We each talked about how we would miss each other and I said, "But we do have each other on social media. So we're not really missing out on each other's lives anymore like we did in the beginning after I'd left. Thanks to the power of the old internet here." Justin said, "I see. I think I have all four of you on there. I know that Josh, Dex, and Kyle post a lot, but I don't see you posting so much. But when you do, it's your family and what y'all are doing." I told him, "I have other things to do than mess around. I mean, come on, I'm a Mama of eight. There is no slowdown and when I do get it, I just soak up every minute." Justin asked, "Are you guys planning on doing any recording?" We looked at each other and said, "Maybe tonight. You never know what's going to happen when one Blake kid and the Conner kids get together." He said, "Let's talk about this gathering for tomorrow night." I came out and said, "Well, it appears that my Uncle Gabe has blown it out of the water, I guess, and pulled us all together. To be honest with you, I'm starting to get stoked up about it. I do believe we are a little overdue to show everyone that, yes, we are still here and playing. I'm hoping for a good show tomorrow. But whatever happens, I am looking forward to having a lot of fun. The show starts at 6:00 PM, so eat your dinner before coming or Timmy will be fussing about being hungry and choose a beer instead." When I said that, everyone started laughing and making a joke about Timmy. Justin said, "Well, since we are here, let's pull out some of those songs." Once we were off the air, we shook Justin's hand and told him, "See you tomorrow for a sound check." He said, "I'll be there to help out. I can't wait to see this." I said, "It's better with age." As we walked out of there, we headed out, and I said, "Well shit. Let's go get some nice clothes to wear for tomorrow." So we went to the western store and I grabbed a pair of jeans and a nice-looking shirt and a pair of boots. I was fixin' to see if I could fit into my old belt, but I picked up one just in case, and we were out of there. The last stop was to go by the music shop. I couldn't get both of my guitars in the van, so I had to buy some new ones. Once we got back to the shop we started on a set list of the songs that we were going to play. They saw the new songs, so we started working on them. They picked one out. I told them I had written how good Steve is to me and other positive things about him. I can tell you that we let time get away from us and every minute with my cousins felt good. It was close to midnight when we quit practicing and figured we better stop. I noticed that Steve had called me a few times so when I walked upstairs and into my bedroom, there was Steve waiting up for me. I told him, "Welp there's no turning back on tomorrow night now. I just need you mentally prepared for tomorrow night. Oh yeah, Kyle and Joshua inspired me tonight, so it should be fun." When I got into bed, Steve said to me, "I was getting worried about you." I told him, "Sorry, the shop is very loud when we get to play." When his arms wrapped around me and pulled me into him, I knew he was fixin' to go out for the night. When morning came, I was looking for some coffee and that's when Mama came out and said to me, "Kerala Jade, you know the rule of no talking and no caffeine." I felt as if I was a teenager and she was telling me what I couldn't have. I looked at Steve, and his facial expressions was who the fuck are you talking to. But it was just for me to perform better. I'm fixin' to break the shit out of it when there was a big knock on the door and Dex came in. I found myself silently laughing my ass off as he was making a dead stare at Steve. Dex asked me, "Kerala are you ready?" I ran upstairs, got my purse and one of my buckles. As I was coming back down Steve and Dex were looking at each other. Dex looked up at Steve and said, "Damn." Steve came out and said, "Who are you?" Dex introduced himself, and it was funny. Dex kept saying, "We have to go." I was waiting for him. When we bolted out the door, I was laughing, and he said, "Damn, I was stuttering my ass off like porky the pig in there. The motherfucker is buff and a huge man. I know why Uncle John let you go with him." I was just laughing my ass off. When we got to Uncle Gabe's, sure enough, I told Josh and Kyle the way Dex acted. They said, "See, that wasn't so bad. Dex your ass is acting like a big baby over a big man." When I saw what Uncle Gabe had done, he rented a stage and a big tent. I was like is that what he financed his bar for? When I saw Uncle Gabe, I noticed something different about him and the way he was acting. I brushed it off. I was giving him a big hug, but there was a smell that was coming from him that I couldn't put my finger on. I went on about it and Uncle Gabe was just a little big over the moon about tonight. When I went upstairs, there was Aunt Donna finishing the bread pudding. I said to her, "I need some coffee please." She started laughing and said, "See, I knew you would do it. Did you see your Aunt Martha last night?" I told her, "No." She told me, "Well, you know the routine. She does your makeup and hair." I smiled and said,

"Aunt Donna, I love you, but right now, I'm making love to your bread pudding." She started laughing. I fixed me a cup of coffee and I said to her, after my first sip, "I'm ready to go for the day, but I have one last dirty thing I wanted to do." She said, "What's that?" I told her, "A shot of alcohol later." She said, "You bet." We goofed off most of the day because Uncle Gabe hired some people to move our stuff from the shop to here. Normally, it's us moving the shit ourselves. About 1:00 PM we did a sound check, and it took about an hour. At about 3:00 PM, when I saw Aunt Martha, I knew it was time for me to go do my thing with her. I asked her, "What's the town gossip?" She said, "Well, you know that Monte girl that you went to school with?" I said, "Yea, she's the one I beat the shit out of." She said, "Man, she's just like her Mama. I did her hair the other day, and she was complaining about her daughter and Shane's daughter." I said, "Dakota?" She said, "Yes. Well she caught them two at the back of her house smoking." I said, "That shit. I wouldn't put it past Dakota. That kid. I just wonder where in the hell my brother and Layla went wrong with her. Oh, I forgot they didn't whip that ass." Aunt Martha said, "You got that right." Once she was done with my hair and make-up she said, "Well I gotta go, be back here in a little bit." When I got dressed I saw Hope come into the bar. She said, "I would like to chat with you, but we have 160 pizzas to deliver because we are closing here in a few minutes. It feels like everyone ordered before the show. But this pizza is on us girls." I said, "Thank you." I was about to go upstairs and raid my Aunt and Uncle's fridge. She said, "Go old school tonight and knock us out like you used to." I told her, "Don't worry, I will." As we got a few slices, I started to eat because I was about to start not talking. After I was done eating, I dug in my purse for my belt and buckle. I put it on and saw a pack of smokes, so I pulled a few out and went behind the bar. Dex, Josh and Kyle said, "Line it up." I poured us a shot of what Shane had given me the first time I ever tasted my first drink. We knocked a few and I lit up the cigarette. They asked me, "When did you start to smoke?" I told them the Asha story and their jaws dropped and said, "Damn Kerala, you were out there being a badass." We knocked out a few more until we got a buzz. And 15 minutes before we started singing, we knocked out about two more. Needless to say we were just in those stages of about drunk and buzzed because my mouth wouldn't shut the fuck up. We were giggling like a couple of little bitches. I said, "Fuck it, let's wing it on stage and see how that goes for us. Hell, we don't have Mama here barking orders at us. We are adults now." And Josh said, "Let's go." I heard people talking and I could tell that there was a lot of people starting to show up. So I said, "Boys let's take a shot for the road because here we fucking go." So we did, like dumbasses. But I can say, I damn sure wasn't feeling any pain. When my cousins took off, and they got up on the stage, I took one last look in the mirror. I took a big, deep breath. When I saw Dex on the drums, I gave him a nod and I let it all go. I came out there with all I had. As I was singing and trying to walk to the stage, everyone wanted to touch me. It bothered me a little bit. Once I got done with the song, I came out and said, "Someone in this crowd thought he could find this song in a retail store and I had to tell him on our first date that it didn't exist. So I started singing Giving Up the Fear, and the crowd started going nuts. When I was done with it, I started that one of how Cole was abusing me, and it's called 'No More'. I looked over at Josh and I could have sworn his ass was about to puke. I gave him a look of suck it up. Kyle and I did a song together. But as we started going through the list, I was being a little comedian, keeping the crowd interested. I was getting into the area of where I was hitting those high notes on my voice. But as we were getting down to no more songs from our list, I said, "This is the last one for tonight. I wrote this for my husband, so Steve, can you please come up here?" And he really didn't want to come to me. I sat down on the stage and told him, "If not, I can fix you behind a closed door with no cuddles." And everyone started cheering for him to come to me. As he stood in front of me, I started singing to him. I have never sung this to him. It was a lot of my feelings about him and telling him thank you for all that he has done for me. That man's smile on his face was far and wide as ever as I was singing to him. As we came to a small break in the song, Steve ripped me off-stage and put me in his arms and kissed me. I smiled at him and told him, "I'm not done with the song." This got the crowd going big time and he had put me back on the stage. I finished the song and everyone wanted me to sing some more. I told them, "Alright, how about three more and that's it. I'll blow the hell out of my voice, and we'll call it past this doctor's bedtime and eight kids are out late." So I picked up my electric guitar, and we started playing. I looked over at my little family and one more shocker down of me playing electric guitar. I'll be damned if I didn't blow out my voice on the last song. But once I got off the stage and Uncle Gabe hugged me, it hit me and I knew that smell. It was cancer. He handed me an envelope and told me, "Don't open it until the day I'm gone." I didn't want to let go of him, and he said to me, "Darling, don't worry about where I'm going. Just remember I'll be up there when you need me in spirit." This broke my heart. And as I had asked him, "How long?" He told me, "It's stage four and it could be anytime. But you made my dying wish and that was seeing you rip the hell out of a stage/ My Jaded Girl, I'm exhausted, and I love you. I'm off for some rest." I told him, "I understand and love him too." We parted ways. We got into the van. The boys started in and asked me, "Mama, can you sing this song or that song?" I really wasn't paying them any mind because I was heartbroken by the news that I just got. Steve told the kids, "Well, you heard her didn't you? Let's give Mama some space please." I was still drunk. We were sipping on the damn bottle behind the stage so we were lit as fuck. The next morning I was hungover and laryngitis sat in my throat. But you can say this, I had a damn good time. With me not being able to speak, this had me worried about me being a little sick. It had Steve worried, so I wrote Steve a note and sent him down to the drug store to get something for my throat. When he came back, he had the right prescription that I needed. I asked him, "How did you get this?" He told me, "The Pharmacist knew what you needed and told me don't tell anyone." I could feel myself more feverish. I was starting to feel cold, so I took the medication. And I told Steve that I was coming down with a fever and I told him I feel like I ruined Christmas. He told me, "Baby it's not ruined, you're still with us and your Mom and Dad. You are just under the weather, that's all. Baby, get some rest." A few hours later, I heard my old bedroom door open and I knew Steve had come back into the room to check on me. But Steve laid down beside me and I asked him, "Why are you so tense?" He said to me, "I know what happened to you, I disrespected you and read one of your journals and I know what that motherfucker did to you. I want to drag his ass to hell myself." And when he said that, I knew what he had read and the abuse that Cole put me through and I saw Steve had mixed feelings about what he had just read. I told him, "You're trying to build a bridge that I burned a long time ago. Yes, it hurt and I had no one to turn to, or even know how, until I got to know Judge Shafer during church. He and the pastor built up my confidence again. Steve, you're letting this and my past get to you. I need you to understand that I'm in my safe place and that's with you. I'm not mad about you reading. If you want to know something, just ask about it." I saw he was very upset, and I was upset with him a little, but this needed to come out. I really should have told him a long time ago. He said to me, "Baby, fair is fair." Steve took a deep breath in and out, then said to me, "Do you want to know why I have nightmares some nights and why I have to take medication? It's because I had to listen to Chase die in the car accident. To this day, I still have vivid dreams of them. I still feel like it's my fault for getting them killed." I told Steve, "I put the puzzle together a long time ago, that's why I changed out your medication for something healthier. You were killing your liver. You have survivor's guilt. You haven't really given yourself some real time to grieve. Maybe it's time to let that happen. And Steve asked me, "Do you think their parents have ever forgiven me?" I told him, "Honey it was fate. We all live on this clock, hell. When we go home, it could be our time to leave here. I can tell you myself it was strange. Look at me, what I was about to do to myself as you read when Noah walked into the loft. I felt something crazy-like in there with me. I can't even explain to you what it was, but for what has happened to me something told me karma was coming. I do believe in that and I find it a crazy question that I've always wondered. If you think this too. Do you think it was fate that put me and you together?" When I asked him that, Steve said to me, "I do believe so. I mean, how crazy is it that you and I were at the same place at the same time?" I somewhat succeeded in getting Steve out of a bad mood. We discussed the things Cole had done to me, but there was one detail that I left out, that I was raped by him. I wasn't ready to tell Steve that because he was ready to get up and go find Cole. I really wanted to leave that bridge burnt. By that Tuesday morning, I felt a lot better. So Mama and I, along with my fab four, took off to town and did a little bit of last-minute shopping. While we were in a small store looking around, I felt as if I was being watched. But in a way I had pushed it off. We had a good Christmas and once we got home, it was back to the basics. As 2014 came around, two weeks into the new year, I got a phone call from the school nurse. She told me that Savannah's history teacher noticed she was still gone during class. She went to the bathroom and found Savannah crying. "Sorry Dr. Nicholas, but Savannah has entered womanhood." When the school nurse told me, I as a Mama was excited about her, but kind of wasn't ready for this. I noticed Savannah being kind of moody in the last few weeks. I had a feeling that this day was coming really soon. So my last resort was to call Steve. When he picked up, I asked him, "Could you go get Savannah from school and bring her to the office?" He asked me, "Why, what's the matter?" I said, "Steve, do this for me without asking me any questions." So when he hung up, and I walked into our lounge, they asked me if Savannah was okay and I told them yes. But to her, I can imagine it's the end of the world for her, she just got her first monthly. I had to call Steve to go get her so this is going to be a little fucked up. He is going to bring her here so I can talk to her. So when Steve brought her in he was trying to come into my office with me and Savannah. I told him, "Sorry babe, but this conversation is not for you. So go into our little break room and hang out until I'm done with her." When I closed my office door poor Savannah wasn't ready for this day. But we had our discussion about when, how and what she should do. She was already carrying around a pad in preparation. I handed her two pills for cramping, and she told me in her little crocodile tears, "You didn't tell me that it's going to hurt." And I told her, "As you get older, you'll become used to it. Within the first few days it's going to hurt. You'll be a little hateful. It just depends on your mood, and please don't act like your Daddy when he gets in one of his moods. I'm going let you hang out at the house for a few days. Because for you, and it being the first time, I know that you're embarrassed. So if anyone asks, just say you got sick. Baby girl, Mama has some appointments coming in the door soon, and I need to get to them." When I opened the door, Savannah and I hugged. I kissed her and Steve was standing at the door confused as ever. I smiled at him and said, "Take her home Steve so she can feel miserable." Steve said, "Like hell Kerala, she needs to be in school." And I said to Steve, "No, and I'm not telling you what's wrong with her, she's embarrassed enough." When I said that he shook his head like oh my no you didn't put me on the spot for this one, and he said, "No." I said to Steve, "Yes." He and I kissed. Out the door he and Savannah went. I looked over at my Nurse Millie, and she said, "Oh my God, that was heartbreaking on his end. He couldn't believe it." Hannah said, "When I kind of told him that she was no longer a little girl, he didn't like what he was hearing." I said, "I know, right. The look on his face was pitiful." I felt bad because my husband was about to endure the first round with Savannah being on her period. By the end of my day I hurried home to see Savannah. When I got into the door Steve was there. I felt sorry for him, so I went into Savannah's room, and she said, "Mama this is a mess down there." I told her, "It's part of being a woman." She told me, "Well, I don't want to be one anymore. It sucks that guys don't get one." I told her, "That's why they're assholes and big babies. You see, us girls are a helluva lot tougher than these guys are because we have to deal with things like this and having babies." She told me, "Mama, the ride home was awkward with Daddy. Don't ever do that to me again." I told Savannah, "Your Daddy will always see you as a little girl and this was one thing that I never wanted to pull him into, but I had no choice. It will be okay. Since this is your first one, you'll need to place a beach towel on your bed tonight, and until it gets controlled. If you're too embarrassed to come out of your room tonight, I understand. You'll be staying at home for a few days from school." Before I walked out she told me, "Mama I love you, and thank you for doing the things you do for me." I told her, "It's my job, and you're very welcome." As I had walked out of her room Steve looked at me, and he had a look of disbelief that this was happening. I just smiled at him and started dinner. I looked up and saw Stephanie going to Savannah's room. I was sure the big sister was going to tell her little sister all about the mess that's going on with her. When I had dinner fixed and I made Savannah a plate, the boys asked me, "Is Savannah sick?" I told them, "No." They said, "Well, why did she just get special treatment for her food to be taken to her room? And you made her favorite dinner. It's not her birthday." I told them, "It's none of your business why." Well, the boys got riled about it and ran their damn mouths. And that's when Steve slammed his fist down on the dining room table, and said, "Like Mama said, it's none of your damn business. It's between Mama and Savannah. If Mama wanted us to know she would announce it to us." When Steve said that, the boys just shut up about it. I knew this bothered Steve a little bit because he well always sees his girls as his little babies, but after dinner I grabbed up the remote and turned it to watch my shows which was a medical mystery and the ID Channel. I can tell you that a few of my boys will watch it with me along with Steve, but it was my night to have the TV. As Steve and I headed off to bed I asked him, "Well how was the rest of your afternoon with Savannah." And he told me, "Awkward as fuck. Thanks baby, for putting me in the line of fire on this issue that I didn't want any part of." And I told him, "Sorry, but her history teacher noticed she was still gone during class. She went to the bathroom and found Savannah crying, so I got the call, and you'll have her again tomorrow. It's just until she has a better understanding of her body and her changes." Steve said, "Great, dear ol' Daddy has to be around for the first one." But as a few months passed, it was a Saturday morning and it was raining outside, so that left Steve and the boys stuck inside the house with me. Savannah and Stephanie had just left to go over to each of their friends' houses. I started doing a room check and grabbing the bath towels from them, or they wouldn't have any. It's the only thing of the kids that I would wash for them. As for the boys we're dealing with the ages of 14 through 16 so in their rooms you never know what your going to see and say what the fuck is that? Well, I had one more bathroom to go to, and it was upstairs. Matthew, Kaden, Seth and Chase have a dirty habit of leaving their upstairs bathroom lights on, and I had just seen Seth in Kaden's room and Andrew and Lucas were in Chase's room. So I headed to the last bathroom and when I opened the door, there was something that any parent never wants to see. I saw Seth masturbating, so I closed the door quickly and yelled out, "Oh fucking God, I did not just see what the fuck I saw. You will not believe what the fuck I caught Seth doing in the bathroom." I slowly started downstairs, and I told Steve what Seth did.He smiled at me and said, "Baby, you just walked in on him?" and I shook my head and yelled out for them and all six boys were on the balcony staring down looking at us. I just blurted out, "Alright God dammit. How many of you are whacking your wacker?" When I said that, Steve busted up laughing so hard that he fell out of the chair onto the floor. He looked up at the boys and they were so God damn embarrassed. I looked at Steve and said, "Steve it's not funny. While they're up playing with their wacker and putting their fluids in the towels, I'm the one who's wagging it around downstairs, and he was still laughing, He said, "Baby, I'm sorry." That's when I got him and said, "I think it's time for you to have the talk with them." When I said that to him, he knew I was being serious about the matter. So Steve stopped laughing and got up and kissed me. He walked into the bedroom and came back out with a bag and a book. The way he looked was like he was taking a bunch of little boys down to the barn to preach to them about sex. What was so funny about the issue is the fact Steve knew I was being serious when I told him if he doesn't shut up I'm going to cut off his cuddling. But as we got ready for bed that night I came out and asked him if he had given them the talk or did he go down there and laugh about how I said it to them. And he said, "Yes baby, I went down there and spoke to them about it." I could kind of tell that he still wanted to laugh about it, but he knew better. A few days passed with Seth and I not really looking at each other, but the next few days we just gave up and started talking again. When February came along Lucas and Andrew got it in their heads that they thought Steve and I would buy their first car. Steve had told them if they worked for it we would meet them halfway on helping them. They were both still studying, working and learning how to drive it, and they had agreed.

But this one night we all sat down to watch television (TV). Seth and Chase had this crazy idea that due to what they saw on TV. They thought we, as a family, should go out in the woods, try to make a shelter, find food and eat it. When they were talking about it, while we were sitting there watching TV, Steve sat up and said, "I think that's a good idea. Y'all are out there all the time. I want you to show me and Mama how you do it. I'm teaching you how to live off the land. You can survive out there and it's time to teach Mama a few things." I looked at Steve, and he said, "You need to learn." The kid's looked at me and Steve said, "Well, there are no ball games that the kids are playing, and no truck pulls, so I think we can do it this weekend. We'll just have to double the feed before going. I looked at Steve and said, "There's no school and you're off on Friday." He said, "Well, then we're going." So when Friday morning came around, the kids were fed, and we trotted off into the woods. We walked about 20 miles until the boys picked a spot alongside the river in a wooded area. Mine and the girls' task was to find wood for us. So the girls and I took off and gathered the wood. We would collect a bunch, take it to camp, and go back out again. We walked back and forth so much that we were getting tired. By noon, those boys alongside their Daddy had a hole dug and a base of something started, cutting every single tree wasn't safe. After lunch, Lucas took off by the river and I followed him, watched him take a soda tab and turn it into a hook. As I was watching, I was taking pictures. Between all of us we had four wagons with stuff in it which the boys packed. I just helped tow them along. I didn't know what I was doing. All I could hear was chainsaws running, so I figured I would back away from Lucas. The girls and I sat down shortly before dark. My boys built a cabin. Mathew was covered in mud. I didn't understand what he was doing until it was put together. He built a fireplace inside the little cabin. I turned around to see Lucas had a mess of fish. I sat back and watched Kaden make a fire while Lucas cleaned the fish. I felt the cool air coming in for the night as the boys put last-minute touches on our camp. I thought this was cool that the kids really worked hard on making a shelter. Steve was really hard on the boys about getting things done in a timely manner. But as I was sitting there, I was freezing my ass off. Matthew finally got a fire built. As we were sitting around the fire, Steve came up behind me and wrapped us up in a small blanket. The kids were telling stories to each other. Steve was telling me good things about me. I love when tells me things that I want to hear from him. As the fire outside started slowly dying out, Matthew made one inside the shelter. I walked in and I thought that we would be sleeping on the ground. But the boys had cheated a little and brought air mattresses, sleeping bags and an ice chest. When we gathered inside the shelter I was looking at their hard work. It was a 20x20 foot little cabin shelter. And as we were getting comfortable for the night, Steve placed me and the girls against the wall, away from the door. He made sure we were warm before he laid down. Somewhere in the middle of the night I woke up to see Steve sitting up with the gun and this crazy look on his face. It's a look I haven't seen in years. He was facing the little door. I heard something outside so I reached out to him. He hushed me. It sounded like somebody was walking in a far distance until we couldn't hear it anymore. I fell back to sleep, but when the next morning came Steve got up and started walking around the camp. Kaden and Chase stayed with us at the camp while Matthew went with Steve and Seth. Lucas and Andrew were looking for wild game.

I went into the shelter and tried to make myself useful by making our beds. After I got that done, I moved some wood in to help keep the fire going. I heard the gun go off, so I stepped out, and I could hear the excitement from my boys hollering from the woods. They were far from camp. Within 45 minutes, they were dragging up a wild hog, and they started cleaning it. I was freaking out because I didn't know what to do once they cleaned it.

Just as they were almost done, Steve and Matthew were walking up and Steve was barking orders at the boys to start digging a hole in the ground, get a fire started and get ready to secure and waterproof our shelter. While they messed with the hog, Lucas started seasoning it. I asked him, "What are you doing?" Lucas told me, "Making it taste better Mama. You don't want it to have a wild taste do you?" I replied to him, "No." As I sat there watching Lucas I was satisfied knowing that he can defend himself, take care of himself, and survive in the woods along with my other boys. They all have mad survival skills. As the night settled in, lightning flashes were lighting up the skyline and you could hear thunder in the distance. We hurried and started packing up things so it wouldn't be so bad in the morning because the walk was going to be six hours. As we settled in for the night, it started storming. I was terrified during the storm, but the next morning Steve got all of us up early. It surprised me that the shelter was dry as a bone. By the time we got home we were exhausted.

When I went to work, I showed the whole office what we did over the weekend. But my legs were sore as ever. Around 1:00 AM Wednesday morning Aunt Donna called and told me, "Kerala, I don't know how much longer your Uncle Gabe will be with us. We rented a van, started packing up things and getting the kids ready, telling them they needed to get their fancy coats, suits and their black cowboy hats. It was about 4:00 AM when we got on the plane. By the time we dropped the kids off with Mia, when we saw Uncle Gabe he was so weak. He saw me and I grabbed a chair and sat down beside him. He said to me, "I see Mama, She's here." I told him, "I feel her here with us." It was a weird feeling like Grandmama Blake was there. He told me, "Grandmama said you have grown into a beautiful woman." I told him to tell her, "Thank you." Uncle Gabe called for Aunt Donna, and he told her, "I love you, and it's time for me to go because Mama is waiting." When they told each other goodbye he looked at me and smiled. Uncle Gabe held onto mine and Aunt Donna's hands. He looked at me and said, "Sing me home baby girl." So I started singing to him and he took his last breath. I couldn't finish singing and the feeling of Grandmama was suddenly gone. I kind of lost my shit and that's when Steve held onto me because Uncle Gabe was like a second Dad to me. Once I stopped crying Aunt Donna and I got it together. I pulled out the envelope that he handed to me and I opened it. Inside were his funeral wishes, for me and my cousin's to sing at his funeral and for my six boys to carry his casket. Aunt Donna said, "I don't know how I'm going to pay for this." I told her,

"I got it. You just take care of the arrangements." I really didn't want to leave Aunt Donna alone, but she insisted that she would be fine. I understood she needed some time to herself. I told her that I would meet up with her in the morning to help her with the arrangements. We thought we had everything settled and ready to go so the next night we went to the viewing. Daddy was so torn over losing his big brother, and it was sad how Daddy said it to me, "I got nobody left now." I told Daddy, "You still have us, and he isn't hurting anymore." While we were at Uncle Gabe's viewing, I was looking him over and he never looked so much better. As we were leaving the funeral home I noticed that Aunt Donna's cousin, Wanda, was hanging around the funeral director. The next morning of Uncle Gabe's service I set out Steve and the boy's suits. As I got dressed and Steve asked me if we were set to head home tonight, I looked up to tell him that our flight leaves at 9:00 PM and I couldn't get some of my words out. Steve made me start flirting with him in the way he looked and my mind thought oh my God Kerala, you're lucky as hell. I said to him, "I'm not a horse, but you can ride me like one if you like. Because damn, my hubby is looking good today." When I had said that to him, he took a drink of coffee and spit it out. I told him, "I've been a bad girl so spank me because in my mind we are having sex." As I was telling him this, he was getting choked up, and he said, "Damn baby, you're being so cute that you made me forget my pickup line that I was about to say to you. But I'll tell you this, you're so sweet that you're about to put Hershey's out of business. Right now, baby your own mind is being a really bad girl. Don't worry, I'll whip you when we get home." I smiled at him and said, "It's a deal." He and I hugged each other and I felt him pat my butt. As we walked downstairs Mama was looking at all of us and said, "Now this is something that we don't get to see every day. The Nicholas clan all dressed up. I know this isn't the right time, but I would like to get a picture of your bunch Kerala." So we got on the staircase, bunched up together and Mama took a few pictures. I asked her if she could take one with my phone, so she did.

As we walked into the church, my cousin's and I planned a few nice songs to send Uncle Gabe off. But as the service was going and it was getting time for us to go up there, someone cut on a CD. I looked at my cousins thinking what the hell. Josh told me your Aunt Donna's kinfolk were telling the funeral home people that she got permission to change some thing's. I lost my shit because I paid for his services. When I saw Aunt

Donna's face she was having a fit. Dex pointed over to Wanda. This pissed me off at the fact that I really didn't get to enjoy sending my Uncle off the way he wanted it. We got into the van to head over to the cemetery and I knew that I was fixin' to let Uncle Gabe have his day. So when we got out Josh, Dex, Kyle, and I were about to go Acapella. They said we'll go up to the shelter area and you walk behind his casket. I told them the song, and they said, "Oh hell Kerala, not that song. You're going to really make everyone cry." I thought I'm going to make it echo as hard as I can on these grounds. That's going to wake Grammy Conner up out of her grave. When the boys and I stood at the back of the funeral car they had Shane and Noah to help them out. They stood there for a few seconds and looked at me. Noah said, "Boys, cover your ears. Your Mama is fixin' to make us all cry." When I nodded my head, that's when it took all I had in me, "He is gone — but within our souls of memories, but left us with a hole in our hearts, but we must carry on while he walks with Jesus." I walked up to the pavilion behind Uncle Gabe's casket. I sang as hard and as loud as I could. Seth kept looking at me and was amazed. I had tears falling as I was walking behind them, but I saw Kaden crying when they lowered him in the ground. Mrs. Morris came up to me. She and I started talking. That's when Stephanie came running up to me and said, "Mama, that woman over there is talking bad about you." I told Stephanie, "I'll deal with her in a little bit," as we had gone back to the church for the family dinner. I was minding my own business. When Steve got up and left me, I got up and that's when Wanda came over and said, "You know we didn't need you singing at the service like that." I told her, "It's what he wanted, and I didn't see you paying for this shit." Wanda said, "You know I think you need a good ass beating since you think your shit doesn't stink miss rich ass." I looked at her and she slapped me. I grabbed her hair, threw her ass out of the chapel door and I went to town beating her ass. I wasn't letting up off of her. Before I knew it, and wasn't paying no mind to what was going on around me, that's when I reared back and knocked her the fuck out. I was still going at it. Suddenly, I felt someone locking my arms behind my back and everyone pulling me off of her with them telling me it's okay. Dynamite, the bombs exploded! When we went and sat over in the area where the vehicles were I sat down inside the van watching her. When she sat up and got up, I was about ready to go for round two with her. But as she started running across the parking lot, Steve pushed me back and ran across the parking lot himself. That's when he drop-kicked her and yelled in her face, "Enough. If I catch you trying to attack my wife once more, I'm really going to hurt you." As we continued to sit there we were all laughing and carrying on about what just happened. I saw her sit up again. She got up and left. I was still so damn pissed off about the whole thing that I helped Steve smoke a pack of cigarettes. As we loaded the van and went back to Mama and Daddy's house, I saw a red mark on Steve's face. I asked, "Did you get hit or something?" He looked at me and said, "Yes baby, you hit me when we packed." I felt bad for the fact that I hit my husband, but it was a lesson for him to learn whenever I go to fight. Don't get in the way. As we got back to my parents' house, Daddy was a little bit disappointed in me because I got into a fight with Wanda. But still, she should have never changed things. Daddy said to me, "This should have waited until another time." He laughed and said, "Girl you looked like you were fighting a broomstick out there. I'm surprised you didn't snap her in half and poor ol' Steve there seems like he's going to have a nice shiner on him." Daddy started laughing while saying, "Well that fight is down in the history books of being part of a memorable funeral." Mama said, "You did a damn fine job singing at the graveyard Kerala. You certainly did echo off those headstones and I had cold chills on my arms. That's the hardest I have ever heard you sing." I told Mama, "Well I was trying to wake Grammy and Grandmama up out of their graves." Daddy said to me, "Oh you definitely did." Steve agreed with them. As we left out and got on the plane, my hands were hurting, but the next morning my fist was all torn up. Steve had a good shiner on him and I felt bad about it.

When March came, the kids had this crazy idea of planting a garden of four acres. I told them that it's going to be hard work caring for it. Normally, I'll have a small garden, just enough for us to enjoy during the summer. But when I took the kids to go buy the plants and seeds, those little shits had every veggie and fruit that they could get their hands on. I knew that once we had it all planted, by the end of the weekend, there was no way in hell I was going to be able to care for almost four acres of garden. I knew that I had to get some mason jars and canning stuff. Somewhere during May, something changed in Andrew and Lucas. They weren't talking to me and Steve. One night, out of the blue, Andrew smarted off to me and that's not really like him. When I asked him, "Did you clean your room? Because you know it's Saturday and I'm going down there to do a room check." Andrew smarted off to me, "Well it would be clean if I didn't have a worthless Mama who wouldn't get off her ass and clean for me. That's why Steve married you to do the woman thing." When Seth heard that he asked Andrew, "What did you say to Mama?" Andrew said to Seth, "She heard what I said." I turned around and screamed at him, "Go to your fucking room and don't come out of there until I say so." This stunned me. When I told Steve what happened and what was said, Steve said, "I'll talk to him and see what's going on with him." When Steve tried to have a talk with him, they were yelling and screaming hateful words towards each other. Lucas jumped in with Andrew and the arguments with both of them were just about every day until Andrew pushed me down, got in my face and said, "You need to start learning to stay out of my business." He started laughing about it and he did this in front of Steve. Before Steve could get to him Chase grabbed him and those two started to fight. Steve and Kaden had to pull Andrew and Chase apart. It was the last straw when Andrew pushed me into a corner and said, "You know what Mama, you're a coward." When Steve heard what he said to me, he pulled Andrew away from me, got in their faces and told them that they better straighten up or else. "You better not ever do your Mama like that again."

And that's when Steve said to me, "Call your Mama and tell her these two are coming. Pack their bags and get them the hell out of here so we can get some peace." I put two and two together. They were acting like Cole. I called Mama and told her what they had done to me. I said to her, "They're acting like Cole. Steve has done everything to make them stop acting this way. Mama, you think Daddy can have a hand on them to make them act better?" Mama said, "Put them on the plane. I'll get Kyle to pick them up." I told her, "Thank you." The morning they left out I felt some heaviness leave the house.

The next morning I had to get ready to clean up the house because I was about to have my first case. I wanted to do this at my own home so I could have at least a few days to understand the child's behavior. During this time, I was in the middle of studying this child to make sure I gave him the proper diagnosis of autism. If I screwed up I could give his primary pediatrician the wrong dosage of medicine for him. I invited the family to stay with us a few days so I could watch his behavior and monitor his tantrums. I think attending to the child gave the parents a break. To this day I get cards and photos of him, thriving, for which they were grateful. But it felt odd to us having a baby around the house. The kids loved it and played with him. He especially loved being around Matthew and Stephanie. They made him their summer best friend. When July hit my kids really figured out that the garden was hard work. I showed them how to do canning. I canned some jams, jelly and veggies, with their help along with Steve.

During this time, Steve took three hogs and six cows to be slaughtered and processed. After it was said and done, the kids appreciated their hard work. My freezers were full of meat with vegetables and canned foods. But as the second week of July came, Phoebe called me and asked if she could come and spend the rest of the summer with us. I told her I did not mind at all and when I spoke to Shane about it, he said, "There's one issue. What am I going to do with Dakota?" I told him, "Go ahead and leave her here since you two are going off to a shutdown." And I told Shane, "Do you realize you are leaving Dakota with me and Shane said, "At this point Kerala, I just don't give a shit. Beat her ass if she needs it. I should have listened to you all along. Now it's too late." Dakota is the same age as Seth and Chase. In the last few years she's done nothing but give Shane and Layla hell and doing things that she shouldn't be doing. Well the morning that they dropped Phoebe and Dakota off, I fully disagreed with what she was wearing. She was wearing very short cut-off shorts, a very low tank top, and make-up so thick that you didn't even know where her face started.

I knew that she would try to influence the girls. I have spoken to Stephanie and Savannah, telling them not to let her talk them into doing things they know that they would get into trouble with. But all in all, my girls and Phoebe are close cousins. I know for a fact that Dakota is no longer supposed to be alone in any room with Noah's girls because she cut off Samantha's hair. Dakota tortures them. Shane is sending her to me to let her Uncle Steve get around her and hopefully change her attitude. I said, "Yea, I'm hoping Daddy will change my boys' nasty attitude." Shane said, "Yea, I saw Daddy have Andrew and Lucas out in the field sweating their balls off the other day." I said, "Good. They need to learn extra hard work the old way." The next night as Dakota and Phoebe settled in with us, I started dinner and went looking for my toothpicks to stab some meat to hold in place. Well, I knew where they went. Kaden's room. As for Kaden, that child loves to build things out of toothpicks. Little houses and barns and stuff. But as I was going into his room to get them, there was Dakota in his room with no clothes on, and I lost my shit on her. I asked her what the fuck was she doing, and she told me, "Oh, I'm just hanging out with Kaden." I knew that Kaden wasn't there. He was at Jason and Dane's house with his other brothers. I told her, "Put your damn clothes on and get to the room where you need to be." As I walked out I had an idea of what she was thinking and that was just plain out nasty. The boy was just avoiding her altogether so I decided I would catfish her. After dinner I told Steve what she had done in Kaden's room and told him my plan. Steve said, "Mama that's a little too far. She just needs a good ass whipping with a belt. But if I get a hold of her it's going to be a different story with us." So I found her hidden social media pages and there were pictures of her in Kaden's room, acting like Santa's Favorite word. So something told me to keep a closer eye on her. The next night is what made Steve sick when we were all in the living room watching a movie. And I for one saw what she was doing as we were sitting there. She had her legs open with a dress on. When Steve got up he smarted off, "I thought it smelled like tuna in the damn house." The boys started laughing, and I said, "Yeah it does and nobody is fishing." When I got up, I went outside behind Steve. He looked at me and said, "Baby, we better count our blessings that our kids don't act like her. The one I feel sorry for is Phoebe, she's always getting left out." And I told him, "I feel for her." Steve told me, "I think we both do." As the month progressed, I was at my wits' end with Dakota. The day before I knew that Jason and Dane were coming over to hang out with Seth and Chase, I knew that Steve had hay to cut. Our home camera was on my work laptop. As Steve and the girls walked out of the house I watched Jason and Dane get dropped off. I stopped watching for a few hours. Around lunchtime I watched her go into our master bedroom and this pissed me off. When I saw that she came out with my string bikini on and went upstairs, I switched to the camera going to the upstairs hall. Within a few minutes she came out of Chase's room and Dane and Jason were right behind her. I was so mad that she went into our bedroom and got into my clothes. I watched Jason and Dane feel up on her and just as something was about to happen, Steve came pulling up on the tractor and those two started getting into it. Steve jerked her little ass up, and he was chewing her ass out. I saw crazy ass Steve come out on her and that's when I called Steve's phone. He put me on speaker and I told Dakota, "If I catch you with anymore of my clothes, I'm whipping your ass. And matter of fact, I'm going to when I get home because don't think I didn't see you let Dane and Jason feel up on you. And while you're at it, throw my bikini away. It's nasty that you had the balls to even go into my room and take something that doesn't belong to you. Every little thing you do in and outside the house I can see it. So that means you can't get away with stuff here. And matter of fact, I don't have any appointments, so I'll be home early to deal with you." I told my staff, "Since it's 2:00 PM and a Thursday, let's call it a day. I've got to go home and deal with some stupid shit. Y'all have a great weekend." I was so mad that I don't think I stopped properly in any of the four ways. Once I got home I busted in the door, and she was sitting on the couch. I took my belt off of her and started whipping the shit out of her with it. Steve had to stop me. Once I was done with her, I said to her, "I'm sorry and not sorry that you have to be such a whore all the time, but then again, a pimp always beats the hell out of his whores when they don't act right and that's the road that you're walking on. I have noticed that you have made a name for yourself which isn't good." When she got up she called Shane and Layla. They both told her, "Well you hit the fuck around and find out button with Aunt Kerala didn't you?" This put her into doing a little tantrum on them, but they were starting to ignore her. For the remainder of the week she only came out and grabbed food and went back into the room. When Shane and Layla came and got them, I was glad to see her go, but didn't like the road she was on.

A few days after they left, Steve and I were waiting for Lucas and Andrew to come home. When they did, those boys were two different kids hugging all over us. And Lucas, I could have sworn he was trying to get Steve to hold him. They were more helpful around the house than ever. But I was glad that they have a good bond with their Papa and Nanny now. Because that's all they could talk about to us. Steve made a good call about sending those two to my parents' house. Because if we would have sent them to Glamy and Poppy's, it would have been worse on us. Before school started, Steve had taken Andrew and Lucas for their drivers exam and they both passed and with that being said, Andrew thought we were going to buy him a brand new ride. Steve flat out told him hell no, but Lucas, on the other hand, had been working his little ass off. He saved up most of his allowance that we had been giving him for the past year and half along with his paychecks from where he was working. So Lucas bought his own ride and I couldn't say much about it. But for Andrew, he wouldn't let it go until I found a car for him and he figured it out that he could fix it up. Steve said to me, "Mama, that's still a little bit too much car for him." My other kids took a lesson from Lucas. As for Andrew, he thought I was going to help him with a sports car. But I made him settle for a 2009 G8, which he figured out that he could fix it up to be just as good as a truck.

Lucas saved his money and bought his own ride

without mine and Steve's help. Lucas was thinking cheap and bought himself a truck that was $6,000.00 dollars. They started working after school. They would jump up early before school and go help Steve feed the cattle. As Christmas of 2014 came around we made plans to go out to my in-laws, but a few weeks back, I had given Savannah the green light to put on makeup. She was very nervous about what her Daddy would say to her. But with a little bit of my own guidance of how to use it she did so the morning we had to catch our flight. Savannah came out of her room with full makeup on and dressed really nice. Steve looked at her and said, "Well shit. I guess this is another one that I wasn't ready for. I'm getting old, baby." I smiled and told him, "Now we're just one step away from them leaving the nest." He told me, "Yeah you're right Mama." When we got to his parents house Shelby was telling me that she wishes the kids would stop growing. I told her, "I know. I think both of us are wishing time would slow down a little bit." Shelby was really busy with hosting a Christmas party which they do every year, but only this time since Steve and I are in, we were attending this party. So the next morning, Shelby, Amy, Leah and I got up and headed off to get our makeover done and pick up our dresses. It was a formal dinner party, but as we were getting our hair, makeup and nails done, Shelby told me that she caught Lizzy keying Mary's car the other morning. And she said to me, "Kerala, I miss you being around here. It's like when Steve dragged you off from us, things got boring for us girls. I'm feeling a little adventurous today. Before we went to the party, I'd asked her what's on her mind. I want to go get a tattoo. I looked at my mother-in-law and thought she lost her fucking marbles, but she was dead serious. I looked at her and said, "Awe want to be a rebel huh?" Shelby said, "Hell yeah I'm being one. I mean, after all, you're here and there is no telling what we can get into before the party." Amy said, "Well, let's get our jolly party started." After we left, we went straight to a tattoo shop and they tried to get me to get one. I told them, "Sorry, but Steve would flip his shit on me if I did and that would give him clues that I'm an undercover gangster. Hell ladies, he already tells me I watch too much of the ID channel." And Leah said, "Well that's why we appoint you as our leader of the jolly club of dirtiness." My mother-in-law got what we call in the south a tramp stamp along with Leah and Amy, but inside the tattoo there's a little tiny Jolly Rancher in those stamps with roses. I was laughing my ass off because we were some dirty deed's women. But I can say that ever since Shelby did that to Lizzy, it's like I opened the floodgates of her to never be ran the fuck over. And Bebe, herself, has done some things to her neighbor. After they got their tattoo's we went to lunch and that's when we had a few mixed drinks. They were fussing about how bad it burned on their backs. I told them, "See, I have an open back dress ladies and that is the second reason I'm not up for one yet." We let time get away from us as we were laughing and carrying on. Leah said, "Shit, it's 3:00 PM, and we need to go to the dress store for our dresses." I ordered mine through the store, and it was shipped back and forth to me for the right fitting, so Shelby called Phil and told him that we were running behind. As we got to the dress store the manager was waiting on us. We were giggling and carrying on from our mixed drinks at lunch. I put my gown on which was a little bit of a mermaid dress, with a nice split on the side up to my thigh, and some sequins at the top. It was a pretty dark blue dress. When I added my jewelry and heels, I was ready to go. I stepped out behind the dressing area and waited on my ladies. When I saw Amy I said to her, "Damn I feel ungangster now." She said to me, "That bitch is in there somewhere." I smiled at her and said, "Well, it's now or never." When we got to the clubhouse Phil and Shelby were introducing me to people when a waiter came by and gave me a glass of champagne.

When I took a sip of it, I thought yuck, that is the nastiest shit I have ever tasted. I backed up to a plant and poured it out. When I saw Steve sitting at the bar it took me a few minutes to recognize him in the way he was dressed. I'm used to seeing him in Wrangler or Ariat Jeans and Cinch shirts and his work boots instead of suit and tie. When I saw him looking at me, I smiled at him as I was walking up to him. When he pulled out a chair for me, I noticed that he had my favorite mixed drink next to him. I came out and said, "Oh hey. I'm wearing that smile you gave to me." Steve said, "Oh I know. I think I can handle the first six deadly sins, but the lust I have for you now is killing me." I looked at Steve and asked him, "Can you be my Santa? I'll let you slide down my chimney tonight." He leaned over and whispered into my ear, "If you are a good girl, Daddy will treat you tonight because baby, you're so hot, you make the equator look like the North Pole." He made me laugh with that one. As we were going back and forth, this guy walked up to Steve, and they started talking. The other guy that was sitting next to me started rubbing my ass and I turned to look at Steve. I heard this guy mumble something about me which was disgusting. As Steve introduced me to the guy that he was talking to I noticed the switch of moods on Steve quickly when the bartender took my glass from me and gave me another drink. Steve told me, "Baby, don't set this drink down. Hang on to it." When Steve told me that I really didn't want it anymore. When Steve walked away from me, I looked over to the left side of me and, thank God, that fucking weirdo was gone. I was starting to feel uncomfortable sitting next to him. Within a few minutes Steve came back to me. He acted like he was rushing and asked me, "Do you want to get out of here?" So he grabbed my hand. As we were leaving, Phil caught us and asked why we were leaving so soon. Steve gave Phil a look and Phil said to Steve, "Oh, okay, I see. So here's my car. Why don't both of you go get a room? Mom and I will get the kids and the both of you go enjoy each other. I'm sure it's overdue." I was like damn, but once we got in the car, I could tell something had happened and Steve asked me, "So are you hungry?" I told him, "Why not." When we got out of the car I gave him my Mama's look. When we walked in, as we sat down, there was crazy ass Steve sitting with me in this nice restaurant. I came out and told him, "I don't mean to piss you off any more than you are, but I'm not having dinner with crazy Steve. Is there something on your mind that I can help you through?" Steve said to me, "Baby, please give me a moment to think before I say something wrong to you." So I nodded my head toward him and gave him a few moments or we would be fighting inside the restaurant. So when he said to me, "While I was in the bathroom, I just beat the fuck out of the prick that was sitting next you for drugging your drink." When he told me that, I was stunned. Before the bartender had taken the glass away, I was about to get a drink. I said to Steve, "How come you didn't invite me to this fight so you and I could've gone full gangster on his ass?" When I had said that Steve started laughing. I smiled at him and I said to him, "There's my Steve. I mean come on, that guy was on my fucking nerves and I had kind freaked out when I heard them talking about me. They were telling him to touch me and I swear to you if I had a vial of Insulin and a needle I would have pulled his tongue out of his mouth, shot the needle into his throat and watched him die a slow death." When I said that to Steve, this shocked him and in my mind I was like damn you're letting your white ass gangster out. Steve said, "Baby don't talk like that. You watch too much of the Investigator channel." I took care of it and it helped me. I got most of it out of me. As we finished eating, Steve asked me, "Do you want a night away from the kids, just me and you, cuddling and having our own fun?" I looked at Steve and said, "A night with you. Hell yes!" So we left and got a room for the night. We both enjoyed every damn minute of each other. Our conversations together were longer than ever. Being selfish with him is all I want to do with him here lately. But when we got back to Phil and Shelby's house, Bebe was going on about Bradly and Leah's kids acting up and bragging hard to Phil about ours. But when Phil and Shelby had taken off, about 30 minutes later I knew where in the fuck the crazy look comes from on Steve. It comes from Shelby, and she came out and said to me, "You mean to tell me that was the reason why both of you left last night?" I said, "Partly." Shelby said, "Don't worry Kerala, I'll take care of this." So the next morning we got up and went over to Shelby's office. Shelby's Secretary stands up and looks at Steve. He and I just walked on in and Shelby's office is filled with family photos. As she and I were talking about Christmas dinner she started digging into some of her boxes that she had on the floor. Steve asked her, "So what have you and Dad really been up to?" She turned to Steve and said, "Living son." And he told her, "Yea, right Mom. I see that tramp stamp on your back." She told Steve, "Hush it. You and Kerala will have the house to yourself soon and no kids, so what are y'all planning to do when they're out of the house and Steve told her, "Mom, you don't want to know." She quickly said, "Okay, put that thought through with me and your Dad." Steve told her, "Don't wanna know." Shelby looked at me like shit. I am glad that he didn't see that hidden Red Jolly Rancher in her back. Until this day everyone is still wondering who did all that damage to the Welshman's cars. Shelby and I did that. When Shelby got on the phone and called that department, she looked at us and said, "Okay, let's go to the boardroom." As Steve and I sat down, and the department started walking in, Steve was texting the boys and Bodie. He asked me about a code text and I had to explain that to him. When Steve saw this guy walk in that he fucked up badly, and I had looked at him, I could tell crazy ass was trying to come out and play again. So I grabbed his hand and when Shelby sat down she started rocking in the office chair and Shelby had told everyone to shut up. She said, "It has come to my attention that an incident happened at the Christmas party. And this incident was very inappropriate. When it comes down to my family, everything is off the table. I would like to introduce you to my son and daughter-in-law. They were attendees at our Christmas party and from my understanding, a few of you in this department like to drug a woman with their drinks. My daughter-in-law almost fell victim, but luckily Steve and the bartender saw this person do it to her drink. I find it disgusting. I see that someone in this room had the honor of meeting my son's fist, so it looks like a few of you will be fired today.

As we left from there, Steve was all riled up, and he had gotten the boys stirred up also. When we got back to his parents, I told him, "You and the boys need to go and find a punching bag to get it out of your system. We had a great Christmas, but we were happy to be back home.

But as the new year came along, around February, Steve and I got a knock on the door with pissed off parents, telling us that one of our boys knocked up his daughter. This Dad didn't know which kid did it. At the time the boys were dating around. That Dad demanded that we pay for the abortion and that set Steve off. Steve told him, "If you don't want this child my wife and I will raise it and pay for the medical bills." Just as this Dad was about to get into Steve's face, Steve stood up towering, and stopped him dead in his tracks. Steve told him again, "No. I'm not helping pay for something that I don't know if one of my sons did or didn't do. In this house we do not support abortions. We are pro-life, so I'll tell you what, if your family doesn't want any part of this baby, my wife and I do. See it may be that it is her body, her choice, But if it is one of my boy's, doesn't he have a say in this and let's just say it is his. But I'll be asking for a DNA test just in case, and if she doesn't want the baby, then my wife and I will raise it. The only thing we would ask is that she give up her parents' rights because I don't need this baby mama bullshit going on in my house. Kerala and I will pay for the visits and the bills on this baby that's coming. The minute that this baby is born, a DNA test will be done. If it isn't one of my boy's, I can tell you that you're welcome for me and my wife paying for your daughter's pregnancy. But the question is again, which one?"

He looked at our family photos, and he pointed out Andrew and said, "That's him. He's the one that's been hanging around my damn house." Steve said, "Alright. When he gets home I'll take care of him."

When Andrew came in the door, Steve told him, "We need to go and talk now." He and Steve took off outside. When he came back in, that boy knew that a lot of things were going to change for him.

But as spring came, Steve and I started our sled season. Kaden and Chase were getting interested in sledding, but with our help in getting their own trucks.

By May, Steve and I decided that it was time for us to sell off some of our cattle, so Steve loaded up a whole pod. Steve took off with them since we didn't sell them here. He took them off to his normal livestock yard and when he came in the door yelling for me, he said, "Baby, look at this check." I knew a long time ago that this farm would start paying us back, and I asked him, "So when will we be getting my milking cows?" He told me, "Soon baby, very soon." Believe me, it happened the next day. When I came home from work there were four milking cows and the equipment. About a week later Marty calls Steve and tells him that it's his turn to be out for six weeks. I really don't care for a 44, nor does Steve. But I laid down some damn rules to him if he drove at night. He can't drive past 9:00 AM and if he gets tired to pull over and get some rest. You need to think of us and not those damn cows. And he understood what I said to him and respected it. The morning that he left out I really wasn't happy because of this summer with the kids, but I tried to keep him entertained. Steve and I video chatted until one of us fell asleep. The boys helped me maintain the ranch while Steve was gone. When he did come home I was one happy ass wife. As August came around, I had to take a step back and look at the boys, especially Andrew and Lucas. They were in their senior year of high school and I just couldn't believe the fact that they were almost grown and out of the house. Both of them had their mind set on what they wanted to do with their lives, but with Andrew having a baby on the way, it was going to be a little bit difficult for him. As a mama I had prepared him for more obstacles to come. I can say for sure that Andrew really busted his ass off to help us pay for this unborn child. Andrew has already made up his mind if it is his, he will raise it. Andrew and I had very long conversations with each other about if the baby is his.

About 3:00 AM in the middle of the night, I get a phone call from this girl's mother telling me she had the baby and they will be leaving it at the hospital. So I got Steve and Andrew up so we can get this DNA test done. When we got to the hospital I was kind of anxious to know if it was really his baby or not. But when we got there somewhere in my heart I felt the way this baby girl looked, like Andrew, and she had a birthmark. Andrew shocked me and Steve when he had shown a little compassion and went to check on the mother. He came out and told her, "Now if this baby is mine, I'm willing to co-parent with you. But if you have nothing to do with this baby, I'm going to lay it down to you now. Once you give her up to me, I don't need you or your parents to come around because I will put a restraining order against you. Because what you are about to do is give up your parental rights. I'll ask you to sign a document." After he told her that, she told him, "I don't care what you want to do with that baby. I'm not ruining my life with a baby on my hip. If it's not yours, then I'm putting it up for adoption." I was floored by what she said and by what Andrew said to her. I, in a way, was one proud mama. So when the lab office opened up I took Andrew down to the lab, and they brought in the baby. They took a DNA test when the baby Mama left the hospital. It hurt seeing this baby girl still in the nursery and it bothered me that she had just thrown this baby away like it was nothing. Within three days I got a phone call from one of my med school buddies, and he told me the baby is Andrew's. I told Andrew and we got her out of the hospital. Steve and I had asked him what are you going to name her? He was lost for words on what name she should have, and he came out and said, " Madeline Marie." When we got her home everyone wanted to hold her, but Andrew was being picky. What he said was mind-blowing. Andrew said, "Okay Maddie, this is Grumpy and Lala's house. We are just here for a few months." Steve looked at Andrew and asked him, "Why Grumpy?" Andrew said. "Because Daddy, no one knows what mood you're in." Steve looked at him and said, "Thanks." I could tell it hurt Steve's feelings of what he wanted Maddie to call him. After everyone settled in for the night, Steve and I had a little time to ourselves out on the patio. I said to Steve, "Holy shit, we're grandparents. I'm 35 years old and I'm a damn grandmother." Steve said, "Baby, I'm two years until 40 if that makes you feel any better." I said, "It doesn't feel real just yet." He told me to just give it time. I've been waiting to hold her and Andrew. Man, he's going to be a good daddy, and I told Steve, "That's because he has a good daddy that raised him." But what got to me was what we were going to be called. I thought it was cute in a way, but for Steve, that nickname for a grandparent fit Steve to the T. A lot of it was because Steve hadn't held her yet. But boy, when he did, it was said and done with him sitting in his chair calling himself Grumpy. When the next weekend came we invited everyone up for a weekend visit. And that's when I saw Steve get nitpicky over Maddie. As for Seth and Chase, when they turned 16, they followed Lucas' path of buying their own ride. Steve and I didn't say shit, but we were proud of them. Chase bought a decent truck, but as for Seth, he bought what he could afford. We asked them if they needed our help and they refused.

As the winter months came Andrew was doing great as a first-time dad. He didn't ask me or Steve to lift a finger for that baby. He had daycare set up and was trying to finish his high school year. I was proud of him. He made up his mind that what he wanted to do for himself was to become a school teacher. At the beginning of the new year of 2016, I noticed that Maddie was getting congested. I advised Andrew to give her a few things to help relieve her. He was doing all he could do and Andrew was very worn out from studying, his testing and caring for Maddie. It surprised me when Steve told Andrew to leave her with Grumpy for the day. She was really sick, but I told Steve what he needed to do. Maddie had an appointment with her own doctor. It kills me that I couldn't treat her. When I left for work I looked at a few medical videos that I got in my email. One really stood out to me about this baby that was congested, a doctor was treating this baby, and it was basically mucus removal. As I came home from my own workday, there was Andrew being the best dad that he could be and caring for her. Steve and I woke up around 2:00 AM with someone beating the hell out of our bedroom door. When we got up there stood Andrew in a panic state and said, "Mama she stopped breathing on me." So I ripped Maddie out of his arms and laid her on the kitchen counter. I told them, "Now the both of y'all know I'm not allowed to treat any of you kids or grandkids. What I'm about to do, I don't need you both freaking the fuck out, and I don't need y'all pushing me away. She's my granddaughter too." Drew came out and said, "Mama just do something!" So I went downstairs and got the humidity steamers and placed it on Maddie. I started boiling water, Steve stepped outside and smoked. I came out and smoked with him and told Steve, "I'm fixin' to do something that I saw on a doctor's video article that I got. From what I studied this might work, but I'm afraid that Maddie has RSV, and it leads to Pneumonia. The way I have to perform this, it's fixin' to freak him out and I might need you to hold him back." When Steve and I went back inside, I let the boiling water cool off and I washed my hands, grabbed towels from our bathroom, a saline bottle, and put some gloves on that I had from the office. I took Maddie to the sink, flushed her little nose out, and allowed Maddie a few minutes to catch her little breath. She started coughing and I said, "Now let's get this shit out of her." So I was squeezing and massaging her little chest. They thought I was choking her and Andrew started screaming so loud that he woke everybody else up in the house, "Mama what in the hell are you doing?" I looked at Steve, and he was preparing to hold Andrew back from me. I saw Chase come flying up behind me. That's when all the kids came out of their rooms freaking out and Steve told them, "Don't intervene with Mama. If you do, you'll be punished with 50 pushups a piece." When I turned Maddie on her stomach, that shit started coming out in chunks and the kids were standing there watching me do my thing. As I laid Maddie back down on the counter, I looked at Andrew and said, "I told you this would freak everyone the fuck out." They thought I was done and I looked at them and told them, "I'm not done. I'm just getting started." When I was done with Maddie, she was breathing a lot better, and it was about 5:00 AM in the morning. I looked at Steve, and he said to me, "Baby, let's just go back to bed." He didn't have to ask me twice. By that late afternoon I could see Maddie was slowly getting back to herself and being Grumpy's Little Diva. As May 2016 came around, it was difficult to see Andrew and Lucas set sail on their own path.

Steve and I had set up apartments for both of the boys so they can have their own space and privacy instead of sharing it with someone else. But for Andrew, it was very necessary since he had Maddie. It shocked me that the career choice Lucas wanted to take in was being an Emergency Medical Technician (EMT) and Fire Rescue. The day before their graduation I found myself looking through their baby pictures and going through their baby stuff. As I was looking at it in the dining room I started crying a little bit because they were fixin' to no longer live in the house. The fact that we raised them here. As I started looking at the pictures the doorbell had gone off. It was right on time for the family to be in for at least a two-day visit with it being a Friday evening. The only kid that would still be at home is Andrew. Since Maddie has come into his life, he has kind of stepped up and stopped going out. Steve and I told him to go be a kid one last time, that we have Maddie. Mad Maddie is Grumpy's girl. That's what he calls her, Mad Maddie. But as I looked at my brother Shane and saw Dakota, who was working on her second baby, I had no right to say anything. But the fact that she was still young and when she walked in, she didn't dare to look at Steve.

As the next morning came around everyone was hustling around the house before 2:00 PM. I, on the other hand, was begging time to stay still. As we left the house for their graduation Steve and I could tell that both boys were on a jagged edge of the unknown to them. But as we were getting a seat this young girl kept her glare at Seth, off and on. He was making gagging sounds to her. I thought it was very wrong for him to do so. I have always told my kids that making fun of others isn't the way to do things because he or she could be your boss one day and the way that you treat them can scare that person. If you need a job and they're your boss, they can treat you like shit and make you feel like shit because of the things that you did to them in the past. As I looked at this girl,

I could tell she had a small crush on him and that's perfectly fine and healthy. That's when Kaden came out and said, "She's the one that likes to chase Seth around, and he is mean to her." I told Kaden, "Remind me when we get home to pop Seth in the back of the head for being mean." Kaden said to me, "I will very well note that Mama." As we sat there I will admit that I had my tears until Steve smarted off, "Two down, six more to go, and the house is ours." I just looked at him and shook my head. We had a nice little dinner for both of them. When the next morning came our family was the first to take off before the boys. They were making sure they didn't leave anything behind. As they were getting ready to leave, Steve was holding onto Maddie tightly and my own tears were flowing as I held onto both of them. I knew they didn't need Mama that much anymore. I watched them drive off and I turned around to Steve. I saw him tearing up a little bit and this stunned me. I said to Steve, "Well we did it. They're grown and gone. One has a baby on his hip. I saw you tearing up." He told me, "Hell no baby, I don't cry." He smiled at me, and I asked him, "What would have been one thing that you could have changed while raising them?" He told me, "Nothing that I would change about them." It was a lie that he was tearing up too. As 2017 came into place, Seth and Chase had their sights set on something else, but they had to wait until they turned 21. So Seth took his course of becoming a cop for the county until he reached the age of 21 to become a state trooper. Chase wanted to become an electrician, so Steve and I sent him to school for that. Seth didn't go far from the house. He was saving money to build his home. It felt odd because time was really flying. Seth and Chase's senior year of high school was gone. All we had left was Kaden, Matthew, Savannah and Stephanie. As for Seth, he was still living at home with us and working for the county Sheriff's office. It felt crazy that I only had five inside the house as fall of that year came. Kaden, who loves to mess with wood working, had a big surprise when I came home one evening. That baby built me a nesting swing on the patio and a gazebo out in the yard. I always told Kaden if he could get his hands on the stuff that's what I wanted him to do for me. And he did it with his Daddy and Seth's help.

As a few days passed and we were out on the patio. Steve and I were in the nesting swing giving each other affection and the kids were fussing at us because Steve and I were being affectionate to each other. Chase came out and said, "There's nothing wrong with what Mama and Daddy are doing to each other. It's showing us that their marriage is alive and healthy." Stephanie came out and said, "Yeah but they're old." Steve asked Stephanie, "How old am I?" She said, "40." Then he asked her, "Okay, how old is Mama?" She said, "37." He asked, "How old are you?" And she told him, "14." Steve told her, "When you get to mine and Mama's age, this is something that married couples do." Savannah came out and said, "I think it's cute to see Mama and Daddy still showing love to each other." And to me, the kids were older and understood a little bit of me and their Daddy wanting some alone time. When Thanksgiving came Andrew and Lucas surprised us. They came home with extras, two young ladies, Meara and Renata. Andrew met Meara in a library during a children's reading hour. As for Renata, Lucas met her during a class and she was going to be a nurse.

But as I got to know them, I liked them. I got to embarrass the boys with family stories about them. But my main worry about Maddie getting attached to Meara was if things didn't work out between them, this would leave Maddie confused. For both of the young ladies, they were down to earth and didn't take crap from Lucas and Andrew. I watched Meara in how she treated Maddie and I was pleased in a way. I felt as if their visit was short because before I knew it, they were back out the door again and gone. I felt as if life was flying by us. One by one the kids were leaving the house. As for both of my baby boys, when 2018 hit, our last set of boys were scheduled to graduate. Kaden had his mind set on building himself a small construction company. When Glamy and Poppy found out what he wanted to do, they set his little ass up with the equipment and things he needed to get it started. Matthew wanted to go to college to become a criminologist and study criminal behavior. He got excited about the fact that he was accepted into a school near Glamy and Poppy. This would be our last summer with them in our home, so Steve and I wanted them to have a great summer with us before Matthew leaves out. Kaden wasn't going anywhere from us yet, but during dinner Kaden asked me and Steve if he could buy some land from us for him to build his own home. Steve had told him that we needed to discuss this in private because we wanted to leave something behind for each of them when we are dead and gone. I knew that Daddy and I had to discuss this and Steve told them, "If any of you kids would like to build on the property that has this house that we live in, Mama would want it to be a place for you to gather in for family things and for just for the ones to have a place to sleep when you do get together as a family, so not one of your families would be permanently living in this house. And I looked at Steve and said, "Steve, I do think this is a good time to discuss this with them and in front of them." I said to them, "As you all know, this is a 800 acre ranch. Each piece of the ranch will be split into small acres for you to build on. If you don't want any part of this ranch, one kid will gain your acres. This ranch isn't to be sold, it is to stay in the family. Your Daddy and I are leaving something behind for you to appreciate when you get older. The kids quickly understood what Steve and I wanted. Steve really busted his ass off on this ranch, and they knew it wasn't until a few days later that we were to deed over a few acres to Kaden. We told him that it was part of his Inheritance from us. I could see his appreciation of what we had given to him. He wanted to build in front of the ranch close to the highway. We were very satisfied with where he chose to build his home.

As the summer started to wind down, the girls and I went on a small shopping trip. Savannah loves her magazines and on our way home Savannah and Stephanie started asking me some questions from the magazines. What they asked me was some pretty in-depth questions about mine and Steve's marriage.

Savannah said, "Okay Mama, first question. In a straightforward answer, when was the last time you and Daddy had a date night?" I asked them, "Redefine the question. The only time your Daddy and I get alone time is every Friday when y'all are in school and in the summer months we don't get any alone time." They asked me another question, "When was the last time Daddy took you out to dinner?" I said, "It's been a long time." And they asked me, "If you could describe one night with your better half and what you would like to see him in?" When they said that, I turned red a little bit, and they started laughing at me and said, "Mama it can't be that bad." I said, "Okay girls, a pair of black jeans, no shoes and a white button down shirt, not buttoned, and his black cowboy hat with his hair down." When I said that I had a small grin on my face because, honestly, it's something that I get turned on about when I see him like that. Both of my girls were grossed out about it. I said, "Well both of you asked, and I told you." They said, "Mama, that's one of your personal fantasy's that we should have never known about." I told them "Well you asked and I told you." They asked me a few more questions and I could tell something was brewing between my girls. It being a Friday evening and as we started carrying groceries into the house my phone was going off. It was Lucas, so I had picked up and there was no hello or nothing. He blurted out the words, "Well Mama we did it. Renata and I went and got married today." I told him, "Congrats. What is this chain reaction between you and Andrew?" He told me, "No Mama, it's something that she and I had been talking about for a while now." The weekend before last, Andrew and Meara got married. I was happy for both of my sons. I just pray that it will be a very lasting marriage for both of them. Both of my boys went to the courthouse and got married. I just wished that I would have been able to meet their parents, but I'm sure it will be soon. I understood the reasons, and it was because both of them played around and got Meara and Renata pregnant.

They were grown men correcting their mistakes and doing the right thing. As the month of September came and both of the girls were in three weeks of their schooling, Savannah 16 and Stephanie 15, and it felt crazy at the fact that my baby boy was fixin' to leave out. I was aware that the kids had plans to go up to spend the weekend with Chase and I was fine with that, but I felt as if something was going on behind my back. When I went to bed I made sure that I set my alarm clock so when I felt Steve waking me up telling me, "Baby you're going to be late for work." When I saw the time was 6:00 AM, I jumped up and out of the bed. I started cussing my phone because it was set at PM instead of AM and I could have sworn I put it on AM. As I was walking to the bathroom, I didn't pay any mind to our walk in closet as I walked past it. I quickly showered, put on my makeup and fixed my hair. I had to quickly figure out what I was going to wear. So as I walked into the closet all of my fucking clothes were gone except this one dress. I yelled out, "Where in the fuck is my clothes?" Steve comes in to the closet and leans against the door shrugging his shoulders at me with a smirk of I know what happened to them, but I'm not going to tell you. The only thing that was hanging on the rack was a sundress and I can tell you I was getting angrier by the minute. I looked at Steve. He just threw his hands up and said, "Baby you're going to be late." I told him, "My clothes better be back in this closet when I get home. If you're doing a dirty trick on me, well played Steven Wesley, well played." I put the dress on and I kissed Steve. I saw that smirk on his face as he walked me out the door. When I got to the office my new hired nurse Alexa, who calls me Little Mama, was stunned by how I looked and asked me, "Looks like someone has plans after work?" I told her, "No, my husband thought it would be cute to take all of my clothes out of the closet and leave this dress." Hannah said, "You might want to check your house cameras because Bodie asked Steve if he wanted to go to the stockyard with him and Steve told him no, I have big plans this weekend. And that dress tells me you're involved." At about 10:00 AM I looked at the camera's and all I could get was nothing but a blank screen inside the house and outside the house. It made me wonder what he was planning. By early that afternoon I saw that I had no afternoon appointments. So about 3:00 PM that afternoon I told Missy and Alexa, "If we don't get anyone in the next 15 minutes let's clean up and head home." Missy said. "Kerala in the years I have been with you I have never seen you in a rush to get home." I told her, "I want to know what Steve is up to." She told me, "I'm sure it's well planned with the kids' help." As we cleaned up the work area's I told my ladies to have a good weekend and I would see them Monday morning. As I was almost to our drive I saw the kids pulling out and thought it was kind of late for them to be leaving to go to Chase's house in St. Louis, but after all it was only just a three and a half hour drive from our house. I put my car in the carport and I opened the door. There were rose petals from the front door to the back door and I smelled food cooked. So I put my purse and work bag on the bar and walked out back. When I opened up the patio door and stepped out there stood Steve leaning against a post in a unbuttoned shirt, no shoes and that black cowboy hat on with his hair was down with a bouquet of my favorite flowers. All I could do was smile and I felt my face flush with redness. Wild thoughts were coming into my mind, but as we walked up to each other he picked me up into his arms. We made out for a few moments, and he had his little grin on his face. He told me, "Happy 20th anniversary baby!" This shocked me and I said, "You're kidding right? Have we been married that long?" He told me, "Yes we have. The kids put this together for us." I thought it was sweet of them to do this for us when he put me down, he told me, "Look here." There was a new set of wedding bands in the bouquet of flowers so we placed them on each other's fingers. He asked me to have a seat, so I did. He ran into the house and brought out some food and I could tell that our girls had cooked this for us. I saw a cake for us as well. He asked, "So are you still mad at me about the clothes this morning?" I said to him, "I want to know something." He said to me, "That's one of my favorite dresses on you and that's why your clothes went missing." I said, "I figured you were up to something and the kids too." But damn, I was so turned on by the way he was looking that I had just said fuck eating to myself. I was being polite because a lot of hard work went into this meal. He handed me two boxes and I opened them. Inside there were two sets of lingerie and two swimsuits. I felt bad because I didn't get him anything, but the grin on his face said it all. With the kids gone, I couldn't contain myself from wanting sex. It had been about a month since we made love to each other because we had been busy. We were well overdue and I wanted my husband badly so I asked him, "What's on your mind for later?" All he could do was just smile and shrug his shoulders. I said, "Well, off the subject, how long do you and I have for alone time?" He told me, "All weekend baby, I'm yours." When he told me that, it put a little smile on my face. So when he told me that I got up, ran my finger through the icing on the cake and slowly started walking around the table to him. As I placed my leg up on his chair and said to him, "So you're telling me that I get to play in my playground and be a bad girl all weekend long?" As I got close to his face and suckled the icing off my finger, I could see what was going on the inside of his pants. So I sat down facing him, unbuttoned two buttons on my dress and I had his full attention. He asked me, "So are you going to be my bad girl tonight?" And I told him. "I'll be whatever you want me to be. This is something that I have always wanted to do to you. So I started unbuckling his belt, unbuttoned his pants, pulled out his hard cock and slowly made my way down. I started sucking on him, and it's always been me receiving and never giving. This was a little treat for him. As I looked up at him, I could tell he was enjoying it. And it had been a long time since I had done this to him, but he stopped me, picked me up, carried me over to the nesting swing and ripped off my thong. When I felt him inside me, I knew he was about to rip into me, and I let him have me. I wanted every ounce of him in me and he was taking his time with me. I love how he and I have this thing with each other when we are done, we don't talk to each other and it's just our vibes that we give off to each other. As dusk started to settle in, I got up and ran to the pool with him behind me. When dark hit I found myself wanting more of him, but I figured I would not wear myself out too much. So I put on those cute little silk pajama shorts that he just got me. When I got into bed he pulled me a little extra closer to him and started cuddling with me. But when morning came I knew it was the weekend for us because Steve kissed all over me and I decided to put his ass back in a happy mood. We started making love again. For some reason I was loving every damn bit of us being alone. He asked me, "Do you want to go somewhere?" I told him, "It's whatever you want to do." When I said that I saw a smile on his face and he said, "Well it's settled. You and I can take a little drive together and go have dinner." So I got up and started getting ready. When I stepped out of the bedroom his face said it all and he was stuttering his words a little bit when he saw what I was wearing. For some reason he seemed to be a little bit nervous as we got into his truck. I sat a little bit closer to him which surprised him a little bit. He was getting giddy before we left the house. I wanted some new pictures of us together as we had made our way to the Ozarks. I enjoy going there and looking in their little shops. I looked at Steve and for some reason got this pleased vibe from him. It's something that I have never seen from him before. As we sat down for dinner he and I couldn't stop looking at each other until he started a conversation and asked me how work was going. I said, "It's good. I have a new nurse named Alexis. She's young, very vibrant, and a goof ball that kind of brings a little bit of fun to the office. Hannah cannot believe that we were that stale in the office until Alexis came along." And he told me, "It sounds like y'all are having fun in the office." I asked him, "What's on your mind around the ranch?" He told me, "Nothing but fixin' to get ready to change out the fencing. I've noticed it's starting to give way." We talked through everything that's going on with the kids and our granddaughter. When we returned home, we went back to having our fun and jumped into the pool. I had a taste of what it was like to be without kids and I didn't want it to end. I was starting to be a little sad about it and Steve had asked me, "Baby what's wrong?" I told him I don't want this weekend to end." He told me. "Baby it doesn't have to end. It's fixin' to be just me and you in this big house alone. Our next chapter is fixin' to start. I've had the best damn weekend with you, and I'm telling you right now I'm fixing to start being selfish with you." I told him, "Good, because I want to be selfish as hell and have you all to myself." Steve told me, "You know I love you and I want you to know dreaming of you keeps me asleep. Being with you keeps me alive."

After he said that, when he told me that, I was melting

again in his arms and I said to him, "I love you and I want you to know you're the love of my life. All through the years, I've watched you go through hell and back for me. I thank you for everything." As he held on to me in the pool, he hugged me, kissed me and said to me,"You're welcome baby. I'll go back through hell again if I have to for you." To me, we had the most perfect wedding anniversary the next evening.

I felt as if we don't really get enough time with each other, even if we do have our Friday's just me and him. By that Sunday evening, I was worn out from us doing things together, and I found myself laying on top of him like a child on the couch. It was late in the day and when Steve woke me up I asked him if the kids had made it back yet, and he told me, "Yes baby, a long time ago, and it's time for us to head to bed." When I got to work the next morning Hannah said, "Damn I didn't know both of you were married that long." I told her, "Yea and I find it odd that this is our first anniversary that we have ever celebrated. I just assumed that he didn't want to celebrate it, but damn, he gave me a good time. The kids were all gone from the house, and it was just me and him." And Missy said, "It looked like y'all were having fun in the pictures you posted." I told her, "We went to the Ozarks, had dinner and went to a couple of shops, then we came home." Missy said, "It's hard to believe Steve liked getting out of the house." I've known all we see him in the office is just once a year and I told her, "I know. He thinks everything is there at the house for him other than the feed store, Marty's, Leo's or over at Hannah and Bodie's." When I came home that afternoon and saw the truck sitting at the front door, hooked up to a pod, I knew that he was fixin' to hit the road. This had me bummed out because I was hoping that he and I would go and do something together this weekend. As I walked into the house I said, "Oh, so I see how this is, you gave me a damn good time, and now you're hauling ass on me?" And he said, "Well baby they had a good sale over the weekend, and I'm going to Colorado to drop them off. So this trip is going to take all weekend. I'm leaving out Thursday night." And when he told me that, I was disappointed. But when I came home that Thursday night and Steve was getting ready to leave, I got out of my car and walked over. He opened up the door and I stood up on the steps watching Steve get everything ready. I noticed that he was still moving things over into his new truck. The other one was about to give out on him and I told him it was time to spend that money for a new one. I will admit that I was being a little pouty about him leaving. Then it hit me and I had just blurred out and asked him, "Can I go with you?" When I asked him that he had the most surprised look on his face and smiled at me. He said. "Get your butt in there and pack a bag, but not the kitchen sink baby." So I went into the house and changed into something comfortable. I packed a small overnight bag with comfortable clothes and brought something that could take off my makeup. As I was headed out the door I looked at Kaden and told him, "I'm going with your Daddy for a few days." Kaden told me, "I'll let Seth know." I told him, "No. I'll text Seth. You and him are responsible for your sisters. So there's no going out for those two and no one over while we are away." He said to me, "Yes Ma'am." As I walked out the door I figured I would text him because in some way Seth is just like his Daddy. He doesn't put up with any bullshit. When I looked at Steve I could tell his head was swelling at the fact that I was going with him. So as he helped me in and closed the door, he was getting more big-headed by the minute. As we were leaving, he had shown out a little bit and I looked at him. He had the world's biggest smile on his face. When we got to the stockyard Steve hooked up and moved out of the way until the others showed up. I texted Seth and told him what I was doing. I told him he was in charge while we were away. He knew what I was talking about. As I looked up, Steve was talking to the other truckers that were coming in, telling them that time is money. I felt that a lot of me really rubbed off on him about people that waste my time and money. He wanted to make sure everyone showed up and got hooked. As we were leaving, there was still radio chatter going on. We passed another truck and someone saw me. They asked about me and Steve told them that I was riding with him. They carried on talking about Steve. I was just busy looking out at the view. I wasn't paying any mind to what they were talking about. I was just happy to be in my husband's presence somewhat. As dark had hit my husband was still on the radio, and it had become quiet there for a little bit. They started to jabber again. I had fallen asleep somewhat then I felt Steve lay down next to me. Steve and I had our conversations between us, but when we got home Sunday morning, he and I were tired. It had taken me until the next weekend to catch up on some rest. The next week came with saying goodbye to Matthew, the last of our baby boys. It was difficult to see him go, but we knew that it was time for us to let him go. We knew that he would be in better hands where he was going because Bebe has already made a room for him in her house. When we returned home from taking him to the airport during the Month of October, the girls came to me and told me that Stephanie was having issues with this one boy. He was groping her, and I told her that he shouldn't be doing this to her and not to let it happen again. Well, it got to the bare wire of where I called the school about the incident and the principal told me he would take care of it immediately. About three weeks later this kid started his shit again. I know that my girls and other students turned him in for what he was doing and nothing was getting done about it. So the week before Thanksgiving, I came home and the girls were complaining about it to me again. I told them, "Well both of you grew up with six brothers, and they would rough house with you occasionally. What did you do to one of them?" They said,

"Beat them up." I looked at them and said, "The only way you're going to get respected is if you beat the fuck out of them, and it might stop." Well around 9:00 AM, I got a phone call from the school staff saying, "Dr. Nicholas, can you come to the office? It seems that both of your girls are in here and have gotten themselves into a little bit of trouble today." I knew what it was about, so I told him, "I'll be in as soon as I can." But what didn't I know was that he called Steve as well. As I pulled in, I noticed Steve beat me to the school. I walked into the school office and saw two boys sitting there all fucked up by my girls. I was looking them over and was looking at the two boys. I smarted off to them, "I see my girls did what I asked them to do to you." And said to Steve, "Honey these two little boys have been groping on Stephanie. She told them to stop multiple times and even told school staff on them." When I said that to Steve he was about to come unglued and luckily as he was about to say something the principal opened up his door and asked us to come into his office. When the girls saw their Daddy they got a little bit worried. But with me there to explain everything that just happened, they knew they weren't in trouble with me because they did what I told them to do. As we sat down, Steve told Mr. Dia that he better start explaining to him real fucking quick or else. Mr. Dia told Steve, "Well Mr. Nicholas, both of your girls beat up two of our students." Steve asked him why. He told Steve, "Both of the boys had inappropriately touched your daughter Stephanie. When she pushed them back Savannah stepped in, and it escalated from there. I told him, "My daughter turned them into the school administration and nothing had been done. Now look where we are." Mr. Dia told Steve, "Well we can't tolerate this behavior so we are going to have to give the girls a week's worth of suspension." Steve said, "So why are my daughters getting punished when they were defending themselves? So what's those boys going to get?" He told Steve, "I can't tell you what their punishment will be." Steve and I looked at each other and Steve looked at the girls and told them, "Well girls, looks like Daddy is going to take you out for a treat for stomping their asses." As we got up, Steve placed both of our girls around his arms, and we walked out. I saw the other parents and I opened my mouth and told them, "If I hear that your children are messing with my daughters again, I'm coming after you, and it's not going to be pretty. You need to teach those boys to keep their hands to themselves or you'll be seeing them behind bars as adults." As we walked out Steve was tickled at our girls for beating those boys asses. When we walked out Steve and I kissed, and I told him, "Well at least we don't have to worry about them two now. We know that they have each other's backs." He told me, "Yea that's a plus on them two." As I went back to the office I knew what Steve and our girls were fixin' to go do. He was fixin' to go spoil them. Steve was never hard on the girls like he was with the boys. When I got back to the office everyone was asking me how it went because they were aware of what was going on. I told them, "Those girls fucked them two boys up. But the bad part about it was they got suspended also. That's okay. At least it's Thanksgiving and they get two weeks off from school." The school issue had put me behind a little bit which made me kind of late getting home. But as I walked in the door my girls had dinner almost ready. I praised them for their hard work. During dinner Steve and Kaden were talking back and forth over why Steve was at the school. When Steve told him I could see Kaden getting upset. Steve explained to him that everything was good now. When he heard what the girls had done, Kaden had a little smirk on his face. While Steve and I were watching my shows he asked me, "Baby does that fucking monkey inside your head ever get any rest on studying things?" I smarted off to him and said, "No babe. He's at slow peddling right now and enjoying the slowdown of the day."

When I had said that to him, he started laughing about it as we were sitting there. I could hear loud music and a loud truck fly by the door and there's only one of the boys that does that, it's Chase. I wasn't expecting him, so when he came in the door I held onto my little boy because it's rare when he comes home. But I was happy that he was here, and I was checking him over. And that's when he told us that he was done with his schooling and home for good. I was happy to hear those words from him.

When the next morning came I fixed a big breakfast and I received a text from Andrew telling me that Meara had gone into labor. I told him good luck son and let me know how everything turns out. He said, I will Mama. Stephanie and I had taken off to town and that's when I got a text message with a picture and his name, Tatuam Drew. My daughter-in-law had just given me my first grandson. I told him, "I'll be up to see him in a few days. I want y'all to get settled in your home before I come." He asked me if I could check him over for us please? I told him I would. As I returned home I showed a picture of our grandson and told Steve what they had named him, Tatuam Drew.

When we went and paid them a visit, Steve was about to break his neck to get into the door just to meet him, but it was more of a want to be with his Mad Maddie. I checked that Tatuam was okay and this eased Andrew's mind a lot. I understood why he didn't want a repeat of Maddie, but I can say that our grandson checked out perfectly.

As 2019 came into play, Lucas and Renata gave us our third grandchild, a little girl named Braylee Jade. I was tickled that they gave her my middle name. She was our New Year's Day baby. Seth had just finished up with trooper school and was patrolling our roadways. As for Chase, he was slowly building his life as a hard-working bachelor and was living in town. Matthew and Bebe were living at their best together. Kaden was working on his house plans. He was ready to get away from us and have his own home. His little business was booming really well for our area. Kaden loved building houses. Seth and Kaden hooked up doing something for Seth. As for Savannah she was going to graduate early because she had taken some summer classes, so this advanced her to graduate from high school early. We just wished Stephanie would have taken Savannah's lead, but she would be heading off to dental school in the fall. She wanted to leave in June to go find a job and an apartment which Steve and I fully understood. It was scary to see our first baby girl leave home and for both of us, as Mama and Daughter to me and Steve. Once she walked across the football field to get her Diploma, it was just like that, she was gone. It felt kind of unreal that we just had one kid in school and that was Stephanie, but we still had Seth and Kaden living in the house with us. It was during a summer day and Steve came running into the house, telling me to get my shoes on. He wanted me to see something. So we rode down to where Seth and Kaden had been spending time. As we got closer I could see a glass window on the upper side of the mountain and the closer we got there was building material. So we stopped. I saw what they were doing. Seth was building a house inside of a cave. He had an upstairs area done. I was amazed by his work. He had a bedroom built and from the looks of it, the downstairs was his kitchen and living room. Steve was so giddy about it because to him this had ensured who was going to stay on the ranch. I told Steve that this wasn't Kaden's house plans. This must be Seth's, but during dinner that night it was revealed that it was Seth's house. Steve and I had bragged on Kaden's hard architectural work and Seth couldn't wait to get in there. As December 2019 came in, I went into work and Hannah dragged me into her office area. She told me, "Did you read your Centers for Disease Control (CDC) Newsletter about this virus going around in China?" I told her, "No." She told me, "Man, this virus looks bad for them. Over there people are dying left and right." I told her, "Hopefully it doesn't make it over here." She told me, "No doubt." But when I got home that night I gave my bunch a heavy warning about this virus that the news is talking about and told them to be extra careful around people. As February 2020 came Hannah had her first case of COVID. We really didn't know what to do with it other than what the CDC was telling us. We did what we had to do according to our guidelines, but by the end of February it was really ramping up. I had to make a choice for the babies that were coming into my office. So my little team did well check house calls by April. Hannah and I were getting our asses kicked just about every day with COVID cases and the school was already talking about shutting down. I didn't want Stephanie's education screwed up so I found a homeschooling program that worked for us. Every night I would come home and pull off my clothes outside. Kaden built me an outside shower so when I would come home that's where I would get myself cleaned off from any germs. As I came into the door one night, Stephanie said, "Mama I'm done with high school." I told her, "I just put you in that program three months ago." She looked at me and said, "Well, from the looks of it, I'm not going to have a senior year." So I had emailed the teacher that was helping her with the assignments. Her teacher replied, Congrats. This is the fastest I have ever had any student to finish. So she's done with her schooling. I asked Stephanie, "So what's your plans?" She told me, "Well I spoke with Glamy today and she and Poppy have a two-year internship program. I can go out there and work with one of them until I decide on what I'm going to do for myself. But Glamy advised that I speak to both of you about it before just jumping into it." Stephanie liked the idea of showing off houses, and she is in favor of being a real estate agent. When I looked at Steve he said to me, "Baby we have to let her do her, I don't like this anymore than you do, but we can at least say that she'll be taken care of, unlike Savannah worrying us sick of not knowing if she's eating or getting enough rest. But you know Mom and Dad would spoil her worse than what we do." When Steve called his parents and told them that we were okay with Stephanie going out to them for an internship, Poppy and Glamy were over the moon about having her there with them.

The morning that the last bag came out of her bedroom she was all hopped up about going. Steve and I were starting to be a little bit lost before we had even put her on the plane. But as she boarded the plane, I found myself holding back the tears from letting our baby go. It wasn't until I watched her plane take off from the runway that the water works started. I tried to hide it from Steve and that's when he held onto me a little bit tighter and told me, "Mama it will be okay. I'm also a little bit lost." I told him.

Part Three

"The last of our kids are gone." He said, "Now, we still have Seth and Kaden at home." I told Steve, "Yea but those two kinda need to get the fuck out." Steve chuckled and said, "Yes they do. But at least we both know that they are building their homes."

When summer came around, Hannah and I needed a big, long break from this COVID mess. So we decided to take a month off and let the office get cleared of germs. We hired some contract cleaners to come in and do a deep clean. With COVID still flying in the air my kids in their own way wanted to high tail it back home thinking Mama can save them. But I told them that it wasn't safe to be around me because I could have it and not know it. With me being off, Steve and I had a lot of time to ourselves. I could tell Steve started getting a wild hair up his ass to go buy something big. When that morning came Steve woke up and we were sitting out on the front porch. That's when he asked me, "Baby when was the last time you drove the damn van?" I told him, "It's been well over two years." He said, "You know it's wasting just sitting there, and I can't believe that you have taken very good care of the SUV that I bought you years ago." I told him, "Yes I have. That thing is about 22 years old." He said, "Baby we have too many damn rides. It's time for us to go and upgrade." So we got dressed and went shopping for a vehicle for both of us. I found two that I liked, but I couldn't make up my mind of what I wanted. So I had to put on my cute little look that Steve loves, and I told him I was unable to make up my mind of which one I wanted. I just came out and asked if I could get both of them. I saw him cave in and told me to get them, so I got a little truck and an SUV.

The minivan, we just about gave it away. It had so many miles on it and the first SUV went along with the minivan and Steve's truck. So many miles and memories.

Steve and I were so glad to see that minivan go, he and I still hated it. But it did serve its purpose for us as a family. Steve got the truck he wanted, and we both settled on our car of choice. As 2021 came we welcomed our fourth grandchild, a little boy named Landon Blake from Lucas and Renata. Steve and I made the 4-hour trip up to see him and meet our new addition to the family. When we got there Braylee thought that Grumpy and Lala were it. So Steve and I get on the floor with our grandchildren and play with them. I'm really studying Braylee and since this COVID mess. It was driving Steve crazy to be apart from our grandbabies. I, for myself, wanted the kids home. But I feared that COVID could be in the house without knowing about it. It could bring death to kids. The one thing that I advised us all not to do is if the shot comes out, do not get it. It's very unhealthy for us and that it was loaded with NATO bites and lead that can mess with numerous organs. But as this was going on, it hit the house and Kaden and Chase got it. So this put me and Steve off from being able to go anywhere. Chase had given us a big scare. So I was studying the shit out of this Man-made pandemic disease. I would take any antibody and mix it with a sample of the mess and see which would kill it. The only thing that I could circle back to help cure it quickly was Ivermectin for worming pigs. So I had given the boys a few drops in some juice. Within a few days, Kaden and Chase were doing well. It affected some thing's on the boys and one was it messed up his vision so that made it to where he has to wear eyeglasses permanently, but he chooses to use contacts. As for Chase, it affected his immune system. When I caught Steve telling people about the worming meds, I told him to shut the fuck up about it because it could make me lose my Medical License. He did what I told him to do. When June 2021 came we had given up on the COVID-19 bullshit and started living life again. By May of that year our baby girl was ready to come home to us with all the hard work she had done for Glamy and Poppy. They bought Stephanie a nice little house and some acres to put her horse Trigger on. It's a beautiful brick home. With Trigger gone, it was one less animal that Steve had to feed.

But during that summer, Chase surprised me when I went on my normal grocery run. I stopped by his house. As I was walking up to his door, I could hear an acoustic guitar playing around the back of his house and a male voice singing all of Chase's life. I taught them music, but Chase was always a little bit shy about singing in front of people. So as I stood at the corner of his house, he had my voice but only a male version of myself. So I started singing along with him, and it startled him. I encouraged him to keep going saying, "Don't stop singing. Come on. Sing with me." We continued and the smile on that kid's face with me singing with him had made him feel good about himself. Once we were done with the song he told me, "Mama don't you ever startle me again." I just laughed and told him, "Stop hiding your talent from people." He told me, "Mama this is just my personal hobby." I told him, "I knew you were hiding it from me. I am heading home if you want to come over for dinner tonight." He didn't decline at all. As I left I noticed that I haven't seen much of my baby girl since she's been back home, but I do understand that she's a busy person herself. As for Savannah, she calls me just about every other day. As April 2022 came around life was normal for us again around the Ranch. It wasn't until that afternoon when Steve came in the door, and he said, "Baby Marty asked me to do a 44." I told him, "Well that fucking sucks." He told me, "Baby when I get back I'm all yours again. You and I might go up and see Andrew or Lucas and roll over to do something ourselves. It's whatever you want to do." We really had a good April, but one evening as we were eating dinner I could see Steve had something up his sleeves and I said, "You did something that you shouldn't have behind my back." When he looked at me, I saw it written all over his face and he told me, "Yes baby I did. Dex, Josh and Kyle are coming up. They want to get together and play with you." I let out a sigh and knew that those three along with my husband had put something together. I thought this would be a good opportunity for Chase to come out and play for us. So I barked orders at Steve and told him to go get my books and there's a new one in my office. As we were looking through my catalog, I could see the excitement on Steve's face. As the weekend was drawing near, Chase and I had a big surprise for everyone. We had written a song together and that boy was starting to become a train wreck when Thursday night came and family had come in. I didn't know that Steve planned a big dinner party for which he hired a catering company. But as Friday morning came around I kicked off my no talking rule. I wanted Chase to stay away until it was time to eat. Chase and I had been practicing, but in a way I understood why Steve did this. He wanted to have a few great weekends with us before leaving on his 44. He and I really missed the kids badly but was grateful for the ones that were there and our closest friends, including my office staff and Bodie. As Dex placed two stools up on this makeshift stage that Kaden built, I guided Chase to look at me and no one else. As I started singing, it confused some as to why Chase was just sitting there, until he started singing and letting it out. I looked over at Steve and saw his jaw drop. I had to keep Chase focused on me. I sang a few songs until Chase felt comfortable. And I let him loose. That's when I removed myself to go and enjoy his music. I found myself in Steve's arms. He said to me, "This is a big surprise. I couldn't be more proud of him and you too baby."

As everyone else left, Chase stayed the night with us and he woke up crying over his voice. I gave him some hot tea with lemon and honey, and I told him the soreness is part of it. By that afternoon, Steve got a call from our sled team asking him if we were willing to do a 4th of July show in our arena. It was to raise money for the troops. I told Steve I was up for it. The weekend before Steve left, I wanted him to have a relaxing weekend with us. Seth made sure that his Daddy didn't have to feed, and Chase and I collaborated on the back patio. Chase and I had plans to go one weekend to the shop and make a demo. I made sure I made Steve's favorite foods. I was spoiling him and I had given every inch of myself to him that night.

When morning came he was acting like a big baby. He told me,"Baby I don't want to go." I turned to face him and told him, "I don't want you to go either, but this was something that you have chosen to do. When you do go, come home safely to me." He said to me, "Yes Ma'am." We both walked out the door that morning. Steve was loving on me and that last kiss he gave me I felt so much love from him. There was a little bit of sadness from him because he was going to be gone and he and I had made sure this kiss would last for the next 44 days. It broke my heart in how he was acting.

By that next weekend, Chase, Kaden and I had packed up and taken the hour and thirty minute flight to my parents. We got our demo's done within two days. When I went into my Aunt Martha's Beauty Salon there sat Tilly. I just looked over at her and walked up to Aunt Martha, hugged her, and told her, "Me and the boys are out of here." As I looked back over at Tilly, she was working the fuck out her phone and I knew she took a picture of me. Aunt Martha said to me, "I guess we'll see you next go around." I told her, "Y'all should come up for the 4th." She said, "Oh I promised my sister already that we would be joining her." I told her, "Maybe next time." She asked me, "Your Mama said to me that Kaden is fixin' to restore your Mama and Daddy's place." I told her, "Yes Ma'am. Daddy is getting into the age where he can't do much anymore." She told me, "Ask Kaden when he is here next time if he could come and fix a few posts on my porch. Your Uncle Joel hasn't done it yet when I have asked him a million times. My boys don't have time anymore, especially with them having their own families now." I told her, "I will." She told me, "Don't worry. I'm frying that bitches hair over there. I think she's spying for Cole." I said. "Way to go, Aunt Martha." Me and the boys got back home and I could see Chase was getting big-headed about that demo. We made sure Steve got a copy of our demo's. We set it inside of his truck. As it was getting close for Steve to come back home, he was counting down the days. What surprised me is when the kids put me on a conference call. We were talking while I was driving. Our kids were beating around the bush and ready to come home to see us. Besides, Kaden, Seth, Stephanie, and Chase had saved three years of vacation and they wanted to spend two weeks with us. We were ready for them. Steve was putting together a small truck pull show for the troops and the community in our area.

Two weeks before Hannah and I would be closing the office, Alexia came into my office with an Autism case. She told me that they were from my home state and she wanted to know how soon I could study the child. I told her, "I don't know because this week Steve will be back home. That Thursday the kid's come home for vacation and I don't feel comfortable with just them and me there inside my house.

Besides, I would have been at work on that Monday

morning. I had to decide how I could fit this child in. I wanted to spend time with my kids and grandchildren and not work. Besides, Steve had that event planned for months, and it was a two-day event, so I called everyone asking the kids if it would bother them to study this child for the first four days after their Daddy's event. They would be at the house from Thursday until Thursday in which they didn't mind. So after I received my family okay, I told Missy to call the parents and inform them that I would be providing room and board for them and sending them a money order for gas and food for the trip up and home. If they don't have a car, I'll rent it for them. If they want to fly, I need to know. I opened this child's folder to get information and the little girl who is one named Payton. I didn't see the last name on the child, but the mother's name was Isabella, so I closed the folder and went on with my day.

By the time that week came, Missy had everything set up for the family. I shifted my focus on my kids coming in and Steve coming home after being gone for 44 days and the event. So when that Thursday morning came, I went to work, but something wasn't feeling right. I brushed it off, but as the day ended, I stopped by the grocery store and got a few things for dinner. Steve was grilling for us.

As I pulled into the carport, it looked like Steve had just come home also, but the kids were around back. I counted the cars that were parked, and one was our guest. I noticed that Seth, Kaden, and Matthew, haven't made it in yet. As I got out of my car, there stood Steve, a little bit on the rough side. He said, "Come here, baby." So I walked over to him, and he picked me up into his arms and said, "Damn baby, I'm glad to have you back in my arms." We kissed each other until we heard little voices from around the back, and he told me, "Listen to that." When I smiled at him Steve said to me, "Get ready for the house to be turned upside down with it just us here the house was too quiet." So we walked into the house and the kids had dinner almost done. Seeing our kids meant everything to me and Steve just smiled as we walked in. Renata and Meara were ahead of us cooking in the kitchen and Andrew and Lucas were cooking on the grill. Steve and I hugged our daughter-in-laws, and I saw the kids looked like they were catching up with each other. The first thing I asked after small talk was, "Where's my case family?" Renata told me, "Stephanie let them into Bebe's personal come and go door. She wouldn't let them come through the house until you were okay with it." I had Bebe's room set up like a hotel room. I asked them, "What time did they get here?" Renata said, "They got here at 10:00 AM." Meara and Andrew just got here and just as I heard a horn honking I was trying to see who it was. Matthew came blasting through the door bursting full of energy and excitement. He gave me a big hug and that's when Meara and Renata ran me off and told me, "Go and visit. We got this." So I told Matthew that I was going to change clothes, and I'd be right out. It was so hot outside, so I had put on a tank top and cut off jeans. As I walked outside, I stepped by Bebe's door and heard the TV going. I stepped away and gave them some privacy.

The kids were getting rowdy and drinking. They were all adults now. I couldn't tell them not to, but we were having fun as the food was almost done. Kaden and Seth had come home. Kaden was all dressed up, and I had asked him, "Why so fancy?" He told me that he had a contract meeting for developing the new houses. Seth, he was in uniform and being cocky as ever, but as dinner was almost done we gathered and ate. Having fun I went back in for another mixed drink. When I came back out and stood next to Steve, Bebe's door came open and who stepped out of there shocked me and Steve. So Steve jerked me up and took me into the house. I was in shock to see Cole, and I was freaking out. I started crying. Steve held me and said, "Baby I don't know what to say." After Matthew fixed up a few shots, Matthew was confused. I looked at Lucas and Andrew and I could tell the mood on them had changed. Steve told Matthew, "Can you please give me and Mama a minute?" Steve and I started slamming our shots together. Steve and I were questioning each other. He told me, "Baby I've been spying on the fucker for years. I did it for the safety of the boys. That cocksucker is a drug addict, an alcoholic, and he goes back and forth to the Bible. And seeing him here in my fucking house, no, he better not dare to destroy my boys. Those are my babies." I was crying and said, "You saved me." That's when Steve told me, "No baby. I've had my eye on you. I watched you inside of the Café while I was standing at the window. I was watching you work when the Major asked me to join them for breakfast. I couldn't resist, so I took the chance of seeing you up close, but when the old chick told me your business I still wasn't concerned about what he had done to you. I knew when I brushed my hand against yours I wanted to be with you and I love you with every bone and vessels in my body. But if this fucker runs his mouth, I'm ripping him apart and burying his ass where no motherfucker will find him. He doesn't deserve to know those boys." Just as we were talking, I couldn't stop crying. That's when Lucas and Andrew came in and asked us if everything was okay and I just shook my head at them and said, "I don't know." Lucas and Andrew said, "Mama, Daddy, we know who he is. We knew it years ago." When I heard that Steve and I just broke down and Andrew said, "We see that he's our hump and dump mama piece of shit, but that doesn't change things here. The man that is standing behind you and makes sure that we were first, along with you, is our Daddy. He stepped up to the plate and how we found out was something we shouldn't have ever been pilfering in, and that was your Journal's Mom. So we asked Nanny and she lied to us at first, for a long time, until someone came out at church and asked us if we were his boys. And another old woman who always begs the church for stuff said yes they are his, so after church Nanny had some explaining to do to us. She told us, but still that doesn't mean that we stopped loving Daddy or changed things that out there is a coward ass crackhead dad. On the other hand, Daddy gave us his last name." After we found out what Andrew and Lucas knew, it still didn't make anything better on our feelings. Steve and I were buzzed and the boys told us to get a quick bite and go to bed. We got shit from here. Well, just feed them and ignore them. Steve and I went to bed. I cried myself to sleep that night.

When I woke up, I got up, made coffee, grabbed a cigarette from Steve's pack, and went outside as the sun started rising. I saw Seth and Kaden feeding. As I was watching them and getting ready to move them to another side of the ranch, we had to open up the road for our event tonight.

But that wasn't even on my mind; it was what was sleeping in my house. It hit me that pure meanness came up inside of me. I was going to rub my life in front of Cole and show him I came out on top. Just as I was sitting there in deep thought, Steve walked up behind me. He kissed me on my cheek and said, "Baby I see that devilish look on your face. Do you want to talk?" I told him, "I do." Just as I was about to say what was on my mind this young girl comes up out of nowhere and walks up and sits down. Steve and I looked at her and Steve asked her in an asshole way and said, "And you are?" And she said, "Oh. I'm sorry. My name is Isabella. I am Payton's mom." I said, "Well Isabella, I'm Dr. Kerala Nicholas and this is my husband, Steve." She quickly said, "Oh, I thought that the other woman was the Dr." I asked her, "Which one?" She said, "The blonde." I told her, "That's my daughter-in-law, Renata. She's a Nurse." She said, "I've heard about you through Cole." I said, "I'm sure your Dad has told you." And that's when she started giggling and said, "Cole isn't my dad, he's my boyfriend." When she said that, my jaw dropped, and I had asked her how old she was, and she said, "Oh, I'm 24." When she said that, Steve got up and said, "Sorry baby, but I've got to get a bunch of stuff ready before 5:00 PM, and I'll need all the help I can get. I've got to get those coolers going to keep people cool for tonight." When I looked at Steve I could see the frustration on him. My mind was blown and disgusted that an almost 50-year-old man was with a 24-year-old young lady. So I just told her, "I'm sorry to be rude. Like my husband said, we have a lot to do on a show for our troops tonight." So I got up and went into the house and there stood Kaden. He hugged me and told me good morning, and he said, "Mama that girl treated me and Matthew like a damn geek last night." I smarted off and said, "Yeah, well she's got a man with a pencil dick so go and fuck with her head. I know you've been hiding those tattoos from me. I don't mind you having them, but don't cover your body and you better not put any on your face. It took me nine months to make you." Just as I was about to say something else to Kaden, my front door busted open. The words were, "Here in comes Shane and Noah." I told them, "I can't bullshit right now. Steve is waiting for y'all down at the arena." As I turned around everyone was out the door besides Renata, Meara and my grandbabies. The older grandkids had taken off to the arena. Meara and Renata took off downstairs to Lucas and Andrew's old rooms. I started cleaning up some things and thought it was Meara sitting on a stool behind me when I heard Cole's voice. I started to cringe. He said, "It's a pretty nice spread you got here. see that he has raised my boys pretty well." When I turned around and faced him he said,"It must be a nice life for you and him to steal my boys from me. After I found out you had given birth to my kids you finished up and married him before I could see them and give them my name. You know you could have had this with me, but I'm going to tell you this you little bitch. If I catch you alone, I will give you a lesson for taking them from me." As I was looking at this piece of shit sitting at my counter I couldn't get my words out. I ran to my room and I was crying because I was so mad. The reason I didn't tell them to leave was because due to a law in the state if you don't treat a patient without seeing them I could get sued. I wasn't going to rent them a room because with an Autism case, you have to spend time with the child before saying if they have it or not. As I sat there, I tried to figure out if what he said was my fault for not trying to notify him. I sat there and Chase came in. He said, "Mama, that motherfucker just gaslighting you. I was standing there and I heard everything and whatever happened before you and daddy is in the past. This dickhead can't let it go. We know what's going on. He fucked up and Daddy stepped in. This dude is fucking jealous. But for right now Mama I need you to hand me that knife." As I looked down, I handed the knife to Chase and he said, "Now I'm starting to get pissed off because the woman that raised me is a really tough person and doesn't take any shit. But seeing my Mama cry pisses me off. She's letting a piece of shit rip her apart when Daddy's back is turned. I think Cole's a coward." As Chase was talking to me Seth comes in, and I know when he's mad, and he gives Chase a look, it's a twin thing. Both of them started getting annoying, cocky, jerks, and something was up their sleeves. Seth said, "Mama I have something for you to see." That's when he showed me that Cole had a history of in and out of jail and I told them I figured as much. As the patio door slammed open, Matthew was calling out for me, "Mama, Mama." And out of breath he said, "Daddy is coming this way and he's about to go ape shit nuts on this retard in there." Just as Matt told us that, Steve comes running in the house heading towards that door. Seth stops him and said, "Daddy, I'm 30 steps ahead of you, and he's not fucking worth it. So go to Mama." When Steve came into the room he sat behind me, wrapped his arms around me, held onto me and asked me if Cole hurt me. I told him, "No." Steve said, "Matthew sent a video of what he said to you. I promise I'm about to get my fucking hands on him. It's over with. Baby we did everything legal. He gave up his rights. You know this. That's why they are my boys. I raised them. I just don't understand why now. I want this motherfucker out of my house as soon as possible." I told him, "I haven't seen this child nor have I heard her in that room." It made us question if this child is even here. Steve told me, "Come Sunday, start studying this child. But right now, your body is stiff as ever. I need you to relax before tonight. I have never seen you so upset and it bothers me to see you like this." As we sat there I started calming down and Steve said, "Go start getting ready. It's almost 2:00 PM and the food vendors have shown up. The staffing we hired is here." I got up, showered, put on my makeup and fixed my hair. I fixed my crown, but what was brewing behind my back with my kids was absolutely fucking revenge.

As the show started, I got ready and settled into my truck. But when it came my turn I had taken all of my anger out on the track. As I pulled out, I saw Steve smiling and laughing. I didn't realize that out of the 30 guys that were there, I whipped the shit out of them. When Hannah and Bodie met up with us behind the gates, I pulled Hannah aside, and she had asked me how my case was going. I told her, "Very uncomfortable. The parents are both drug users, and I'm trying to figure out a way to get them the fuck out of my house. I believe I will start studying the child Sunday, so I can get them going. Steve is freaking out about it." Hannah told me, "Girl do what you gotta do." I asked her, "So when are you and Bodie leaving?" She told me, "Some time Tuesday. Hey, why don't we take an extra week off? Hell, we've earned it as much as we bust our asses." And I said, "If I had an extra week off, I could really use it with the bullshit that I'm dealing with right now." After everyone was gone Steve and I took off up to the patio and laid in the nesting swing until Cole came outside. Steve had told me, "Go in the house through the front door." So I got up and made sure Cole didn't see me when I went inside. I peeked outside watching him pace back and forth until I saw Steve get up. I went into our bathroom and started a shower. As I got in, I made sure it was Steve there with me. As he stood behind me that's when he started kissing on my neck and I had melted into him. I let him fuck me against the bathroom wall. It really wasn't how we have sex with each other, but it would make due until we are really alone. But the second night, the more I thought, shit the harder on my rig I was doing and I had done some damage to it. After I unhooked, I put it up in the shop and I walked over to my grandbabies to watch Grumpy and my brothers with Uncle Kaden and Chase. As we sat there watching Shane hook up I could see Steve was next and Braylee and Maddie were getting excited about their Grumpy. But once he hooked up and got the green light, he let into it and wasn't letting up off it. But for the boys, they lost against a guy named Adam. After the night was said and done and everyone was paid, we had raised $40,000.00. Steve and I are in the works to do it again. As we settled in for the night, we were still trying to unwind from our adrenaline rush.

When the next morning came, I didn't want to rush up away from cuddling with Steve. I wanted to spend the day by the pool, but as I looked, the bedroom door was open. My problem, across the living room floor, was standing around looking at our family photos on the wall. As I laid there watching him and her wander around my house, I pretended to be asleep. While I was watching them, I looked up at Steve, and he looked at me and said, "Baby I need to get up. Me and the boys are moving cattle back up here closer to the pond. So as we kissed each other he got up and got dressed. He closed the bedroom door. I rolled over and Steve came back in with coffee for me. I thanked him. He kissed me and rushed out the door. About 10:00 AM I put on my bikini and grabbed a few towels. Renata was making the rest of us some margaritas to enjoy by the pool as we lay out. But I saw them two out there in my pool with the child. So I stepped out to watch this baby's play behavior. I proceeded and grabbed a layout chair. I had some good dark sunglasses on as I watched in my pool, but as soon as Cole saw me lying there I could hear them talking shit about me. Savannah was about to start running her mouth until I gave her a look of shut up. I had something in mind that I wanted to say to myself, but keeping my mouth shut was going well. In the midst of it I was plotting revenge and knew karma was coming. In a twisted way I think my own kids were thinking, Mama how and the hell are you sitting back and letting this dickhead run over you. But what they didn't know is fixin' to be game on as I'm lying there Stephanie yelled out, "Mama." I looked at her and my phone went off so I looked at it. She sent me a text saying, "You've got this crazy look on your face that I've never seen before." I just smiled at her.

But as we laid there talking, something had pissed him off, and he left the pool. I went inside and he came back out and said to her, "I'm going for a drive." I thought good get the fuck out of here and get lost. As soon as he left Isabella felt out of place so she sat there with her feet in the water watching the kids play in the shallow water of the pool.

As I had heard the rumblings of the cattle coming closer, I knew that my guys were coming in for the day. The closer they got, something caught my attention and got my ass sexually thirsty when I saw my husband up on his horse with no shirt on, sweat dripping from his muscles, his long hair not put up and his cowboy hat on. My own husband was putting fantasies in my mind of me and him. I had his favorite bikini on me. Steve whistled at me and smiled. I just giggled and Steve was smiling, shaking his head. He turned the horse around and grabbed his junk. I knew what was going on in his pants and I guess he left the boys behind. He sat there watching them come up. As soon as I saw them, they had their shirts off. Renata and Meara nudged me to look over at Isabella and I noticed her face was beet red. Her jaw dropped as she was watching them ride up. I thought oh shit. She let out the word oh damn. My boys were just like their Daddy. They work out, lift weights and have a good size six-pack of abs, especially Kaden. Kaden, Steve and I work out together. But generally, it's just him and Steve. Seth and I would go for a jog to catch up and talk.

But as we sat there watching her gushing, I thought dammit girl, but went back and watched Steve and the boys put the saddles up in the storage room. As Steve was walking his horse beside him, I couldn't resist taking a picture of him. As I watched him put his horse away, I felt my skin burning, so I got up and placed my feet and legs inside the pool and sat down. I watched Steve walk up and into the house and the boys followed in behind him. Within a few moments Steve sits down beside me and whispers in my ear, "Thinking of me Baby?" I smiled and cut my eyes at him and I started slightly chewing on my finger nail and leaned over to him and told him, "I'm slightly turned on when I see you riding up the hill. Don't worry, I got a picture of you." And he said, You're being my naughty little girl aren't you? You look so fucking hot." I giggled, and he told me, "You'll pay for it later." After he said that he jumped into the pool and turned around and pulled me into the pool with him. I wrapped my arms and legs around him as he held on to me and told me, "Oh I almost forgot to tell you, I'll be visiting the Veterans of Foreign Wars (VFW) tomorrow for a luncheon to donate the money." I told him, "That sounds good." He added, "But I won't be long because I'm already worried about leaving you around that sack of shit." I told him, "I think the boys will be around to handle him. Besides, I think I'm about done with the child. I'm going to take her to my office tomorrow and work with her skills and her behavior." He said, "Please baby next time change up your questioning page for more information in detail." I told him, "I think after this experience, there are no more families here." He said, "I don't mean to piss you off, but it's mind-blowing that he's in our home and thinks he can get a relationship with Andrew and Lucas. He's been watching you and Andrew and Lucas like a hawk, and it's pissing me off." I told Steve, "Cole is a manipulator and he's trying to get to you. I'm shocked at the fact that he's with this young girl that's barely in her 20's. I almost got sick." Steve said, "Matter of fact, where is this fucker?" I told him, "Something pissed him off. When I came out and started sunning he left." Steve said, "Good." I asked Steve, "You know talking about them is ruining my mood?" He said, "I'll make it better in a little while." But as Steve, and I were talking about other things I glanced over Steve's shoulder and saw my four unmarried boys flirting with this nasty ass girl. When Kaden looked at me and smiled with a nod, I knew something was way up my boy's sleeves.

Later on that night after everyone went to bed Steve, and I were feeling adventurous so we turned down the pool lights and had fun with each other. I just couldn't get over the feeling that someone was watching us so we both got out and went to our room. The next morning I closed the pool and made an appointment for it to be cleaned out. As I walked into the kitchen Kaden was making the kids breakfast and moved along with making us adults a plate. After everyone had eaten there was one plate left. It was Cole's. I became a petty bitch and ran to the medicine cabinet and got some melatonin that Steve has to take every once in a while. Steve has small Post Traumatic Stress Disorder (PTSD) because of being guilty of the soldiers that he's trained that never came home. There are nights that he's dreaming about the ones that died along with his two best friends that were killed in the car crash. It's more like survivors' guilt. I crushed it up and put in Coles food. As I was crushing it, Kaden looked at me and said, "Damn Mama you're a savage person." After I crushed it up into a fine powder I walked away. But as I was sitting in the dining room I saw Cole come in and Kaden handed him his plate. He sat down at the bar and I watched him eat every bite. He got up and went outside, so I proceeded to finish my breakfast. I could hear the kids making plans to do something. Andrew and Meara were taking his kids to a movie and invited Renata and Braylee. Lucas was taking his little man fishing. Steve had his luncheon to go to and Savannah and Stephanie were going shopping. I got up, took Payton to my office and studied her. By noon she was tiring out on me. I had my office door kinda cracked and as I was trying to set up some blocks I kept hearing moaning and thought shit, the boys are watching their dirty movies. As I looked over this baby passed out on me. So I got up and was fixin' to have a fit on them. Something caught my attention. Cole passed out. So I took a piece of paper and started cutting his hands, but as I was getting ready to paper cut his throat, the sex sounds were getting louder and I could hear beating against the wall. I looked around for Isabella and she was nowhere in sight. Matthew's door was closed and it fucking hit me. I saw the pool guy showing up. I ran out to meet him and paid him. As I went into the kitchen I was embarrassed of what was going on, so I went to my room. I got up and in came Chase through the patio door. He looked at me and upstairs, and he shook his head and said, "Nasty. I didn't think Kaden, Matthew, and Seth would stoop so low. She's not their type." Chase stepped over to Cole and said. "Listen to that motherfucker. Your old lady getting fucked by my brothers." My ears went numb. I told Chase, "Go get that baby out of my office and lay her next to him. We'll leave." So Chase and I went to town. He and I rode around for a while until about 2:00 PM. I called for a carry out of eight pizzas.

When we got home, for some reason, I couldn't look my three boys in the face, but something just set me off as Kaden was sitting at the bar. I walked up to him, grabbed him by his ear and dragged him out of the house. I asked, "What the fuck?" His exact words to me were, "She's a whore and we did it out of spitefulness. Look at you. Mama, I saw what you did. So we're even. You drugstore his ass, and we screwed his crack whore." I told him, "Y'all better have used a condom because I don't need that shit being back at my door, and I'm getting rid of them on Wednesday, so I can relax and spend time with y'all."

As I laid in bed watching TV with Steve, I thought about telling Steve what the boys did, but I just left it alone.

The next morning I quickly finished testing this baby and all I could see was she was slow developing. Tensions were rising in the house. I could tell that Andrew and Lucas were kinda moody. So they went down to the shop with Steve and I had advised my other three to go somewhere for a few hours until dinner. Isabella all of a sudden got clingy. I had Chase and the girls in the house with me.

But as I gave the child back to Isabella, I asked her to let her play. I planned on feeding my grandbabies early because I figured we would have an adult night. So I started to prepare some things and I asked Stephanie if she could run into town and get some shrimp for our steak dinner tonight. So I proceeded to make some dinner rolls. I tried to keep myself busy, and I had thought about a dessert. I saw we had some blueberries and I had the flour out so I had decided on a blueberry cobbler. I moved along with a summer salad. As for the kids, I made them nuggets and macaroni and cheese with mixed veggies. When Lucas came in he jumped in and helped me out. I haven't really bonded with them since they came to visit, but could tell that this Cole mess was getting to him. I told him, "Don't worry, they'll be out of here in the morning."

He said, "Daddy is getting sick of them." I told him, "I'm sick of them." We fed the kids and put them in bed. As we sat down for our dinner out on the patio we were laughing and carrying on. As soon as Isabella and Cole came out we just ignored them and continued talking to each other. Out of the blue the shit show began when I heard Cole calling my name, "Kerala." I ignored him and all of a sudden, he raised his voice, slammed his fist down onto the table and screamed my name, "Kerala." Everyone got quiet. Cole asks me, "When are you going to tell them I'm their real daddy and you and him took them away from me?" I grabbed Steve's hand and I asked Cole, "Do you need fucking closure because that damn window closed a long time ago. As for your closure you can go fuck yourself and get the fuck out of my house and out of our lives. You've done nothing but brought me teenage misery, and you're a fucking pedophile that likes to play mind games with little girls that don't know any better. The only thing that came from your ass was the boys, and thank fucking God the love of my life raised them, or they would be just as fucked up as you are." As I was about to say something else Lucas got up in his face and told him, "Andrew and I know who the fuck you are and you are not my Daddy. That man sitting at the end of that table right there next to my Mama is my Daddy. That man right there put food in my stomach, clothes on my ass, and made damn sure all of us kids had everything we needed, put Mama through school and taught me right from wrong. I'm glad Mama saw who you really were and left your ass on that ground. Oh, thank God for that man right there for taking a chance on Mama or Andrew and I would be two different people. As for you thinking that we would ever have a relationship with you, it's never going to fucking happen. So you can go fuck yourself. As for your bitch, my brothers had their way with her upstairs yesterday." After Lucas said what he said to him, Andrew said to him, "Don't contact me either." Cole looked at me and said, "You fucking bitch. You never gave me a chance." Just as he threw something at me, Steve came undone and ran across the table, jerked Cole up by his neck and out of the chair and started beating the shit out of him. The boys ran over and tried to stop him and Seth got slammed on the ground. Seth got right back up. I wasn't about to go near what was going on. By the time the boys pulled their Daddy off of Cole, Steve was covered in blood and walked up to Isabella. Steve told her, "You get in there, get your shit and get off my property." She quickly got up, looked at Steve and said. "I'll leave after the cops show up." Steve told her, "Call the mother fucks. Did you forget that my son is a state trooper and a matter of fact the sheriff is my buddy." When she heard that she got up and went inside. Meara had opened the door and told her, "I need you to leave this door open so nothing else is taken." As I sat there being numb from what just happened, Savannah and I couldn't stop staring at each other. Steve was pacing back and forth around the pool and he and I locked eyes with each other. That crazy psycho look on Steve's face that I hate was there. But with all the chaos going on no one was paying attention to Isabella. When I turned my head she had a gun pointed to my head. My heart started beating faster and tears started swelling in my eyes. I started getting mad, and I moved when my boys grabbed her. Somewhere during the grab she shot me out of nowhere. I couldn't breathe and my ears were ringing. I felt a pain like bees were stinging me. I started blacking out. Subsequently, I knew nothing, but when I woke up, Lucas and Stephanie were sleeping in the room. It had taken me a few moments to recall that this shit happened. It was still kinda fuzzy to me. I felt sore. The pain on the right side of my throat was intense. I got tired of just sitting around watching the kids sleep, so I turned up the TV and shut it off. Just as I thought one of them was fixin' to get up I sometimes forget that I have three heavy sleeping kids. Bombs could be going off and nothing could get them up. So I hit the nurses buttons. When the nurse came in she was surprised to see me awake. She checked me out and I had asked her to wake Lucas up which she did. When she pointed to me, Lucas jumped up, smiled, hugged me and said, "Thank God Mama, you're okay. But Daddy is such a train wreck right now, worried about you. He just left. We had to make him leave. Just as I was fixin' to tell Lucas to let him go get some rest, he was on the phone with him. Within 30 minutes Steve came through the door. I still saw the worry in his eyes as he pushed my hair back and kissed me on my forehead. He held on to me for dear life. When I looked at Steve I saw tears rolling down his face and that man that I married never cries. He said to me, "Baby I thought I lost you." I assured him that I wasn't going anywhere. Yet, when I tried to speak to him, my throat wasn't ready. I looked him over because the last time I saw him he was covered in blood from a dumbass. I noticed Steve had scabs on his knuckles. Not much was said between us, and all Steve could say to me was, "Baby I'm sorry that I wasn't there beside you when it happened like I should have been. Baby he finally got you and I failed you." I tried to tell him that it's ok that he didn't fail me, but the burning in my throat was preventing me from talking. I could tell that my breathing pattern was off. As Steve was sitting beside me, he seemed to be very upset with himself. I was looking him over just to assure myself that he was okay. But I didn't know who was checking on whom to make sure we were both okay. Steve and I fought hard to stay awake, but when I woke up there was Steve at my bedside, with his head laid down on my bed. I ran my fingers through his long black hair and as I was doing so the smile on his face made me happy. When he opened his eyes and looked up at me, I could tell he was exhausted from being there. As he kissed me, he said to me, "Baby I love you." All I could do was just smile at him. He knew I would say it back to him in a heartbeat if I could. The nurse walked in and came in to change my bandage. Behind her was the doctor. He introduced himself to me and Steve, and he said, "Well after your bandage changes we're fixin' to get you up to walk." I just smiled and was ready to go. When the rehab nurse came in I got out of the bed, and she said, "I guess we are ready to go." As we walked just about every single hallway there was, we made our way up to the Pediatrics Wing and some nursing staff knew who I was because I pay them a visit occasionally. I knew that one of my tot's parents was about to give birth soon and I wanted to see if the baby had made its arrival. Once we got to the nursery window and the rehab nurse said. "Now Dr. Nicholas, you dragged me and your husband up here to try and work. Now I know why you are so dear minded and push yourself." Steve said, "Kerala Jade, your little mind monkey is wounded, needs some rest, and you're forcing it to work." I turned to Steve and smiled at him. The nurse laughed and said, "Oh Mr. Nicholas, she looks like she's going to fight you over this. I bet y'all are a mess behind closed doors together." Steve told her, "We can be at times." When Stephanie came by she brought my catalog book and her Daddy some more clothes. Steve told Stephanie, "Mama went upstairs and tried to work." Stephanie looked at me and said, "Damn Mama take it easy. For God's sake, you just had a big brush with death. I don't think I can see Daddy be a train wreck again." After she left, it wasn't until later on that afternoon that Steve laid it all out for me, about going back to work and getting the much needed rest. All I could do was tell him that I would. Each one of my kids came by along with Mama and Daddy. They didn't want to leave the state until I was awake. After being in the hospital for 16 days, we saw prayer and support signs all over town for me and my family. Steve slowly placed his hand into mine and slowed down to let me look at so much support from folks that I really didn't know. In the office there were balloons and flowers all over the sign. As soon as we got home most of our kids were still there. Savannah, Seth, and Chase had to go back to work. Our baby girl wasn't too far from us. As for Lucas, he was going to stay around for another week and Matthew was home until fall. Kaden was there and Andrew was going to stay for a few more days.

As Steve parked in the carport I was getting babied. He refused to let me walk in the house. Once Steve placed me on the couch, they kept asking me if I wanted anything and I didn't want anything but rest. Before I knew it Steve wasn't letting me out of his sight, nor the boys. I had so many questions of why Isabella shot me. I didn't do anything to her and it bothered me that Cole couldn't let the past go. As I got up Steve was hot on my ass, so I walked out onto the patio. My blood was still on the concrete and I could see where the crime scene tape was marked off. I just shook my head and Steve asked me, "Baby what's on your mind?" I looked at him and asked him, "Why? What did I do wrong?" He told me it was premeditated. Matthew was studying them while they were here. Isabella and Cole looked you up online, on your medical profile, and planned this. He's butt hurt over not having input on Andrew and Lucas. Matthew had a sense of jealousy from him. Cole lost you. I gained a very beautiful person and I watched you become someone that I love and care about. We've raised good kids. As for dumbass Cole, when he threw the knife at you, he hit the fuck around and find out button with me. The whole entire time he was here he was pushing my buttons. The boys told him how they felt about him. He's nobody to them and that sets him off more. I've looked up the other kids he has and they have no chance in hell to become something of themselves. It's an off and on relationship he has with them. He'll get on the Bible belt and off when it suits him. I was just as shocked as you when I saw him here in our home. Yeah I was mad, but then again I thought that he wouldn't say anything. But the moment he saw you I knew shit was about to hit the fan for us. Attacking you was the biggest mistake he ever made. Nobody touches my baby or my kids, and you know this."

As Steve was talking, I could tell he was getting angry about it all over again, so I always have to get him to settle down before he gets too out of hand. I let him ramble on for a few minutes and the result was me getting hurt. So I got up as he walked in behind me and got a few more pillows from our room. He placed them on the couch because we were fixin' to do his favorite pastime, cuddle. When I raised my voice at him and told him, "Get your ass on the couch, I need you." Without flinching he made a fast move where I told him. I placed myself into his arms. I always feel safe and warm when he holds me, and it never fails that I fall asleep in his arms while he's watching something on TV. Somewhere in the middle of the night I thought I heard something outside. I got out of bed and sat there. My biggest fear was one of them coming right back through my door. I thought damn you're on edge. So I got up and went to the door. I felt someone standing on the other side. As I took a step back, Steve scared me, and he said, "Shh, I hear it too." When he opened the door Odie, our dog, was digging in my damn flower bed. I was mad. I found myself not really being able to sleep. I still had so much on my mind. I got up and I let him sleep. He needed it more than me, so I made my cup of coffee. As I walked on the patio I stood where I was sitting when I was shot. I was looking at my blood and the thoughts of how I was tricked. I sat down in what my family calls my meditation spot. As I watched the sunrise, my thinking kicked into high gear of wanting revenge. I wondered how and why this little girl shot me over a worthless piece of shit. I was dying to get my hand on more information. Thinking how I would go through Steve to get to Brian and out of the blue my mind shifted to thoughts of what if I didn't make it. How would things really be for Steve around here and how would the kids take it. I started crying. While I was in my thoughts Steve started moving my hair from my face and telling me, "Baby, I know you're processing a lot of shit, but if and when you want to discuss anything, I'm here." I told him, "I find it crazy that the thought of how you and the kids would handle it if I didn't make it keeps coming in my mind." I asked him that. He took a deep breath and said to me, "Wow baby, you're really in your dark thoughts. First off, you have almost given me a stroke along with a heart attack. I'm just gonna tell you that it wouldn't be the same around here, and I would go into a deep depression. So please get out of your dark thoughts and let's start on positive things, getting you long overdue justice. Brian will be here later on today to speak with you." When he told me that I was satisfied knowing that I'm going to get some answers. I found myself tired and getting frustrated from my thoughts. I figured since I was home, I knew I would be bored as ever. Matthew came over and said, "Mama you have that look of I need to do something." I told him, "Yup." Steve said, "Well I have things to do. Matthew, don't let Mama do a whole lot." Matthew looked at him and said, "Daddy I can't control Mama. All I can do is help her." Steve told Matthew, "That's what I want to hear." As Steve walked off, I told Matthew, "Welp, I guess you and I can go get into something until Brian gets here." The only thing to keep shit off my mind was burying myself in work. So I sent a text to Hannah and asked if we could have a staffing meeting on Friday, at the house. I got dressed for the day. When Hannah responded back she said, sounds great. I'm glad you're home. I bet Steve is happy you're home. I had told her, yes he is but being moody as ever. I've only been home for 24 hours and bored as ever. She said, get some rest and the girls are ready for you to come back to work. They'll be excited when I tell them we'll have a staff meeting on Friday. I told her, I think I need some of y'all time anyway. After I walked away from my phone, I kinda pushed myself into the kitchen. I'm thinking ahead and getting my house back in order. I started baking a cake and I thought of a meal for tonight. I started prepping it. By the time I had just about finished, the doorbell rings and I saw through the glass that Brian had made it here. I opened up and let him in. He asked how I was doing, and I had asked him the same. He said, "Man you're lucky to be here with us. Well I know you want answers, and you have every right to have them. I have y'alls home security video of that night, but I have another video for you. When he pulled out the phone, there was a confession from Isabella of why she shot me. It premeditated Cole had put her up to it. As I sat there listening and watching her tell the police their plans and how they used the baby, she said, "It's time someone knocked the bitch off of her high horse. She got away with stealing his kids. Cole told me if she was out of the boy's life he might get a chance to have a relationship with them. So they'd be a big brother to their little sister. We could be a big family. She's got it all, the mansion, the money, everything she could possibly ask for." As I watched the video, all I could do was shake my head. Cole was playing her like he did me back then. That's when my own journals came out. If they told her why I didn't have anything to do with him, they let her read my old journal of my past. I'm guessing Steve gave them an insight of the bullshit that I went through as a teenager by Cole's own hands. The look on her face was lies to her of what I had written. That's when Brian said, "Kerala, I didn't know that you had gone through this, but may I ask you this? How did you and Steve take Lucas and Andrew away from him?" I told him, "Judge Shafer married Steve and I I didn't want the boys around Cole due to his abuse and drug use. Judge Shafer knew Cole's dirty habits and the morning he married Steve and I, Cole was sitting in jail for hitting a female. Judge Shafer said that he thought Cole was unfit to be a father to Andrew and Lucas and waved his parental rights away from him, so that's how Steve adopted them. And that's why Andrew and Lucas have Steve's last name." After I told him that I had asked him, "So what's next?" Brian said, "The District Attorney (DA) wants a trial, and he's asking for one." As I was about to say something, I didn't even know Steve was in the house, and he told Brian, "She's got one. I dislike our laundry being aired out, especially Kerala's past with him, but maybe this will put him where he really belongs." I agreed with Steve, "I don't like our personal and private information about us being out in public, but putting his ass in the ground is where he really should be. I just couldn't believe I got suckered into his old ways." I had to excuse myself from our dining room because my cake was almost done. Steve and Brian sat in there and talked.

I became mad at the fact that I kept to myself for years, far away from him, and he wanted me dead. It all backfired on him when Andrew and Lucas told him they don't want anything to do with him. The boys were 24 years old. Grown men, making their own life decisions. They had their own kids, but they made their choice of who their Dad was, and it's Steve. As I stood there, deeply back in my thoughts, Lucas came in poking his dirty fingers in my homemade icing. I smacked his hand and he said, "There's my Mama." I asked him, "Can we talk?" He said, "Yes Mama." So I told him, "In private. Just me and you." Lucas and I went out back, and he asked me, "Mama, what's on your mind because you've got something built up inside you?" I asked him, "I really want to know how you feel about this?" He told me, "Mama, it's like a bad dream. I never in my life knew this is how he was. I'm just going to say this, the night I found out is when you and Daddy went out. I broke one of Daddy's rules. I went into the safe room and got my bow out. Your box got knocked over. As I was picking it back up, one of the books was open. I read it and all of my anger and hate towards you and Daddy came out. I hated both of you. When Andrew read it, it also made him feel like an outsider. The last straw was when us and Daddy got into it. You shipped us off to Nanny and Poppa, We were glad to go that weekend. When we went to church and his Mama was looking at us like crazy, to the point of being uncomfortable. She came up and said, "Y'all look like your Daddy. I wish he would have come to church today. Nanny lied until we told her no more lies Nanny. We know. She quickly got mad at us and said, "Y'all don't know what kind of hell you can bring on your Mama." She said, "Yes, that is your biological father." After she walked off mad at us, we went to bed that night. But, soon as Papa laid down, Andrew and I snuck out of the house, and we rode down to Uncle Gabe's bar and asked someone where Cole lived. So Andrew and I went back to Nanny and Papa and decided to wait until the next morning. So we got up and took off. When we tracked his ass down, we didn't like what we saw. He was so drunk that he couldn't stand up. As he was passing out, we got a better look at him and the way he lives is a makeshift shack. We left him there like you did years ago. Papa was out looking for us and when he saw us he snatched our asses up. He wasn't much on words on the way back until we got in the door, and he said to us, "God works in crazy ways on people, especially your Mama, and He has a strange way of putting people together when they're not looking. Your Mama was preparing to be a single Mom until the man that's raising you two stepped into her life. I, for one, disapproved until I saw the love in his eyes for her when he asked to be your father. So he stepped up to the plate. The man that's raising you two was there when you were born. Cole was very abusive to your Mama. She didn't think we knew, but the situation and signs were starting to show. Steve loves both of you. He's hard on you two in fear of either of you turning out like what both of you just saw. Steve has done a lot for you and Andrew. Lucas,

I'm telling you this now. Your Mama and Daddy did what was best for both of you, so whatever is going on inside your head needs to go. But I'm going to ask you this, what has he done for you and Andrew?" After Papa asked me that we answer him the best we could, and we told him Steve's been there for us, will do anything for us, takes us places, buys us stuff, puts food on the table, and makes sure ours and Mama's needs are first before his. After Andrew and I said that, Papa said, "There you go. That's your Daddy and that's the man that's raising y'all." Lucas said, "I knew when I read it, Mama, that Papa was right, and we were being dumb kids. Daddy was teaching us right from wrong and our attitude changed." After I got a deeper understanding on how Lucas felt, and his view, I was surprised that my Dad had a good talk with them. But Lucas realized that I did right by them. I didn't ask or force him to be their Dad or beg Steve to marry me. He just did it. Each and every day I thank God for him being in my life and I love the hell out of that man. He has a sweet side, even to his moody side. He and I will go to hell and back for each other.

As Lucas and I sat there I asked, "So when are you leaving us?" He told me, "Sorry Mama, but I'm leaving in the morning." I told him, "Stop staying away from me." He told me, "No Ma'am. I'll be back home soon Mama. After what happened this taught me a lesson that life is precious. But Mama, can we please get off this mood you're in? I saw my meatloaf you're making." I told him, "Yes I am, but not as quick as I used to be. It's going to take a few more weeks until I heal better. After we talked my mood was still mixed. I went back to finish the cake. I got busy planning for dinner this week.

When I made dinner, nothing was being said, which was abnormal for us. In my heart we had a lot to say about what happened, but chose not to discuss it. I figured if there was going to be a trial what better way to say what needs to be said. I know when Steve gets a little distance, he's processing his thoughts, but in a way I feel this is ripping us apart.

After I cleaned up the kitchen, I figured I would call it a night. So I soaked in some hot water to stop it from hurting so bad. I got into bed. I found a book to read on my Kindle. When Steve came to bed he said, "You and I have been running in circles around each other all day. And dinner, that was some weird shit. I know we have a lot going on, but I'm saying this to you, your heart is safe with me. And You'll always have my heart. You give a lot, and I appreciate how much you give. And this isn't your fight alone. No more. I can't pretend to know how you feel, but I do know how strong you are. This won't keep you down. This is temporary. I've got you. Because My soul and your soul are forever tangled. We just had an asshole that tested the waters, and he finally fucked around and found out. But I felt that my actions caused you to get hurt, and I'm not happy with myself. I've always told you I never wanted you to see that side of me, but he gave me no fucking choice when he threw the knife at you. What you said to him was brave. I knew when you grabbed my hand, you were scared."

"Damn baby, you look like you're in pain." I said, "I'm sorry. Yes, I'm hurting." He said to me, "I told you not to suffer. I'll get it." He got up to get something for my pain. When he came back I took it and told him, "Thank you and I love you." He said, "I love you more." Within minutes of taking it, I was out.

The next morning I hated to see Lucas go, but he has his family that needs him. We only had a few more days with Matthew. Seth had just finished up his place.

Matthew and I decided to go down to the gate, remove the dead flowers, and rearrange my flower beds the people had damaged. I still had to fix what the dog dug up from the other night. When we reached the gate, I loaded up as much as I could. The stuffed animals I set aside. After we fixed my mini roses we headed up to the house. I told Matthew I can't do anymore which he understood. He finished up. I found my spot on the couch and went back to reading. I looked up and Steve was standing over me, and he asked me, "Is everything okay?" I told him, "Yea, I'm just tired and kinda not feeling well. It's the next day pain pill thing. I'm resting right now." He said, "Good. Because you've already done too much." I told him, "Hannah and the ladies will be over Friday for lunch." Steve said, "I think that would be good for you. And no work baby. I know your habit. You bury yourself into your work, and right now, you need to be resting." I truthfully told him, "Sorry babe, but it is a little bit of work. Hannah and I are discussing a different way for me to study cases instead of here." Steve said, "Yup. No more here. It liked to get my baby killed. Don't worry about dinner if you don't feel like it." I told him, "Stephanie is coming over to cook for us." He said, "Stephanie hasn't mastered your cooking, but we shouldn't fuss." I told him, "Be blessed. She's my mini me." He said, "No shit with her. Both of you are savage and sarcastic women." I told him, "Me, sarcastic, never. But other notes, I'm the tornado and Stephanie is the hurricane with a little twist of sunshine. That leaves Seth being sarcastic as well. Besides I'm not savage, I'm just brutally honest." I had him rolling, and it looked like he needed a good laugh. I hadn't seen him laugh like that in what seemed like weeks. He said, "There you are." I asked him, "Instead of Stephanie coming here, can we go somewhere, please?" He said, "Yea, yea, we can go. You're wanting to get out of the house."

I told him, "I figured it might make me feel better." He said, "That's a good idea, but it will be this afternoon. So you have a while so you can rest up. I've got to finish up doing what I need to do." When he walked out of the door, I figured I should find something to wear and start getting ready. I horse assed around with my hair until I liked it and got my makeup on. After I got dressed I stood in the mirror looking at myself.

Even though I was carrying a war inside my head, I shook it off and thought of something I needed to do. I went into my office. I requested this child's medical records the week they were here. So I busted out my computer and got them. As I was about to start digging more into the records, I heard the patio door open. I closed my computer and went into the living room. My guys were home from work, and they were getting ready for dinner. So I opened my computer back up. Something wasn't adding up with Isabella and Cole over this baby. The thought of them kidnapping a baby pissed me off. I had to walk away. I stood behind the kitchen bar and Seth asked me, "Uuh Mama, who pissed in your cereal?" I told him, "I think that baby was kidnapped." Seth was stunned, and he said, "Mama, there's only one way to find out before you start jumping those curves at ninety miles an hour with your theory, but don't let Daddy catch you working." I told him, "Let your brother's know because I may need one of them to come home to do a DNA test." Seth said, "Mama, I'll bring my laptop up here when we get back from dinner and do some digging. But you know, you gotta do your best." After thinking about this question, I had to rush to find out something. I wanted to see before jumping, but during dinner, Steve noticed that my mind was elsewhere, and he said, "Kerala Jade, that little monkey inside your head is peddling like a motherfucker to save his life." I couldn't deny that the bastard was working, and I blurted out, "The baby isn't theirs." When Steve heard what I said, he sat there looking at me, and he asked me why I thought that. I told him this baby looked nothing like the boys or the other siblings that he has. Steve said, "Okay baby. When we get home, we're going to work. I'll help you so you can sleep tonight. Because if you're not working, you're not sleeping well. I know you miss working, but you're treading on our rules and boundaries that we have for each other when we're home. If you're right, I'll let you go back to work early. If not, you're still staying home with me, and I'll make sure you're clinging to me." So I told him, "You got it." He said, "Please let's enjoy the time we have with Matthew since he is leaving Sunday." As this was our topic, Matthew was very interested in my thoughts on this baby. Matthew told his Daddy, "If Mama is right, this could get them two lethal injections." This made Steve more interested. On our way home, I still had a bone to pick with Steve. I said, "A little dirty birdy told me that Seth pulled you over when you were coming home off your truck, what was the reason? Now if you were in a rush to get home to me, don't be a dumbass just because you weren't around me for 44 days. So did you get the Mama Blues, and the one that told me was Stephanie. She was showing a house right where he pulled you over." After I said that, he looked at me and said, "Sorry baby, it won't happen again." I wanted to lecture him, but from what I heard, Seth tore into him already.

When we got home, all of us piled into my office. I went back into this child's record and there was no birth certificate and I couldn't find a social security number or any hospital records with this baby's name. I looked at Kaden and I asked, "Okay nasty ass So you and her were doing it in my house. Did she have stretch marks, and he said, "Don't all big girls have them?" I told him, "Yea, good point. Okay, when she got arrested here, did Brian get their things out of the house?" He said, "The only thing I know of is child welfare came in there and got that baby and left Mama. There was too much going on." I got up and went into Bebe's room. When I opened the door and turned on a light, I couldn't believe what the fuck I was seeing. I called out for Steve to come see the room. I saw burnt places in the hardwood flooring, holes in the wall, clothes everywhere, flooring a mess. Steve saw it, he was pissed. I, for one, was mad. The mirror in the bathroom was broken, cuts inside the cabinet tops, trash and broken lamps.

Steve called Kaden into the room and the boys just came in with disbelief. I asked Matthew to go get us some gloves. I'm looking for her purse when Matthew bought them back. I started going through their shit and when I found it, I found her identification, but nothing on the baby. So I handed it to Seth and Kaden said, "Leave everything alone. I'll start to demo the room in the morning." But as I continued to dig through their stuff, I found drugs. Seth took it and flushed it down the toilet. I was mad, but   was fussing and taking pictures. Seth and I took off to check Isabella's identification, and she has a record of minor crimes. With that, I used it to check her medical records and there's no sign of her having a baby. I asked Steve, "Is there any way you can call Brian and have him come over in the morning?" He said, "Yea. What have you found out?" I said, "Well the only thing I know is to call Dr. Dunbar in the morning and go from there." I started looking up missing babies from this child's date of birth until I got tired. So I figured I would put this on pause until the morning. I found myself in a damn good mood of feeling hopeful. I sometimes catch myself dancing when nobody is around, which I call my happiness dancing. As I was dancing in the closet, and straight up I didn't know Steve was standing there, he said, "I see someone is in a good mood." When I turned around to face him he said, "You better not be leading a wild chase on this child. If it is, I'm gonna bend you over my lap and whip your ass." I smarted off and said, "Oh, is that a threat or a sexual suggestion?" I had blown his mind again and made him laugh, but my own mood had changed like a bipolar roller coaster. This sad feeling came to me and I just blurred out, "I miss you. I know you're standing in front of me, but I just feel like something has changed in both of us since this has happened. I feel like I'm not all here and you're not all here." When I said that to him, he walked up to me and carefully picked me up into his arms and told me, "Baby I'm here. I've been here. I'm just a little bit more protective of you. I'm still trying to wrap my mind around this. just like you are. But today, seeing you smile and laugh with me, you're making me laugh. I say you and I had a good day." As he was talking I couldn't help but take a stolen moment and kiss him. As he walked out of the closet, he carefully placed me on the bed. I caved in and gave myself to him. I could tell that we both hadn't made love to each other in almost a month. Steve said to me, "When I first got together with you, I did not expect our love to run this deep. I am here, I will always be here." I told him, "I'm here as well, and I'm not going anywhere. I love you too much." As we laid there cuddling, we enjoyed our time alone.

The next morning, I got my ass up. I still had a lot to prove. I went to my office. I had a picture of this child and kept looking at her and dumb ass Isabella. No resemblance to her or Lucas and Andrew in this child. I was putting in great effort until Seth came into my office. He said, "Damn Mama, you're working harder than the FBI." I told him, "I just want to clear my mind. Something isn't right." Seth kissed me on my cheek and told me, "I love you Mama, and I'll see you later." I told him, "Be careful and have a good day. I love you too." When Steve came in he told me, "I was making sure you're decent because Brian is here." I told him, "Bring him back here." So he went out in the living room when Brian came into my office, and he said, "Steve called me last night and said you were up to this crazy idea that this baby might be kidnapped." I said, "I'm on a wild ride Brian, and I'm fixin' to make phone calls. I need you here as a Witness." He said, "Well, let's get started." I called my old hometown Dr. Dunbar. When Faith picked up, I said, "Hi Faith. This is Dr. Nicholas." Faith said, "Oh hey girl. How are you feeling?" I told her, "Sluggish, but it's a day by day thing, and I'm running on too much caffeine today." Faith said, "I'm glad you're still here with us. Your Mama was a wreck worried about you." I told her, "I hate to be rude, but I need to ask Dr. Dunbar a few questions, or maybe you can answer them." She said, "Okay." I asked her how long Dr. Dunbar has been treating Isabella and this baby?" She said, "Geez Kerala, come to think of it, he's been treating Isabella for a few years now. The baby, we just started seeing her in the office about six months ago." When Faith said that, I asked her, "Okay. Did Dr. Dunbar treat Isabella for any maternity or deliver the baby?" She said, "No Kerala. And come to think of it, oh my gosh, oh no they didn't." I said, "Faith, if you're thinking what I'm thinking." And she says, "Yes I am thinking that this baby was kidnapped." I told her, "Yup and I told her there's no medical history on this baby." Faith said, "You know I don't recall Isabella ever being pregnant. She just showed up at the office with that baby in her arms. You know Dr. Dunbar is the only doctor in town that is a MD and licensed for Obstetrics." I asked her, "Don't say shit to anyone, but can you fax me over the medical records on both of them?" She told me, "Give me about 20 minutes." I gave her my fax number and I said, "I'll be in touch." When I hung up the phone Brian looked at me and said, "Damn girl, I need a Investigator at the office. I'm starting to think you're right." I told him the only way I'm right is if we get a DNA test done from this baby and our boys. I told him, "Hold on. I have one more phone call to make." So I called Judge Shafer and he and Brian talked about me and the past. He still couldn't believe that we let Cole in the house. But what caught us all was when Judge Shafer said, "I've had my suspicions for a while over her and that baby. You know there was a kidnapping about a year ago, about four Counties over. Do you believe this could be the missing baby?" Brian said, "I don't know, but I think we could work together. Maybe if this is a kidnapping, it might be that we can get this baby back home to its real parents. We just have to do a DNA test and go from there." When he hung up, all I could do was smile and Steve's mind was blown away. He looked at me and said, "That little monkey inside your head should be a fucking Gorilla by now." I smiled at him. As the fax machine was going off I started looking at Isabella's medical records. She had broken arms and fractures from his abuse. As for the baby, a small injury to the arm and well visits. I handed it over to Brian and let him see, and he said, "Shit. I need to go ask questions again." As I looked up Matthew asked him, "May I join you to study their behavior?" He said, "I don't see why not. You're about done with your schooling, right?" Matthew told Brian, "Yes. I may need your help to understand them." I asked Matthew "What about your flight?" He told us, "Oh, I changed it Mama, to next week." I told him, "Cool." Steve asked Brian, "I would like to press charges. I need you to see what they have done to my house." Steve and Brian went in and looked at it before Kaden got started. On Saturday Steve just sent him on a run to get the stuff. I sent Andrew and Lucas a text asking them if they could come home? They need a DNA test done. Lucas told me he'll be there Saturday and Andrew said he will be home tomorrow. For some reason I wanted to dig in this shit deeper, but I figured I better let Brian handle it.

I finished up other cases that were long overdue. As I looked up, Steve was standing there watching me, and he said, "God Kerala, I hope you're right. If not you've opened up a big can of worms, but I do see your point of view on this. Baby, I will keep my word if you're right and let you go back to work sooner than we agreed upon." I told him, "I know." He said, "But if you're wrong, it's more time here and since when did I become a bad person to be around?" I told him, "You're not. I have bills to pay." He told me, "Baby, I've told you this so much that I'm blue in the face. It's my job to worry about our bills, not yours. It's always been my worry." I told him, "I like to lighten the load off of you." He said, "Awe, I'm not going to fuss with you." As he walked away from me I told him, "You're an asshole." He yelled back at me, "Would you have me any other way?" I told him, "Hell no." He said, "Good. Because I'm not changing. Love you." I just started laughing and told him, "I love you more." When I heard him leave out the door, I knew he would be back in the house soon. It's still too hot for him to be out past lunch. I decided since I was home, getting bored, and needed time away from this Cole mess, I figured I would spoil Steve for dinner. He's really put up with some shit in the last few days. So I made one of my casseroles that he likes. After I got it going and ready to put into the oven later, I figured I would enjoy the pool. I changed my clothes, put my music on and went out to the pool. I was really in a damn good mood so I found myself singing along with the song that was playing. I placed my feet inside the water. I was fighting back who I was. As I was sitting there, I saw Steve prop up against the barn door watching me. This made him smile. I shook my head and continued singing away. Before I knew it, here he comes. He started smiling at me. I motion him to come to me. When he starts taking his clothes off, I knew what I was doing to him. Just about down to his underwear and in the pool he went up to me, pulled me in and held on to me with nothing being said between us. We both weren't paying any mind and Kaden came blasting around back yelling out say, "This is the reason why I'm moving the hell out. God damn Daddy, please don't tell me you're in your undies." Steve smarted off, "Boy this is how you were made." Kaden said, "Too much information Daddy." Steve kissed me, and we got out. Kaden said, "Well hell, I still don't see how I came out of that little bitty body of Mama." I told him, "Well you did and dinner will be in a little bit. If there are any leftovers, it's your Daddy's." I went in and got dressed. I started with the rest of dinner. I looked up and Steve was just walking through the house. He said, "I miss them in ways. I don't miss the damn disruption between me and you." I smarted off and said, "Well we had the little cock blocker, so there you go." He said, "I don't regret our kids. It just gets worse when they're adults. I'm just happy to know that we are still wanted." I just shook my head and told him, "Well, the grandbabies will be here this weekend. So we get a second chance to be with them." When I told him that, he got excited. With me and him, we get to spoil our grandbabies and send them on their way. Especially our Mad Maddie and Braylee. It drives Andrew and Lucas crazy because if they do something wrong in their eyes they can't touch them. Steve and I jump their butts now. For the grandsons I'll go ape shit on them. As he stood Matthew came in, and he said, "Oh my God Daddy." He walked back out the door and I pointed, "You better go get some clothes on." He took off, so I walked outside and told Matthew to bring your butt in, and he said, "Damn you two."

I snapped at him and Kaden and told them, "If your Daddy wants to run around the house butt ass naked, so be it. Enough with it." As I turned around there stood Chase, "Mama are you on one and how are you feeling?" I told him, "I'm fine." When I turned around there stood this girl. Chase says, "Mama this Jessa. Jessa, this is my Mama, Dr. Kerala Nicholas." I looked at her and said, "Hi. Nice to meet you. Will you be joining us for dinner?" Chase, "Yes. we will Mama." I turned around and thought bad timing son, bad timing and my phone went off. It was Andrew, "Mama I'm about 15 minutes away. Do you want me to pick anything?" I said, "No. I'm good." It surprised me that he was coming in early. I turned to the kids and I said, "Guess what? Andrew will be here in 15 minutes." I told this young lady that this household gets a little crazy. I ran into the bedroom and told Steve, "You better be fully dressed. Chase brought a girl here and Andrew called and said he'll be here in 15 minutes." Steve said, "Oh, it's bad timing for us to meet someone." I told him, "I know, and I don't have enough food made for us all." Steve said, "Baby you always make enough. Sometimes too much." So I ran out of the bedroom and went back into the kitchen. I turned around to speak to this girl and I asked her, "So how did you and Chase know each other?" She said, "I met him in school." So you're in college?" She said, "Yes." I asked her, what are you studying?" She said, "Finances." When I looked over at the fridge, Steve was standing there like a Wildman. As he was pulling his hair back, Kaden comes out and says, "Daddy you're a mess. I'm surprised you're not in your birthday suit." I told Kaden, "You're really pushing buttons today." He said to me, "No Ma'am. I just wanted to give him a hard time, that's all." I said to Kaden, "If only closed minds came with closed mouths." He said to me, "Mama no, you did." I smarted off to him again. " I am busy right now, can I ignore you some other time?" And he said, "Man Mama, you can be the devil sometimes." I came back and told him, " I'm closer to hell than you think. You'd be in good shape, if you ran as much as your mouth." He just wanted to run his mouth. Steve gave him a look and he said, "Okay Mama, I'll leave you alone." Steve stepped behind me and Chase introduced him to Jessa. I heard loud music coming from a car and in blew Savannah. Steve and I looked at each other, as she was unexpected. When she walked in the door, I hugged her. She broke down in tears. It made me cry, and I told her, "Mama's not going anywhere yet." I looked up and saw Seth coming in the door. Savannah and Seth started their little slapping games with each other. So I left them alone and finished cooking. Andrew and Meara come in and Mad Maddie puts Steve in a better mood. She comes over to me and raises my shirt and I told her, "That's rude. We have company." She asked me, "Lala, can you fix me some special food tomorrow?" "I told her tomorrow, I'm not sure." Steve picked her up and told her, "Let's not ask too much from Lala right now. As soon as Meara came around the corner into the kitchen she and Savannah told me,"Get out of here. We gotcha." I sat down. I felt that I had done too much, and I was hurting. After I sat down Steve sat next to me and said, "You're doing too much." I told him, "I wasn't expecting all the kids to be home this weekend." He told me, "Well baby, they're here."

As we gathered at the dining room table I wanted to ask this girl more questions, but my mind was elsewhere. It was with Matthew, but it would be rude to speak about personal things at the table while we have a guest that we don't know. Yet I felt rude, but I started not feeling well. So I got up and laid down. When Steve came in he asked me if I was okay. I told him, "No. Suddenly I got a sick feeling." Matthew knocked on the door and I told him, "Come in." He said, "Daddy, I'm sorry to interrupt, but Mama is right about the baby. When Brian asked her to do a swab for DNA she refused and her facial expression changed so much.

I thoroughly couldn't believe what I saw on how their faces changed. I called my Professor today and asked him if I could study this case. I had to quickly shut Matthew down and told him, "I'm sorry baby boy, but I don't think it is a good idea because you're fixin' to discover dark things in my past that's not going to make you happy about me. If we go to trial, you're a witness." Matthew said, "Sorry Mama, but it's been assigned to me, so I have to do this, so I can graduate." As he left the room I told Steve, "Close the fucking door." When he did, I told him, "Is there any way that you and I can run away and not come back for maybe a week? I need a real vacation." Steve says, "Wherever you want to go, we're gone." I told him, "As long as I don't have to be here. We can just pack a bag and leave Tuesday. All Steve said to me was, "Let's go." I told him, "You pick the spot." He said, "It's a deal. We'll have to drive because your lungs can't handle cabin pressure right now." I told him, "I don't care."

He said to me, "You're hurting, aren't you?" I told him, "Yes. I will deal with everything tomorrow." As we were talking, in comes Mad Maddie. She runs and starts jumping on the bed.

She grabbed my phone and this set me off. Somehow she kicked me where I got shot. Steve ripped her up and gave her a few spats. This shocked her and Andrew came in afterwards. He really got her, but I think it was by accident. It broke my heart, but I wasn't feeling well. This put me in a lot of pain. Then I reached over and got a pain pill. Within 10 minutes I was out.

The next morning I got up, and I started making breakfast and lunch. I saw Maddie climb on the stool. She was watching me, it was just me and her, so I raised my shirt and showed her my wound. She told me, "Lala I'm sorry. I didn't mean to. I just wanted a picture of me and you." I snuck her a cookie from the jar and told her, "I've forgiven you." I asked her, "Why are you up so early." She told me, "I wanted to see you." I told her, "Okay. What do you want for breakfast?" She told me, "Your blueberry muffins." I told her, "Well give me a few minutes and I'll have some done." So I turned on some cartoons for her, but when she saw Steve, she had nothing to do with him. So he sat next to her and I knew she was mad at him. I watched him with her for a few moments, and she got up and came to me. I asked her, "Why are you sticking to me like glue?" She told me"Because I can." So I told her, "Okay." Steve had said to me, "Something isn't right with her." I told him, "I know." She's kinda running from and holding on to me. He told me, "See baby, that's why I'm fighting you to go back to work." I told him, "I see now. I'm still hurting from her kick." When everyone got up Andrew wanted to get this DNA test over with. I understood him needing to get back home because school was starting on Monday morning. He told me, "Since you're doing your staff meeting here, we'll go and do that. Do you need anything?" I told him, "Yes I do." He said, "Let me guess. Go get groceries." I told him, "Yes please. I'm down to the wire of nothing in the house." He said, "Okay. Just make a list." I told him, "I've already got one done." So I handed him my debit card and I asked, "Why is Mad Maddie so clingy?" He told me, "Mama, ever since this happened, she's had nightmares." When he told me that, it explained everything to me. She must have seen it all after everyone left the house. Savannah had taken off with Matthew for the day and man did the house feel peaceful. As I was catching my breath, Steve comes in, and he said, "Did everybody leave?" I told him. "Yes, and I told him I think Mad Maddie saw it all. That's why she's clingy." He told me, "Maybe you need to ask her some questions." I told him, "I will." When Hannah and Bodie arrived, Steve and Bodie took off. I figured he needed some guy time. Hannah said, "Girl, I can only imagine you're going crazy." I told her, "Hell yes, but here's the thing. Maddie kicked me last night and I'm having serious thoughts about coming back too soon right now." She told me, "See, Steve is saying you need another week and I can't wait until you come back. That asshole that's filling in for us is a dumbass. He treats your patients like shit. No compassion. Alexis is about to ring his neck." When she told me that, I was getting pissed off. I have boundaries and bondage with my patient's parents. I told her, "Let this pain go away, and I'm coming back." She told me, "Yeah. The girls have count down clock, and they told him,"You see that my boss is coming back in this many days." I started laughing, and she asked me, What's this about the baby? Brian came into the office wanting the health application. Something about him needing a DNA test." I told her, "The baby isn't hers or his, and she refuses any test to prove the baby is hers." Hannah said, "Do what? So you mean to tell me that you had someone else's baby in your house that wasn't theirs?" I told her, "Yup, and we need to cover our asses or the board of health is going to rip us a new one for sloppy ass work." She told me, "You did everything correctly, Kerala. I went back and looked over everything at least a million times. I'm still stunned over this mess." I told her, "You know when I came home this week, I found myself thinking of the what if's." She said to me, "No you didn't go there." I told her, "I asked Steve what if I didn't make it?" She said. "Girl, I already know that answer. He would square away everything y'all have and hurt himself." I told her, "Yea and I found myself not liking it. I guess I was too deep in my dark thoughts." The other day, just as I was about to say something to Alexa, and being silly she told me she passed Missy up and she told me, "I miss you Mama." I told Alexia, "Miss y'all too, but the boss said I can't come back just yet." When Missy came in, Alexia was talking about how she drives and told them, "You know I got Steve's ass the other night for whenever he came home before this shit, Seth said he was doing about 90 when he caught him. They said it was dangerous and I told them I know." Hannah said, "I don't want to know how fast Bodie drives in that thing, but if Seth catches him, yes, then I do." When Abby and Tara came in we went out to the patio and had lunch. We had a lot of catching up and Missy said, "We need to do an office prank on that asshole." I told them, "Put dish liquid in his coffee and he'll shit for days." We started laughing about what I said when Steve and Bodie came up to the patio. Steve said, "Y'all can reverse the whip and put it on her." They said, "No, that's your job." Steve told them, "I got the whip in the barn." I smarted off, "Oh so that's where it went to when I wanted to use it the other night on you." I couldn't help but to laugh and us ladies said, "Oh you stepped into that one Steve." He took off in the house. I truly enjoyed their visit. After they left, I knew I had to get dinner started for everyone. When Andrew came in he yells out, "It's done Mama and Lucas did his with me, and he's behind me somewhere." I told them, "Don't drive me up the fucking wall. As much as I love you all, I'm tired and if you don't like what's on the table, tough shit." I didn't eat as much due to lunch. I found myself being irritated. So after dinner I went outside and walked down to the end of the fence to pet Stephanie's horse, Trigger. When Blue saw me, he made his way and pushed the other horses out of the way. I handed him his treat. I didn't know Steve was standing behind me while I was talking to Blue. Steve said, "You know you've spoiled him rotten and he's so damn fat that I can barely get him to run." I told him, "I enjoy treating them." He said to me, "You seem irritated." I told him, "I am. A few things are getting on my nerves. I'm thinking my blood pressure is up." He placed his arms around me and asked, "Am I getting on your nerves?" I told him, "No." He told me, "You need some rest and we're heading out Tuesday for you to get some." I asked him, "So where are we going?" He told me, "I want you to just enjoy the ride." I found myself kind of excited about getting away. I'm guessing because it's hard to get away from the ranch. As Steve and I walked back up to the house, instead of going in, we took the opportunity to watch the sunset. When we went in, the kids were in the middle of playing Monopoly. When I looked at them, there was Jessa again. So I told her, "I'm sorry to be the brew of a woman yesterday, but I wasn't feeling well, and I assume you saw our granddaughter got her butt torn up after kicking me where I was shot." She told me, " I'm sorry for showing up unannounced, but Chase told me there's no perfect timing." I told Jessa, "If I would have known then a better meal would have been planned." I asked her, "So are you staying in town?" She told me, "No. I'm staying with Chase." I told Jessa, "Oh. Okay." I minded my own business because it's his. and told them, "Y'all remember the last time y'all played that game. Kaden cheated, and a fist fight broke out. I told them it better not happen again or someone will be doing push-ups." "They laughed and said, "Shit Mama, that's our morning routine."

I sat there with them until I got tired. I knew it was going to be a long game for them. After I showered, Steve and I found this movie. I couldn't get comfortable on my side when Steve raised up my shirt and there was a bruising from Mad Maddie. I was starting to get disappointed because it was a movie I've been wanting to watch. So Steve got up and left the room and when I looked up the kids came in, and they told me, "Mama you don't have to get out of bed. Within ten minutes, Steve had them rearrange the bedroom furniture. They moved our bed to the far side of the room and put the TV on the other side of the room. When they were done Lucas locked the door behind him. Steve got back in bed and asked me, "There baby. Is that better?" I giggled and told him, "Thank you and yes, it's better." As I got comfortable and started watching, about ten minutes before the ending, I looked over and Steve was out. I turned off the TV and went to sleep. About 3:00 AM I woke up because it was thundering pretty hard. I don't know what it is, but ever since Grandmama Blake's death, I hate storms. As I'm laying there, Steve kinda wakes up and tells me, "Come here." So I moved in closer to him and placed my head on his chest. He rubbed my back to soothe me, as I'm laying there listening to his heart beat after 24 years of marriage. I find it crazy that if I move my hand somewhere else on him, his heart starts to beat faster, but it's called a bondage heart rate. The first time that I ever did it, Steve couldn't figure out why, until I did it a few more times during storms and he fully understood it.

When morning came it was still storming. Steve was out cold. I had finally got to have a coffee chat with my daughter in laws and I asked them how are they holding up since they witnessed this mess? And they told me they were having nightmares. Renata said, "He's never seen Steve cry so much and get so mad. It had him and Andrew worried. And you, I don't know how to react if we lost you." I told them what Steve said to me. It shocked them and Meara said, "Lala, I still see her shooting you." I told them, "I don't know why I didn't ask them to leave, what I should have asked them." Meara told me, "Lala you were trying to help a child and do your job. Your home is a small side clinic for these babies so you can get the right type of diagnostics. From what I understand, since you opened up your home for study, you couldn't make them leave. I think they studied on coming here and knew the laws. Andrew wants him dead. I've never seen so much hatred come out of him since this has happened." And I told them, "I think, right now I'm still in disbelief. I felt that when I told Cole off, I think he thought I wouldn't do anything to him. There are two different people in Steve and crazy ass Steve came out fully when the two of you met him. I'm pretty sure crazy Steve will be tucked away for a long time now." Renata told me, "Grumpy feels like he failed you." I asked, "Why?" She told me, "Because he wasn't right beside you." I told them, "He was trying to calm down and Steve knows that I have nothing to do with crazy ass Steve."

I had to explain to them why it was a funny story to tell them. I told them, "Okay, let's change the subject." Meara said, "Okay, so what do you think of Jessa?" I told them, "I'm really not clicking with her, I'm guessing it's because of bad timing or her shyness. If Chase would have informed us, maybe I would have been prepared for her. Unlike Savannah, she told me she has a boyfriend, and she's been seeing him for a while now. She wants us to meet him and this is something that I get to sit back and watch Steve go nuts about because this is something he's not ready for." We started laughing about it and kind of making fun of the situation. As we sat there and talked, Andrew came up and hugged me and told me, "Good morning Mama." As I was about to say something Stephanie came up beating the door and ringing the doorbell. As I was walking to open it up, Steve was at the door, and she was pissed off. Right behind her was Savannah and Matthew, and she said to me and her daddy, "We've been calling everyone in this damn house, including your office phone Mama. A God damn tree fell in my house last night and crushed my car and Savannah's car."

244

I asked, "Matthew, where's your car?" He told me, "It's here. I rode with Savannah to Stephanie's, and we got here by Brian." Steve told Stephanie, "Hang on Daddy is getting there." So I figured I'd go get dressed and see the damage. As I was getting dressed, Steve comes in, and I asked him, "Is it Tuesday yet?" He told me, "Baby by tomorrow it will be me and you alongside Kaden and Matthew." I said to him, "If her house is bad, I'm sure Steph is going to stay here." He said, "Right so we pack up." Steve, Stephanie, Savannah and I rode over to her house and poor Savannah just made her last car payment. Steve was giving Stephanie hell and told her, "See Steph, this is what you get when I told you need to cut that oak tree down;" She said to him, "Daddy, don't make me even madder this morning. I'm feeling hurt already." I wanted to change the subject and I fucked up and opened my mouth and said, "So Savannah, when are we going to meet this boyfriend named Trevon?" When I said that Steve stopped the truck in the middle of the road, turned around, looked at Savannah and said,"What the fuck?" Savannah said, "Thanks a lot Mama. Now you've woken up the madman." Steve asked, "How long?" Savannah told him,"Oh, so I'm not supposed to date? Daddy you're gonna have to stop picturing me as your little girl. I'm an adult now. I am entitled to see someone if I want to. Besides, bringing him here has been bad timing. I'm not Chase just bringing that over unannounced. I was waiting for you to meet him at the right time. Besides, Stephanie is seeing Clayton." When Savannah said that, I was unaware of this. Steve said, "I know Stephanie is seeing him. He asked me for my permission. There's a difference between just starting to see someone and when a guy asks the father for permission. And if the father says no, then he should respect the father's wishes." Savannah said, "Well did you ask Papa when you started seeing Mama?" When she asked her Daddy, Steve said, "Well kinda, but Mama was in a different situation and Papa threatened me." When Steve said that I asked him, "Okay, so my Daddy threatened you?" And he told me, "Yes. He said if I hurt you, he and your brother's would hang me from the cotton loft, but didn't I do right? I did ask him permission to marry you. So my ass isn't hanging there yet." Steve told Savannah, "I want to meet Trevon as soon as me and Mama get back from vacation. I need to figure out if he's worth something. As for Clayton, Mama and I know his parents and know they're hard workers. So there is a big difference. When we got to Stephanie's, Steve looked at everything and said, "They're lucky. It just tore up her kitchen and living room. The girls' cars are totaled out. They need a ride so they can come and go. So, as of right now, all you and I can do Mama is go get the girls a car. I looked at him and told him, "We better get going." Just as we were about to leave, Kaden said to Stephanie, "Looks like you're going with me in the morning because if I'm fixin' this, it's not going to be cheap. I have to pay my hands. From the looks of it, your whole roof needs to be replaced and new cabinets in the kitchen." I told him, "Just do your thing Kaden." As we left I told the girls, "Think cheap until your insurance company pays you." We stopped by the bank and I ripped out enough for the girls. Within 40 minutes of getting what they wanted, the paperwork was completed and the girls had brand new cars. They made a deal with me. I get the insurance money out of their old cars, so that they pay me back. Steve is going to fix Stephanie's house and the boys were working quickly to get the tree removed. I saw Kaden called his hands to help. As Steve and I were standing there, I saw Clayton pull in. I yelled out, "You come here now." He stood straight and Steve said, "Mama leave the boy alone." I looked at Steve and said, "You knew about this." He said, "Yeah. Well you knew about Savannah's boyfriend. So we're even." When Clayton walked up to me, he boycotted me and shook Steve's hand. He turned to me and said, "Yes Ma'am." I asked him, "So how long have you and Stephanie been together?", He told me, "Well Mrs. Kerala, for about four months now. Your husband said I could date her." I told him, "If you hurt her, I'll be coming for you." He told me, "No Ma'am, my dad taught me not to hurt women. I have a saying if she's done with me, then I'll let her be." I was pleased with what he told me and I asked, "Will you be joining us for dinner tonight?" He looked at Steve, and he said, "Yes Ma'am." After he said that to me he said, "Excuse me, but I would like to check on Stephanie." That kind of impressed me. After he checked on her, he jumped in and started helping the boys. With everyone being there I figured there was an opportunity to be alone at the house. So I stole Steve's truck and left. When I got back in the door, I started cleaning up mine and Steve's room. After I cleaned up the house I went into our closet and started packing. I reached up on Steve's shelf and felt something. I got the stool and looked. There was a shoebox, so I moved it and when I did, there was a jewelry box. I put the shoebox like it was. I knew what it was for. Our 24th anniversary was coming. All I could give him was a transferred recording of me and my cousin's band put on his phone. I had the link to download. I packed up a few more things since I didn't know where we were going. Only he knew. As I was sitting there, thinking this would be our first vacation. Just the two of us, alone and no disturbances, I kinda got a little excited about it.

I saw the time and my bunch knows it's 5:00 PM for dinner on weekends and 6:00 PM for weekdays. It was 3:00 PM and I needed to get my ass in gear. I enjoyed the peacefulness and my time alone. I decided that I would treat my grandbabies and make us strawberry crunch poke cake, spaghetti with summer salad, and scratch garlic bread. As I was about done, right on time, Steve comes in. He looks at me and says, "Come here now. So I figured I pissed him off by leaving. I followed him into the bedroom. When the door slammed I stood there waiting for my ass chewing. He said, "There are two things that haven't made my damn day, my coffee and a little bit of you." I knew what he meant by a little bit of me. Our normal morning habit of kissing each other and telling each other good morning. I smiled and told him, "Come here. After he kissed me I asked him, "There, is that better?" He told me, "Well just a little more." I told him, "I spoil you too much." He told me, "You did it." I told him, "I know, and I love you." He told me, "I love you too." I told him, "I hate to interrupt our moment, but your dinner will be burned if I don't get back to it." When he kissed me again I walked out of the bedroom. I had to run and get my bread out of the oven. During dinner Steve and Clayton were chatting. I could see he was very well mannered and I could see Steve's approval for him. After dinner all the kids scattered which I understood. Andrew and Lucas had to get up early. As for Stephanie, she had to retire to her old room. Steve and I went to bed ourselves. When he closed the door, I started picking on him about Clayton, and he said, "Mama, he's just a good kid, that's all. Isn't that what we want for them?" I told him, "Yea it is, but I'm waiting on Savannah to bring that Trevon home." He said, "Me too. Did you enjoy your time alone?" I told him, "By the time I finished cleaning the house there was no time for me." He told me, "Just think, this coming week, it's just going to be me and you." The next morning as Lucas and Andrew were leaving. We had agreed on Thanksgiving. I told them we were overdue for family photos. So I booked a session early that morning for Thanksgiving week. After they left, it was just our fab four in the house. Kaden got up and started on the room Cole had ripped apart. By that afternoon Savannah left and Matthew had to go back to school. All that was left was Stephanie and Kaden. When Monday morning came around I had to go to the doctor and get checked out. Steve went with me, which he never does. As she was reviewing me, Steve was trying to tell on me about my recent activities. She told him, "She is doing alright." By the time we got home, we started packing and got in bed early. By 3:00 AM I was ready and we were out the door. Somewhere along the way, I passed out until Steve stopped. He said, "Damn baby you're missing the whole trip." I told him, "We're finally about to get there, soon it's going to be me and you." He said, "I know it's long overdue. No worries about being disturbed. I finally get you alone and to myself." I looked over at him. He was getting excited and I told him, "Hey calm down and save it. That horse dick in your pants can wait." When I said that he started laughing. My own mind started running dirty thoughts of us. I started blushing and tapping my nails against my teeth, kinda chewing on it. Steve was looking at me, and he said, "Woman, whenever you do that shit you have some wild and freaky shit on your mind." I told him, "You'll find out really soon because I'm gonna make you my bitch." His jaw dropped and said, "I knew it. My wife is a freak." I giggled and smarted off to him, "Yea, and she's coming out to play." As I looked at him, he was bright red, which that shit is very hard to do.

Just before sunset, we arrived at this cabin out in the middle of nowhere. As I walked out on the deck, there was a small town out in the distance. I realized it was one of the screens on my computer. I always told Steve if this place existed I would love to see it in person. I couldn't believe he did it. I love looking at small chapels. I often think of how many of the towns people go to just to attend Sunday services. Ever since I was a little girl, I loved Thomas Kinkade's villages. When Noah told Steve that I always wanted my own collection, Steve made it possible. As I'm standing there thinking and looking out, Steve comes up behind me. He told me, "There's nothing more satisfying than to see you happy. It makes me happy." When I turned to him, he picked me up. I told him I loved him. The next morning things got a little freaky. While he was still asleep, I handcuffed him to the bed. I placed a piece of ice in my mouth and he woke up to be surprised by what I was doing to him. I made him shake. After I got done with him, and unruffled him, things got sexually serious from there. Steve and I stayed in bed the whole day, but the next morning Steve's phone started ringing. When he answered, he said, "This better be fucking worth my time." Steve sat up quickly and looked over at me. I was trying to eavesdrop, but the look he gave me was I better run. So I got up and made coffee. As I stood there watching it, he came out of the room, smiled at me and snickered. He said, "Guess what baby, you were right. They kidnapped that baby. But here's our bad news, the District Attorney wants a trial." I told him, "Okay. I would rather not discuss this right now. My focus is on us. Right now, my mind is on you." After I said that it had put him in a better mood. I asked, "So what do you want to do today?" He told me, "We can go and explore the town." So we got dressed and went on a tour of the caves. We have this stuff close to home. After we toured the town, we went back to the rental. The next morning I texted Andrew and Lucas, Happy 24th Birthday Mama loves you. As I'm sitting there, watching the sunrise, something behind me was making noise. I turned around and there stood the biggest buck I have ever seen in my life. I carefully turned around to take pictures of him and I posted it in our family group chat. Steve missed out on seeing this deer. Seth said, "Damn Mama, Daddy isn't up and where y'all at?" I told him, "I don't know what state I'm in. Only your Daddy knows." I had to lie to the kids because it was mine and Steve's secret from them. Steve, and I were in the Shenandoah Valley. I stood there a good ten minutes looking at this deer out of the damn blue. The thought that the baby isn't theirs and there is a court trial. So I texted Andrew and Lucas and told them the news. Your Daddy was the one that spoke to Brian the other day. I told them we'll do a family conference chat when we get home. When they replied to me it was, "Alright. Go Mama."

As I stood there watching the sunrise, my own mind started running over my past and the thing is, my teen years were kind of ripped from me by Cole. All of his physical and verbal abuse, him telling me that I was stupid, I don't deserve to have things, or I don't need friends, or I shouldn't speak to this person or that person. As I'm standing there, thinking of all the times he hit me or choked me, my anxiety started to go to the roof and I started crying. I was getting upset at myself for how and why I put up with it. I began to question myself about what if I had never messed with him, who would I really be. My thoughts were running wild when Steve grabbed me and placed me in his lap. Steve held on to me and told me, "No baby, not here. Whatever is going on in your mind, let it go. I'm here with you now. That's the past. You and I are moving forward together. Kerala, you have moved mountains for us as a family. You're strong, smart and beautiful. You are the woman that gave me everything that I asked for in my life. The moment you took your very first step into my life, you became my life. Meeting you was fate. Becoming your friend was a choice, and loving you was not in my control. That's why I love you, and you are my everything in my world."

I told him, "I'm sorry. I know I shouldn't have been thinking about it, but with it back in my face again, my anxiety is kinda high." As I was trying to explain how I was feeling, I could tell he was upset with me because this wasn't our ideal kind of getaway. He said, "Well, I forgive you. I think it's time you let yourself loose tonight and fully relax, baby. You just had a traumatic experience and I get it. You're trying to put it away, and it's not going to leave your mind until you're done with this shit. But please, for the remainder of this week, let it just be us." I agreed with him. I did need a good drink. When he pats me on my butt, I showed him what he had missed. This got him in the mood to go look for it. As he got up he told me,

"Hey, I love you and you and I we're fixin' to have fun in a little while." I got up and fixed us some breakfast, so we sat outside to eat. Out of the blue, I just took a piece of food and threw it at him. At first he thought it was by accident and I did again and started laughing. I took some of my oatmeal, put it in my hand, rubbed it in his face and started laughing. He and I started throwing food at each other until there was nothing left. I was laughing so much that we were laying on the ground. We couldn't help but to kiss each other, and he told me, "You're a mess, and you've made a mess." I told him, "No. We made a mess." As we started to clean up, we started laughing and picking on each other. After we cleaned it up and ourselves, I grabbed my book and lounged around and read while he took off fishing. By that afternoon, we had a quiet evening with each other. I wasn't in the mood to drink. My focus was on him. The morning of our anniversary I sent him the link to Dex's small website for the song catalog. The way he acted like I had just given him the world and a million dollars. He told me, "I can't give you yours yet, but I promise it's worth it." I was happy to know that he enjoyed what I gave him, but later on that night we sat out by a fire. As it got dark, he went in and came back out. He told me, "I know you love looking at the stars, so I got this for you." He handed me a certificate. I have a star named after me. I thought that was sweet of him and said, "Thank you." I asked him, "Do you ever regret anything in our marriage?" He said, "Baby there's only one thing I do regret and those are the years that I was an asshole to you, but the rest I don't regret." He asked me, "What about you?" I told him, "Loving you better." He told me, "No, you have always given me the best of you and still do." I told him, "Let's not go into those rabbit holes." He said, "Yes, let's not, because I fear it will lead to us having a disagreement and I don't like fighting with you. Fighting with you is like digging in a box of dynamite. When I pick the wrong word to say it explodes." I

252

said, "I do not." I giggled, and he said, "Yes you do." I started picking at him and I took a drink. "He said, "Oh now I see why you're being so spicy. I got your other if you want to take a few shots with me." I told him, "Why not." He ran into the house and got it. I swear I barely blinked. Because he was right back in front of me and I said, "I sometimes swear you like to get me drunk." He smiled and said, "Uh huh, there's a little bit of a wild woman inside you that needs to come out and play." I smarted off, "Oh, so is asshole Steve gonna come out, so the wild woman can tame him?" He and I started laughing. After my fifth shot, I was gone and didn't remember anything.

The next morning I woke up on the kitchen floor, sick as a dog and with no clothes on. I got up and on the other side of the kitchen Steve was passed out. I'm guessing he tried to cook something because the kitchen is a mess and no clothes on him. It never fails. When he gets plastered he somehow thinks he's a Chef. I'm glad we didn't burn the house down, or we would make some owner really pissed. I got up to shower. As I was showering, I felt sticky shit in my hair, so I washed it. When I got out and walked back over to Steve, he was covered in syrup. I'm guessing Steve and I did something freakish. As I'm standing there, I'm hearing a phone ring. I go outside and our clothes is scattered in the yard. I see Steve's phone on the table and ringing. Its Shelby. I answered it and she said to me, "Hi Kerala. I am glad to know that both of you had a great time last night, but I didn't need to see the images of you being physically intimate with each other." When she said that to me, I was embarrassed. I apologized and told her that both of us had a little bit too much to drink last night and I promised it wouldn't happen again. We talked a few more minutes and we hung up. I went through Steve's phone and the photo was only sent to his Mom. But still, it was bad on our end and Steve was the one that took it. I looked for my phone. When I found it, I checked to see if I sent anything stupid, and it was clean. But I saw the last text was to his Mom and nothing else. I went through his pictures and there's my answer. Things got crazy between us. I walked back into the kitchen and woke him up. When he got up, walked into the bathroom and showered, I slowly started cleaning up the mess. I figured I would let him wake up. I found myself drag assing to the couch. When he got out of the shower he looked at me and said, "God damn baby. What did we do?" I told him and I told him I'm still trying not to replay what we shouldn't have done. For instance, we shouldn't have made a porn and sent it to your Mom last night. I just got off the phone with her. He looked at me and I gave him his phone. I saw the instant regret on his face. He said, "Oh God. Next time we need supervision around us." When he looked at it, his face was red as ever, and he said, "Well we must have had a good time." I told him, "You might better call your Mom." I rolled into a small blanket. He was on the phone for about ten minutes with her. When he came back in he got on the couch with me and we both said, "I think we don't need to talk about this ever again." I told him, "No, not ever."

The next morning, I made sure everything was clean before we left. By noon, the hangover was still with us. Steve and I were starting to make a joke about the situation over getting drunk. Later on, when we got home, Chase surprised us with a few things. When we pulled in the fence next to the house was down. Out in the field where Steve takes the new mama's and calves was a double wide trailer in the middle. Steve started in and said. "Son of a bitch. I've only been home for a minute and I'm looking at this shit in my door." So we go out there and Chase comes walking out. He said, "Mama and Daddy, what do you think?" I got out, walked inside and there's Jessa. I looked around his house. To me, it was a little bit too much for Chase's budget. I walked out and Steve was on his ass. Chase said, "Daddy, I got bigger issues going on. When they brought the house in, I got fired and in between this, Jessa and I got married this morning." Steve told him, "Well, there's a truck and an extra trailer. You've got a CDL. You need to go talk with Marty, son." Steve turned to me and said, "Guess what Mama, one less mouth to feed in the house because he just blew all of his savings on this house that's gonna fall apart on him in a few months. And congratulations on getting married, but come tomorrow, you better fix this fence." As we got in the truck he told me, "Hold on." We drove over to Kaden's and that poor baby was working on his house, but he had his walls up. Kaden said to me, "Mama, I got done with Bebe's room. I'm working on Stephanie's house. And boy, as soon as y'all left, Chase got a bunch of wild hair up his ass. I told him don't go putting a house where you want because Daddy has it all mapped out for us to be even. The only odd ball is Seth because his house is made of natural material. But yet here we are, Chase not waiting. This girl, or should I say his wife, is making him do some crazy shit. Sorry y'all had to come home to crazy ass shit. But did y'all have fun?" When Kaden asked us that, Steve and I looked at each other and our faces turned red. Kaden said, "So I have taken it y'all did." We just shook our heads and laughed. Kaden said, "Daddy I bet you had a fit seeing that deer." He told him, "No I didn't get to see it. Mama did. I saw a picture of it." Kaden had shown me around I saw he had his cabinets in and flooring. The only thing he was doing was putting in his trim and last-minute touches. He told me, "I'll be moving out by the end of the month." It kinda broke my heart a little because he's the last one to leave out of the house. As we went home, Steve and I were tired so we went to bed. The next morning, Chase was at it. I was preparing to go back to work. This would be my last full week with Steve. He and I were ready for a little bit of normalcy. But for Steve and Chase sparks were about to fly with those two. I fixed Steve something to drink and took it to him. The small bickering between them was only getting worse and Chase asked me.

"Mama, where's my drink?" I told him, "You have a wife now. She should be bringing you something to drink. What is she doing?" He looked at me and said, "Watching TV and painting her nails." I looked at him and asked him, "So did she make you breakfast and make sure it's sitting on the table for you or did you cook together?" All he could do was look at me. Steve smarted off with a laugh, "Damn boy you got a lazy wife." This made him kinda mad and I told him, "Look. I love you, but if she's not doing it for you, she needs to find a job quickly, and you're doing all the work. You come home and there's no dinner sitting out, then what good is she? I understand she's in school, but a part-time job would help out." I reminded him I went to school, worked, then came home and took care of all of y'all. I don't think she could handle one step in my shoes." He said, "Yea, but Mama, you're a workaholic." I said, "Not right now I'm not." He said, "Mama, you and Daddy got married after just seven months of dating." Steve said, "Yes we did, but we had our damn heads on and we were mature. See, boy, we grew up having to know the how's of life because we had the GI and the baby boomers raising our asses. As for your Mama, they didn't take shit. So when we were about 16, and on up, we were kinda adults because of how we were raised." So I advised him to text her to see if she would bring him something to drink. Well he did and her reply was come and get it yourself. He walked off pissed. Steve said, "Mama, me and that girl just isn't clicking." I told him, "I'm the same way right now, and I'm trying to butt out of it on those two. I think it's best for you to do as well." Steve told me, "I am, but I'm fixin' to test them." I looked at him, and he said, "I called Marty, and he's willing to take on Chase, but he's told me that Clayton will be joining us. Somehow that boy is trying to prove something to me. Hell Marty said he went and bought him a truck, unless mama and daddy helped him, which it's a good thing."

As the week went by, Steve and Chase were getting ready to head out on Sunday night and I was getting ready for my first day back myself, but as Sunday night came around, Steve was stalling a little bit until Kaden came to stay with me.

The next morning came. I put myself together. I was kinda ready and kinda not, but once I got in my car, I told myself we're going to have fun today. When I got to the office, I was the first one there. When I was unlocking the door, a deputy was making his last-minute rounds and came around. It was Austin. He saw me and was complaining about my step in because he liked to hurt his baby. I told him, "Tell Erica to bring the baby in today if she can. Just tell her to call. I won't charge anything." He told me, "I'm glad you're back." I asked him, "Are those two still in the jail over there?" He said, "Yes Ma'am and boy ol' Steve put a hurting on that Cole. Just remind me not to piss him off." I told him, "Well, have a good day and stay safe." When I turned around, Austin made sure I was in the building. I locked up behind me and went into my office. I could tell he didn't take care of my things. When I heard the door unlock, Hannah came in, and I startled her a little. I asked her, "Was he giving my patients the right kind of meds because I just had Austin telling me that he gave baby Milian the wrong medicine." She told me, "He's been screwing up a lot in the last week." So I looked over my charts and this was pissing me off because he's not doing his job. When Alexia came in and she saw me, she asked, "Why the resting bitch face for Mama?" I told her, "Because you and I have our work cut out for us." She said, "Oh, you know me and him got into it Thursday over him giving the wrong dosage to a baby. I went behind him and fixed it." I told her, "We'll have a staff meeting before the first patient this morning." So I sent an email to the Dean of Medicine of where he was attending and told him that Mr. Miller needed to relearn his Pharmacology before graduating. He needs improvement in people skills as he was rude to my patients, parents and staff. If there's anything you need from me, please call me. When I got up I went into our little break room. Hannah asked me, "So what's the big story about Chase being put in the truck?" I looked at her and said, "Hannah, the boy is fucked up. He made some poor decisions while Steve and I were gone. When we came home, there's a double wide sitting in the field where Steve had intended to build a winter shelter for the cows. Chase said to us, 'oh Daddy I lost my job and I wasn't thinking while buying the double wide and Jessa and I got married.' So yay me, I have a daughter-in-law that I haven't bonded with yet. I just don't know with her just yet. I'm trying, but I guess there's too much going on." Hannah said, "Damn. You've really got too much going on. When Bodie said that Chase was in the old truck he saw Chase and Steve getting into it." I said, "I figured they would." She asked me, "Something that's been on my mind, do you think this girl is using Chase?" I told Hannah, "That's on our minds because Chase just blew all of his savings just to get this house and that's not what he wanted. His attitude has changed a little bit towards Steve and I." Hannah told me, "That's crazy. What about the Mitch boy? He's rolling with them as well." I told her, "He's seeing Stephanie and Steve is head over heels with him." She shook her head and I told her, "I know the madness never ends at my house." I saw the time and I told her, "Well, let's get this first day back over with." When I saw my step in I asked him to step into my office, and he comes out and says and you are? I smarted off and said, "I'm the bitch that's fixin' to make sure you don't graduate." He and I started arguing in front of everyone and I told him, "If you had killed a child, it would have been on your hands and this is my practice. You're damaging it with the wrong dosages for a child. Whatever hole you came from, it's time for you to get the hell back to it. Leave, so I can gain my parents' trust again since you've just about fucked it up." When he walked out, I locked the door. I took a

258

deep breath and was ready to scream. I told Missy, "Okay, here's what we're going to do. I want to recheck all the kids. It might take us a week, but get them in here and tell them no charges. I just want to check them over," She told me, "I'm on it, boss." When I saw Alexia, I looked at her and she was being Alexia. She said, "Be you." She made a funny face at me. I laughed and walked off. I heard Hannah say she's back, and I popped off, "You damn right I am."

During the whole day I've cleaned up what he fucked up. By the end of the day I was ready to go home. When I got in the door I dropped. I fixed myself a small salad and sat down. My phone started ringing and it was Chase. The first words out of his mouth was, "Mama." I said, "What?" He said, "Mama, you're gonna have to get Daddy off my ass." I told him sorry boy, as much as I love you, you're on your own with him! But I'll see what's on his mind. Right now, you should be asleep." He told me, "Nope. Daddy's up and about ready to come home." I caved and told him, "I'll speak with him and see, but I can't promise you anything." After I hung up with him, I called Steve. I asked him,"You okay?" He told me, "Yea baby, I'm good. How was your day:" I told him,"A fucked up Monday. I'm having to go back through about a month's worth of patients and fixing this guys fuck-ups. And I'm having to backlog all of his mess." He said, "I'm sure it's a pain in the ass, but to you, it's a challenge." I asked him, "How's Chase?" He told me, "Mama I caught him on his phone and not paying attention, so we got into it a few times. He's going to get someone hurt or himself and I think this so called wife of his is lazy. I don't want him working himself to death over this girl." I told him, "Let's stand back. It's kinda none of our business until it becomes our business." Steve told me, "I know Mama, but I want them to do right in their life and have things." I reminded Steve, "We can't hold their hands forever. We have to let them go." He told me, "I know." And I told him, "Just kinda lay off of him please. I think he's confused right now. I think in my own heart and gut feeling she pressured him. All we can do is stand back and watch." Steve agreed with me, and he told me, "I'll be home in the morning Mama. Maybe, if I get home early enough, I can cuddle up with you." I told him, "If you drive carefully, I will spoil you a little bit." When I told him that I could hear him getting excited and he asked me, "Can you put the pecans in it? How 'bout some chick pick too? Will there be extra?" I told him, "Yes, and extra coconut on the cake." He told me, "I smell misery." I laughed about it and he told me, "Well Mama, if you want me home before you leave for work, I need to get this train moving." I told him, "Yes, you do." He said, "Baby, keep my side of the bed warm for me and I love you. See you soon." I said, "I will and loved him too." When I got off the call I finished eating and knew he just asked for a banana split cake. So I started preparing for it. By 9:00 PM I had my butt in bed. Around 3:00 AM I felt him get in the bed and wrap his arms around me. It didn't take him long, he was out. But I was locked into his grip, so I waited until he was relaxed. By 5:00 AM I had to get up so I did. I got ready for a day of hell, cleaning up someone's mess. Just before I left, I made sure to kiss him and out the door I went. When I got to the office I had started with the charts. I knew by the end of the day things would be back to normal and I could move forward by 9:00 AM. I received a call that couldn't wait, so I took it. Our lawyer told me, "They're setting the court date for February, so everyone can enjoy the holiday. I want you to be ready for the date." I told her, "I'll be there." I just couldn't believe that this was turning into a trial. My name is about to be smeared and my personal past for the public to hear.

By the end of the day I dragged my ass into the house like a little toddler into Steve's arms. He thought it was funny the way I came in. I fixed dinner and Chase came in. I only fixed enough for just me and Steve, planning to give the leftovers to

Steve for tomorrow's lunch. I said, "Uh, I thought your house was out there?" He told us, "Yeah, she didn't fix anything. She told me she's not messing up the kitchen." I told him, "Boy, get up to your house and cook yourself something. That's your house." He looked a little mad at me and walked out. Steve said, "I believe he's thinking being married is all fun and games. This is why the other three are not rushing into a relationship. And she's as lazy as ever." I said, "I'm not concerned about him, it's her after dinner." As a mom, something in my gut told me to go be nosy. Steve looked at me and said, "Baby you have that concerned look on your face." I told him, "Something in my gut is telling me to go check on Chase." He said to me, "I'm not ignoring any more gut feelings, like I did a few weeks back, and besides I've been wanting to measure for that area anyway." So we got the stuff to measure for the cattle shelter. With us having 2,500 head of cattle they needed something larger. Steve and I slowly sneak our way to Chases. The closer we got, we could hear them fighting. Steve and I were debating on if we should interrupt them or leave them alone. So we walked up towards the door and I knocked on the door. When Chase opened up I asked him, "Have you eaten anything?" I could tell he was so pissed off, and he told me, "No Mama, I haven't." I pushed him out of the doorway and came inside. I saw she had everything to cook with and she hit me with the wrong words. I have been holding back my anger. When she said, "He can cook his own meals and mine too. You baby your children too much so why don't you just get out of my house?" When she said that to me, I hit her back and told her, "Is your name on the title of this house? No. It's not. Is your name on this land? No, it isn't. It's mine and Steve's. So before you try running me off, you're a little fucked up in the head over this. What's pissing him off is the fact that all he is asking you to do is to cook him a meal. Now, he has busted his ass off for you and all he has asked is to keep his house clean and cook him a meal. It can work 50/50. In return for doing so, there won't be any more of me coming up here making you look like a damn lazy ass wife. And as for my kids, I'm gonna tell you this, I was there for their first breath and I know damn well they'll be there for my last. If they need it, and I got it, I'm damn sure gonna make sure they have it. On this land here, you don't have any say so. Now, as for him, I don't have a choice in whom he wants to be with, but from the looks on his face you're about to hit the fucking door and be single." When I got out of her face, I grabbed Chase by the ear, and out the door we went. I told him, "Come on, get your ass to the house. You need to go do some thinking. I think you've been eating too many bowls of stupid here lately." When we got back into the house, I made sure he was fed, and I went to bed to read my book. But for Steve and Chase, I could hear them talking. Chase admitted that he thinks it was a mistake. I heard him tell his Daddy, "I want what you and Mama have." I love what Steve told him, "We all fall in love with three people in our life, and it's been said that we really only fall in love with three people in our lifetime. Yet, it's also believed that we need each of these loves to happen for a different reason. We enter into the first with the belief that this will be our only love, and it doesn't matter if it doesn't feel quite right, or if we find ourselves having to swallow down our personal truths to make it work because deep down we believe that this is what love is supposed to be. Because in this type of love, how others view us is more important than how we actually feel. The second is supposed to be our hard love—the one that teaches us lessons about who we are and how we often want or need to be loved. This is the kind of love that hurts, whether through lies, pain, or manipulation. We think we are making different choices than our first, but in reality we are still making choices out of the need to learn lessons—but we hang on. Our second love can become a cycle, oftentimes one we keep repeating, because we think that somehow the ending will be different than before. Yet, each time we try, it somehow ends worse than before. Sometimes it's unhealthy, unbalanced or narcissistic even. There may be emotional, mental or even physical abuse or manipulation—most likely there will be high levels of drama. This is exactly what keeps us addicted to this storyline, because it's the emotional roller coaster of extreme highs and lows. Like a junkie trying to get a fix, we stick through the lows with the expectation of the high.

Now, as for your Mama and me and on both ends, we weren't looking because she is the love I'd never see coming. The one that usually looks all wrong for us and that destroys any lingering ideals we clung to about what love is supposed to be. This is the love that comes so easy it doesn't seem possible. It's the kind where the connection can't be explained and knocks us off our feet because we never planned for it. This is the love where we come together with someone, and it just fits—there aren't any ideal expectations about how each person should be acting. Nor is there pressure to become someone other than who we are.

To tell you the truth son, your Mama and I weren't looking for any person to be with, it just happened. I can tell you this, when I first kissed Mama I felt like a lightning bolt had struck me. Our connection between us was there until I knew I couldn't let Mama get away from me. Yes, it's true that we got married within a few months of knowing each other, but we were a helluva lot more mature and knew what we got ourselves into. To be honest with you, our marriage isn't perfect. Hell, I have my flaws that Mama doesn't like, and she has hers. We have our small spats where we get mad at each other, but we come back to each other and talk it out." Somewhere in their conversation I fell asleep. The next morning I got into work and I was checking on some newborns. I take my time checking them out because I'm studying them a little bit. I try to get them in early so I check their stool to make sure their mom's feeding choice is not upsetting their stomach. I look for any possible hernias that could arise for the baby's later on. I ask a lot of questions to the parents. When I walked out of the patient room I saw my office door was closed. Missy told me, "Steve is in your office." I told her, "Okay, I've got this tot to see and we're on lunch. So I stepped in, checked my tot and this baby was covered in fire ant bites. I smelled the tots' clothes, and it was Gain laundry soap. I explained to her parents that, "Anything with a sweet smell might bring ants around. Despite this being true, ants can actually get poisoned by laundry detergent. So it's not like they will be picking up laundry detergent and carrying it around back to their colony. So for him, and the bumps, I want you to use Campho-Phenique. It's an old cold sore remedy. Rub it on him after his bath and again in the morning. This will help to keep him from scratching and leaving scars. I would change the laundry soap to one that doesn't have any sweet perfume smells. After my tot left, I opened my office door. Steve had his head down looking at the floor. The look on his face had me scared. I could tell he was thinking hard about something, so I closed the door behind me. He looked up at me and said, "Baby I came here to talk to you about us." When he said that my heart sank and I started shaking. He asked me, "Why are you shaking?" "Because those words I dislike." He told me, "No, no baby, I'm sorry that I said it like that. What I'm asking is did you and I paint a perfect picture for the kids of our marriage? Was their image of us, what they grew up seeing of us, too perfect?" When he asked me that my own mind was blown. I asked him, "Do you want to go to lunch and talk about this?" He said, "Yea at least get this off my mind." I told him, "I know because you just transferred it to my head." So as we sat down not much was being said between us. Because what he had thrown at me, as I was about to say something, he and I spoke at the same time. He told me, "You go. Ladies first." I told Steve, "I'm guessing it's because we never really had any big arguments in front of them. If you and I disagreed on something, we never did it in front of them." Steve told me, "You know, I was thinking the same. It did feel good last night to have that deep conversation with Chase. To get him to kinda understand our marriage." I asked him, "So why did that make you think about our marriage?" He asked me, "When was the last time you and I had a big fight?" I told him, "When we were kinda on the rocks before Bebe came to the bedroom that morning. Our disagreements are once in a blue moon." He said, "Damn, it's been that long." I told him, "You and I may get mad about things, but it's been a while since I've been upset with you." He said, "I guess I'm doing something right. Back on the subject of Chase. I know he told me he's going to give her another chance. But if things don't change for him, he told me this morning that he's getting rid of her." I told Steve, "I hate this for him, but it's his own fault for not thinking straight about things." Steve agreed with me. And he said, "Baby I didn't mean to scare you with my words in your office. You know I'm not going anywhere. I love you too damn much." I told him, "Please don't ever use those words again." He said, "I promise." When he took me back to the office he said, "I didn't get my morning kisses from you." I told him, "I'm sorry. You were out cold and sleeping hard this morning." So we kissed each other, and he said, "Now the rest of my day will go right until you get home." When I got back into the office, Hannah asked me if I was okay. I had to ask her, "Do you think Steve and I have the perfect marriage? I'm asking you this because I want your point of view, how you see us." She said, "Well for one thing, the man is absolutely fucking crazy about you. Half these women in town would love to kick you out of the way just to get his attention. But he doesn't bat an eye for any other woman. He's only got eyes for you, but behind closed doors, no one knows if it's that way. Why are you asking?" I had told her, "Chase and his new little thing isn't working out too well. Last night he told his Daddy that he wants what we have, a perfect marriage. Steve just asked me if we painted a perfect picture of their viewing of us." She asked me. "I know y'all have had y'alls fights and no marriage is perfect, so what makes Chase think marriage is easy." I told Hannah, "That's a good question I might need to ask him. One thing is that he jumped onto the marriage train with a girl that's refusing to cook for him." Hannah said, "What?" I told her, "She's a lazy wife." Hannah said, "That boy just did three days out with Bodie and his Daddy. He should've come home to get a good meal from her." I said, "See this Mama is fussing about the same and she told me to get out of her house last night. I basically told her to fuck off. I tell you this, if she stays, she'll be the one out of my boy's wives I will not get along with." After I told her that, Hannah said, "Maybe you should really ask her if she's in love with him or vice versa, not just a heat of the moment thing."

By that Friday morning, I got up and had my coffee in my meditation spot. As I was thinking of my own children and their lifestyle choices, Chase comes over and says, "Mama, can I speak with you?" I told him, "Sit, I want to speak with you as well." He asks me, "Mama, is it wrong for me to think two things? One of them wants me to see if she would change and make this work and the other is going to the courthouse and filing for divorce." I asked him, "Well my question for you is, has she called or texted you since you've been here?" He told me, "No Ma'am." I asked him, "Okay, so what are your methods to see if this can work?" He told me, "Well, I'll go and have it out with her. If she doesn't bug me and tells me she's gonna change things, I'll try and make it work with her. If not, then I'm going to ask her to leave and go from there." I told him, "Well Chase, it sounds like you have a plan already in mind.

The question that I want to ask you is why do you see me and your Daddy as a perfect marriage?" He said, "Well Mama, y'all don't really fight. You make sure Daddy is happy, and you cater to him." I told him sorry son, but I'm gonna have to correct you a lot on what your Daddy and I have. I'll be honest, yes your Daddy and I used to fight badly, but it was behind closed doors, away from y'all. And two, your Daddy and I were kinda on the brink of a possible divorce once. We were ignoring each other and our needs with each other. We were basically too busy with our jobs and you kids. We did not stop to attend to each other. It wasn't until Bebe came here and gave us some advice on what we were doing to each other. Her advice to never stop dating each other, and we used her books as our tools to become close again. I spoil your Daddy in my own heart and my own way." He said to me, "Daddy doesn't spoil you enough." I told him, "I hate to say this Chase, but what you're looking for in a person that you want is Mama, and my child there's only one of me. It's like your Daddy told you the other night, the next will come along when you are not looking. But it's whatever you decide." He sat there for a little bit and I could tell my own child was thinking hard about his choices. He said, "Mama, you're right, maybe I am looking for a little of you in a girl I'm after." Before he got up, I told him, "If you still want to try with her, and you get to the point of having an uncomfortable feeling, get out of there." As he got up, he hugged me and said, "I love you Mama." I told him I loved him too, and he walked off. A few minutes later there stood Seth. I said, "If one twin has an issue so does the other." Seth said, "Nope. I just want to sit here, have coffee with my Mama and help Daddy out today." I told him, "It's 5:30 AM Seth and your Daddy isn't up. The way he is sleeping here lately he has a lot of worry and stress on his mind. With your twin pulling his shit, it has him worried more. With him showing up at my office the other day, saying the words we need to rethink our marriage, it kinda freaked me out." Seth said, "What? Daddy doesn't go to your office but once a year. That's Valentine's Day, if you're working. Why did he ask you that?" I said, "Your Daddy worded it wrong. Chase thinks we have this picture perfect marriage." Seth said to me, "Bullshit. I've heard you two go at when we were kids. Y'all just didn't want to do it in front of us. I told Chase to get rid of her. She's after something and it's not love. Besides to me, she doesn't fit in the family. She's too high maintenance." I told Seth, "You know Meara and Stephanie said the same thing." He said, "Why is Daddy stressing out?" I told him, "The trial that's coming up in February, and he's still afraid that they're going to arrest him." Seth laughed and said, "Mama, if they were going to, they would have already done it. Besides that mess right there, Daddy was just protecting you. I've never thought of the day of him losing his shit. Speaking of him, he is up." When Steve told me, "I was searching the bed for you." I told him, "Sorry, but I heard Chase moving around." He told me, "Yeah he kinda kept me awake last night. He needs to go back to his house." Seth asked Daddy, "What do you need help with today?" Steve told him, "Well, I've been wanting to measure that side of pasture up there, but Chase fucked it all up." Seth said, "Yea, the mama and baby pasture. We can do that." I knew when Seth asked to help him it was going to be an all day thing, so I got up, went inside and started breakfast. As I'm making biscuits, I hear two vehicles and in comes Kaden. Behind him was Clayton. I had to stop what I was doing to go get dressed. When I got back into the kitchen there was Chase, and he said, "Mama I just put a lot of thought into it, and I'm just gonna divorce her." I told him, "If that's what you want to do. But you need to take your house back, because Daddy and I want our alone time. I'll feed you today, but the rest you're gonna have to learn on your own." He said, "Yes Ma'am." After breakfast they were out the door. I cleaned up and figured, since we have company, that I'd figure out what to cook for dinner. I finished getting dressed for the day and around 12:00 PM I got something for them to drink. I walked out to where they were and watched them do some planning. I only stayed out there for about 45 minutes and went back to the house. I started cleaning up mine and Steve's room, did our laundry and started dinner for the night. When I was putting things away, I heard the door open and Steve breezing by. I heard the bathroom sink come on and I turned around. Blood drops were on the floor. I stepped into the bathroom and I looked at him. He was slinging blood everywhere. I saw he cut himself pretty deep in his arm so it was the doctor/wife/ mom to the rescue. I put on some gloves and put a tourniquet close to the cut to slow the bleed down so I could see the damage. I asked him, "What did you cut yourself on?" He told me, "My knife." So I proceeded to wait until the bleeding slowed and cleaned his arm. I asked him, "Is it numb?" He told me, "No it hurts." I was trying to see if it damaged any of his nerves. I cleaned it up and got it ready for me to stitch up. I started in and after I got done with him, he wanted to go back to work. I told him, "To hell you are. I have to watch you now. So on the couch you go. I handed him some pain medication, and he acted like a little kid about wanting to go back outside. I had to bite into his ass and told him no. Within a few minutes he was starting to get drowsy and he went out like a light. I made sure his heart rate was good and blood pressure, but I was concerned about any nerve damage because he couldn't explain his pain to me. When the boys came in looking for him, I showed them why he was passed out. Before dinner I had to wake him up. He bounced up and was trying to go at it again. I told him, "No, that's it for you today." He told me, "I have a lot to do." I told him, "If that shit gets infected, then it's your fault for not listening to me." He raised his voice at me and said, "Fine." I told him, "If you raise your voice at me again, you'll be sorry." He said, "So what are you going to do?"I told him, "I'm going to whip your ass." He told me, "Bring it baby." So I went to the dining room and got a chair, dragged it up to him, got in it and faced him. He started laughing, and he said to me, "You're a mess baby, and I wouldn't have you any other way."

By Sunday night, Chase made Jessa move out and that was the last we saw of her. By October, we got a phone call from his parents saying that Steve needed to come home. They didn't know how much longer Bebe would hang on. So we packed our bags and left. Steve was very upset during our flight. My own worries were how my in-laws were going to treat me since the truth has been out. But once we got there, they still embraced me. I was relieved and my father-in-law wanted to make sure they had everything out of their way for the trial. He told me they wanted to be there for support and asked if Steve and I were holding up mentally. I told him we're trying not to think about it. I had spoken with him some more about it when Matthew came in, and he asked me, "Mama can I talk to you or can we go for a walk?" I told him, "Sure." So we got up and started walking. He told me Poppy is trying to keep his mind off of Bebe." I told him, "I figured as much." As we turned the block, I stood there looking at our old house and Matthew said, "Mama, so many memories were made in that house with us." Matthew asked me, "Have you been to Bebe's yet?" I told him, "No, we just got here. I need to go say goodbye." We walked over there. As I walked in, I knew that it wasn't going to be long. She was in and out of it, talking to Steve off and on and seeing stuff in hallucinations which is part of dying. So I texted the kids and told them to get on the first flight out here. I knew she wasn't going to make it through the night. I told Steve that I'd help take care of her in her last hours. Steve fell asleep in a chair next to her, holding her hand. I got up and down periodically checking on her. I made coffee and as I came back into the room, I noticed her death rattle was gone. I noted the time. It was 4:00 AM. I dug out my stethoscope from my purse to confirm, and she was gone. I easily woke Steve up and told him. I held onto him and let him have it out for a few. We started making phone calls. I stood back and sat down until they came and got her. Bebe was a remarkable person. I can say she put a good mark on me and our marriage. I found it odd about my in-laws. Each was an only child and how they found each other. When the kids made it in, the sleeping arrangements were crazy. Steve and I put the kids up in Bebe's house. Our grandbabies stayed with their other grandparents, so we didn't get to see them. Steve was mad about it. I told him, "They're coming to see us for Thanksgiving and we were having Christmas here. They don't need to learn about how we leave this earth just yet." The next morning Steve and I hung out while my in-laws went and made the arrangements, just in case someone stopped by. Of course there were a few that dropped food off and gave their condolences to the family. As I'm talking, the elderly lady pointed out, in the backyard, through the patio door, asking are they alright. I looked back and Steve and his brother were going at it on the ground. Our kids were watching. I told her, "They're horse playing around. They do this every time they get together." She handed me her food and told me, "Well I have to go." I said, "Thank you." I hated to rush her out the door, but I wanted to see what the hell was going on. As I stepped out, Chase said, "Uncle B's gonna get his ass whipped." I said, "What in the fuck is going on?" Matthew said, "Mama they're horse assing around with each other." As I stood there watching them be jocks and pushing wrestling around, I kept waiting on his brother to cave in. Steve knocked him down. When he got back up, our kids just started playing tackle football with each other until I finally said, "Are you two old geezers done yet?" Matthew went in and gave me a break from people stopping by. That's when those two were out of breath.

271

Phil and Shelby returned, but during dinner, Phil kept looking at me and looking at Steve and clearing his throat and Steve said, "Kerala, Dad wants to ask you something." I looked at Phil. He cleared his throat again and said, "Kerala, can you or Chase sing for Bebe's funeral?" Chase said, "Poppy I'll do it if Mama doesn't." I said, "Why don't Chase and I do it together, just in case I get winded?" Phil was pleased with our yes to him. To me, it was an honor to sing at my grandmother-in - laws funeral, but with my lung still healing I wasn't sure if I could sing my high notes. But I could also tell that Phil was happy with my yes. With Chase being a bonus, it was a plus for him. The next morning, Chase and I were working together on a few songs. Stephanie, Meara, Renata, and Savannah were hanging out back with us. I got a text from Kyle saying that the overnight package of the non-Vocal CD has made it to the FedEx office. I needed to go and pick it up. So Chase and us girls decided that we would run to get it. I disrupted Steven and Phil's conversation about cows when I needed the rental keys to go and get the package. But as we walked out of the house I saw that blonde bitch standing in her driveway. I just looked at her. I didn't have the time nor did I want to put up with any of her bullshit. The way I saw it, this was Bebe's week. Before leaving I stopped by and checked in with Matt. He was so torn up over Bebe, but as I walked in, he had big brothers looking in after him. I knew he was okay. After we got the CD, Chase and I went over the sounds and tried to put the words together with each instrument. I felt as if we were doing some justice for Bebe in the songs that we were going to do for her. We had it narrowed down to five songs. There was a walk in song which was something that wasn't mine and that was, Ave Maria. As we got back to Phil and Shelby's, I noticed that Shelby was on one about something. I looked at Steve. He said, "We need to talk." So off to the bedroom we go. When the door shut, Steve said, "Baby, there's something I need you to be

272

aware of. Just after you left that thing I dated, well she stopped by with her mom. She's up to no good. When I saw her, I got up and went outside. Drew is my witness, along with everyone else. You know where I stand, and it's with you. As he was sitting there, I said, "Gee, it's the season of the exes coming up out of the woods this year. Honey I know where you stand with me. If you would've wanted her back, you wouldn't have married me. Because the man I married is a little bit possessive of his wife. It might just take a woman to put a little girl who is in her 40 something year old body in her place." Steve said, "Baby if you do, I'm just going to let you do it." When Steve and I walked out of the room, Chase was looking at us. Shelby was still hot about what Lizzy and Asha did. Those bitches just did this out of spite to let me and Shelby know that this little war that we have had going on with them is still there.

Around 6:00 PM we went to the funeral home. I, in my own way, saw that blue Jolly Rancher pen on her jacket. I didn't know if I should laugh or cry. When I looked at Seth and Lucas they both winked at me. They knew what the Jolly Ranchers meant with us. I looked at Amy and she saw the same and she started giggling about the pen. Phil just didn't know why she wanted something like a type of pen to be buried with her, but for me, Shelby, Amy, and Leah, we knew what that meant. As for Bebe, she looked so peaceful and no more pain for her. As we were sitting there, I had to help Steve through this difficult time, along with our kids. The next morning of her service we were asked to wait until the attending people were seated. They asked us to go in behind Phil and Shelby. As Steve and I walked in, our kids came in behind us in order and as I was singing Ave Maria, we were walking. I looked over and saw that Lizzy and Asha were sitting in the back row. I gave her a go-to hell look. As Steve and I sat down, the pastor gave me another mic, and he waited on Chase to come in. Once the kids were settled, Chase and I started with this one song we wrote. I was sitting there next to Steve and I made sure I didn't let go of his hand which was my way to let him know that I was there for him. But when Matthew stood up and said his speech, I couldn't be more proud of a man that Steve and I raised. His speech talked about how it was a blessing to be part of a great-grandparents lives, and he took it hard because he lived with Bebe, but as that part of the service was about over, I looked at Chase and shook my head to let him know that I was about to sing her send off song. As I sat there between Chase and Steve, Chase had his hand on my back to let me know that he was there to take over. But as I hit that high note, I didn't let up. It hurt like hell a little bit, but I sang it as good and as hard as I could for Bebe. After we got to the cemetery Steve asked the kids to not run off. He wanted to talk to the kids. So we placed Bebe in her forever place and Steve grabbed my hand. He called for the kids to follow him. As we got to another section of the cemetery, we came upon two graves. I saw the names on the headstones and Steve sat down on a visit bench in front of their graves. I knew who they were. It was the original Seth and Chase. Steve's high school best friends that were killed in the car crash with Steve driving. As our Seth and Chase saw their names on the headstone, they kinda got freaked out. Steve told the kids, "You wanna know why I'm so quiet sometimes. Well the truth is that I watched those caskets close too soon on them that had a lot of life in them and I haven't been the same since. I watched them both get lowered in the ground. I miss them and I wonder how their lives would have turned out. I heard Chase in the back seat of my car dying and Seth died instantly when he flew out the window. We were hit head on by a drunk driver. I was the only one that had a seat belt on. This is why I was kinda hard on y'all in fear of losing one of you just like their parents lost them. I blame myself in my own way for wishing I could have taken a different way home that night, but instead we weren't ready to go home." As Steve stood there, I saw a lot of pain in his eyes and I knew it was time to knock this door down. He explained to the kids very well about these things. As we sat there, the kids and I sat in silence with him. He has had a hard day of crying over his grandmother and I see him still hurting from losing his friends.

When we left the cemetery, Steve looked at me and told me, "I have to go and do this like we talked about. I think it's time to close the door on this. I knew what he wanted to do, so when we showed up at the parent's of Chase, Steve wasn't too sure about himself. I gave him a little push of encouragement, and he proceeded. I, on the other hand, stood there beside him. When a woman opened up the door she recognized Steve. I could feel her hatred toward Steve and the unwelcomeness. What she said to him had almost set me off. She said, "What do you want? It must be nice to live a full life, unlike Chase. It looks like you're doing well for yourself. The more I think about him the more I wish it was you laying in the ground instead of my son." After she said that to him this pissed me off. She was making Steve feel like shit. My dumbass just had to open my damn mouth and I told her, "Look, I don't know your pain or anything, but Steve has survivor's guilt. Every night I have to make sure he takes his medication to ensure that he doesn't have to relive that night in his sleep. All he is trying to do is seek your forgiveness. But I can see that he can't move forward with you. Thanks for making his day even shittier. We just buried his grandmother, so it seems you could have gained something from having a relationship with him, so have a nice damn day." I was mad in my own way, and I moved Steve like a child that refused to move. I could see this made him depressed, and I told him, "Okay, I know I shouldn't have said what I said." I said to him, "Next house. If this mom is cold and bitter then it's their issue, not yours." Steve didn't want to, but I told him, "Let's just go and see." Steve and I rode three blocks down and we rang the doorbell. When the door opened, both couples had a smile on their face and welcomed us in. Now Seth's mother was crying while hugging Steve and Steve was crying himself. All he could say to her was, "I'm sorry, I'm so sorry. She told him, "It's not your fault. I've waited for years for you to come back around to us." As I'm looking at pictures on the wall of her Seth, there's one in particular that looked like my Seth and Chase. It was mind-blowing, so I quickly texted Seth and asked him and Chase to bring their butts to this address. I stood back and let them talk about how it happened, and I introduced myself to the man of the house. Steve told her, "I'm sorry. This is my wife Kerala." As we sat down with them, Steve asked me, "Can you ask our second set of twins to come here?" I told him, "They are on the way." This lady said, "Oh my, you have twins?" I told her, "Yes Ma'am, three sets of twin boys and two daughters, they are fully grown."

When their doorbell rings, she gets up and answers it. The look on her face was white as ever like she saw a ghost. Steve told her, "I'm sorry, but I should have told you, these two are named after them." She guessed Seth right off the bat, which freaked us both out. Seth was ready to go, but we visited with them. To me, Steve got one part of his closure. As we were leaving Steve and Seth's parents exchanged numbers. I could tell that it was kinda closure on both ends and a new beginning for them with us. It was heartbreaking for Chase's mother that she couldn't find closure. When we got back to Steve's mom and dad's house, it was full of people and my mother-in-law asked me where we went. I told her we visited Seth's parents, but for Chase's mother, and she told me, "That woman has called me so many times after it happened and blamed Steve for all that mess. It drove Steve into a deep depression, but I'm glad he finally went and visited them." As me and my girls helped out cleaning up from people, I noticed that my father-in-law was off to himself. I think the realization of the fact that his mother is gone is finally settling in, so I stopped what I was doing and went over to him. I sat down next to him and asked him if he was okay. He told me, "It's going to be hard not having the boss come into my office whenever she wants to interrupt my business meetings just to tell me something isn't working in her house, or I'm doing something wrong." I told him, "She was something else. I can tell you that you have a little bit of her in you. Because in the years I've been a part of this family, I see her spirit come out in you from time to time. You may not notice, but give it a few months, and she'll pay a visit inside you with her sassy attitude." He and I laughed about her being a mess, and he told me, "Did you know that we love you deeply and dearly." I told him, "I love y'all too. I must confess that I had this fear of rejection since the truth has come to light." He told me, "Lord no, you're part of us. You and Steve have given us the best gifts, our grandbabies and great grandbabies. You keep that grumpy butt of a son of mine happy and that's all I ask of you." I started laughing and told him."There's a different mood swing on him on the hour, every hour." He said, "Hey, thanks for talking with me." I told him, "If you need to talk about anything, I'm a listening ear." He asked me, "Are you and Steve coming back for Christmas?" I told him, "That's the plan, but with those grandbabies in tow." He asked me, "Before you leave, can I have a Kerala meal with bread pudding?" He described the meal to me and I told him, "Sure." We continued talking for a while until someone came up to us and started talking to us. I told him, "I better go help out. We'll catch up in a few." I got up and figured I would run to the bathroom before I got too busy. I didn't use the one in the hallway. There was one in Steve's old room. As I walked in the room, Steve was sitting on the bed. I walked up to him and asked him, "Are you okay? Is there something on your mind or if you're not ready to tell me, I understand. You've had a crummy day. "As I sat down I started rubbing his back. He was tense. But as I got up and started to walk away, Steve grabbed my arm and pulled me back to him. He looked at me and said, "Thank you for being there. You're the best damn wife any man could ask for and helping me close that chapter of my life is appreciated more than you know." I told him, "Honey, I'm always going to be here for you and beside you, even when I'm not. Closure was long overdue for you and their families. I think it's great that you're rekindling a relationship with Seth's parents. As for Chase's mother, I don't see closure for that woman in sight." He told me, "It felt great to have them embrace me again. I felt a lot of heavy weight has lifted off of me."

And Steve said, "I saw what you did for Dad. You got him to smile and laugh." I told Steve, "I noticed the reality of Bebe being gone now had finally hit him and a whole lot of people were in there not talking to him. I know you are grieving also, but it's a good time for you to go spend some time with him." He told me, "Yea baby, you're right." Steve stood up towering over me, he bent down, kissed me and told me I love you." I told him I loved him as he walked out of the room. I had to go, but as I rejoined the family, I went back to help clean up and return the dishes back to the ones that brought it. By the end of the day I was worn out. I kept my word to my father-in-law and did what he asked, but it felt so good to be back home. The Monday morning that I returned I saw Brian go into one of my rooms. I was very curious as to why, so I walked in there. The baby that Cole and Isabella brought to my house and a woman I have never seen before was there. Brian said, "Kerala, this is Lacy and the baby's real name is Trinity. Lacy is her birth mother. Brian handed me a DNA test report to let me see. I extended my hand out and shook her hand. I asked her, "How did she get taken from you?" Lacy told me, "I opened up her bedroom window to let out a fresh paint smell. My husband just painted the room before we brought her home. I laid her down for a nap. When I went back into the room to feed her, she was gone." The day before I noticed this girl following me around in our local grocery stores and I asked, "Are you or your family any connections to Isabella?" She told me, "No, I've never met her before, and I'm sorry what happened to you. My family and I want to thank from the bottom of our hearts for all that you've done. You brought my baby back home to me." I told her, "You're welcome, I'm just happy that she's going home to her rightful place." She asked me, "What made you think she was kidnapped?" I told her, "My son's biological father, whom the asshole is a part of this mess, has a family trademark. All of them do, and my twins also have it. I noticed that the mark wasn't on her and she didn't look anything like them. When I looked for her birth certificate, nothing was provided. So it really got me wondering if this dummy would go that low just to get to me. Cole is a drug addict and I didn't want my boys to witness any part of it. In the mix of this, my husband comes along out of nowhere. We started dating until I had them, and we got married. He took my two oldest as his own and raised them. Ever since then, Cole has had it out for me. But before that, Cole would beat me. That's history and I definitely want to see him locked up for good. But that's fixin' to be a story to tell in a few months. As for Miss Trinity here, I did study her behavior. I'm not sure how she was treated by them, but please keep in mind that she's behind a little on her motor skills because of them. I'm sure she will be in classes requiring an Individualized Education Plan (IEP) when she starts school." She asked me, "Can I get a picture with you?" I told her, "Sure." We took a picture and I asked the same. We said our goodbye to each other and I left. It felt good to reunite that baby where she belonged. Lucas and Renata were just about to request to adopt her. Steve and I were going to help them. We didn't want this baby to grow up without a family. So I sent the pictures to our family group chat and my kids congratulated me on it. It surprised us all when Steve joined in and said, "Good job Mama. That little monkey inside your head has worked hard for a break from his hard work. I'm very proud of you and I love you, see you when you get home."

By that afternoon, Brian kept his word and came back into my office with new toys and bought us all lunch. When I got home, Steve greeted me and we discussed meeting the real mother. Each day, I'm still helping Steve and the kids through the loss of Bebe. She made sure that we weren't going to suffer and left Steve and I a nice looking penny. So if I wanted to quit being a doctor I could, but I wanted to stay working so we put it aside for our retirement. As I came home from work that evening from meeting that baby's mother, I was kind of proud of myself. Just wished that Steve was home, but he and Chase were out on their normal cattle run. As I was about to sit down and eat my own dinner Mama was blowing up my phone. When Kyle called me I answered, and he said, "You're not going to believe this shit." I said, "What?" He said, "Your Mama, aka my Aunt Barbara, stuck her foot in her mouth and told the Fall Festival Committee that we were going to play at the Fall Festival." I sighed and said, "Boy she really did it this time." Kyle said, "Well I told my Daddy since she's done this to us and thrown us under the bus, I think their band needs an old-time reunion." I said, "You're damn right they do. I guess since we automatically got signed up by Mama. they're joining us. I'll see if Chase wants to do this with us, and in the process I'll put my foot in Mama's ass. I'll call you in a few days." Kyle said, "Okay." When I got off the phone with Kyle, I called Steve. When he answered I said, "You will not believe who just called me." He said, "Who?" I said, "I just got off the phone with Kyle. He told me that Mama just told the Festival Committee that Chase and I will be there to put on a show." As I was talking to

Steve, I could tell that Mama had already called him because he was giddy as ever and started snickering. He said, "I know all about it baby and so does Chase." I said, "Well, is Chase up for it?" He said, "Yes Mama, I'll do it if you do it." I said, "Welp, looks like Nanny is fixin' to get it. I'm fixin' to get her." After I got off the phone with Steve, I called my Mama. When she picked up I said to her, "Look here old woman. Since you think you have a say in when we should play or get together, then I have a say when the old Rockabillies should get their asses back on the stage. If you and Uncle Joel don't play, then my band and I will not, and I'll make you look like a fool. I love you Mama, but you need to just check with me first before throwing me under the bus. Since I'm under the bus, I'm putting your ass under it too, do you understand me Barbara Noelle?" I could hear the gasp coming from the other side of the phone and Daddy fussing in the background saying you did it, you did it Barbra. I have a tune for you. Time to pay the piper, time to pay the piper. As my Daddy was saying that in the background and laughing at the same time, I told her, "See, Daddy is singing the words for me. My foot is going up your old ass. So you got two weeks to get your shit together." I just hung up on her because Mama just thought she was going to get the upper hand on me. I reversed it on her. The next morning, before my alarm went off, I felt Steve getting into bed and loving all over me. I was glad to know that he was safely home. Before I got out of bed Steve was out. Just as I was getting into my car, Kaden called me and said, "Boy Mama, you sure know how to stir up the pot with Nanny and Papa." I said, "Why?" Kaden said, "Well when you hung up on her last night she was madder than a wet hen. Her and Papa got into it over you and what she had done. It was hilarious as ever. I believe I will come home to my house for a few weeks until we all come back down here." I asked him, "So how much did you get done on their house?" He told me, "The dining room and kitchen are done. I just need to get the den done, and I'll be done with the house." I told him, "Okay, I'll see you when you get here." Kaden had been working on my parents' old Victorian style home off and on for well over two years. I found it crazy that my Daddy came to my defense when it came to something like this. As I walked into the office, I asked Hannah, "Did Bodie and Clayton make it to their drop spot safely?" She told me, "Yea they made it there last night and should be home tomorrow night." I said, "Good. I'm going to close my office for a week because my Mama put me in the Fall Festival show this year." When I told her that I gave her the details about it." She said, "Don't be surprised that Bodie and I will show up there. I'd like to know where our singing doctor comes from." I smiled and told her, "Bring your butt in the morning for us to leave." I made sure Chase had a nice looking stage, thanks to Savannah coming home a few days early to help me out with a lot of things. During our little flight, Kaden was placing bets with his siblings over if Nanny and Papa would get into it. That boy is still laughing about their little old people spat. This had us all laughing because he was reenacting how they were acting that night. I had called Mama when we landed. We had to wait on my in-laws because Steve had invited them to join us. I called Mama and told her, "Don't worry about dinner for us. We will grab something before going there. When we met with my in-laws, they were looking around like they were on another planet, and it was funny. But as the next morning came, Mama and I made breakfast for everyone. When Steve came in and gave Mama a big hug, I knew what he had done. He placed some money in her apron. Steve and I are tired of seeing my parents struggle, so we figured it was time to help them out and give them a break in life. After breakfast Chase and I took off. Before I walked away from Mama I got cocky and told her, "Old woman me and the boys are going to mop y'alls ass all over that stage." Mama looked at me and said, "Oh, so this is

282

going to be a competition?" I said to her, "Maybe." I knew where they were practicing, at Uncle Gabe's old bar, that was still in the family. I made sure the bank didn't get it. I just have my cousins run it. Chase and I made it down to the shop where we were waiting for Kyle. When Kyle walked in he told me,"This is how I think we are going to help Chase out." and in came Kyle's son, Nate. Chase started talking, and I looked at Kyle, and he said, "I think this should be a good fit. Our kids and Chase could make a good band." So Chase has Nate, Tucker, Riley with Noah's girls as back up. We stepped back to see how good they could work together. It impressed us. This isn't our kids first meeting. They hit it off well with each other growing up, so they started getting their music together. Dex and I started trying to put our songs off and on. By the end of the day we stopped and figured we would meet up in the morning. When we got back to Mama and Daddy's house, I said to everyone, "Why don't we take everyone out to eat? Mama isn't back yet, and she said she would meet with us at the café. I smiled at Steve. It was a treat to go back and really show the kids the place where we met for the first time. And Steve asked me, "I thought they closed it years ago?" I told him, "Yes, but they just reopened it with new owners." As we got to the café, Steve was happy to tell the kids and my in-laws our back story of how he and I came together. I looked at the spot that I had gone into labor with Andrew and Lucas and told the kids, "This is the spot I went into labor with Andrew and Lucas." They asked their Daddy, "Where were you?" He told them, "Soaking wet chasing after my troops." As Steve was talking to the kids and telling them things we were waiting for Mama to show up. Within 15 minutes of standing around, Mama finally shows up. As we walked into the door, I was taken aback. As we were getting ready to sit down this kid came from behind the counter, and about to break his neck, he said to me, "I know you." I looked at him, and he said, "You used to work for my grandfather. He would talk about you all the time." I asked this kid if his grandfather was still alive. He told me no, and it was a little heartbreaking to hear that Joe is no longer here. He told me, "Grandpa would talk about you to his sons and grandchildren all the time." He and I were swapping stories of myself and Joe to each other until my bunch was getting frustrated with me. This kid and the waitress were waiting on me and this kid to get done talking with each other when I told him, "I guess you better get busy." He said, "Yes I better get yall's order done." After we ate, Steve and I took the family down to our old apartment. I can tell that since Steve and I moved out, the base closed two years after we were married. As we stood there looking at the rundown old apartment, Steve was talking away to the kids about where he and I started. I'm looking at the burned down building that Cole burned. I just shook my head and thought why in the hell did I ever get with him. I keep asking myself over and over inside my head, why.

As soon as we got back to Mama and Daddy's house, Chase and I started going over our song catalogs. I brought out my very first catalog and Daddy pointed out one song and said, "Do you remember this one?" I said, "Oh yea, that one has a little history." Daddy told me, "I want to hear it." I told him, "Okay, to me that's the very first song I had ever made. It was the bomb song that started it all with me and Mr.Doven." I had assured Daddy that would be my opening song. By Friday morning, Kerala Jade and the Bomb Band was set and ready to go for Saturday night. As we're having breakfast, I could tell my own Mama had forgotten how much hard work it is to just put it together for one night because her old ass was dragging after breakfast. I walked into the kitchen and helped Mama with the dishes. She and I started pointing at each other about who's going to get the crowd moving better. That's when she told me, "I will make you cry just before your ass gets up on the stage." I looked at her and said, "Really. I doubt that shit Mama. I noticed that my own Mama was getting to be a big head over thinking she's got things on her side nice and sweet. When she reached into her apron her facial expression changed so much. She read the note that Steve had written to her, and she started crying. So I shoved her into the mudroom and sat her down. I told her it's time that I start taking care of them. I was confused if it was tears of joy or something else. She told me, "Kerala I can't." I told her, "Yes you can. Take it and enjoy retirement. Hell, Daddy is working himself to the bone, and you're doing the same right next to him. It's time to relax." When Mama pulled out her money bucket she placed it in there. I told her to pay your bills off and I walked out of the room. My Mama was in her emotional breakdown moment. When she would have one of those, she would always run me, Shane or Noah off. A lot of tears had fallen in that room and that was Mama's space when things were going wrong or for tears of happiness. Mama always refused to let us see her cry.

It wasn't until that afternoon that Mama was back to being herself. I knew she hadn't told Daddy about the money. I knew that once everyone left after the weekend activities, she would tell him. My parents had a full house with my in-laws. I could tell that they were having a great time and learning about my background of culture. Later on that night Steve and I attended the Fall Festival and each turn Steve and I made, there was someone that I knew wanting to talk to me. It felt good knowing that I didn't have to worry about Cole popping up anywhere in sight. My kids were getting a chance to explore my hometown without Steve or I hovering over them for their safety. But with being in my hometown, I started to feel like I was being pulled, once again left from right, by people which always draws me out of my comfort zones. I hate that feeling. It makes me feel depressed in my own way. But it wasn't until Steve and I got back to my parents' house, while we were laying in bed, that I told him, "I don't want to do this singing mess anymore. Everyone is doing it again. Treating me like I'm someone I'm not." And Steve told me, "I don't want you to feel pressured into doing something that you don't want to do. But I'll promise you this, that I'll make sure it's on your own terms. Tomorrow night just go and give it your all and have fun." He was right. I did need to look at this way. It was for fun and to help out with my hometown to restore the downtown area. That's what the money was going towards with this show that my family, and I were putting on. When morning came around, I just rolled out of the bed and put my hair up in a messy bun. I already knew the routine of who was doing my hair and make-up. So I walked into the room that Chase was sleeping in, and I told him,"Get up, you gotta get up on stage and shake your ass in front of a bunch of girls tonight." As I walked back into my old room, I got dressed because Dex was fixin' to come and get us for the day. When I got up fully, I told him, "Did you get your clothes so you can change later on?" He told me, "I gave them to Aunt Martha yesterday." So as he got up he came out and said, "Girls huh." I told him, "Uhh yeah, you're single, remember?" Chase said, "Mama, these girls around here might whip my ass." I told him, "That's the type of woman you need to keep your ass whipped and in line. These young ladies around here are just like your little ole'mama. You said you're kind of looking for a little bit of me in a girl. So here you go. Get rid of that nasty ass mistake on your finger. It's bad luck." He said, "You know Mama, the old saying is girls go after men with wedding bands on." I snapped at him and said, "Yea, they're called whore's and homewreckers son. There is an old saying, you can't turn a whore into a housewife. Get moving. Dex is outside waiting."

As we were heading downstairs, I looked over at Daddy, and he said, "Kerala Jade, go whip your Mama's ass on that stage tonight." I told Daddy, "Don't worry. We will." I had given

Daddy my old devilish grin. As I walked out the door, Dex was showing Steve something on his phone. Dex was trying to put his phone quickly away. I knew both of them too well. They were hiding something from me. But after Steve and I kissed each other I got into Dex's car. As soon as we took off, I started drilling the fuck out of him about what he was showing Steve. Dex was looking at me out of the corner of his eye. I said, "Start telling me, or I'll make you squeal like a little bitch and start talking like porky the pig." He said, "Alright, it was a funny video of a cat." I looked at him and said, "Bullshit." I decided to drop it. When we got to the fairground, mine and Dex's eye's were in disbelief of what he and I were seeing. There was a real life concert stage setting at the end of the county's rodeo arena. This is something that we have never been on or played on. The town's Mayor Walker came up to us and said, "I hope this fits you perfectly for tonight Kerala." I was so lost for words all I could say to him was, "This could work." He said, "Good, good, anything to please our hometown girl." I just looked at him, smiled and said, "Well, we have to do a sound check." Dex and I walked up to the stage and I looked back at Chase. I asked Chase, "Are you going to be able to handle this?" He told me, "Mama, are you going to be able to handle this type of stage?" I told him, "Son, I don't know." He said, "Okay, there's your answer from me, I don't know either." On the edge of the stage sat, a baby grand piano and I knew Mama was fixing to bring her game on with that joker. When I saw Uncle Joel he said, "So what do you think of this Kerala?" I said, "It's too much." He said, "Well this is all for you girl. You better get it up there and cut one hell of rug up there tonight." I told him, "With what this country is doing, I'm going to have to." When we started our sound check, it went great for us. When we got off I saw that it was going to be a family reunion behind the stage area. When I saw Aunt Donna, it was said, done and over with. My confidence was up. She and I were catching up with each other. I saw other family members that I haven't seen in a long time from my Mama and Uncle Joel's side. I asked Uncle Joel, "After we get done, do you think we can all collaborate for fun?" He said, "That's what I was going to ask the four of you." I told him, "Yeah, I think Mama and I can sing a few songs together." So as we were all chatting it up, Aunt Martha came in. She tells me, "Girl, that messy bun bull isn't going to work for us." As my kids sit around me, they are starting to see the hard work that's being put into this mess. I looked at Matthew and told him, "Run to the store for me please, and get me a bottle of lighter fluid." Everyone looked at me and I said, "What? I'm out of my lighter fluid." Which was a damn lie. I'm fixin' to rip the hell out of that piano. If they want a show, by God, I was going to give this county what they paid for. By 4:00 PM that afternoon, Josh comes up to me and says, "I got that little drink that you like sitting in a cooler behind the cattle gate if you want one." I told him, "Can you let me eat my food first?" When I got done eating, Aunt Martha started working on my hair. When she was done with my hair and make-up I went and got dressed behind this makeshift curtain. When I came out Josh, Dex and Kyle were motioning me to come to them. I saw they poured me a shot of whiskey. I told them. "There's no better time than before show time." As we were standing around, trying to get our buzz on, I could hear the arena start to fill up. Three minutes before Chase had gone up there, the Mayor was flapping his jaws about my life and where and what I was doing now. I really disliked it, but it was what it was and it was the truth. As the four of us were standing back there watching Chase, I could tell he was a little bit nervous about being up there in front of that many people. From what we could see, the whole damn county and plus was sitting in the stands. I can say we were getting a little excited. When Chase got off the stage, he looked at me and said, "That shit out in front is a monster Mama." I said, "Really?" When I

288

heard Mama up on the stage, it shocked the shit out of Chase. He said, "I guess Nanny did have to pay the piper and that is you Mama." I said, "Yes she is." Chase said to me, "Damn Mama, you and Nanny sound alike, but her voice has got a little bit of raspiness to it." As I stood there, I missed the sound of her songs and seeing them playing. But she was really kicking my ass up there already. As we were hanging out behind the stage, kicking back a few, we thought we better scale back or this would be a train wreck on our end. As Mama started talking, she said to them, "I wrote this for my daughter and her husband." When she started singing, my damn tears were falling. It was beautiful. It explains Steve and I, in three minutes, how he spoils me and how we both are with each other. The boys had to make me stop crying or my make-up would start running and I would have to fix it. When Mama and Uncle Joel got off the stage, I told her, "You're a mess, Mama for making me almost cry." When my cousin's got up on the stage and started playing the bomb song, before I could join them, the crowd started cheering. I had to just start singing before I could join them. I looked out there and a little bit of stage fright set in on me. I couldn't believe the turn-out. So I started singing loud and proud within the middle of the bomb song. I started letting loose and dancing a little bit when I saw Shelby, Amy, and Leah at the end of the stage taking pictures of me like crazy. I started singing to them a little bit. I was trying to work both sides of the stage, but I can tell Kyle, Josh and I let loose on that stage and put a hundred percent in what we had on our songs. When we got down to the last song on our list, I sat down at the piano and I started ripping into it. Mama and the rest joined in with this collaboration. Once Mama and I got started trying to outdo each other. It was a mess between me and Mama. Once we were finished and standing behind the stage, I was dripping with sweat, along with everyone else. When Steve came back there, I took one look at him and told Steve, "I'm ready to go home." He said, We're going, baby. You did a damn good job. You have my side of the family thinking that you're famous. I told them just around here, but baby, you never did tell me that you almost had a contract. Now I see why they are crazy about you around here." I told Steve, "I'm sorry. I thought I did." He said, "Baby, it's okay, because if you did, there wouldn't be me and you." As Steve and I were talking to everyone, I started gathering my stuff. The newspaper staff came behind the stage and wanted to get a picture of us, but I was ready to blow this place and go home to my own four walls. But as we were leaving, there was a small line outside waiting for me. All I could do was just smile and start signing their stuff. I overheard Amy talking to Steve, "So she's not famous, huh little brother?" And Steve had said to her, "Well, just around these parts, I guess." My mother-in-law started taking more pictures of me signing things for people. I think my in-laws went a little gaga over what they had just seen. But as Steve and I were walking out of the place, I felt his arm around my back, and he had kissed me. I was so hyped up when we got back to Mama and Daddy's house it took me until 1:00 AM in the morning to finally go to sleep. I felt bad for Steve because I was keeping him up. When the next morning came, Kaden was going to take Glamy and Poppy back to the airport for us. I felt as if a small hangover and throat Chakra had hit Mama, Chase and I, but when Steve and I boarded the plane, I was out. When Steve and I got into the door, I went and soaked in some bath water. When I got out and put my clothes on, I made it to the bed and passed out. It had taken me a full workweek to get my rest pattern back into normal. When the first weekend of Thanksgiving came around we had our family photos done, but what was on my guys mind was hunting. I knew there had been a lot on Steve's mind. It was time for him to go and clear his mind. So the next morning he took off by mid-afternoon. Savannah's boyfriend finally made it to our home and I had been calling him the wrong name the entire time. He corrected me and told me his name is Trey, I apologized to him for Savannah making me misunderstand his name. I could tell he was a city boy. As we were getting acquainted with each other I knew I had to start dinner. He sat on a stool and we continued to talk. I wanted to watch his actions with my daughter. Steve had Stephanie's boyfriend wrapped around his finger and the two are buddies. Clayton is good to Stephanie. Steve and I know who wears the pants, and it's Stephanie, she has him whipped. I could tell that Tray had a different accent than ours and asked him, "So how did you and Savannah meet?" He told me, "We met at a dance club while I was in town for a business meeting, and I've been flying back forth ever since for a year and half now. After he told me that I asked him, "So where are you really from?" He told me, "New Hampshire." As I'm talking to him, Clayton comes in and right behind him is Steve. They were all chatty. Steve comes up to me and I look up to him. We greeted each other and I asked him, "Did you get me a deer?" He told me, "No Ma'am, but I can try again tomorrow." He turned his head to Trey, and he asked him, "Who are you?" Savannah said, "This is Trey." Steve started drilling his ass and came out and told him, "I'm only going to say this hatefully to you once, if you lay a damn hand or gaslight my daughter, I'm the last fucking face you'll see. Do we have an understanding? He looked at Steve and told him, "Sir, I've been seeing her for a year and a half now, and I have no intention of doing any harm to her." Steve told him. "Well you said something I want to hear, so welcome." They started a decent conversation with each other. As we sat down for dinner, small conversation was still carrying on between us.

When Steve and I went to bed he said, "Baby I need my lucky charm to go with me, so can you please go with me?" I looked at him and said, "So you're asking me to go play with you in your deer stand?" He said, "Oh you mean we can play with each other instead of really looking for deer? Hmm, you're gonna make my mind run wild." I told him, "Slow down cowboy. If I pull that trigger and get us a deer, you're cooking dinner with me for a week. And if you pull the trigger, I'm all yours of where, when and any time, so I'll go with you." He said, "How about I help you anyway, because you and I always make it fun and loving, and you throw in some extra cuddling before you leave for work." I told him, "If that's what you want, you got it." I told him, "You seem like you've kinda cleared your mind." He told me, "Just a little, but my focus is on you right now. Woman you've already got my mind running crazy." I had snickered at him, and he moved me closer to him. He said, "You know baby, you and I have kinda been running in circles, and you know I hate that shit." I told him, "We've had a crazy year." He said, "Yes we have and some of it is fixin' to drag into the new year. But my blessings are you're still with me. That was the biggest scare." I told him, "The circle is closing and we're getting back to us."

The next morning I got my ass up and got my clothes on. I still found myself wanting to sleep more, so when I got to his stand it was 2:00 AM and Steve lit up a small heater. I saw the cot, and he got a sleeping bag and I went for it. He asked me, "Is there room for me?" I told him, "There's always room for you, but I thought you were supposed to be hunting for deer?" He says. "If I get my extra cuddling with you, I'll choose you over a deer." So I padded the cot and we passed out just before sunrise. I got up and sat in the chair and waited. When I saw a deer with bigger antlers than the one I killed before, years ago, I looked over at Steve still out. I told myself this is going to be fun with him in the kitchen, so I raised up the gun and fired one shot, one kill, down went the deer and woke Steve up. He looked at me and snickered, and he said, "Well baby, let's go see what you got. As we walked up to the deer, he counted the points of the antlers. I bagged a 15 point deer and Steve looked at me and said, "Damn baby, this one is bigger than the one you killed years ago. Good job! So I guess you got me in the kitchen for two weeks." I smiled at him and told him, "It will be fun." As we got back up to the house, our boys were just now waking up and Steve told them, "Y'all done and fending for yourself on breakfast. Mama killed this one, and I think she deserves a good little nap." Our boys looked the deer over and said, "No way Daddy. You helped her get it." He told them, "Nope. I was asleep on the cot." Kaden said, "Man I guess I'm gonna have to take Mama with me." Steve told them, "I'll be damn. Mama's my lucky charm and don't ask her again to go with you." As they were picking at each other, I walked off. I asked the grandkids if they wanted to come to Lala's room and watch cartoons. I told them, "Let me get a shower and when I open up the door that's when you can come in." So I went and took a shower. I figured I would lay up with my grandbabies. I put something comfortable on and opened the door. There they stood. So they climbed in the bed, and we picked out a cartoon. By that afternoon, Lucas came in and told me, "Mama, I'll make dinner for us." I told him, "Okay." The next morning, before the rest of the family came, Thanksgiving went on with a blessing. I knew my side of the family would be back for the trial in February because they have been summoned as a witness. That was something Steve and I weren't looking forward to. I was happy to get my family photos. To me, that was my Christmas present. But as Kaden walked out the door, peacefulness and grandbabies' messes were everywhere. As soon as I turned around to see Steve, I walked over to where he was sitting and placed myself into him. We were finally alone and we weren't holding back from each other. But somewhat that morning, I felt as if it wasn't enough. So I said to him, "I think I need a little bit more of you." When Steve placed himself inside of me he didn't hold back on loving me. I felt every single thrust of love from him. Both of us expressed our feelings of love for one another. And I, myself, loved every inch of being selfish and having my time with him. Each time that he and I make love to each other I never rush up after we make love. I enjoy feeling his naked body next to mine. I got up and took a shower. When I got out, Steve came back into the room with coffee. He kissed me. I looked at him and asked him, "Are you ready to have fun with me tonight in the kitchen? I think I want to make the very first meal I made for you." When I said that, I could see he was a little giddy about it because I haven't made that for him in years. I told him, "You're helping, and we will start at 5:00 PM." I saw he got a little excited about what we're going to do. As he was fixin' to say something to me, his phone started ringing. When Steve answered he just said, "This better be fucking good boy. You are messing up my time with Mama." I knew it was one of our boys and when the word, well?, came out of Steve's mouth, I knew it wasn't going to be good because we were starting to be at the beginning of calving season which is kind of hard on Steve. It begins during this time of year and goes through March. I figured out which one of our boys he was talking to, it was Seth. When he told him, "Hang on. I'll be there. As Steve started getting his pants and boots on, he looked at me and said, "Sorry baby, but we've got an abandoned calf." I asked him, "If you don't mind, I want to go with you to see it?" When I asked him that, he had a shocked look on his face. He said, "Hell yeah, you can come." So I ran into the closet and got dressed. I breezed by Steve who was still trying to get his stuff gathered up. I was standing outside waiting for him. As soon as he came out he told me, "It's cold, so go get in the ranch truck." We drove over to where Seth was, and I was sitting inside the cab. I saw Steve and Seth pick up the calf and place it inside the cab. I asked Seth if he had fed the horses yet, and he told me, "No Mama, not yet." When we got back to the barn, I got out and went in to check on Lilly. When I got to her stall, there stood a foal beside her. I started flipping out. I couldn't believe my eyes and that's when Seth came in. Seth was in disbelief himself. When Steve came in this shocked him too. All of us had waited on Blue and Lilly to hook up. We were about to give up and there stood a beautiful foal with a mix of Blue and Lilly. I asked Steve, "Do you think I should call the vet?" Steve had told me, "Yes." So I called the vet. Once I was off the phone with him, I called Kaden and told him, "Get your butt to the barn. It's Lilly." Once he made it to the barn, Steve and Kaden were discussing Lilly and the new foal. As Steve and I got back into the truck, we took off to find the mama cow. Steve said to me, "Baby, they need to hurry with my mama and baby building. I feel like they're milking us on getting it done." As we reached the west side of the field, there stood the mama cow. Steve was reviewing his papers that he kept on every cow we have and with this one, Steve and I had lost so many calves out of her. He said, "Well, off to the deep freeze she goes." We headed back to the barn and I stood there looking at both of the newborns. I found myself getting attached to this calf for some reason, the same for the foal. When we went back to the house, Steve showered while I started making dinner. When I saw Steve sit down I wasn't going to ask him to help me. He had a lot going on today. As I had my back turned from him, I felt him come up behind me wrap his arms around me and started kissing on my neck. Steve stopped, smiled at me and asked me, "So can I help?" I told him, "Yes, please cut these up for me." I moved my little step stool by him. I looked over at him and kissed him. As I started nibbling on his ear, I knew he was about to hit the floor and I walked away from him. I turned around and smiled at him. That's when he took off running through the house, closing the blinds and locking down the house. He started flirting with me and I stood closer to him. As he took my bra off, he suggested that I go get comfortable since it was just the two of us. So I walked off and thought since we were having pot roast and I kinda wanted to recreate our first time with each other, but only the kitchen edition version, we were literally all over each other and flirting at the same time. I could tell Steve was loving the hell out of this kitchen fun that we had going on. Surprisingly, we got dinner done and went for round three of loving each other. When Monday morning came I kissed him before leaving out the door. But once I got into the office, before I had seen my first child, I got a phone call from the Board of Health. They said, "Dr. Nichols, we have come to the decision that we feel it is no longer safe for you to practice studying Autism cases. We feel you have put a child in danger. So, as of today, we will revoke your Autism License. When I heard those words, I was pissed. I just lost it because of Cole. I got up and walked into the front office. I told Missy and Alexia that, "We can no longer schedule Autism cases. The Board of Health just called and revoked my license. All over this stupid shit that just happened." I was mad in my own way about losing it and bummed out. When Missy asked me, "So what about your Pediatric License?" I told her, "We're safe there. They are not going to take that away from me." By the time I fully simmered down about my license being taken away from me, I began to get pissed again. Around lunchtime, when Amy called me, she said, "Asha is spreading rumors about you and Steve getting a divorce." I just chuckled, laughed, and said, "This is another thing I need on my list. Amy, it sounds like our treaty between each other is over. I'm tired of her shit and I need to put her in her place. I know it's all a damn lie. She's just trying to make herself feel better. Jealousy is what she's trying to make me feel. That's it. The gloves are off, and I'm ready to go start fighting." That's when Amy told me, "Girl, it's not worth it." I told her, "Yeah, maybe you're right." Amy told me, "Perhaps Mom will call Steve today and tell him what's going on. That might diffuse it there." By the end of my day, I was so tired of the bullshit. I just wanted to go home and lay it all out on Steve. But just before I went home, I stopped by the local grocery store that we have in our town. As I walked up to the checkout counter I saw the little girl that had a big crush on Seth when she was in school with him. As I'm standing there, I noticed that she is with child and smiling at me like you wouldn't believe. I had asked her how she was doing, and she said to me great. I waited on her to ask me how Seth was, but I had to look at it the opposite way, that she found her person and hopefully that she was happy. I still laugh and giggle about how she used to chase Seth everywhere, and he had nothing to do with her. I thought she was a very beautiful young woman. As I was driving home, I had the feeling of me just wanting to throw in the towel and give it all up. Sitting at home with Steve and helping him take care of the ranch sounded good, but in a way with my practice, I felt a little bit burnt out also. As I walked in the house, he looked like he was ready to start cooking with me. Then all of a sudden, I just started letting out my problems to Steve, like I should be, and I had asked him, "Do you ever get so burnt out on something that you worked so hard to get?" Steve asked me, "Baby, are you implying on wanting to give up on something?" I said, "Yea kind of, sort of, like today for instance. I got a phone call today from the Board of Health that my Autism License is revoked until further notice. They feel that since this shit has happened that I'm putting a child in danger, and they may or may not give it back to me. I won't know until after the trial is done." He asked me, "Did they take your Pediatric License?" I told him, "No, that is safe." Steve hugged me, gave me a kiss and told me, "It will be okay baby. I promise this here was just a little push, and you know how to stand tall up on your ladder. My advice for you is to push that license off of your ladder and go bigger or come home. I'm sorry you had a crummy day." I told Steve, "I believe I will retire in the next three years." Steve asked me, "Then what are you going to do?" I told him, "I'm going to drive you carefully up the wall." Steve said to me, "I can't wait." When he said, "I was joking." As I was going back and forth with him in the kitchen, he was just hearing me out, and I guess you could say that I did have a crummy day. But after dinner Steve asked me if I wanted to go to the barn to see the calf and foal. Before he could finish, I told him yes. He just smiled at me. As we walked down to the barn I grabbed up a bottle and filled it. I walked over to the calf and started feeding it. As I did that I felt as if my daily issues left me. By the next day, Asha was still stirring up the fucking pot. I knew that the little treaty Ed and Steve had with each other was about to be broken. This chick must be on some meds the way she's posting lies. I know that she blocked me on my own page, but the dumb bitch forgot that I had my business page for a media outlet. I was watching everything she was posting. When I went back into my personal account, I loved what Steve was telling everyone, that basically she's a liar.

When I got home that afternoon, Steve surprised me big time. As I walked into the house, Steve cooked dinner which was out of the norm for him to do. I thought it was really sweet of him to cook for me. But what got to me in a sad way, it was a dish that my grandmama used to cook for us. I had not eaten it since she passed away. I knew that Steve went digging into my recipes to find it. All I could say to him was, "You're kidding me." He told me, "No help whatsoever." I was being sarcastic to him and said, "You trying to earn extra cuddling points?" Steve said to me, "Hell yeah, baby I am." I told him, "If it's anything close to my great-great-grandmother's, I'll throw in getting in the bath with me tonight. And you and I both know where that leads." When I said that he started smiling, and he said to me, "Baby, I made this for you since you had a shitty day yesterday." I said, "Awe, I'm proud of you. This really has made my day for sure." I could tell he put great effort into making dinner for us. I said, "You're close to how she used to make it." I asked Steve, "So what have you done today besides cook your first dinner for us?" Steve told me, "Nothing, but carefully making this for you." I said, "Is there something else that you need to tell me?" Steve truthfully told me about what Asha was going around saying, and I told him, "I know Amy and Leigh called me yesterday and told me. We were all laughing about it, and then again, I'm not because she sounds like she's sick in the head. She wants your attention, and I better not catch you messaging her. I see what she's been doing all over Facebook. She's blocked my personal account, but no one knows I control my pediatrician business account. I saw what you posted this morning. You couldn't have put it any better in wording than fuck off and leave us alone." Steve asked me, "Are you mad at me?" I told him, "No, but please don't interact with her in person or on social media." Steve said, "Baby, I'm not." Steve and I were getting ready for bed, Steve asked me to step on the scale and I looked at him like he was crazy. So I did. The week before I weighed about 98 pounds, which is perfect for my height. As I got on the scale, I noticed that I had lost eight pounds. I was 90 pounds and the look on his face said it all to me. I knew this was dangerous, but there had been so much going on that I found myself not hungry at all sometimes. And that's when Steve started in, "Baby, please at least try and gain some of it back." I promised him that I would. As we were laying there, Steve and Marty were texting each other back and forth. Steve asked me, "Do you want to go on his cattle run with me? Hannah is going." I told him, "Sure, I'll go." He told me, "We will be close to Mom and Dad's house so we can go over there and stay a night or two." I told him, "Your Mom and I can go and get Christmas shopping done the next morning."

Just when I thought my week couldn't get any worse, I got a phone call from one of my patient's parents telling me that her kids were hit by a car while trying to get on a bus and one of them was my five-year-old tot and her brothers. She was just in my office the other day. My heart was breaking for Mona, so I had given her my personal cell phone number. I told her that I would rent a hotel room for a few weeks, so they could get some rest. Later on, before we closed the office, I found out that the kids were in critical condition. So when I got home, I kept telling myself this is part of the job Kerala. I cooked Steve and I something to eat before we left out on his cattle run. As Steve and I had got ready to leave, Bodie called Steve and something set him off. When he told Bodie, "If he says one word to me or opens his mouth, I'm putting my foot in his ass." I found myself amused a little and I knew that asshole Steve might pop up somewhere tonight. I wasn't in the mood to see him tonight. I found myself still busy with my three that were in critical condition and I still was mad about the driver that wasn't paying attention. Looking at his phone, but as we pulled into the yard, Steve asked me if I needed to go to the restroom. When he asked me that, I knew I better go, because with this bunch, there's no stopping. As I walked inside the sale barn to use the bathroom, I heard someone walk in and a raspy voice said, "It's me Kerala." I knew it was Leo's wife. I was glad that she let me know that she was there with me. As I left the restroom, she came out right behind me. She said, "Kerala I hate to ask, but do you have any info on the accident this morning?" I told her, "I can't give you a lot of information due to the Health Insurance Portability and Accountability Act (HIPAA) regulations. But I can tell you that they are in critical condition." She told me, "I saw Brian and Seth at the Casey's this morning. It was a few hours after it happened and your son, Seth, looked disgusted at the accident." I told her, "Thank you for letting me know this." I thought I'd better call Seth and check on him as soon as I can. But as Hannah came up to me, she hugged me and told me, "You've had one hell of a week girl." I told her, "I know. I just wish there was a reverse button for this week, but then again, I would be looking for the fast-forward one too." When Stephanie came up to me and gave me a big hug and told me the news is all over town about the Morrow family." I told her, "We know." She said, "Mama, I'm sorry that it's one of your patients, but Seth came into my office this morning before going home. I could tell this was bothering him a lot." As I was about to say something else, we could hear the guys yelling at us to get in the trucks. As I got in the truck Steve said to me, "Come on, we've got to go." I said, "Well we were waiting on y'all." As we were traveling, I focused on my charts and my tot while hearing the road chatter that was going on. Steve asked me, "How was your day?" And I told Steve, "I have three of my kids that were involved in a car accident this morning before getting on the bus. The driver of the car was on the phone and passed the bus before realizing that they had hit the kids. I have a tot who is five in critical care, and I'm texting the hospital pediatrician staff for a check in, I've been doing this off and on all day today since they got into the hospital. I'm sorry, honey, that I'm not off the clock with this case." Steve said to me, "Baby you're just checking in with them and being a good doctor. Not a whole lot of them will do that." I told him, "I don't need you mad at me, but I've rented the family a room for two weeks, so the parents can get some rest." Steve told me, "Baby I'm not mad. It's awesome that you're just trying to help them out." I said to Steve, "It just makes me so mad that a person was more worried about where they were going instead of paying attention to what was around them. My tot is such a sweet little girl and brave as ever when Alexis gives her a shot. Her mom said she gets excited whenever she sees me and her brothers are a mess. They reminded me of Seth and Chase, always asking me questions about our boys." Steve said, "Awe baby, I'm so sorry that you have had such a shitty week." My phone started ringing. I picked it up, and it was

Chrissy, Mona's sister. She told me, "Kerala, I'm going to be the first to tell you Dianna just passed. She's had too many seizures today and a tonic-clonic just hit. Her little body couldn't take it anymore." All I could say was, "I'm sorry about this. If there's anything else I can do for you, please let me know. And please reach out to me when the services will be." She told me, "I sure will." When I hung up the phone, I started an office conference and told them that, "Little Dianna had just passed away. The brothers are comatose to keep the swelling down, they'll let me know when the service will be. I'm asking my side of the staff to join me and Hannah said my staff will be with you." When I hung up the phone I thought of that first time when the baby passed away in my arms. That's when Steve asked me, "Baby is this your first?" I told Steve, "No, my second. The first one was when we lived in Arizona. When I was doing my clinical work, the mom just delivered the baby. The doctor handed the newborn to me, and it died in my arms as I was taking it to the weight table. The newborn had asphyxia. It was born with birth defects. It fucked me up for a little while and I had to come to terms with that possibility being a part of my job. It's really something they don't teach you in med school. The reason I didn't tell you is because we just had Stephanie, and you got mad as hell when I moved her into our room. I laid there watching her sleep, it took me about a month to kind of understand and unwrap my mind off of it. And Steve said to me, "Baby, I'm sorry for those years that I really wasn't there even if I was there." I told him, "It's water under the bridge now." Bodie comes on the radio, and tells me sorry that I lost one of my patients. And Steve told him. "She's still trying to swallow down the news back here." They all got to talking about how the accident happened. And that little motherfucker named River, who Steve can't stand, is really rude and disrespectful, just had to put in his two cents, "Awe little baby gets squished, the doctor is going to squall about it."

Marty said, "I think we need to take a fuel break." So we pulled into a place and I had enough of the day, so I got up and went into the bunk. With what had just been said, everyone was pissed off. As I was laying there, within 20 minutes, Steve came inside the bunk and asked if I was handling this okay. I told him. "Just a little bit, but that little dumbass just made me mad." Steve told me, "Well, River isn't going anywhere for a while. We fixed his ass up." I asked him, "Are you going to be upset if I don't come back up there?" Steve said, "No baby, if you want to rest go for it, from the week that you're having you sound like you could use some rest." Steve had kissed me and said, "I love you too. Get some rest. You need it." After he left the bunk, I laid there looking through my phone and I thought I'd better check in on Seth. I told him the news, and he said, "Mama I've never seen a mess like this before." I told him, "Son this is something that you never get over. It's part of our job. It will fade away in time. Yes, there will be some days when you think if I could have done something better. While you're present, the facial expressions of others will never leave you after you tell them the news." When Seth texted me back, he told me, "Mama, you're right. When I looked at Mrs. Mona this morning it was as if her soul had left her body. The numbness. It's all kind of haunting, but it is something that I have signed up to help others. Mama I need to stop texting. I have company over and I would rather not be rude to them. Love you Mama. Make sure Daddy keeps it under the speed limit." When he told me that I stopped texting him, rolled over and went to sleep. By that Friday afternoon we made it to Phil and Shelby's house. As we were pulling in there stood my Matthew, waiting for us. When Steve opened the door for me, I got out and hugged my baby boy. He told me, "Sorry Mama about your loss of one of your tot's." I told him, "It will be okay on my end. Just pray for the family because it's going to be a long and hurtful road for them." I looked up and saw Shelby. She looked a little antsy for some reason. Matthew said, "She's cooking one of Nanny's meals." I told Matthew. "Okay what is it with this bunch? Your Daddy cooked for me the other night and I do believe he is loving being in the kitchen with me." When I said that Matthew said, "I knew he would. Thanks for helping Faitha over the phone with our dinner. I know that you are helping her." I said to Matthew, "So when is this Mama going to meet this girl?" He told me, "When you get back here on the next trip. She's working overtime since it's the holidays." We sat down for dinner. I noticed something was amiss with my grandmother's recipe that Mama sent to Shelby. I wasn't going to be rude to my mother-in-law and tell her she forgot to put some extra spice in the dish. I politely told her, "It is almost just like my grandmother's." I was bragging hard to her about Steve finally fixing dinner for me for the first time. After dinner I helped Shelby clean up. She and I were talking about the stores to hit up tomorrow and what time we should get up. The next morning came and we shopped until we dropped and headed back. But as always with Steve, as soon as I had put the grandkid's gifts in Steve's old room, Steve was ready to roll out. So I told Phil and Shelby, "See both of you in a few weeks." As we headed home, I could tell Steve wasn't going to let off of it, so I just let him be. When we got home that Monday morning I got ready to go to the hospital and attend little Dianna's service's. As I checked on Mona's boys, the swelling was slowly going down, but when they both woke up they were going to get the most heartbreaking news ever about their little sister. When I arrived at the church, Missy and Alexa were waiting for me. We got to talking about the accident and both of the boys, but as we waited on Hannah and her staff to show up she said to me, "That was a wild ride." I smiled and told her, "Yea it was." As Hannah and I stood there with our staff we kept getting looks and whispers of I have never in my life heard of any office of any doctors closing their doors to show support to the family. I had to hold Alexa's mouth because she popped out with, "Yea we are here to show compassion." But once we saw the viewing of little Dianna, Hannah and I noticed a lot of mistakes that were made while she was in their care. I told her I'm going to ask for the chart while she was there. As we walked over to Mona and gave her our condolences, I just couldn't get past seeing her pain of losing a child. I understood her pain. After the service Hannah and I, with our staff, left. That's when Missy said, "Did you guys see that baby's arm?" I said, "Yes and I'm going to say this once. They blew that baby's arm to where no meds could get into her system. Everything looked rushed. I mean sure, at the moment when everything was happening, someone should have checked their work." They agreed with what I was saying. When I got home Steve had a mixed drink ready for me. I was well overdue for the bullshit that I have been through. As a few weeks passed, we all packed up and headed back out to Phil and Shelby's for Christmas. As we got on the plane, Chase was having one hell of a fit to be seated next to me. He traded his seat with Seth and I couldn't figure out why until we got in midair. Chase handed me his song catalog and I pulled mine out of my purse. I asked him, "Is this why you brought your guitar?" He told me, "Yes, Mama, I'm skimming something. Yea, it's time to bust it fully out. Besides Mama, you look stressed out and you've been singing all over the house when I'm around." I told him, "I was hoping you'd sing with me." Chase said, "Mama, all you gotta do is ask." I was reading his lyrics. I felt every word he wrote had his heart, soul and a lot of feelings poured into them. While I was reading Chase's, Steve grabbed my catalog and read what I had written so far. I gave it back to Chase once we got to my in-laws. I always find myself feeling jet lag and sick as ever after a flight. Steve still had my catalog book. As I was laying down, he came in with it and pointed out a song to me, telling me he wanted to hear it. I told him, "Okay, just let me get over this midair hangover." By the next morning they were preparing for the dinner party that evening. Whatever Chase had going on, I was involved with, along with his Poppy. As I laid there watching Steve sleep, I placed my head on his chest. Each move I would make, I could hear his heart beating faster. Somehow he woke up and put me in his death lock. I figured whatever Chase had going on, I better not talk. Steve says, "Yup, you better not say one word because Dad is scheming with Chase's butt and right now, I'm being a little bit selfish with you and you can't say anything. All I could do was smile at him. By mid-morning I had to go to my hair appointment with my two daughter in-laws, Savannah and Stephanie. After that it was back to my in-laws and I finished getting ready. Matthew drove me and Chase over to the clubhouse. As we walked in, there were my damn cousins Dex, Joshua, and Kyle. I knew this shit was going to be a fun night. I wrote a note and told them now we have to play fancy or else. I'm not going to be singing my ass off all night. That's why Chase is doing his thing. They told me, "Oh you think the rest of us are a broken church choir. You're full of shit Kerala. We've got a surprise for your ass tonight, but we have to go and get our fancy suit on." It just bothered me that I didn't get to show up here with Steve. As I was watching for him, he walked in smiling at me, asked if I was mad at him and I gave him a little grin. He told me, "Baby you've got Mom and Dad hooked on your music. And yes, I helped put this together for him." I wrote a little note and told Steve, "Your ass is mine later." He popped off, "Is that a threat or a promise later?" I told him, "Both." He said, "Bring on it baby and beat me." My fear of these types of people was starting to set in. This may not be their type of music, and I was thinking that Steve would start to build me up. He tells me, "I know that look baby, so don't worry about what they think of you. Some of them are here to show off their mistress and get free food. Baby, I don't know how much I tell you this, and I'll say this until I'm dead. You're very beautiful and very special to me. You're a very multi-talented person, you are a damn good role model to our kids, and you've made me who I am today. You inspired me so much that I'm a rich man because you are my wife. And I know my Kerala Jade, she's a fighter and a showstopper, and she fills all the emptiness in my heart." After he told me that I didn't realize I was about to start crying and he told me, "Baby don't cry, and I do mean every single word I say to you. I know that we are trying to circle back to each other. I've not been myself lately and nor have you since the accident, but I know damn well for sure we both haven't left each other's sides." As he was fixin' to say something else, I placed my finger on his lips and smiled at him. I knew he was hyped up on me singing. He always gets hyped up over me singing. As I was sitting in his lap, I kissed him. We were having our moment. I nipped on his ear and felt him getting excited, and I stopped. I looked at him, he told me, "Damn you woman. Just wait for it. I don't think we will be going back to my parents house tonight. We are long overdue for us, we've had too many things in our way. I shook my head at him and agreed. During our deer kill bet I did make it fun for him. And so much so that ever since he and I have had this thing in the kitchen with each other. As Steve and I were sitting there Josh and Dex came back fussing and said, "Kerala there is no way in hell I'm eating that shit they're going to serve these people. Steve got up, went and looked. He came back and said, "Nope, I'm not eating that shit either so I'll go get us something. While I'm at it, I'll call the kids and tell them to grab something before coming. I noticed the time and as I looked up, there were my cousin's and their wives. I got up and hugged them. They said, "Girl, we got your back." I patted Chase and told him, "It's time to warm up our voices." So we started and within 30 minutes we were ready. When Steve came back, I asked, "What's cooking back there?" He told me,

"They're cooking squid and snails. Mom's going to shit bricks when she finds the dinner menu." As we ate our own dinner, I looked at Steve and said,"Oh by the way, your ass is mine later, with passion." He smiled and said, "Good."

Before the guests started showing up I had taken a few shots and smoked a cigarette. I finished up my hot tea with lemon and honey. Chase was fussing about how nasty it tastes and I told him, "Well you wanted to start this mess of singing and this is the process. But I'm wondering what y'all have going on behind my back and which kid has finally found their voice. Josh looked at me and snickered, "Kerala, you'll see." As we're sitting there, Phil comes in and asks if we could go into a room after we are done eating and wait for an introduction? I told him, "Sure, but that food, nope." He asked, "Why?" I said, "I'm not eating squid." He told me, "That's not what we asked for. It was steaks. Hold on. Let me go see what's going on." When Phil came out, he said, "That's for another dinner party. You had me worried Kerala." I said, "Sorry, but we saw their food and we freaked out. Oh, by the way, by putting this together, I'm going to punish you and Steve." Phil looked at me, and he looked at Steve. He asked Steve, "She's joking, right son?" Steve told him, "No Dad, she's not messing with us." Phil asked me, "Okay, how I'm I getting punishment?" I told him, "I'm not cooking you a Kerala dinner. This turns into a disappointment for us. Ask Steve. He knows where I get him." Steve told him, "Well Dad, you and I will be up shit creek together, but the band will be in tow behind us if it happens." I giggled a little bit and got up to walk into the area where everything was happening. I started watching some people come in. My mother-in-law comes walking in, and she's all excited about tonight. I told her, "Thank you for getting my cousins here and their equipment." She told me, "Kerala, it's a big thing for us to have you to sing. You have so much talent and I love hearing you sing, so does Phillip." I somehow still find myself embarrassed over what Steve or I sent to her while we were drinking during our anniversary getaway. And that when she nailed me, she said, "Honey if you and Steve intend to get drunk tonight, please shut your phone off." I told her, "We'll do that." She hugged me and said, "You look great tonight. I'll catch up with you soon." I had gone back to catch up with Steve and saw my bunch made it. I saw Kaden was extra dressed up with Savannah and Stephanie. The three were smiling from ear to ear and Matthew was acting like Steve, making me laugh. As for my other three, they dressed up nicely, along with my two daughter-in-laws. Steve and I were ready to go find a seat and I wanted to be close to where we set up. About two hours after everyone arrived, I looked over at my sister-in-law, and she's flagging me over to her table. She told me, "Okay, I know it's been years ago, but do you remember when Steve bought you the SUV here? Well, Asha just popped up here." I told her, "Yea, how can I forget because she called me a hillbilly and thought my damn name was Elle Mae." Amy told me, "Well Kerala, here's your chance to get her back for those remarks." Steve's brother looked at me and said, "Kerala, that little bitch isn't worth it. And dammit, Amy, I hope you know what Steve told me. It takes an army to get Kerala off someone when she starts fighting." I looked at Amy, smiled and told Amy, "Go distract Steve, and we go from there." This woman was standing at the bar. I figured it was time for a shot of whiskey. So Amy got up and walked over to our table. My brother-in-law was getting pissed. He told me, "Kerala, leave Steve's past behind." After he said that to me, I looked at him and said, "Why did you say that?" He knew he fucked up by what he said, and he told me, "Her and Steve used to date each other in high school until they broke up. You know Steve was going through depression, and it's best to leave things where they are. You know it all too well Kerala. Besides, you have my baby bro wrapped around your fingers, and he's not going anywhere." I told him, "Stop sweating balls man. I just want to see her reaction. Besides, it's been well over 20 years since then." So I walked off and up to the bar. I got my favorite shot of whiskey. As I stood there, she looked at me and said, "That's a very nice jumpsuit. Is it Genny?" I told her, "No, it's Maje. My husband bought it for me as a gift with my mother-in-law's help. He always buys me sweet little presents. As I took my shot of whiskey, I heard my father-in-law on the microphone talking about me and Steve. It caught her attention and Phil said, "Our baby boy and his wife blessed us with eight grandchildren." She smarted off, "I wonder where that fat cow is now?" I asked for another shot and said to her, "Maybe stuffing her face." She said, "I don't think I could've handled that many kids." As I took my last shot, I turned around, looked over at my brother-in-law, raised my whiskey shot at him and knocked it back. I smarted off to her, "It's okay if you don't like me. Not everyone has good taste. If you find me offensive. Then I suggest you quit finding me. And I see that you showed up with your AARP card member holder. What's next? You become a thunder cunted cougar. And I'll tell you this, Steve married me, not you. So get the fuck over it. Life's good, you should get one. And my fucking name is Kerala, not Ellie Mae." The look on her face was so fucking priceless. I made her look so stupid standing there, that my brother and sister-in-law's, especially Steve's brother, was kinda wondering what I said to her. As I walked off, Phil was bragging about all of his grandchildren. When I got back to my seat he   said, "I see you're a few shots ahead of me. I'll see if Seth will go get me one. I would rather not move once you start." Kyle looked at me and said, "Time to assemble in our spots." I kissed Steve and got up. My father-in-law introduced us to the people and away we went. I wanted to start out soft so I could hit my hard hitting notes last, so I can kill my voice. But as the night went on, we had people in the palms of our hands, so that pulled Phil and Steve out of the dog house with me. My biggest surprise was when Kaden got up there with Chase. I knew in my heart what those boys had, but my shock to us was Stephanie, she sang her heart out. She still needed some work on her low notes. I could see she was nervous, but Steve and I were proud of their hard work which had surprised us both. Steve and I left and wanted our own adventure. I was pretty buzzed. When we left, we made sure Kyle, Dex, and Josh were okay. As I looked around and saw miss thing looking at me, Steve grabbed my hand and we were gone. As we walked outside Steve looked at me and said, "Baby, I've been drinking and so have you. Let's be safe rather than sorry. Your words are starting to slur, and you know how we are when we get drunk. We do some weird crazy shit together." I looked at him and we both started laughing. Just before Steve was about to get us a ride, Seth came and said to us, "Mama and Daddy, I pray that both of you don't intend to do something stupid." We looked at him and said, "No." So Steve handed him the keys and Seth said, "Come on you two." As he pulled the car up Steve's words were slowly slurring, and I don't recall some of the words, but it made our son speed up some. When we got back to his parents house, Seth walked us into the room and he said to us, "Now that y'all are safe, I don't want to know the rest." Steve looked at me, flashed some keys, and said, "Baby, do you want to go to our old house?" I asked him, "How in the hell did you get the keys?" He told me Amy is renovating. It's back under Mom's name. She hasn't started on it yet." I said, "Hell yea, let's go. How in the hell are we going to get by our Dudley Do-Right of a son?" Steve said, "Wel, I guess we can go old school." So he walked over and raised up the window. He helped me out and grabbed a bottle of Whiskey. As he was walking by the door, he started showing his butt in the glass, made a whistle sound, and we took off laughing. As we opened up the door, so many memories were made there. We stayed in our house until we decided it was time for some rest. The next morning Steve and I woke up puking our asses off. We kinda spent the day in bed. He told me, "Baby, the older we are, the more the damn hangovers feel like we're dying." I couldn't agree with him more, but by that afternoon we both stumbled out of bed. From the looks of it, both my father and mother-in-law had worse hangovers than we did. So I ordered take out for us all, but behind my back, Steve bought our old house back. As Amy was visiting, she asked if Steve and I wanted to join her and her husband Rex, alongside his brother and his wife, Leah. Steve told them sure. As for my own kids they were scattered all over the city visiting old friends. Since we left there years ago, the kids had kept in touch with their friends. My in-laws were going over to their annual dinner with friends. The next morning came. I had taken my time on my makeup and hair. Amy reserved a table at a high-end restaurant. I had this cute dress that has been sitting in my closet for years. I just grabbed it and brought it with us. After I finished my hair and fixed myself up, I walked out of the room. Steve looks at me and smiles. When we got in the car he said, "You're putting the hurt on me so bad right now. Sometimes I think you do it just to punish me. Because baby it looks like you made yourself extremely gorgeous tonight." I asked him, "So it bothers you what I have on. I see my flagpole trying to make his stand and I think it's cute. Oh shit, you know what, I think I might "forget" to wear panties to dinner tonight." And he looks at me and says, "Baby, I'm not sure if I can wait another week. If you don't stop looking at me like that, we're going to have to go somewhere private. God damn baby, you've got a way with your words sometimes. And sometimes all I've got to do is look at you and you have me going." I giggled a little bit.

When we got to the restaurant and got seated with my in-laws, Amy, Leigh and I started a conversation about odd medical things to crazy houses, and they asked me about a few cases that I have done. I told them I hate when a baby comes in with fire ant bites all over them because the mother will not change out the family laundry soap or check their bed for old food. This one baby came in with them in her ear building a colony in her ear. As I was trying to get them out they were biting her on the inside. She wouldn't stay still, and she bit me on my arm. The mom got mad at me when I put a mouth guard in the baby's mouth. But my worst parent is one that came in smelling like Marijuana. She came in with him a few times. Everything she did I would leave out of the room searching the break room for snacks until I had enough of her. I asked her if she had a medical license for her habit and she said I don't know what you're talking about. I said to her every time you come here this baby is high as a kite, and you get mad at me because I can't diagnose your kid because the baby is high. So I ripped up the baby, took it to my nurse and told my receptionist to call Child Welfare. When they ran blood and urine that baby's TC levels were out of this world. The back storyline is the mother would put the baby in between her legs and she would blow the stuff in his face. As we continued swapping stories, I looked up and saw about six women sitting at the table next to us. I went on talking. I looked up again and there Asha stood standing over Leah. She said, "Well hi there ELLIE MAY. I figured this place is way out of your league." I looked at Steve, and he said, "Get her." I said, "Nope, Trixie it's not. Oh, I see that you must have forgotten to bring your AARP card member holder. Or, you weren't in the mood to change his dirty ball sack in the bathroom tonight. I know what the fuck you're up to and I think I've got Steve pretty well managed. Our marriage is on the fireproof side. We don't need a third wrinkle in the mix. From the looks of it, you have quite a few. Maybe you should go get Botox for it. Oh holy shit, do you hear those banjos playing? Trixie, they say in the south when those fuckers start playing you better run." As we got up, I smarted off in a dumb blonde mouth and said, "Like have an awesome, fun dinner, Trixie." The ladies were laughing their asses off, and I looked at her. I guess I humiliated her. As we walked out, Steve and my in-laws were laughing their asses off and I was just standing there when they caught their breath. We said goodnight to them. When Steve got in, I apologized to him. He said, "What baby? You and I talked about what you could do if she did it to you again. And dammit, you really humiliated her." Steve just couldn't stop laughing about it. And he asked me, "So baby, why don't we run somewhere and get us an air mattress so we can stay at our place?" I told him "Let's go." We went into bed and bath to grab some thing's then ran next door to Target and got some more stuff. He reminded me that we would have the grandbabies for a little bit. So we walked over and got the girls some sidewalk chalk and a few other girl things. We got Tatuam a little push car and Landon some toys. I found myself happy knowing that we were going to have our old house here again, even if just for a vacation or to visit the house when we come to see my in-laws. While we were putting the stuff together, Steve was still laughing his ass off about what I told Asha. The next morning Lucas and Andrew wanted to go do some last-minute Christmas shopping. Steve and I told them to go. It was a nice warm day, about 80 degrees. Landon had just recovered from a bad cold and I figured he needed a little sun to dry him up. So Steve and I grabbed the grandbabies and went out to the front yard. I sat Landon up. Steve and I sat down on the ground with the babies. I gave sidewalk chalk to Madi and Braylee. Tat and Steve started building his Lego truck. While he was telling him to hurry, with our backs to the street, Steve and I didn't have a care in the world of what was going on behind us. We were busy with the grandbabies. When I looked up at the glass door, there stood Asha with a red can over my head. I reached around, grabbed her leg and tripped her. She slapped me in my face and I let loose on her. I held her down. Seth came out to hold Asha down and Steve pulled me off of her, letting crazy ass Steve out to play. Stephanie and Kaden already had the babies back in the house and my ass got up. Steve told her, "I told you to stay away from us. Looks like my wife gave you something to remember her by and it was something you needed." As Steve was getting in her face, I saw our girls coming. That's when Savannah and Stephanie came bowing up. I knew my daughters well enough to know what they were fixin' to do. I saw Savannah move slowly on the right side of Steve. Before Steve could turn his head back to Stephanie, Savannah pushed him down. Savannah and Stephanie went in beating the shit out of Asha. I wanted more of her, but I was being held back and the words that came out of Steve. I saw Asshole Steve come out. He told Asha, "My wife gave you something to remember her by, and it was something you needed you dumb bitch. And this is something you need to get through your head. I will never leave my wife for your ugly ass." He grabbed her by the hair and made her look at him. He told her, "See, the real me you could have never handled. I would have become someone who would have beaten you for your stupidity. The only person that can handle me is my wife, Kerala." I was so pissed off at myself for what she just tried to do to us. When the police came, she was arrested. She had gasoline in the red can. She was fixin' to dump it on me and light us on fire. When her mother came down to my in-laws, Phil got in her face and told her that her daughter needs to be locked up and forgotten about. That's when Steve got in Lizzy's face and told her off. When the police came and got Asha, it was humiliating to Lizzy. The whole fucking neighborhood got an MMA fight for free. As Steve and I walked back over to our house, Shelby was very hyped up about what I had just done. I was still mad because this happened in front of my grandbabies. As for Steve, I knew it was going to take a few days for him to settle down. Andrew and Lucas were not happy about the news when they came back. We both assured them that the kids would be safe with us for the night. Steve literally begged the boys to let Maddie, Braylee and Tatum stay the night with us. Lucas finally caved in and said, "That's fine." That's when Andrew let us have Maddie and Tat. During the next few days everyone on Nicholas Lane was watching me and I knew the whole neighborhood was talking about me. I didn't care, but that shit was so long overdue. I was chuckling at the fact that Shelby said, "Damn Bebe, you missed it." I told her, "Yes she did."

As Christmas morning came, we received a gift that was a big shock. Seth handed me a picture of a sonogram and told us that he was fixin' to be a father. I asked, "Who is the mother?" He said, "Breanna." That shocked me. Thinking every time I go into the grocery store, she's carrying my grandchildren. I thought you finally gave her a chance. I was fucking beyond tickled pink, and he told us, "Oh, by the way, we are having twins and getting married." When I got home, that's when Kaden came and gave me a five, and it was the foal. We had more like a paper Christmas in which, I thought, was cool as ever. After Christmas morning we packed up and headed home. I asked him, "Could we please have a quiet New Year's Eve?" He told me. "If that's what you want to do, then we'll do it?" As New Year's Eve came I made us dinner. Steve was kinda quiet and as we were eating. "I asked him, "Is there something on your mind?" He gave me his crazy look and I lowered my head. I finished my dinner and went in and cleaned up and grabbed a blanket. When I walked back into the living room, he was nowhere in sight. I went out to the fire pit and wrapped myself up with the blanket. I sat there listening to the outside movement. As I got lost looking at the fire, Steve scared the shit out of me. He walked up behind me and told me, "I'm sorry for the way I looked at you. I'm trying to wrap my fucking head around this year and I think we're going to call it a year of the exes. If I could put it in reverse I'm dredging February like the fucking plague for us." I told him, "It's best for us to put one foot in front of another and we keep moving forward." He asked me, "Baby, I've always wanted to know how in the hell did you push through this shit without going crazy?" I told him, "It's like a band-aid you know you're not supposed to rip it off. If you do, all that hurt and pain flows out like blood. If you don't keep it covered, you'll have more issues than you want. The issue that you and I were trying to keep covered showed up at our door. That was unexpected. It's like life. Did you expect us to have eight kids?" And he said, "Nope. Let alone each set of twins. But each day raising them with you was worth it." I told him, "What are you saying? We are still raising them. They can't stay away from us so we must have done something to make them stay around us. Especially three of the boys. Stephanie is down the road from us. Steve, I never asked you to be a part of my life nor did you ask me to be a part of yours. It was our destiny to start our journey together." He came out and said, "Baby, I know and our life and marriage isn't over until one of us is put in the ground. Baby, what's been on my mind for the past few days is how close our grandbabies were, and I'm thinking of the worst that could have happened. I failed to protect you once and this psycho bitch got a taste of her own medicine. She has been treating people awful for years. I guess you humiliated her so bad that she didn't know how to take it. With you beating her ass it was long overdue. She has blood on her hands because she bullied a girl so badly in high school that she took her own life and Asha got away with it. That's another reason I dumped her." I said, "Well, I guess my banjos came out of the woods after her." When I said that, Steve laughed, and he said, "That they did baby, I heard them when you grabbed her leg."

Steve and I stayed outside until the snow started falling. We came in and went to bed at about 2:00 AM. Steve's phone started ringing. With Seth working night patrol, that scares anyone with a loved working in the line of duty. Seth said, "It's on speaker. Daddy, I don't know how to tell you this, but Chase and Kaden just broke one of your life lesson rules: they were drinking and driving. The little rookie cop that the county just hired got them. I'm impounding Chase's truck." Steve told Seth, "Do your job son. Stay safe and come home to us." Seth said, "Yes sir."

When Steve hung up the phone he started cussing and laid back in the bed. He looked at me and said, "Mama, what was that you said about them not kinda growing up.?" I said, "That's the shit I was talking about, we still have to hold hands with a few of our kids." He raised up really fast and said, "Holy shit, you know who's still sitting there?" I looked at him and said, "Yes." That's when I started to worry about my two boys and I didn't go back to sleep that night. I just laid there watching the clock tick down until the morning light. When the morning light came, Brian called Steve and told him, "Come and get your boys. They've messed Cole up. I'm going to sweep this under the rug because the kid fucked up when he put them in the same cell together." When Steve told Brian, "I'll be there shortly." Steve looked at me and said, "Kerala, I need you to ride with me so I don't lose my shit along the way." Steve is rubbing my hand like crazy, and I said to him, "I think their 20s is just as bad as their teen years." He said, "Naw Mama, this is just a touch of it." He looked at me and I said, "But come to think of it, I can disagree and agree with you. It's confusing right now." When we pulled in at the county jail, there they were. Steve got out and started talking with Brian. Chase and Kaden got in the truck, and they're talking, "Well little brother, I guess we pissed the old man off. I haven't seen him this fucking mad since Lucas shot the M24 carbine. I'm

318

guessing Daddy is handing him our get out jail free card and using the good old boy system." I looked back at Kaden and gave him my look. Kaden said, "Chase shut up." Chase kept at it and Kaden said, "Chase shut up." I started tapping my foot on the floorboard and Chase said, "Aww naw, Mama you mad?" Kaden said, "You remember when Mama slapped the shit out of Seth? He's still trying to find his ass to come back. Welp, from the looks on Mama's face sitting up there, you're about to join him." Being a little on the cocky side, when Steve got in the truck, he told them, "Not a fucking word." Steve looked at me and said, "Who pissed you off?" I said, "The one sitting behind me." When we got home I went into the house. I let Steve have at it with them. I was still sleepy, but when Steve walked in and sat down on the couch, I cuddled up to him. I still didn't know what in the hell the boy's problem was.

As January flew by us, like a ball of lightning, I felt like I woke up in the month of February. The month we were both dreading. Saturday evening the family showed up to stay. As for my in-laws, they were there for support. But somewhere, as I was sleeping, I had a bad dream. I woke up kinda screaming at the top of my lungs. Having to face him again dreams of Cole hitting me, when Steve touched me, I flinched. Steve was letting me know that he was there for me. He rolled me up into his arms and said, "Baby, this week is going to take a toll on us both. You are so stressed out right now, try and go back to sleep, you need the rest." Somehow, the next day I woke up at about 12:00 PM. I haven't slept like that since I was a teenager. When I got up, I got dressed and went to sit on the couch. I could hear everyone in the dining room chatting it up. I grabbed a blanket and rolled up into it like a child. I got quickly irritated by the dining room noise, so I got up and went back to our bedroom. As I closed the door and turned on the TV I laid back in bed. A lot of those old memories came to my mind, thinking why didn't Noah say something or save me.

I began to get mad about it all. So I got up, put on my boots and went out the front door. I made my way down to the horses. I got Lilly, saddled her and I took off with a nice run. Lilly reminded me so much of my first horse, Flower. I took so much care in pride in that horse it killed me when Cole lied to my Dad about me falling off of her. In fact, it was Cole that ripped me off of her and gave me a head injury. When my Dad took her away, I was devastated. But as I was riding Lilly, I somehow felt young again. My worries about tomorrow are gone. I feared that my own thoughts were about to put me into a depression. As I rode upon a small trail, I followed it for a little bit. I saw where Steve had the cows in the back pasture. I let the time and my thoughts get far away from me and I knew I had better get back to the house. By the time I did get back, it was dusk. Steve was standing by the gates and he asked me, "Did your inner you wanna come out and be a kid again?" I told him, "Yea, it felt good." He said, "Good baby. I'm happy that you got out of the house. You had everyone flipping out about your whereabouts. But I saw you take off through the dining room window. So I didn't worry."

Steve helped me off of Lilly and told me, "Baby, I'll put up Lilly. Can you just imagine how upset Blue is?" I told Steve, "Blue had a small fit on me as we were leaving." I walked in the stalls, gave Blue a treat, and waited on Steve. As I was petting Blue, Steve wrapped his arms around me and said, "Kerala, I know there's a lot going on inside your mind. You're having nightmares. I hear them as you're reliving things in your sleep. Tomorrow we're fixin' to close it for good. Just like you helped with mine. I know that I'm going to hear some things that I'm not prepared for, and I will get upset. But it was all before me and you. I know that there's some things that you haven't told anyone, and I'm going to hear about it this week. I may be a little bit upset about it, but not with you. I'm giving you fair warning so that way you can give me time to cool down. I don't want to say anything hurtful. After I cool down I may come to you with questions. I just want you to understand that." I told him, "Let's go talk in our room, but please don't raise your voice for what I'm about to tell you." As we got into the house, Steve and I went into our bedroom. I sat him down and pulled up a chair in front of him. I sat there and as I started crying I told him, "I had forceful intercourse those three times with Cole." Steve said, "Baby he raped you." I told Steve, "The first time he said if didn't, he would tie a rope around my neck and drag me with it. The second time he hit me and told me we had to do it. The third time, I just gave up and felt that if there was no fight, he wouldn't hit me. After he was done, he beat me. When he passed out, I ran out of his house. When Kyle came up on me while I was running down the road, that's when he turned around and went back to Cole's house and Kyle had beat him. The last time I saw him during that period was to go tell him about Andrew and Lucas. When I saw what I saw, it was my chance to run from him forever."

As I sat there in tears, Steve was ghost white with his own tears. He finally spoke and said, "Baby, I'm so sorry this happened to you. How can I help you mend this?" I told him, "Don't stop loving me because I'm putting that son of a bitch away forever." He asked me, "Kerala, have I ever forced myself on you?" I told him, "No, never. You have kinda always asked me or we're in the moment with each other, and it leads to us doing it. But there are days when I wished it was you that took it instead of him. You have taught me the right way to love you." He told me, "If I do anything sexually bad to you, slap me, so I'll know. Tomorrow, yea, we are definitely closing doors, nailing them and burying them shut. But I'm having some difficulty processing what you just told me. Just   hang with me while I cope with it, with you. It's like what you said to me over the bandages and I kept picking at it. I'm so sorry. I knew that you weren't ready to tell me a lot of things baby. But do you feel better now that you told me?" I told Steve, "To be really honest with you, I was hoping to go to my grave with it, but it needed to be told. It was time to cleanse my past." He told me, "Baby, nothing has changed between us. I'm just as crazy about you now as from the day I met you." As I sat there in tears, Steve wipes them away and puts me into his arms. It felt good to finally tell him more. I felt something left off my chest. Whenever I'm in Steve's arms, I feel like I'm in my safe place where no one can harm or touch me. Steve looked at me, he said, "Baby I love you so much that it kills me knowing what he did to you. Not a lot of people know what kind of person I am underneath when it comes down to you." I told Steve I loved him too and said to him, "No they don't because there is a crazy motherfucker in there hiding." He jokes and says, "He might make an appearance soon if I get mad enough." I told him, "Nope, not on my watch unless I'm mad at the same time." He says, "Yup, that'll do it." Steve suggested that we need to try and sleep. I felt I could use some more, but I was in the fear of having another dream. As we got ready for bed, I realized that I had not eaten anything and Steve has been on my ass lately about my weight. I had gone from a healthy 105 pounds down to 80 pounds since the shooting. But in reality, I wasn't hungry at all. When Steve fell asleep I laid there thinking about things and I rolled over to my right side looking out the crack of the curtains. I heard Steve mumble my name, so I turned over to my left side, and I'll be damned if my husband wasn't having a wet dream about me. I was tickled, and he said, "No baby, oh yeah that's it." So I decided to really mess with him. I whispered something dirty in his ear and I started nibbling on his ear. He told me in his dream, "Again baby, I can't get enough of you Kerala." I said to him in a very sexy way, "Steve, take me however you want to." And he started talking dirty. I found myself so fully in the fucking mood. So I took my night wear off, put my body next to him and rubbed my fingers across his chest. I was trying to figure out how to wake him up. So I got on top of him and started kissing him all over. I kinda turned on his lamp and he was still out. I slowly shook him and when he woke up, he was a little surprised. I said, "You summoned me because it must have been really wild what we were doing to each other in your dream. Do you want to make it really happen? If not, I got hot and bothered for nothing." He started kissing my body. With everyone in the house, we had to be extra quiet while being intimate. When we finished we cuddled up. I passed out. I woke up about 6:00 AM with him rubbing on my body. As I opened my eyes I was facing him. I smiled at him and we kissed. He tells me, "Good morning baby. Let's go and put this motherfucker where he belongs." I smiled and told him, "Let's do this." We took our showers and when I got in our closet, I sat on our dressing bench and Steve sat beside me. He tells me, "Kerala, this the day that you are actually telling Cole you mean fucking business and you're done playing his mind games." I leaned against him and told him, "I know. I'm just tired. You know you made me a very happy wife last night by being in your dirty dream. He blushed a little, smiled and said, "Baby, you're always in my fantasy and dreams. I guess I must have let you in, and you heard me and made it come true. I love you for that." As I stood up and picked out a suit of clothes, I figured out a business type or what I wear to the office. So, I put it on. As I sat there I wrapped my arms around his neck and held onto him. He told me, "Baby, I'm going to be right there beside you. My advice for you today is to go in there so pissed off that you can satisfy yourself knowing that your telling that jury the truth." As I held on to him, I heard those words of, "Mama, Mama where are you at?" I yelled, "I'm in here." As I looked, it was Andrew. He told me, "Mama, I'm sorry for busting in, but I don't know what you want me to wear." I told him, "You're a grown man, son. Be comfortable. Be Andrew." I kissed Steve and told him, "Adult kids and their little mini crisis. You wipe their asses and teach them to piss out of their Lillie, and they still get it wrong." As I walked out, everyone was in the living room waiting around. When I saw my cousins, Josh and Kyle, with Dexter, I looked at Dex. He said, "Kerala, I have those demos done if you want to match the lyrics to it. You can listen to it on your way. It might help you to keep a little bit of stress off your mind." I told him, "Send it to my phone. It should make Steve happy this morning." As 8:00 AM rolled around, we all started to leave. I hooked up the Bluetooth and started going through the instrumental places. Something in me started spitting out the lyrics. Poor Steven had to cover his ears when I hit my high notes. But as we pulled up to the courthouse, I didn't want him to turn the truck off. So he got out, and I rolled the window down. People were looking. I was basically singing songs that I wrote. And how I felt I was about to go in there like a lamb and come out like a fucking lion. As we walked in our lawyer sat down and she told me. "Kerala, I'm going to let his lawyer go first for the opening arguments. Then instead of me opening mine, I've decided to let the juries hear what they really need to hear, and I'll close out my opening argument. We're hoping to start asking questions by the end of the day. So we can try and be done with it this week and have him and her off to the prison. I'm hoping for life, but with him and her stealing the baby, it might be an injection. So deep breath here, Kerala." As we went into the courtroom I felt Steve grab my hand, and we sat down. Our lawyer was getting set up. I looked over and saw Cole staring right at me. I could definitely see that he was well over dried out since he's been sitting in jail. I looked at Steve. He was shaking mad and staring Cole down. When the judge came out, I saw who the hell it was, Judge Thomas. I treat his grandchildren and he or his wife comes in when they are attending to them. Steve looked at me because Judge Thomas has his small ranch down the road. The Judge and Steve talk frequently. I saw a few jury members who Hannah treats. I leaned back in my chair and looked at Steve. He smiled at me and shook his head at me like we got this shit in the bag. But as his lawyer started his opening argument, he started pissing me off by saying Cole was the victim. He told the jury that I invited them to my house. My damn mouth opened up and said, "Like hell I did." Everyone looked at me and Steve said, "Baby, don't let your anger get the best of you." As he stood there trying to make Cole look good, I looked behind me and I saw my brothers getting mad. Once he was done making his speech to the jury, my lawyer got up and informed them that she's going to let me do her opening argument. When she told me to stand up, I took a deep breath and stood up. I walked over to the jury box and I looked at a few of the people and I just let it go. "I know that some of you don't want to be here today, nor do I. But from the time I was 16 years old until now, I have done nothing but lived my life quietly in fear of Cole. I really didn't get to finish being a kid because of him. I didn't get to drive around the town square with my friends or hang out with them like I was supposed to do. At the age of 15 when I had first met Cole at a rodeo in the back of the shoots, I was waiting for them to start the barrel racing event. It was just small chatter about my horse and why I got into barrels. I knew he was older, but we all have that older friend who you know growing up, that how it basically is. But I wasn't worried or even had the thought of dating. My mind was on horses, music and being with friends. Throughout the year of 1995, I would see Cole off and on at the rodeos and he and I would speak. My parents knew his parents. As the end of the year came close my Mom noticed that his Mom had started coming to our church. By then, Cole was hanging around my Dad and my brothers, Shane and Noah. Before I knew it, I was dating him. It was common back where I'm from for a younger girl to be dating an older guy, but with parental supervision, guidance and permission. Within six months of courtship between us, he picked me up from a Wednesday night church service. Something in him fully changed before he arrived. I was standing outside, talking with the preacher's son about getting our driver's license, school friends and the coming service for Sunday. I was the youngest person to ever lead the church choir. When Cole pulled up, I had given Isaiah a hug and got in the truck with Cole. I felt a sense of jealousy from Cole about my actions. We had driven down the road and he pulled over. He grabbed my neck and started slapping me. He hit me so hard that my nose began to bleed and he told me that I should be ashamed of myself for leading the pastor's son on. I was so scared to say anything or defend myself. I'm wondering what I did. After he realized what he had done, he kept repeating to me that he was sorry. I was in shock and confused. When he dropped me off at home, he told me, please don't say anything to your Dad about this. I've had a hard day at work today and me seeing you talking to another guy just makes me insane. All I could do was shake my head at him as I walked into the house. I didn't even look at my Mom or Dad, but as I passed by Noah in the hall he asked me what did you get into, so I had to lie to him. Within a few days later, there was Cole standing next to me in church, kinda having his hand on my shoulder like nothing had happened. When the service was over he handed me a few roses and begged me to forgive him. He promised that he wouldn't do it again. As a young girl, I fell for it and didn't know any better. A few months went by and I decided to go for a ride on my horse. But as I was almost at the end of the road, I saw Cole coming. And when he stopped, I could tell he had been drinking. He ripped me off of Flower and I hit my head on his truck. I felt him hit me with his full fist. When he hit me, he kicked Flower to make her run away. He threw me in the truck and took me straight home. He pretended that Flower hurt me. Dad was furious and quickly took Flower away to sell her. When I saw Shane I shook my head, kinda telling him that's not what happened. The next day when I realized that my horse was gone from me, she was like a child I had cared for like she was my first child. I had my hand on her since she was a colt. To have something that meant a lot to a 16-year old broke my heart. I had to miss a few days of school due to a concussion after he ripped me off my horse. And this had become a pattern for Cole to do to me. It came to a point of where I felt we're okay, just get this monthly beating over with, to the point of where I was done with my own life. The thoughts of me leaving this earth had been playing a big role inside my mind. Regardless of what I do or say, my Dad told Cole he could date me. With no other dating experience, I didn't know his abuse wasn't normal. One day I went to the cotton loft and set up a pitchfork where I could land on it head first. It seemed like it was the only way out of this torture from him. As I was about to do it, Noah came into the loft and I pretended that I was doing something else. For a 17-year-old girl to think about killing herself is awful. I'm glad my brother came in, or I wouldn't be standing here in front of you. By the summer of 1997, I started noticing track marks on his arm and him drinking heavily. During this time period of my life I felt that this was how my life was going to be and started to slowly accept it. I had become so good at hiding my bruises that you couldn't tell, but things took a turn on me when I turned 18. He took me to his house. As we walked in those words he said to me still haunt me to this day. He said, well since you're 18 now, I think it's time for me to turn you into a woman and do what I've been wanting to do to you for the past few years. I think I have broken you so that you'll do whatever I tell you to do. So go on and take your clothes off. When I told him no, I'm not ready for that, he got mad at me and slapped me. He told me if I didn't have sex with him, he would tie me up behind his truck and drag me down the road. He then said, so take your clothes off. As I stood there in front of him, taking my clothes off, I began to cry. That's when he grabbed me by my hair and dragged me into the bedroom. He proceeded to do what he wanted. When he was done with me, he beat me. I felt that I couldn't tell anyone what he just did to me because I felt shameful. The next weekend it was a repeat of the last weekend. By the third time, I had just caved and gave up. That night something changed in myself when he beat me and passed out, I got up and ran. When a vehicle came up on me, I was scared that it was him. But as I looked, it was my cousin Kyle, so I got in. Kyle turned around, and we went back to the house and Kyle beat him up. When I got home, Kyle and my Dad got into it. Kyle told my Dad what happened to me. During that time somewhere I got pregnant with my first set of twins. When I found out that I was pregnant, my Mom had kinda begged me to go and tell Cole, but when I saw a friend of his, and he told me that he was with another girl, I felt free from him. About three days later, when my cousin Dex told me what he had seen, I got in my car and I drove over to his house to tell him I was pregnant. There was my answer from God to move along. Cole laid on the ground with a needle in his arm, a crack pipe in his hands and beer cans all around him. I knew I couldn't let this baby be near him. After all he had done was hurt me and my feelings. I was breathing again, but with the constant fear of him waiting around for me somewhere after my husband and I started dating. I was working to support myself and the twins. Cole found out that I was pregnant and seeing someone else. One night he caught me after the Café closed. Cole slung me against my car and threatened to harm me and the babies. The owner came out and ran him off. During this time I was seeking help from our pastor and the local judge on how to regain my confidence back. When Steve and I got married, after the birth of Andrew and Lucas, Judge

Shafer saw that Cole was unfit to be a parent. I didn't want them to have any part of him so he gave me all parental rights and Steve had adopted them on the day we got married. Throughout the years my husband has had a big part of helping me learn who I really am. When Steve and I moved away from my hometown, Cole prepared to burn down the apartment that Steve and I were living in, but the stupid fool burned down the wrong building. When we would come in to visit, Cole would stalk me and my children. My parents never really told him anything about where I lived. I'm guessing he figured it out and used a child to get to me. That's why we are here today."

As I sat back down, I didn't really realize that I had cried so much. I was looking at a few jurors and they were crying with me. But as I looked at Steve, he wasn't there. It was crazy asshole Steve sitting next to me and Judge Thomas set a recess for 30 minutes. I placed my hand into Steve's. When we got up Steve didn't let go of my hand. We walked outside and he sat down on the steps. He placed me in between him. I knew he was pissed off when he placed his arms around me and held onto me. He was breathing hard, and he kept kissing me. He told me, "You got his ass baby, finally." When our kids gathered around us, I saw so many questions in their eyes. I lit up a cigarette and I told Steve, "I need a few minutes." So I got up and walked off. I looked at my Dad and brothers. The look on their faces was one of shock, as well as my Mom. I needed a few minutes by myself. When I saw Lucas and Andrew coming towards me, they were crying and they both hung onto me. I told them, "It's over, but the one that needs the support, or he's going to lose his shit, is the man that raised you." Andrew said to me, "That man who raised me is my Daddy and I love him just as much as you do. He might be a pain in mine and my little brothers' ass, but he's the man, the myth and real legend." Andrew made me laugh. As he walked off Lucas said, "Mama,

do you regret having us?" I told him, "Son, not a day in my life."
He told me. "Mama. I'm sorry for what that piece of shit put
you through. Our 30 minutes is about up so we better get in
there." As I walked up to Steve, I asked him if he was okay, and
he told me yes. As we settled back into the courtroom and got
seated, the judge's face was   disgusted by what I just told
them. My lawyer said to me, "We might have this in the bag
soon." I thought, good job Kerala. I couldn't have said it any
better than you for you. Cole's lawyer called me to the stand,
so I got up and went up there. He asked me to state my name
and I said, "Dr. Kerala Jade Nicholas." He asked, "Dr. Nicholas,
have you ever been in trouble with the law?" I told him, "A few
minor traffic tickets." He said, "Are you sure about that? I don't
think you're telling the truth to the court. Judge Thomas, what
I have in my hands here is a little bit more than she's telling us
about her past. Here in my hands it said,"That you did
something. Can you tell me about what you did to your
parents' neighbors car and the town drunk?" When he said
that I started to smile. He said, "With that smile on your face it
tells me everything." I smarted off and said, "The son of a bitch
shouldn't have stolen my dog." He smarted off, "Did this
involve building a bomb?" I said, "Yes it did." He said, "So you
and the town Alcoholic blew up your parents neighbors' car
over a dog?" I told him Ace wasn't any kinda dog. He was the
dog that went everywhere with me." He asked me, "Can you
explain to the court?" So I said, "That Christmas month Uncle
Gabe and Aunt Donna got Shane, Noah and I a puppy for a gift.
So we named him Ace. That dog went everywhere I went.
Mama and Daddy got us bicycles for Christmas. As the new
year came in the spring of 1990, I asked Mama if I could ride
into town, and she told me to be back before dark. So Ace and
I took off on our 10-mile trip. But as I passed by the crazy
neighbors he stopped me and ripped Ace up off the ground. He
told me I didn't need the dog. It was his. That my Uncle Gabe

stole it from him, which was a lie. I told him to give my dog back or else. Well I figured I would go and tell my Uncle Gabe about what just happened. I was crying and upset. When I went to the back door, Mr. Doven asked me why I was crying. He told me if I would sneak him a bottle out of my Uncle Gabe's bar, he would help me get Ace and make sure that my dog wouldn't be touched or taken from me again. Well, I went in and Uncle Gabe's back was turned. I got the closest bottle and I was out the back door again. When I handed it to Mr. Doven, he told me give me about 25 minutes and we'll go get your dog. Sure enough Mr. Doven pulls up and loads my bike in his truck and down the road we go. In the front seat with us was a funny-looking box and other things. When we got to the neighbor's Ace was in a hot car and Mr. Doven got Ace out. Mr. Doven told me to hang here, we're not done yet. So Mr. Doven takes out the funny box, he wires up some greens and blues and Mr. Doven tells me it's time for three hots and a cot. Summer's coming. He asked me if this is good enough, and I told him it's good enough for me. So he got my bike out and told me to push that in and get down. When I did it all, I got on my bike and rode away with Ace. But Mr. Doven, I told the truth about how it happened. Mr. Doven went to jail. All I got was a slap on the wrist, but I was ten years old and that has nothing to do with this case."

As I looked up my family and boys were laughing. Steve had a smile on his face. But my in-laws didn't know what to think. The lawyer said no other questions at this time. So I got down and went back to my seat. Our lawyer called Cole up to the stand. She asked him if he ever hit Dr. Nicholas. Cole stuttered and said, "I might have a time or two, to get her to understand me or when she would set me off."

As I was sitting there, Steve started rubbing my leg, and she asked him, "When did you find out that Kerala was carrying your baby and seeing Mr. Nicholas?" Cole said, "I found out she was pregnant about four months later and a friend of mine told me and he said she's got a new boyfriend too, so with her brother's running sled trucks I knew where I would go and see if my friend was right. So we went out to the county fair and I saw him have her wrapped in his arms, pregnant. When me and him locked eyes, it made me mad. I saw him stand up. I followed him to the bathroom." She asked, "Did you have any conversation with Mr. Nicholas?" Cole said, "I was trying to bluff him away from Kerala, but what I said to him didn't phase him." She asked him, "Do you recall what you told him?" Cole said, "I told him I see you priding my girl around. I knew she would turn out doing tricks. He turned to me and peed on my boot. He told me the bigger dick wins and walked away from me." She asked him, "Were you on any kind of drugs?" Cole said, "During that time I was off and on them." She asked, "What made you think you could have Kerala back with the way you treated her? In my opinion, after all, you did force her to have sex with you and that is technically raping." Cole said, "I knew she was carrying my child. The lawyer said, "Kerala said that the last time you put your hand on her was in front of the Café, why?" He told her, "I went there to tell her that I was going to take the baby from her thinking this would push her into coming back to me, but the Café owner ran me off. She was about nine months pregnant during that time." She said, "Did you try to hurt her?" Cole said, "I pushed her. The lawyer said, "Your records indicate that a few nights after this incident Kerala had gone into labor. Who told you?"

Cole said, "I was drinking when I found out that she gave birth to twin boys. I tried to see what they looked like, but I got arrested because her father, John, had placed a restraining order against me and the girl I was seeing at the time turned me in for hitting her. About three days later, when Judge Shafer came down to the cell, he told me to sign this piece of paper. The Judge told me I need you to stay far away from Kerala. If not, I'll arrest you so many times that I'll see to it that you stay in here. Those babies are no longer yours. They're his. I stripped your parental rights away because you like to hurt her. Don't think I don't know what you've done to her, and I'm pretty sure the man she just married will make you regret it." She said, "During this time, did you do what Judge Shafer said?" Cole said, "No. When he let me out, I sat out in front of the apartment building for a few weeks until I saw her leave with them. She took them to her parent's house, so I backed off from there and went home. I did a few lines and grabbed my gun and sat back up at their apartment. I planned on doing away with them so I could get the babies. After a few days of learning his routine, I figured I would slip in and get her and the babies. But when I saw them leave, I followed them to the grocery store and I didn't see them. But when I saw her mother with them, I got my first look at them. When I saw the MPs, I thought they were after me for being on the edge of the base, so I left. So I planned on doing what I need to get them back around Thanksgiving time. I slipped into their apartment and saw who he was and saw some money in her jewelry box and I took it. I found out both of the boy's names, took a few pictures of them and left. About a week later I saw a new car sitting in front of the apartment door so I assumed they were back from wherever. I went and set up a plan. I was going to kidnap Kerala and the boys. A few days later I got high and burned down the wrong building. Judge Shafer told me she's long gone from here, so for one year of prison I went. When I got out of prison a year later, I had given up, until I saw her and the boys with another set of twins. She was out shopping with her mother, so I tried to look at them again and that's when the sheriff saw me and locked me up. I always knew when she was coming because Judge Shafer would lock me up." Steve whispered in my ear, I think he's playing mind games with Andrew and Lucas. I couldn't agree more, but it freaked me out that he stocked me and Steve for a year. When the Judge saw the time he told us we have a recess for one hour and 15 minutes for lunch. As we walked down the street Steve told me, "I need to check in with Andrew and Lucas. We're going to sit beside them. As we got to the restaurant and seated, not much was being said between us all. I said screw it. I got myself a margarita with a double shot of Patron. Steve was right behind me on drinking, and he told me, "Kerala Jade Nicholas you better not get too buzzed or your mouth will start flying. With your weight right now, I'm pretty sure it won't take much." I said, "Steven Wesley." I smiled at him and told him, "Okay." As we were sitting there, Steve and I asked Andrew and Lucas, "How are you two handling this shit?" They said, "It's crazy Daddy, but I still feel the same way I told you before." Steve told them, "I am happy that I raised both of you." Lucas said, "You know he is literally telling on himself up there about what he did. But I dislike that lawyer. He's trying to turn Mama into a bad person. I mean he dug up what she did when she was ten years old." When they said that Steve looked at me and said, "Baby, now I know why the kids call you the undercover gangster. Just remind me not to make you mad again." I told him, "Well the neighbor didn't fuck with me or anything around the house after that, but I still feel that ass whipping from time to time from Daddy after my third sip of my drink." And it hit. Oh I tried to eat a lot of bread to sober up. I knew that Steve would be on my ass. As I was sitting there, I saw Chase exchange numbers with Lacey Thornfield. But as I took another sip, Steve took it away from me. As we were leaving, I was looking Lacey up and down. I smiled at her. When we got back to the courthouse, Judge Thomas looked like he was about to just throw in the towel and that's when they called Steve up to the stand. As Steve got sworn in, Cole's lawyer asked, "Mr. Nicholas, when did you first see Dr. Nicholas?" Steve told them, "I first saw her in her Uncle Gabe's bar with her brother's. He asked Steve, "Did you encounter her there?" Steve told him, "No." The lawyer asked, "When did you first meet her?" Steve told them, "She was a waitress in the Café." He asked Steve, "Okay, so what made her attractive to you?" Steve told him. "There are a lot of things about her that I found attractive." He asked, "When you were there at the Café, the day you met her, did you even notice if she was married or seeing someone?" Steve told him, "No, but her Uncle had already told me what was going on, so I proceeded into getting to know her." "So Mr. Nicholas, with her being pregnant by another man, didn't that bother you?" Steve said, "No. We all have our troubles in life. She told me she was pregnant when I asked her to go do something with me. So, no, it didn't stop me from seeing her." He asked, "So, when did you have your very first encounter with Mr. Caney?" Steve said, "At the fair, in the men's restroom. I didn't like what he said to me. It was really more or less calling her the next town whore. So I said what I said to him and I expressed myself." He asked Steve, "So after that, you still proceeded to continue to see her?" Steve said, "Yes." He asked, "So when did you ask her to marry you?" Steve said, "While she was giving birth to the boys. I had asked her Dad for his blessing a couple of weeks beforehand." He asked, "So the day both of you got married was the day that the Judge stripped Cole's parental rights away, and you put your name on the birth certificates?" Steve said. "Yes, Judge Shafer felt that Cole was unfit to be a parent. So, I raised them as my own. Kerala and I left Cole in the dust, so we thought." He asked, "Did Dr. Nicholas ever come out and say that Cole abused her?" Steve said, "No. But there were signs of it. If I raised my voice or reached up to grab something that was nearby her, she would flinch or bat her eyes or close them a little. It wasn't until some years later that I accidentally read her journal where I found out all the things Cole did to her." The lawyer asked, "Did you ask or confront her?" Steve said, "Yes, we had a very long talk about it." He asked, "And how did you feel when the truth was finally out?" Steve said, "I had my feelings that he did do something to her, but I wanted her to talk with me when she was ready to tell me. When I read the journal, I was disgusted by what he did to her. I'm glad I adopted the boys and protected them from him." The lawyer asked, "Mr. Nicholas, how do you treat your wife behind closed doors?" Steve said, "I treat her with respect and love her the way she needs to be loved. Kerala is my world and my baby. I give her anything she needs or wants and my undivided attention. I'll admit that I spoiled her like any other wife should be treated and I baby her." He asked, "Do you have any arguments?" Steve said, "Yes, we have our disagreements, but it's been a very long time since we've had one. But what marriage doesn't have disagreements? And when we do have one, I may raise my voice a little when I get mad, but she calms me down, so we can discuss the issue." He asked, "Have you ever raised your hand at your wife?" Steve said. "No, never, I'll die before I do." He asked, "You're a veteran, aren't you?" Steve said, "Yes, I'm a retired master drill sergeant." He asked, "So you trained to teach others how to protect our country and kill?" Steve said, "Yes, if you want to refer to it that way." He asked, "So you're willing to kill anyone for your wife?" When the lawyer asked Steve that question, I could tell he was about to unleash on this guy because he was asking the wrong things in a way. That's when Judge Thomas slammed the gavel down and told Cole's lawyer to please reframe the question. The lawyer asked. "Would you do harm to someone for your wife?" Steve said, "If it comes down to protecting my wife or kids or any of my family members, then yes."

When he said, "That's all, I have no other questions." When Steve sat down next to me, I grabbed his hand to let him know that it's okay, but I do know where he stands when it comes to me. Within a few minutes Judge Thomas said, "I'm going to adjourn court for the day. But tomorrow, I need to get to the real point of why we are here and move forward from the past. What happened in the past we can't change anything. We just need to move forward with the now of why. I believe our jury has a complete understanding of why Dr. Nicholas did what she did. Court will be back in session at 8:00 AM tomorrow. As I stood up, a big headache kicked in. But I thought of the way Cole's lawyer looked and man I could say some mean shit to him. When Steve helped me into the truck, I smiled at him, and we kissed each other. When he got out I just asked Steve, "I wonder where that lawyer got his nose hair extensions? I just want to say to him, I love what you've done with your hair. How do you get it to come out of your nostrils like that? When I said that, Steve started laughing about it, and he said to me, "Kerala Jade you better not ask anything like that you'll be held in contempt." I had Steve going, and he said, "Baby the silly shit that comes up out of your mind sometimes." I just smiled at him as we headed home on our little 45-minute drive, I started checking messages, but as we were pulling into the driveway, I looked down at the arena and looked back at my phone. I realized that it was Black Betty sitting down there and I had screamed at Steve, "STOP THE TRUCK". My jaw dropped, and I climbed into Steve's lap just about and rolled down the window and looked at Steve and said to him, "You got to be fucking kidding me, this isn't real. That sled is retired. I broke the sled gears on it when I was a kid." Steve started smiling and snickering, and I said, "Steve, look at her all nice and shiny." Steve said, "Baby, I called Marv this morning and had him bring it down. It's all for you baby. So if you blow this engine up, you know I'll just put another back in for you." And I looked at Steve and said, "I smell fun and fuck-ups in a few minutes, so step on it baby." I put my butt back in the passenger seat and I felt like a kid again and felt as if Steve wasn't getting to the carport fast enough. Before he could park the truck, I was out and ran around back. I couldn't believe what was sitting in my backyard, the sled that people think I'm a legend over. I ran in the house, ignoring everyone, and changed into some different clothes. I still had to stand there looking at that sled, so I grabbed Daddy's hand, and we took off down there to it. Once I walked around it, I started talking to it like a fool, "So we meet again, you ready for another round with me, you and I, we go way back don't we." As I was looking at the sled, I saw the new stickers on it. And it had Dynamite 94 run 4.95. As Daddy stood there he said, "Why didn't you tell me what happened to you?" I hung my head to the ground and said to Daddy, "Sometimes our lives have to be completely shaken up, changed, and rearranged to relocate us to the place we are meant to be. And you have always taught us you can't change what has already happened." Daddy said, "I should have never let you go out with him." I told Daddy, "There is no need to beat yourself up over it. Steve saved me by taking a chance to be with me." Daddy said, "I know he was our saving grace. If not, you would be somewhere else in your life. But why couldn't you have just come to me and I could have ended it?" I told him, "I was scared of Cole and what could have happened after I said something to someone." Daddy asked me, "Can you forgive me for turning a blind eye?" I told him, "I have forgiven you a long time ago. But Daddy can we talk about this another time? I have a date with ol' Betty here. We need to finish what she and I started a long time ago. Need to see who's tougher, me or her. She's been on my list of things to finish." So I took off to the shop. With the weather being cold, it was going to take my sled truck a few moments to warm up. So I put my protection suit on and covered my ears. She fired right up. I waited a few minutes and moved it to the arena floor. When I saw Daddy in the sled, I thought okay old man lets go for a ride like you taught me. When I saw Steve walk up to the truck he said, "Baby don't rip it apart." I knew what he was saying, don't rip Betty up. When I hooked up and tugged it, I waited on someone to give me a green flag. When I did get it, I was gone. I felt as if my worries and thoughts of the day were gone. It felt good to pull that sled again. We all had a little fun that night, up until midnight. But as the next morning came, I noticed my daughter-in-law Renata, who was carrying our fifth grandchild, her stomach had dropped. I asked her if she felt okay, and she said, "Oh yea, I feel great. Lots of energy this morning." I thought, yea this baby is coming soon. So before we left out the door, I packed some towels in my bag. When we got in the truck, I sang my heart out again along the way. When we got to the courthouse and Steve turned off the truck, I looked at him and Steve said to me, "Baby something tells me that it's fixin' to be over sooner. As of today, if not the first thing tomorrow morning. I said to him, "I'm just ready for us to move along." I wondered what stupid questions we are going to get asked today. Steve said, "Baby, there is no telling." I smiled and said to Steve, "Thanks for last night." He told me, "I enjoyed watching you, that's what made it worth it." I said, "I think my Dad's ears are still ringing. My Dad is beaten up from the ride." As we got to the courthouse and settled in, I heard a gasping sound from behind me. I pulled out the towels, handed them to Renata, and smiled at her. She and Lucas took off. As Judge Thomas came in, he said, "I don't think we need anymore witnesses other than what needs to be told of the leading event that got Dr. Nicholas shot, so I'm asking for Isabella Whitmer to come to the courtroom and up to the stand." When she walked in and we saw the shamefulness all over her face as she was sworn in, our lawyer said, "I'm just going to ask you a few questions, but please don't hesitate to continue with as much information that the court needs. When did you first meet Mr. Caney?" Isabella said, "I met him three weeks after my 21st birthday and we started seeing each other. When he picked me up, I noticed pictures of some babies on his dashboard and I asked him about them. He told me that they were his twin sons and their Mom took them away from him when they were about three days old. I kind of felt bad for him and wished that she hadn't done that to him." The lawyer asked, "Isabella, were you aware Cole had a drug and alcohol problem?" Isabella said, "No, not until eight months later, when we both started using together off and on." The lawyer asked, "Has he ever hit you?" Isabella said, "Occasionally." The lawyer asked, "But were you sexually active with him? If so, did he force himself on you or was it consensual?" Isabella testified, "It was both, sometimes." The lawyer asked, "Do you have any children together or with someone else?" Isabella said, "No, I can't have kids." The lawyer asked, "So when did you kidnap Trinity Barsom and why?" Isabella said, "It was three weeks before his twin son's birthday and I had observed that he was looking through her Facebook pictures and his and going through the boys, and he said to me, looks like I have grandbabies now. Once he passed out, I looked her up and saw she was a pediatrician who specializes in autism. I thought of ways of how he could finally meet his kids after all these years and let him see his grandchildren. So I looked through the birth announcements in the newspaper. I took off for about a few days in the next state over and followed this woman around and followed her home. I waited until that night to see where the nursery was and the next morning I saw them open up the window. Later on that day, I reached through the window and took things that were needed for the baby. I left what money was in the diaper bag, got a car seat for the baby and went back to Cole." The lawyer asked, "Did he ask you questions about the baby?" Isabella said, "I told him it was our baby." She asked, "And he didn't ask anything other than he thought you carried his child?" Isabella said, "No, he didn't ask me anything and yes, he thought it was his." The lawyer asked, "So when did you fully put a plan together to do something?" Isabella said, "It was after I got the baby, but I couldn't do anything until she was about two years old." She asked, "Did you ever have an encounter with the Nicholas family whenever they came in for family visits?" Isabella said, "Yes, I knew when she was in town because Cole would have to go sit in a jail cell. So I packed a bag and went to where there was an old house and I parked until I saw that her Mom had some extra people in the car with her. So I figured I would get a closer look at Dr. Nicholas. I followed her into a clothing store. She had a few other girls with her." The lawyer asked, "When you got an up close, personal view of her, did you want to harm her then or were you studying her?" Isabella said, "I was thinking she would be taller than her pictures. After I got a good look at her, I left and went home and studied her some more. I looked up articles of her medical profession and found her home address on the internet. I liked and followed her on her pediatrician business page. When they let Cole out, he was mad. I told him that we can go and do something to her so you can finally get a relationship with your boys. He asked me how? I told him, well we can use the baby and fill out an Autism application. She does the in-home study on her ranch. When I told Cole, he said that bitch gotta ranch? And I showed him pictures of it and I told him, but we have to wait until the baby is two or three. So during that time, Cole and I waited it out until the time came and I filled out the application for it.?" The lawyer asked, "Do you mean this application?" Isabella said, "Yes. When we got approved, I spoke to the receptionist, and she told me that Dr. Nicholas would be on vacation with her family at home. When I told Cole that the boys would be there, he got excited. About a week later, when we got the travel voucher, Cole and I were packed up and we both talked about hurting her or her husband if it doesn't go our way. When we arrived, Cole said to me, I could've had all this stuff instead of him. I'm going to kill him and get my woman back. When he said that I was high at the time. As we got up to the house, her daughter let us into an area of the house. The door to the main house was locked, but the room that we were in was like a little apartment. When all of her kids started showing up, Cole stood at the window watching them." The lawyer said, "Judge Thomas, I have no further questions other than to show the entire video events of the Nicholas ranch, inside and outside leading up to the night Dr. Nicholas was shot. What we are about to see is very graphic."

Our own security cameras played the entire week that happened in the courthouse. When the video was done, Cole's lawyer asked Lucas up to the stand, but Andrew stood up and told them Lucas had to leave due to his wife just going into labor. So Andrew went up there. Cole's lawyer asked him, "Are you willing to have any relationship with your biological father?" Andrew said to him, "That man isn't my Daddy nor will he ever be. You are just asking me to have a relationship with my Mama's rapist. And the answer to that will be a no. The man that is my Daddy I'm looking straight at him. He's the one that has taught me to be a real man and put clothes, food and shoes on me and helped me through life's problems. He taught me how to treat a woman and I can speak on behalf of my twin brother and me. We want nothing to do with him. After we found out about him, who he was and what he did to our Mama, when we were kids we knew that Mama was just trying to protect us from him and we're happy to have the man that we call our Daddy in our lives. So as for his actions and what he did to him, I know how far my Daddy will go for Mama and us."

When Andrew got off the stand he walked straight to Steve and hugged him, saying, "It's over for Mama and us. Now we can live without watching behind our backs." Steve told him, "Yes, son, we can." When Judge Thomas said, "As of right now,

I ask the jury if we have enough evidence for a deliberation." When the jury stood up they said, "Yes, far more than enough." Judge Thomas said, "Court will go into recess and we'll be back in session within two hours." So Steve and I went outside and Steve asked, "Mama, can we go get a fun toy?" And I looked at him crazy, and he said, "A side by side?" So we walked down to the dealership with the boys in tow. But while they were looking around my mind was elsewhere. If all of this shit was planned out well, and I had fallen for it all, I knew what Steve was doing. He was trying to keep my mind from thinking of this mess that has happened. He was looking for things to keep me busy, and of course with Bodie having a side by side, I knew that Steve had been itching to get himself one so he and Bodie could hang out more. This was more of Hannah and Bodie's hobbies together. As I was just standing there, Stephanie came up to me and said, " WOW. I wonder what wild hair crawled up Daddy's ass for him to want a side by side?" So I walked over to where he and this guy were talking, I smarted off money talks and bullshit walks. This salesman looked at me and started cutting deals with Steve. I was up for an adventure so why not. After I said that I kind of walked off and looked at my boys. They were acting like little kids in a toy store. I just wanted to go round them up and start spatting their little hands while their Daddy did business. During lunch I wanted to talk to Mama but the more I thought about the past of when something went wrong between Cole and I, she would have a small fit on me. I was glad that Daddy and I had a small talk last night. In a way, I wanted to just push my parents away from me, temporarily, until I was ready to set them down and scream at the top of my lungs at them for not seeing the first set of signs of abuse. But as I put my focus back on what was going on, Steve was on the phone with Bodie making plans to do something later on. But as soon as we got back into the courthouse, I was wondering what Steve had planned for us to do. I was up for anything other than putting up with this courtroom bullshit. As everyone settled back into the courtroom I looked over there at Cole and gave him a go-to-hell look. Steve said to me, "Baby this is the last time you'll ever see that son of a bitch again." As Judge Thomas walked in, Steve grabbed my hand and he and I started praying together for what we both wanted to hear.

In the case of Dr. Kerala Jade Blake Nicholas vs. Cole Caney, we, the jury, found Cole Caney guilty of First Degree Assault and Battery.

We, the jury, found Cole Caney guilty of First Degree Rape in the case of Dr. Kerala Jade Blake Nicholas.

We, the jury, found Cole Caney guilty in the First Degree of Conspiracy to Commit Murder against Mr. Steven Wesley Nicholas.

We, the jury, found Cole Caney guilty in the First Degree in the case of Dr. Kerala Jade Nicholas and Mr. Steven Wesley Nicholas, Felony Stalking.

We, the jury, found Cole Caney guilty in the First Degree of Attempted Murder charges in the case of Dr. Kerala Jade Nicholas.

We, the jury, found Isabella Whitmer guilty of Felony Stalking in the case of Kerala Jade Nicholas and Steven Wesley Nicholas.

We, the jury, found Isabella Whitmer guilty of the First Degree Attempted Murder in the case of Kerala Jade Nicholas.

We, the jury, found Isabella Whitmer guilty of Kidnapping in the case of Trinity Barsom.

We, the jury, found Cole Caney and Isabella Whitmer guilty for Property Damage on the Nicholas family ranch.

We, the jury, found both individuals guilty of all charges.

When Steve and I heard all of those charges, Steve picked me up in his arms and held onto me. Steve said, "It's over baby.

We can live in peace." Again, I couldn't agree with him more. I was free of Cole and free of not looking behind me or worrying if Cole was anywhere near me.

As we settled down, Judge Thomas came out and said, "This is the quickest case I've ever done. You should have been put away a long time ago. I laid my head down last night, thinking of Kerala. I knew that she'd been through it, but I didn't know it was this bad as her and Steve's neighbors watching their children grow up. I think Judge Shafer made

the best decision to take your rights away because you did take something away from her that wasn't even yours. It's meant for a special night when two people get married, and I can't imagine for both of them how their wedding night was because I'm sure both of them were taking care of Andrew and Lucas. As for a man, Steven is one. I have seen him many times on the far east side of our properties with the boys, teaching them how to hunt, fish, learning about and trees and nature. When Lucas and his little brother were out in the pasture as youngsters they had accidentally knocked my fence over. When I went and saw Steve about it, he stood out there with them, making them fix what they had broken. I didn't see it as a punishment, I saw it as tough love for them. As for Mr. Nicholas, that's all he had to give to them was life lessons, learning and love, but if Judge Shafer didn't do what he did, I'm fearing that you, Mr. Caney would have wrecked their marriage. I'm pretty sure you would've put a strain on it with your foolishness. Now I know why Mr. Nicholas beat the heck out of you, because you wouldn't let old dogs lay. I find it very disturbing that you seek out young girls for your fun and games. It's sad that Kerala was your first victim, so I'm about to put the last nail in your coffin, for good, so Kerala and Steve can live their lives. This is justice for Kerala, and I'm still debating if I should put you on death row or or give you life without the possibility of parole. Then again, death would be an easy way out for you. So, I sentence you to Life in Prison Without the Possibility of Parole.

As for you, Isabella Whitmer, you just got caught up in his narcissism and manipulating ways. I'm going to sentence you to prison for 45 Years to Life With the Possibility of Parole and a No Contact Order for Mr. Caney or the Nicholas family. I advise you to seek help and counseling. As for the kidnapping, I'm going to add another 15 years on to your sentence. As for both of you, I order you to get with work programs to pay for the victim fee and damages on the Nicholas Ranch. Now, that to me is justice for Kerala.

Dr. Nicholas, do you have your victim impact statement?" I said. "I do." As I stood up I grabbed Steve's hand, and he walked up to the podium with me. I looked up at Steve for reassurance and when he told me, "I'm here baby." I knew I had my words for Steve and I knew that he was there for me. I took a deep breath, I looked at Cole and said to him, "For years I lived in fear of you. Today I am free. I came in here like a lamb and I'm leaving out of here like a lioness. You both thought that you could mess with my cubs, but there's always a lion laying in his den waiting for someone to poke or harm his pride. Well Cole, you got warned so many times, and you kept poking inside the den until the lion came out. This time Cole, I beat you. As for you Isabella, this is a very long road of understanding why and how come, of why I do what. You almost made my family lose me by your dumb actions. You made a big mistake in thinking you and Cole would have a relationship with mine and Steve's oldest twins if I would have died that night. I can't bear how my husband or our kids would be today if I was no longer here with them. It would have been worse for you. As for baby Trinity Barsom. It takes a very sick individual to go that far to hurt her family to come and cause damage to another. Thanks to you, I have almost lost my pediatric medical practice and my autism license was stripped from me. Therefore, I can no longer study or help any families with autism and there is a child who really needs my help. I hope both of you will think long and hard about what you've done. I'm fixin' to bury you where you need to be, in my past, and finally go finish living mine, so goodbye." Steve and I, along with our kids and family members, felt this ordeal lift off of our chests. That had been a burden on me for years. I knew that I would no longer be hiding from Cole. I was FREE.

As we walked out of the courthouse that afternoon and got into Steve's truck, I looked at him and said, "I think my monkey just packed his shit, bought a plane ticket and headed for vacation." When I had said that, Steve just busted up laughing at me over the monkey joke. I could tell that Steve was about to break his neck to get to the hospital to see our new grandbaby. I told him, "There's no need for us to run to the hospital. We need to let Renata have a comfortable birth. The one I'm going to be pacing the floor for is Breanna in the upcoming weeks." Steve told me, "Mama those two are gonna need our help and with them being twins, yes. I'm ready to see Seth as a dad." I said, "No doubt." When we got home I stopped Steve before he got out of the truck. I told him, "Steve, I'm thankful for you stepping into my life. Without you there's no telling how me, Andrew and Lucas would be today." Steve said to me, "Aww baby, you were meant to be in my life. We were just two people that were broken and God made us cross paths. We have Him to thank for you breaking the hard ass shell I built around my heart. You more or less shattered it. I loved you from the start." When we kissed, I looked and saw Matthew was acting like his Daddy and mocking his old ways. I started laughing at him and Steve asked me, "Do I act like that?" I said to him, "Honey you used to." He just shook his head. Matthew opened up my door and said, "Mama Hannah and Bodie are coming over. They're getting some take out and Uncle Shane wants to see you around the back. So I got out and waited on Steve. I said to Steve, "After our little celebration, as much as I love them, I'm ready to be selfish with you." Steve said, "Baby you got it, and I'm hoping it will be Thursday morning when everyone goes home." I told Steve that Lucas and Renata will be here with the new baby tomorrow night so she won't be able to travel that far. As we stood there under the carport Hannah and Bodie were pulling and there was Steve and Bodie running their mouths to each other. Hannah got out, walked over to me, hugged me and said, "Damn girl, I knew your journey, but I didn't know it was such a long fucking road for you." I told her. "It's been one hell of a ride. Come on, my brother's are up to no good. When it's no good, it means fun as fuck. We headed around back, there was Shane. He had some shots lined up. Hannah said to me, "Think it's time to let the gangster Kerala out for the night?" I told her, "Oh hell. It's time to let the old me from the past out." Shane said, "Oh fuck. So Steve is in for it." I gave him a grin and Hannah said, "Do you want to see who can beat each other in some shots?" I told her, "Why the hell not!" As we were at it, everyone was cheering and chanting. I just grabbed up the bottle and got down on it. That's when Noah stopped me. He said, "You need to eat. Your skeleton is showing. It's time to close it up and lock it up for good." I told him, "I'm burning that motherfucker." Just before we grabbed a plate Clayton yelled out, "Can I get everyone's attention please. I hate to rain on the celebration of Dr. Kerala, but there's no better time to do this with family around." As I looked at him, he kneeled on one knee and faced Stephanie. Clayton said, "Stephanie Nicholas, you've captured my heart in ways I never thought possible. Today, I want to give you mine completely. Will you marry me and make me the happiest person alive?" "Yes," she said to him. When she did, my mouth opened up and I yelled out "FUCK!" Everyone started looking at me and I said, "No, no, not what y'all are thinking. My monkey's flight just got canceled."

348

And everyone started laughing. I knew that my daughter would be up and over here every day stressing me out over planning a wedding. I am proud that Steph found her person. I walked up to Clayton and Steph. I apologized to them for the way it came out as we left out to ride. I was already feeling good, and so was Hannah. But as we were hitting an area of the pasture where Steve blocked it off years ago, we sat there watching Chase and Andrew. I asked Steve what he was thinking, and he told me, "Baby we should be ashamed because Chase and Andrew are making it look fun." I said to Steve, "Do I need to show you how the boys took most of the blame, but I'm the one that showed them how years ago. So not all this is the boys' mess. It was mine too." Steve got out and said to me, "Okay baby, show me what you got." Steve put on his seat belt and I said to Steve, "Pass me that bottle over there, will you please darling." When he did, I took a big drink and put it in reverse. Then I drove and I looked over at Steve and smiled at him. I stomped on it. When I saw the mud fly up I started laughing because Steve was over there screaming his head off. When we got out of the hole, Steve and I watched everyone go through it. Shane said, "Damn was that you or Kerala screaming?" Steve said, "It was me God damn. Kerala, thanks baby, for the tutorial, but I can get it from here." We started laughing and I nodded off and said to everyone, "By the way, happy early Weiner Christmas to you guys." Hannah was laughing and everyone asked what does that mean? Hannah and I said, "Valentine's Day is Saturday. It's the one-day out of the year where guys buy sex from their wives." Everyone just busted up laughing and Bodie told everyone, "See this is the shit we put up with. No wonder their office is a fucking fun house, because they come up with dirty shit to say." Hannah said, "Well, I married a cow hauler and the shit you and Steve say to each other." Steve said to Bodie, "Man you're letting our secret jokes out." Hannah said, "I got one for you. A doctor accidentally prescribes his patient a laxative instead of cough syrup. Three days later, the patient comes for a check-up and the doctor asks, "Well, are you still coughing?" The patient replies, "No, I'm afraid to." We all busted up laughing. Bodie said, "Steve that's our cue to shut the fuck up." I yelled out, "Line them up." Kaden poured this round of shots. When we got back in to ride some more, I told Steve, "That really did happen. It was her first medical error." Steve said, "No shit." I said, "Yea, the guy just about shit himself to death until she saw what she gave to him." Steve said, "Baby you better never do anything like that to me." I told Steve, "I don't think I have the balls to hurt my big baby unless, nah just joking." He looked at me and I started laughing. All throughout the night, we all laughed so fucking hard at each other and were covered in mud until I passed out. The last thing I recalled was Hannah and I, mud fighting with each other. When the next morning came it felt like the devil himself had dragged me to hell and back. But the biggest blessing is the fact I knew that Hannah and Bodie didn't drive home. Hannah and I were more wasted than anything. With a little bit of family help we cleaned up the house and had breakfast to help with the hangover. By that late afternoon we got to meet our newest grandson, Marcus Hunter. As I held onto him, I could tell Steve was getting fussy and ready to get territorial. He was very impatient while waiting for his turn to hold Marcus. Before Hannah and Bodie left, they helped to take a family photo of us with Marcus. Before bed I could see Steve was very upset because he didn't get to hold him. As he was laying in bed I told him, "You'll have the entire day with him tomorrow after everyone leaves. Lucas will be leaving Friday morning." When I told him that he got out of his grumpy mood, he told me, "Baby I'm getting like you. Ready for everyone to go. Steve and I were ready for the house to be empty again. It was just me and him with no one else around by that afternoon. After everyone left Steve had

Marcus all to himself. I got a few pictures of Grumpy holding his number five before Lucas and Renata left. I made sure that Marcus checked out fine. When I closed the door and turned around Steve said to me, "Come here baby." I walked over and got into his lap without much being said to each other. And it wasn't until that afternoon Stephanie came blowing in the door with books, wedding things needing her Mama. I just took a deep breath and looked at Steve. I got off of his lap and Stephanie was going at it ninety to nothing over wedding stuff. I looked over at Steve, like why me, and that's when he opened up his mouth. He started asking her some questions. Steve asked Stephanie, so where and when is this going to happen?" She told him, "Daddy in about seven months. I wanted to know if you cleaned out the shop so I could have the reception in there, and I'm not sure of where I want, yet the arena is my thoughts so far." I was hearing the conversion between them and that's when Steve looked at me like get me out of this one. That's when Steve slammed into her and told her, "We didn't get a wedding like you're fixin' to get." Mama and I have a big project coming. We're buying and restoring her grandmother's old house so we can go and stay there for a while when we visit. You know I'm not on your ass, but Mama and I didn't get this so you better be happy with what I'm doing for you." Her little face was in shock. I said, "Steve, are you going to help me with dinner?" He said, "Yes Ma'am I am." Stephanie continued to talk. I said, "Steph, can we please wait until next weekend? I want to enjoy the rest of my weekend since I've put up with some bullshit for the past few days, and it's Thursday. I love ya kid, but I want to have it quiet around here, so my damn Gorilla can get on his bike and help you." Stephanie's face was disgusted. She grabbed her books and slammed the front door on her way out. I knew what she was fixin' to do, that's call the party line of siblings and tell them what I had done to her. I was proud of my Chase that he had asked the Thornfield girl out. I, as a Mama, had good feelings about her. She doesn't take any shit off of anyone. And I started talking to Steve about doing a joke during Steph and Clayton's wedding. He was full on hearing about it.

As I was cooking dinner, I made sure to make enough extra for just in case one of the kids came in to eat. Sure enough in comes Seth and Breanna. Seth was needing help putting the cribs together and asking his Daddy to come and help him. Steve asked Seth, "Where are the instructions?" He told his Daddy, "I didn't need them at the time." Breanna started laughing and so was I. That's when Steve told him, "Just a heads up, Mama and I will not be here Saturday or Sunday." I said, "We are?" Steve said, "Yup baby, you and I are taking a little trip to Eureka Springs since you're off on Monday. Hannah said she's not going to open because of President's Day, so I figured we do a mini getaway." I said, "Shit I better call Chase. He asked me to press him some clothes." Steve asked me, "Why are you doing that for him?" I said to Steve, "He has a date with Lacey." Steve said, "The Thornfield girl from the Café?" Mama said, "Yup. You didn't see him and her exchanging phone numbers the other day. This one here I'm butting out of. She looks like she can handle his ways. Besides, he's been going in and out of there for the past three months now. I guess you haven't noticed all the empty cups in his truck. I went in there and grabbed lunch about a month ago, and she asked about him. When I got to talking about him her face lit up. Breanna said she saw both of them flirting with each other outside the Café doors." Steve said, "What is it with you boys picking up girls at a Café?" Seth coughed and said, "Damn Daddy, you just put your ass in the dog house. Isn't that where you met Mama?" Steve said, "No, I saw her in Uncle Gabe's bar." He turned around, and I was tapping my foot on the floor. Steve tried to play it off and said, "Well at least I know that they'll get fed, and I wasn't talking about us baby." I said to

Steve, "Keep it up, and you'll be in the dog house and that's when the three of them took off out the door. I got a little bit of peace. I just cleaned up the kitchen and when Steve came back, he was giggling about how Seth had put the two cribs together. Telling me that Seth told him Grumpy was going to put all the toys together for the grandbabies. I just laughed and told Steve that, "Seth is on his own in that area. We're just going to buy the most difficult toys for him to put together." Steve just laughed. He said, "You're right, it's payback time." Steve and I had a nice little trip over that weekend. We had a big discussion during our trip about us, and the outcome of the trial. and I had felt that we had come back to our full circle again and life was getting back to normalcy for the both of us.

As March came for us, we sat back and waited for Breanna to give birth. But the grand twins came to us, but with a panicked Grumpy, When Steve called me at work, he told me, "She's having them, and I'm on the way to the hospital. Call Seth now." Steve hung up on me, so I called Seth and when he picked up, I said to him, "You might want to get your butt to the hospital. Your babies are coming, and your Daddy is taking her." I finished up my charts for the day and a memory hit me like crazy about Seth. It was hard to believe that he was fixin' to become a parent. We feared him treating girls like shit. As I told my office ladies that I was gone for the day to meet the grandtwins they said to me, "Congrats Lala on your new grandbabies." I met up with Steve and saw Seth pacing the floor. Steve and I were there to support them both, especially Breanna. I hate the fact that her Mom is no longer here to be part of this moment. Her parents were killed when she was ten during a home invasion and both her grandparents co-reared her. That is why Steve and I are there for her when she needs us. Steve and I sat there. He and I were talking about things Seth would always do to us. But as time passed by, Steve and I waited for the grandtwins to make their appearance. It was close to 11:00 PM when they did. When we walked into the room we were introduced to Aliyah Destiny and Rhett Steven. As I looked at Seth, I saw Steve's personality all over him. He was being so loving and caring. I knew that Steve and I raised him to be a damn good man. Standing right in front of us when we got our chance to hold the grandetwins I saw a lot of Breanna in Aliyah and as Steve and I had traded babies Rhett looked like Seth. Steve and I couldn't be more happy at the fact that our family is growing like it should be.

As several weeks passed by, I found myself being consumed by Stephanie the Bridezillia. Steve had to settle her down a time or two. One morning I got up and started making my coffee. I had gone outside to watch the sunrise and by 8:00 AM there was Steve taking off to say good morning to the grandtwins. I get tickled at him in the way he cares for them. As the summer months came and went, the day we finally got our bridezilla to the altar Steve and I had a rough ride with Stephanie. This made Savannah run to the courthouse like Steve and I did. She made a beautiful setting in the side of the arena as our friends and family gathered waiting. I saw Clayton sweating like crazy. But as Steve and I walked our baby girl down the aisle, I saw that my husband was being a little bit emotional in his own way and a little cocky. I knew he was fixin' to say something crazy. I'll be damned if he did. When the preacher asked who gives this woman to be with this man, Steve said to Clayton, "I'm going to come out and say this to you once. She's a little bit on the expensive side, and she's not cheap. The price tag that comes with her has no refunds and no returns." When Steve said that, I started laughing and our guests were also. Just like that Steve turned his other switch on and said to Clayton, "Boy all I ask out of you is to keep her high as you can up on that pedestal like I do her Mama and along with the rest of the women in this family." And as I looked over at Steve I saw a little bit of tears swelling up in his eyes, and he said, "Well, I guess her Mama and I give this woman to this man because he can have her now, she's his problem now." Everyone was just laughing about what Steve said. As Steve and I sat down, I told Steve, "You know you couldn't have said that any better or no refunds whatsoever." And he said, "Mama I meant what I said to him since she was such a bossy person in the past few months." After the exchanging of the vows and the cake was cut, that's when we had to set up the little jokes on you. From me and Steve, and we had three boxes set up there and in two were Clayton and Steph's baby things. So we watched them dig into each other's baby things. But when it came to our marriage to murder box, those two started laughing about the floor cleaner, a Kool-Aid, the box of grits, the cooking pot and the cotton candy that was supposed to be fiberglass. That's when Clayton started laughing harder, over the cotton candy. I told them both well when all else fails Steph, call your Daddy. When things get ugly, and that's when Steve walks out with a shotgun and shovel. As we were laughing about it, and it was a cute joke, others were criticizing our humor. We saw Clayton and Stephanie off on their honeymoon. Steve and I found ourselves hanging out in the nesting swing. Steve said to me, "Baby I don't think life can't get any better than this. I've got you wrapped up in my arms every night and what else could a man ask for in his life." I smiled at him and said, "Five down and three more to go." He said to me, "Yes, but at least they're out of the house."

A few years passed us by, and I watched each strain of mine and Steve's hair slowly starting to turn gray. Steve was right, life couldn't get any better since I finally put Cole's ass away. But as the month of June came around and our grandbabies were spending the summer month's with us. As a morning routine with them, I was feeding them breakfast. Steve had taken off to the barn to get a few horses ready for Madi and Braylee to ride. I saw Brian and Seth walk into the barn and within 30 minutes later Brian came walking out of the barn. Brian looked up at the house a few times as he was walking away. Something kept telling me that whatever is going on isn't good. When Steve and Seth walked out I saw that old worry look on Steve's face that I hadn't seen in a long time. As he came onto the patio, he was in a panic. I asked him if everything was okay? He said to me, "Oh yeah, baby, everything is fine," as he kissed me and walked into the house. The news that he got from Brian and Seth was news that I had to learn the hard way.

To Be Continued